THE TH
DETECTIV
THE COMPLE

Featuring:

The Third Pig Detective Agency
The Ho Ho Ho Mystery
The Curds and Whey Mystery

BOB BURKE

The Third Pig Detective Agency: The Complete Casebook

THE
FRIDAY
PROJECT

The Friday Project
An imprint of HarperCollins*Publishers*
1 London Bridge Street
London SE1 9GF
www.harpercollins.co.uk

This collected edition first published in Great Britain by The Friday Project in 2015

The Third Pig Detective Agency first published in 2009
The Ho Ho Ho Mystery first published in 2010
The Curds and Whey Mystery first published in 2012

MIX
Paper from
responsible sources
FSC
www.fsc.org   **FSC® C007454**

To Gem, for believing

Contents

THE THIRD PIG
DETECTIVE AGENCY

Contents

Contents

1

A New Client

I t was another slow day in the office. Actually, it had been a slow week in the office. No, if the truth be known, it had been a lousy month for the Third Pig Detective Agency. That's me by the way: Harry Pigg, the Third Pig.

Where did the name come from? Well, I was the pig that built the house out of bricks while my idiot brothers took the easy route and went for cowboy builders and cheap materials. Let me tell you, wood and straw ain't much use when Mr Wolf comes calling. Those guys were pork-chops as soon as he drew in his first breath and filled those giant lungs of his. Blow your house down, indeed.

And while we're on the subject, don't believe what you read in those heavily edited stories you find in children's books of fairy tales saying how the wolf fell down the chimney into the pot, scalded his tail, ran out of the house and was never seen again. When that wolf came down my chimney and into that boiling saucepan, I screwed the lid on and made sure it stayed on by weighing it down with a few spare bricks (never throw anything away, you never know when it could come in useful). He didn't do too much huffing and puffing then.

'Little pig, little pig, let me come out,' he'd begged in a scared whimper.

'Not by the hair on my . . .' I began, but then gave up. I just couldn't come up with something clever to rhyme with 'I won't let you out' so I just left it. Hey, I can't come up with a witty reply every time.

By the time the pot went quiet and I opened it again all that was left was some scummy hair floating on the surface and bones – lots of bones. The little dog sure laughed a lot that day. He hadn't seen that many broken bones since the cow's first attempt to jump over the moon, and they'd kept him in three square meals a day for over a week.

After that I was kind of a cult hero. Apart from that Red Riding Hood dame, no one else had ever come out on top in a skirmish with the Wolf family so I became a local celebrity. After the usual civic receptions and TV appearances, I decided to capitalise on my new-found fame and become a detective. Well, why not? Someone needs to do it and there's always an opening for a good one.

At first business was booming. I was the one who not only found those two missing kids, Hansel and Gretel, but I also fingered them for the murder of that sweet old woman in the gingerbread house. Their story was too pat: wicked old lady plans to eat the kids, only way out was to kill her; you know the drill. In my book their story stank. Two kids, a house made of gingerbread and an old dear whose only crime was to get in the way. It was always going to end in tears – primarily hers.

As I said, I was on the pig's back (excuse the pun) for a while but then things kind of dried up. No one seemed to want the services of a good detective agency and, with the exception of the kids in Hamelin (which wasn't even one of my cases), there didn't even seem to be too many missing persons any more. The bills were mounting up. Gloria, my bovine receptionist, hadn't been paid in a month. Even her legendary patience was wearing thin. And no, before all you politically correct fairy tale readers get on my case, I'm not casting any aspersions on her looks; she really is a cow and the meanest typist in Grimmtown (even with the hoofs). Unless I got a big case – and soon – I was going be neck-deep in apple sauce and Gloria would be back to cheerleading for the Lunar Leapers Bovine Acrobatics Team. Things were most definitely not looking good.

But I digress (a little). On this particular slow day I was sitting in my office (cheap furniture, lousy décor, creaky wooden floor – you know the type) with my rear trotters on my desk, trying to work out 5 down. 'Sounds like fierce brothers in the fairy tale world. Five letters ending in "m". Hmmm.' I mulled this over while nibbling the end of my pen. Crosswords really weren't my strong suit.

As my creative juices attempted to flow I became aware of voices in the outer office. Voices meant more than one person, so Gloria either had a debt-collector or a potential customer on her hands – and there was no one in town more adept at evading debt-collectors than me. Once I heard her say, 'Mr Pigg is quite busy at present, but I'll see if he can squeeze you in', it meant an obviously discerning client wished to utilise my services. I swung my trotters off the desk, smoothed down my jacket as best I could and tried to look busy while squashing the newspaper into the wastebasket with my left trotter.

The intercom buzzed.

'Mr Pigg,' crackled Gloria's deep, husky voice. 'There is a gentleman here to see you. Should I get him to make an appointment?'

As my diary was conspicuously blank for the foreseeable future I figured that my need for hard cash far outweighed any need to impress a potential punter. I pressed the intercom button.

'I can see the gentleman now, Gloria,' I said. 'Please send him in.' I stood up to meet my potential cash cow.

Through the opaque glass in the connecting door, I could see a large shape making its way through reception and towards my office. The door slowly opened and an oriental gentleman the size and shape of a zeppelin entered. He was wearing a silk suit, the amount of cloth of which would have made easily the most expensive marquee tent in history, and he was weighed down with enough gold to pay off all of my debts for the next twenty years. His shiny black hair was pulled back from his forehead and tied in a long plait that stretched all the way down his back to a voluminous rear end. The guy exuded wealth – and I hadn't failed to notice it. If this were a cartoon, dollar signs would be going 'ka-ching' in my eyes.

It was time to be ultra-smooth, ultra-polite and ultra-I'm-the-best-detective-you're-ever-likely-to-meet-and-you-will-be-eternally-grateful-for-employing-me.

I extended my trotter, 'Mr?'

'Aladdin,' he replied, grasping my trotter in a grip like a clam's. 'Just call me Mr Aladdin.'

Although I didn't recognise him, of course I had heard of Aladdin. Everyone in Grimmtown had. He was probably the most famous and most reclusive of our many eccentric citizens – and quite possibly the richest. Rumour had it he owned half of the town but very few people had seen him in recent years, as he preferred to live behind closed doors in a huge mansion in the hills.

His story was the stuff dreams (at least other people's dreams) were made of. He had started off working in a local laundry. After a few years he bought out the owner although no one knew, despite much speculation and rumour, where the money had come from. Over the years his business had expanded (as had he) and he had begun to diversify. Apart from the chain of laundries he had built up, he owned bars, restaurants, department stores, gas stations and most local politicians. The key word in the above description is, of course, 'richest'. If Mr 'Just call me' Aladdin wanted to employ my services, it would be most churlish of me to turn him down

– especially if he was prepared to throw large wads of cash in my direction.

Ka-ching! Ka-ching!

I took a deep breath and prepared to tell my new best friend how wonderful I was and how he had showed exceptional judgement in availing himself of my services.

'Mr Aladdin, how may I be of service?'

That's me: cool and straight to the point. Inside, my mind was screaming, 'Show me the money', and I was trying not to dance on the table with joy.

Mr Aladdin looked carefully at me, raised his left hand and snapped his fingers.

'Gruff,' he said. 'My bag, please.'

Someone, hidden up to now by his employer's large mass, walked out from behind him carrying a large leather, and undoubtedly very expensive, briefcase. My heart sank. Things had just started taking a turn for the worse. It always happens to me. Just when I think things can't get any better, they inevitably don't and take another downward slide into even more unpleasantness. Aladdin's employee was a sturdy white goat. Not just any goat however, this was a Gruff. And, unless I was very much mistaken, he was the eldest Gruff.

The Gruffs were three brothers who had come to town a few years ago. After sorting out a little (well big, actually) troll problem we were having at a local bridge (a trollbridge, if you will), they had decided to stay and give the town the benefit of their 'unique' skill set – which usually involved threats, intimidation and the carrying of blunt instruments. Starting out as bouncers at 'Cinders', one of Grimmtown's least reputable clubs, they had subsequently branched out into more profitable (and much less legal) operations. Whether it was smuggling live gingerbread men across the border or evicting the old lady in the shoe for not paying the rent, the three billy goats Gruff were usually involved in some capacity.

Eventually the eldest brother had distanced himself from the day-to-day operations of the family business. I'd heard he'd gone into consultancy of a sort usually described as 'security', but not much had been seen of him recently. Now I knew why. If he was employed by this particular client, I suspected he worked for him to the exclusion of any others. Mr Aladdin was that kind of employer; apart from total commitment, it was rumoured he also demanded total secrecy from his staff. If Gruff was involved, it stood to reason that there were some less than legal factors of which I was yet to be made aware.

Wonderful!

Gruff handed the briefcase to his boss and looked me up and down.

'I don't like you,' he sneered.

I shrugged my shoulders. 'You don't like most people.'

'But I especially don't like pigs.'

'Well then, perhaps you'd be more comfortable somewhere else – an empty shoe, a prison cell, maybe propping up a bridge somewhere?'

Snarling, he made to move towards me but his employer restrained him with a large and heavily bejewelled hand. With that amount of rings on his fingers it was a wonder he actually had the strength to lift it.

'Gentlemen, please. Enough of this petty squabbling! Gruff, keep an eye on the door, will you? There's a good goat.'

Reluctantly the goat backed towards the door, never taking his eyes off me. I met his gaze all the way. No goat was going to outstare me.

Happy that his employee was a safe (or at least a less-threatening) distance away, Aladdin turned towards me.

'Might we continue?' he said.

'Of course,' I replied, returning to my chair while, at the same time, ensuring that a large and heavy desk was strategically placed between a highly unstable goat and me. Picking up a letter opener in as non-intimidating a fashion as possible, I began to clean my front trotters and looked expectantly at Aladdin.

'Mr Pigg,' he began. 'You have a reputation as a man – I apologise, of course I mean pig – who not only gets results but knows when to be discreet.'

I nodded politely at the compliment.

'In my experience, an indiscreet detective doesn't stay in business too long,' I pointed out.

'Nevertheless,' he continued, 'in this particular instance, discretion is of paramount importance. I must insist that you do not discuss what I am about to reveal with anyone other than my associate Mr Gruff, and me.'

I nodded, wondering what was going to come next.

Opening the briefcase, Aladdin took out a large sheet of paper. 'I have recently mislaid an item of immense personal value and I wish you to locate it for me.'

He handed the sheet of paper to me. I looked at it with interest. It was a photograph of a very old and very battered lamp.

'It's a lamp,' I said, stating the blindingly obvious.

'Not just any lamp,' said Aladdin. 'This is a family heirloom and one which I am most anxious to have located as soon as possible.'

'Where was it mislaid?' I asked.

'It was last seen in a display cabinet in my study. Last night it was most definitely there; this morning it was gone.'

'Lost? Stolen? Melted down and sold for scrap? Can you be a little more specific?' I looked at the picture again. The lamp didn't look up to much. It was about the size of a gravy boat, coloured an off-shade of gold and had more dents than the Tin Man. I clearly needed more information.

11

'I . . . ah . . . suspect it may have been stolen but I am unable to prove this at present.'

'Have you spoken to the police?'

Again, rumour had it that local law enforcement was more akin to Aladdin's private security force than public servants. If anyone could locate an artifact of this nature quickly and with a minimum of fuss, it was them. In all likelihood, their jobs would depend on it.

Aladdin looked at me carefully. 'The police have been more than helpful but, at this time, they have neither a suspect nor a specific line of inquiry. It is my firm belief that someone of your talents might be of more use in this particular instance.'

'Because?' I enquired.

'Because, as I have already mentioned, you can be discreet. I think that perhaps you can exploit particular avenues of inquiry that may be outside the scope of the law and you have your snout in all the right information troughs – forgive the analogy, I mean no offence.'

'None taken,' I replied. Offended or not, I wasn't going to abandon this client just yet, certainly not on the basis of a less than politically correct analogy. 'However, I don't normally take on cases that are still under investigation by the police.'

'Trust me,' came the very smooth reply. 'The police have exhausted all avenues and will not bother you during the course of your investigation.'

In other words they'd come up with nothing – or at least nobody they could pin the theft on. Either that or this lamp was something that Aladdin would prefer not having the police involved with. This case stank higher than an abattoir in a heatwave – and I should know, my office looks out on one and it wasn't a nice place to be in the summer.

My only question now was should I take this particular case

on? If the lamp had been stolen, chances were that someone with more than a passing grudge towards Aladdin had taken it. By extension, they were probably not nice people. Not nice people didn't normally worry me – in my line of work I come across quite a few – but I suspected this particular category of not nice people probably wouldn't have too many qualms about serving me up for breakfast along with some scrambled eggs. I decided cowardice was the better part of valour in this instance.

'Mr Aladdin, I'm flattered that you saw fit to choose the Third Pig Detective Agency but I don't think I'm in a position to take you on at the moment. My caseload is somewhat heavy.'

He looked at me extremely carefully. 'I think, perhaps, you might reconsider,' he said, very quietly but very ominously.

'No, really. It's just not possible right now. I am sorry.'

Aladdin turned to his henchgoat. 'Mr Gruff?'

Gruff opened the briefcase again and took out a large folder which he handed to his employer. He was smiling at me as he did so.

Aladdin opened the folder and began to flick through the pages. 'Mr Pigg, what I have here, among other things, are your last six bank statements, a number of bills from certain of your suppliers – most of which are, apparently, very overdue – and a number of demands for rent, which seems considerably in arrears. Your former landlord seems particularly unhappy with you.'

I was about to launch into a robust defence of my financial situation, which would include claims of invasion of privacy, how unjust certain of my suppliers were in their demands and how things weren't actually as bad as they looked, when the last part of his statement suddenly sunk in.

'Former landlord?' I said.

'Oh yes, didn't I mention? As of . . .' he glanced at his watch, 'forty-five or so minutes ago, I now own this building. You appear to owe me quite an amount of rent.' He handed the folder back to Gruff. 'Shall I have Mr Gruff here organise for collection? I do believe he is a most effective debt-collector. I certainly haven't had any complaints about his methods.'

That sealed it for me. I could have lived with owing half of Grimmtown money and having Aladdin as my new landlord, but I wasn't going to give the goat the satisfaction of coming around with a large baseball bat to collect any outstanding rent.

With as much dignity as I could muster, I caved in.

'Mr Aladdin, you are a most persuasive client. I assume you would like me to start immediately?'

Aladdin smiled at me. It was the kind of smile that suggested one of his grandparents was a shark.

'Delighted to hear it. If you need anything, Mr Gruff will be more than happy to accommodate you.'

I decided to make Gruff suffer a bit. 'I'd like to see where you kept the lamp. Can your goat make himself available to show me around?'

The expression on Gruff's face at this comment suggested that he'd sooner play catch with dynamite. Hey, it was a small victory but I had to take 'em where I got 'em.

Aladdin was heading for the door. Barely looking over his shoulder he asked – no, told – me to call at the house at twelve the next day and Gruff would show me around.

As the door closed behind him I sank back down into my chair and exhaled loudly. My client was now my landlord. He was missing something that he wanted to get back badly. He wanted little or no involvement with the law and, for reasons known only to himself, he had chosen me rather than any of the other detectives operating in town to do the recovery. Sometimes I just got all the breaks.

'Oh Harry, Harry, Harry,' I breathed. 'What kind of mess have you gotten yourself into now?'

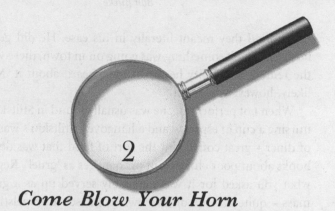

2

Come Blow Your Horn

If television is to be believed, we detectives have contacts every-where. All it takes is a quick phone call to Izzy or Sammy or Buddy and, hey presto, there it is – information at your fingertips. Barmen, bouncers, paperboys, waitresses; you name them, your average detective has them in his little black book. They have their ears to the ground and are always willing to give exactly the information you're looking for exactly when you need it, in return for a small fee.

Wrong!

Forget what you see on TV. Most detectives I know, myself included, can muster up one informant if we're really lucky; usually unreliable, rarely cheap and never around when you want them. My particular source of 'useful' information was a lazy former shepherd. He had got himself into a spot of bother when – after falling asleep on the job one day – his flock had disappeared. Blacklisted and unable to hold down any other kind of agricultural employment, he eked out a living playing the trumpet in some of the town's cheaper bars. He usually then spent the money drinking in the same bars. When people talked of someone with his ear to

15

the ground they meant literally in his case. He did get around, however, and if something was going on in town, there was always the remote possibility he might have heard about it. More than likely, however, he hadn't.

When not performing, he was usually found in Stiltskin's Diner nursing a cup of espresso and a hangover. Stiltskin's was that kind of diner – great coffee, but the sort of food that was described in books about poor children in orphanages as 'gruel'. Regardless of what you asked for it was inevitably served up as a grey lumpy mass – quite like the diner's owner, in fact. Rumpelstiltskin was surly, rarely washed and had all the customer service skills of a constipated dragon. In his defence, however, he did serve the best coffee in Grimmtown.

Well, he had to have one redeeming feature.

I entered the diner and headed for the counter.

'Blue here?' I asked, trying to ignore the smell.

Rumpelstiltskin was cleaning a glass but from the state of the cloth he was using I suspected all he was doing was adding more dirt to an already filthy inside. He grunted in reply and nodded towards a booth at the back of the diner.

'You are as gracious as you are informative,' I said. 'Any chance of a coffee, preferably in a clean mug?' I looked pointedly at what he had in his hands.

Another grunt, which I assumed was an affirmative, but it was hard to tell.

I made my way to the back of the diner. It was a little early for the evening rush but some tables were already occupied. A few construction trolls were sharing a newspaper, or at least looking at the pictures. They also seemed to be the only ones eating what might have been loosely described as a hot meal. That was the thing about trolls: they were a chef's delight. They ate anything thrown up in front of them (and my choice of phrase is deliberate), never complained and always came back for seconds. They single-handedly kept Stiltskin's in business – and they had very big hands.

My contact was sitting in a darkened booth and barely acknowledged me as I sat down. He was still wearing that ridiculous bright blue smock and leggings that all our shepherds wore. The only sop to his status as a musician was a pair of sunglasses.

'Blue,' I greeted him. 'How're tricks?'

He grunted once and continued to nurse his coffee. It was obviously a day for grunts. Conversation wasn't his strong point either. It seemed to be a feature of the people who frequented Stiltskin's.

'I'm looking for information,' I said.

'Ain't you always,' came the reply. He still hadn't bothered to look up.

I pressed on regardless. 'Rumour has it that one of our more upstanding citizens has lost something valuable. He seems to think I might be able to help him locate it. I figured if anyone had heard anything on the grapevine, it'd be you.'

'Anyone I know?'

'That stalwart of Grimmtown high society, our very own Mr Aladdin,' I replied.

At the mention of Aladdin's name he suddenly became less disinterested. He sat upright so fast it was like someone had pumped 5,000 volts through him. Now I had his complete and undivided attention.

'Well, well. So he's come to you, eh? Must be scraping the bottom of a very deep and very wide barrel.'

I ignored the insult. 'He obviously appreciates the skills that I provide . . . and I appreciate the skills that you provide,' I said, slipping a twenty-dollar note across the table to him. There was a blur of movement and the note disappeared off the table and into his pocket. I'd have sworn his hands never moved.

He leaned forward so much our heads were almost touching. 'Word on the street is he's missin' his lamp,' he whispered. 'Not good from his point of view.'

'Yeah? Why's that? What's so special about it?'

Boy Blue leaned even closer, pushed his shades up onto his forehead and, for the first time since I had arrived, looked directly at me. His eyes were an intense blue – just like his ridiculous outfit.

'Rumour has it that it's a magic lamp and he somehow used it when he was younger to make himself very rich.

'There he was, didn't have two coins to rub together, working for peanuts in a laundry. Suddenly he was the talk of the town, appearing at all the best parties, escorting dames like Rapunzel; quite the overnight sensation.'

I groaned inwardly. Magic! I hated magic. As a working detective it's bad enough running the risk of being beaten up or thrown into a river with concrete boots on, without having to live with the possibility of being changed into a dung beetle or having a plague of boils inflicted on you. If you think humans were disgusting covered with boils, imagine how I might look. No! Magic was to be avoided where possible and if it had to feature in a case, I wanted the Glenda the Good type – the type that had lots of slushy music and sparkly red slippers. With my luck, however, this was probably going to be the other type. I was already having premonitions of waking up with the head of a hippo and the body of a duck, going through the rest of my life only being able to grunt and quack.

'Any idea if this magic lamp actually worked?' I asked.

'Nah. I don't even know if it's true. You know how these things are – he probably arrived in town in a stretch limo and with a pocketful of dough. Twenty years later, the rumour becomes the truth because it's just so much more romantic.' He laughed quietly.

'One thing's for sure though, he's certainly not a man to be messed with. He has some interesting hired help.'

'I know. I think I got off on the wrong trotter with one of them this morning.'

'Big guy, scruffy white beard, perpetually angry and smells of cheese?'

'Yeah, that's the fellow; the inimitable Mr Gruff. We've had run-ins before.'

Boy Blue swallowed the dregs of his coffee and pushed the cup away. He belched loudly and with great satisfaction. 'Amazin' thing about this place: lousy food, great coffee. Didn't think it was possible.'

'Well think about it,' I replied. 'Stiltskin's got to have something going for him – apart, of course, from his scintillating personality. But let's get back to Aladdin.' I tried to gather my thoughts. 'Thing is, why would anyone want to steal this lamp, if the story about it is, in fact, just that – a story? Can't see this particular gentleman being overly upset at the thought of having a family heirloom stolen – certainly not upset enough to hire me. It certainly didn't look valuable from the photo he showed. Then again, what do I know? I'm no antiques expert.'

Boy Blue's eyes didn't so much as flicker. 'What if the story's true? Think about it, what could someone do with a magic lamp?'

I thought about it. More to the point, I thought about what I could do with a magic lamp – and I didn't have too fertile an imagination: big house, big car, gold-plated – maybe even pure gold – feeding trough. One rub and all my troubles would be over and, before you ask, it's a convention in this town: you always rub any brassware you might find on the street, just like you always wave any ornate stick when you pick it up and always click your heels together when wearing any kind of sparkly red jewelled shoes. I may not like magic but that's not to say there isn't a lot of it about and people certainly know how to check for it.

It also hadn't escaped my notice that if the wrong people got their hands on this particular source of untold wealth and power then it could create quite a lot of problems – assuming it was the genuine article. There were too many stories of people in Grimmtown who bought pulse vegetables from total strangers with the promise of great things happening to them. With the exception of a guy called Jack (another client whose story I must tell you someday), these great things didn't ever amount to much more than a hill of beans, unless you happened really to like eating vegetables.

My chat with Boy Blue, however, gave me the distinct impression that we were dealing with the bona fide article and a client who wanted it back urgently – presumably before someone else could do what he did all those years ago. Even worse, maybe they had stolen it to use against him. Even worse again, he had hired me to get it back. Ah yes, things were definitely on the expected downward spiral. This was turning out to be a typical Harry Pigg case: much more trouble than it was worth, the potential for great harm being inflicted upon me, and probably impossible to get out of unless I actually found the artifact. I seem to attract these cases like a cowpat attracts flies.

I turned my attention back to Blue, who had now started on my coffee. 'Don't suppose you've any idea who might have taken this lamp?'

'Take the phone-book; stick a pin anywhere in it. Chances are you've found a likely suspect.' He leaned back and looked at the ceiling. 'Any idea how it was stolen?'

'I'm going out to Casa Aladdin tomorrow to have a look. It strikes me that it must have been a professional job. I imagine a man like him would have state-of-the-art security. Someone that rich with something he treasured that much is hardly likely to keep it under his bed beside the chamber pot.'

'That narrows it down a little. Depending on how good his

security system is you're lookin' for someone with enough dough to hire the right help, or the technical smarts to do the job themselves.'

I thought about it. 'Maybe, but if they had those kind of resources, they probably wouldn't need the lamp, would they?'

Blue sniggered. 'Think about it. Ever seen a Bond movie? The kind of guys who would want to steal this are probably thinking about taking over the world, not how they might put the owner of a laundry out of business. We're not talking washing powder and scruffy underwear here, we're talking big weapons, thousands of thugs with large guns, huge secret headquarters hidden under water. Think big and you have your likely villains.'

This really wasn't what I wanted to hear. I was hoping more for a pawnshop and an easy recovery not megalomania and super-weapons. A small-time detective probably wouldn't have much of a chance against that kind of opposition – particularly not this small-time detective.

It was time to go and detect. I slid out of the booth and put my overcoat back on. 'Enjoy my coffee,' I said to Boy Blue. 'It's on me.'

He didn't acknowledge either my generosity or my departure. Typical informant!

I waved goodbye to Rumpelstiltskin on my way out and left the restaurant. Night was falling and, as I headed back to the office, I tried not to laugh out loud as Grimmtown's bright young things made their appearance. I'm no connoisseur of fashion, but to my non-discerning eye this autumn's look was clearly vampire. Lots of black: shoes, clothes, capes, lipstick, hair and eyes. In fact, if there hadn't been any street lights, it would have been difficult just to see them. But, unfortunately, you could still hear them and, in keeping with the theme, there were lots of 'velcomes', 'do you vant a drink' and other stupid vampire sayings from cheap

Hollywood B-movies. Nothing like an idiotic trend to send the fashionistas flinging themselves like lemmings over the cliffs of good taste. Six months from now it would probably be the Snow White look and Dracula would be 'so last year, darlink'.

Outside the Blarney Tone Irish bar, a small man in a bright green outfit was trying to entice customers inside to sample the evening's entertainment. At the Pied Piper Lounge a group of idiots dressed as rats tried to provide an exciting alternative to the more discerning client. It was just as well it was getting dark. No self-respecting punter would enter either premises if they had seen it in daylight.

A number of fast-food sellers were hawking their less than appetising wares on street corners. Hungry though I was, I restrained myself – rat-on-a-stick with caramel sauce didn't engage my senses as perhaps it should. It looked like another busy night in the town's social calendar and one I was, in all honesty, looking forward to missing – not being the social type at all.

I walked the mean streets of Grimmtown back to my office – the further I walked, the meaner they got. I turned into an alleyway that I frequently used as a shortcut. As Grimmtown Corporation hadn't seen fit to light up the alley, I made my way carefully along in the dark, trying not to kick over any trashcans (or any sleeping down-and-out ogres – they were never too happy when suddenly awoken).

As I stumbled along I became aware of a shuffling noise behind me. As a world-famous detective, I had developed a sense of knowing when I was being followed and now this spidey-sense was screaming 'Danger, danger, Will Robinson!' I spun around, trotters raised, ready to fight and, in the same fluid movement, flew backwards into the rubbish behind me when a large fist punched me powerfully in the stomach.

Gasping for breath, I shook old potato peelings and rotting fruit off my suit and slowly came to my feet, trying to see who had hit me. In the darkness I could barely make out my fists in front of me let alone see anything else. I heard the shuffling as my adversary moved towards me again. This time I was ready and aimed a powerful left hook-right hook combo (one of my favourites) at where I guessed my assailant to be. Both punches made satisfying contact with absolutely nothing and, as my momentum carried me forward, I received another blow to the stomach and a kick on the backside. The impact spun me around and I became reacquainted with the pile of rubbish that I had struggled up out of just a few seconds earlier.

This time I elected to stay down. I knew when I was beaten. The question was just how beaten was I going to become. I was also kind of worried. What kind of creature was I dealing with that could hit me so hard yet not be there when I hit back? Having been in more than one brawl in my time, I knew I wasn't that slow so I didn't think I could have missed my assailant.

I felt rather than saw the presence beside me as it bent down and grabbed me by the head with both hands. A voice whispered in my ear.

'Stay away from things that don't concern you,' it said in an accent I couldn't quite place but one that sounded vaguely familiar.

This just added to the mystery: a powerful creature that hit like a hammer, had a body that let punches pass through it, spoke like an extra out of a cheap '40s movie and had powerfully bad breath. I had to ask, of course.

'What kind of things?'

'Your new client and his missing ornament. It might be much healthier for you if you found another line of work in the short term.'

'Says who?' I was getting a little braver (and a lot more foolish).

'Says someone who thinks that you mightn't like hospital food and might prefer walking without the aid of hired help.'

I was now even more confused, as well as smelling like a cheap fruit and vegetable store. How had someone found out about my new client so quickly and, more to the point, why didn't they want me involved in the case? Before I could ask anything else the voice said, 'Remember our little conversation, otherwise I'll call again. Now it's time for sleepies. Nighty night.'

There was a firm tap to the top of my head by something hard, a bright explosion of light and then darkness as what was left of my faculties took command and wisely elected to shut everything down. Unconscious, I slumped to the ground.

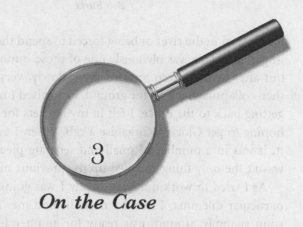

3

On the Case

Two things struck me almost simultaneously when I woke up: the sky was incredibly blue and the only part of me that didn't actually hurt was my left elbow. My mind then went from neutral into first gear and started to tie the two thoughts together into a coherent concept. As I could see the sky, it meant I was lying on my back and the fact that I hurt all over was probably something to do with why I was lying on my back. Then the memory of the previous night's encounter sauntered casually into my head to force my brain into a higher gear. I'd been beaten to a pulp by an invisible someone who I couldn't touch, who had fists like mallets and knew about my current case. This was not a good start to the day and the prospect of another encounter with Gruff at my new client's residence meant it was only going to get worse.

I groaned as I hauled myself to my feet, shedding bits of cardboard, rotten food and used magic beans. I smelled like a garbage cocktail and figured that my new employer wouldn't take too kindly to my turning up at his residence in my present state. Like all good gumshoes, I always kept a spare suit at the office for those important occasions when I needed a one – like being roughed up, thrown in the river or being forced to spend the night sleeping in garbage. This was obviously one of those important occasions but after taking a step forward (very slowly, very carefully) and then collapsing back on the ground, I surmised I might be a while getting back to the office. I felt in my pockets for my cell phone, hoping to get Gloria to organise a cab. When I eventually found it, it was in a number of small and separate pieces. Obviously I wasn't the only thing roughed up the previous night.

As I tried to work out how exactly I was going to resolve this particular dilemma, I heard a noise behind me. I'd like to say I spun snappily around, fists ready for another fight, but I'd be lying. If I had to spin around it would probably have taken me the rest of the morning to do so.

'Hey Mr Pig,' said a boy's voice. 'Why are you covered in beans?'

I eventually managed to look around very slowly and very carefully. A boy of about nine, keeping a very safe distance away, was looking at me with interest. Presumably he didn't get to see a pig in a suit covered with garbage every day. He was dressed in faded jeans, sneakers and a white T-shirt with Hubbard's Cubbard (Grimmtown's latest music phenomenon) emblazoned loudly across the front.

'I fell,' I said, keeping it simple.

'So how did you get that black eye?' he asked. Great: a small nosey boy.

'Fell against those boxes there.' I pointed to the pile of flat cardboard that had been boxes before I fell on them.

'And the cut lip?' A small, nosey, perceptive boy.

'Banged off the wall.'

'And how did your clothes get torn?' Now he was becoming irritating on top of being small, nosey and perceptive.

'Look,' I said in exasperation. 'Shouldn't you be at school or out begging or something?'

26

'Nah,' he replied. 'I don't go to school on Saturdays.'

In my defence, I can only say that my deductive powers were still impaired as a result of the previous night's incident, otherwise, of course, I'd have worked that out in a matter of seconds. That's my excuse and I'm sticking to it.

He finally decided I was fairly harmless – or at least wasn't in a position to do him any real harm – and asked if I needed help. As his chances of carrying me were about the same as Dumbo falling out of the sky on us, I asked him to find a payphone and call Gloria.

'Tell her Harry needs a cab,' I groaned, throwing some coins and my business card at him. 'There should be a phone box out on the street somewhere.'

He looked at the card with great interest. 'Wow, a detective. How cool is that?'

'At the moment, not very,' I replied. 'Just make the call and I'll make it worth your while.'

'You mean I can work for you; be your informant or something?'

'No. I mean I'll give you ten bucks.'

His face dropped. 'But I hear all kinds of cool stuff. I could be really useful, specially with my contacts.'

'Look kid,' I said with as much patience as I could muster (which wasn't really a lot), 'if I need to know who stole the Queen of Heart's tarts I'll contact you, OK. Now can you just make the call? Please.'

He trudged down the alleyway to the street and I tried to clean up my clothes. Apart from used magic beans there were a number of wet newspapers, a variety of vegetables, an old bedspring and spaghetti on various parts of my person. I wasn't sure if I was removing them or smearing them in. When I was finished I certainly didn't smell any better and my suit would never be worn again thanks to the many non-removable stains it now sported. Moving very carefully and very painfully I made my way back towards the street, one aching step at a time.

To my surprise, the kid had made the call and a cab was waiting at the kerb for me. When the driver saw my condition (or smelled my condition, to be more accurate), he was understandably reluctant to let me into his cab. After looking in the back of it I didn't see how I could have made conditions there any worse as the back seat and floor were covered with candy wrappers, old newspapers, apple cores, melted chocolate and various strange and unsavoury-looking stains. If I hadn't known better I'd have assumed the cab had spent the night in the same pile of garbage as I had. When I pointed this out to the driver – and waved a twenty under his nose – he not-so-graciously consented to take me back to the office. As I was getting into the cab I reached into my pocket, drew out a ten-dollar note and handed it to the kid.

'Here kid,' I said. 'Thanks for your help. By the way, what's your name?'

'Jack,' he replied, examining the note for authenticity. 'Jack Horner.'

'Well, Jack Horner, maybe I'll see you around.'

'Count on it Mister.' He turned and walked back down the alleyway.

The cab pulled away and made its way back to my office. I wasn't in the mood for chat so after the cab driver had covered the usual in-taxi topics (weather, sport, vacations, weather again and traffic) without a hint of a response from me, he wisely chose to drive the rest of the journey in silence. At least I gave him a tip when we got to the office: I told him where he could find a good car cleaning service. He didn't seem too impressed as he drove off.

As I entered my office, Gloria tried (none too successfully) not to laugh.

'I shouldn't ask,' she giggled, 'but what happened to you? You look like you slept in garbage.'

I was about to point out how accurate she was and then decided not to give her the satisfaction. I have my pride, you know. With what was left of my dignity I slimed my way into my office. Within a matter of minutes I was clean, well, clean*er* at any rate, sartorially more elegant and, more importantly, smelling a lot less like rotten vegetables. That kind of thing can have a negative effect on clients and this was a client I didn't want to affect negatively, especially on my first day. I opened the top drawer of my desk and took out a spare phone. I had a running supply of spares; cell phones tended to have a limited life expectancy in my pockets. In fact, I suspected that the phone company had a special factory just making phones for me, such was the rate I went through them.

Gloria was still smirking when I came back out.

'That's a bit better, but not much,' she said. If anything, her smirk had gotten wider.

'Thanks for the beauty tips,' I replied. 'Maybe you should take it up professionally. You're obviously wasted in this job.'

'Now, now, I'm only trying to help.'

'Well, try harder.' I headed for the door and walked down to where my car was parked. Sliding into the driver's seat I gave myself a last once-over in the mirror.

'Presentable,' I murmured. 'Not at my best, but I should pass muster. At least they won't know that I spent the night sleeping in an alleyway.'

I started the car and drove uptown to see how the other half lived. Nestling in the foothills on the north side of town, Frog Prince Heights – possibly Grimmtown's most exclusive residential area – was home to the richest, most famous and probably most downright crooked of our citizens. Most of the very large and tasteless mansions had their own security service and enough electronic surveillance to make even the most paranoid of residents comfortable in their beds at night. As was the case with all residential areas of this type, the higher up the hills you went, the bigger the estates got. To my total lack of surprise, my client's home (if a word like home could do justice to the palace I drove up to) was right at the top of the hill overlooking the entire town.

'Master of all he surveys, no doubt,' I said, as I pulled up at the very large, very imposing and very closed gates that were embedded in even larger and more imposing walls. Just to the left of the gates was a small speaker underneath which was a bright red button. Pressing the button, I waited for a response. As I sat there, I imagined that very hidden, very small, very expensive and very-high-resolution cameras were even now trained on me, watching my every move. I didn't have to wait too long.

'Yes,' crackled a voice from the speaker.

'Harry Pigg. I have an appointment.'

'Just one moment.'

A please would have been nice, but I imagined detectives were as high in the food chain of visitors to the mansion as the mailman and the garbage collector so I figured manners weren't part of standard operating procedure.

The gates swung open very quietly and very quickly. I was a bit disappointed; I had imagined they'd be more imposing and ominous with lots of creaking and rattling.

The intercom crackled again. 'Drive through,' said the voice. 'Follow the road around to the side. You'll be met there.'

I followed the driveway up to the house, past lawns that looked as though they were manicured with nail scissors rather than mown. The house itself was a monument to bad taste or blind architects. Someone had clearly tried to incorporate my client's eastern origins into a gothic pile. It was as if a giant (and we have plenty in the locality) had dropped the Taj Mahal on Dracula's Castle and then cemented bits of Barad-dûr on afterwards for effect. Minarets jostled for space with pagodas, battlements and some downright ugly and bored-looking gargoyles. It hurt my eyes just to look at it, and I was wearing shades.

I drove around the side of this tasteless monstrosity to be greeted by another one. Waiting for me at what I presumed was the tradesman's entrance was an ogre, proudly displaying his 'Ogre Security – Not On Our Watch' badge. He was an imposing figure – all muscle and boils. Slowly he checked my ID before letting me out of the car. I could see his lips move as he read the details. The fact that he could actually read impressed me no end – most ogres I knew preferred to eat books rather than read them. Good roughage, apparently.

'So you weren't watching the other night, then?' I asked.

'Huh?' he replied.

I pointed to his badge.

'The other night?' I repeated. 'On your watch? Did you guys take the night off when the lamp was stolen?'

'What lamp?'

'Your boss's lamp. The one that . . .' Seeing the blank look on his face it was obvious that Ogre Security provided the muscle to keep the grounds free of intruders but didn't have too much input to the more sophisticated security inside the house. 'Never mind. Can I go in now?'

He even held the door open for me as I entered the house. A polite security guard, whatever next?

Inside, my good friend Gruff was waiting for me and, by the look on his face, wasn't relishing the job.

'Ah Mr Gruff, so good of you to meet me. I recognised your foul stench as soon as I came aboard. Showers broken, eh?'

He looked at me and I could tell he was struggling to come back with a witty reply, or indeed any reply. I smiled at his discomfort.

'Never mind,' I said. 'If you practise hard in front of a mirror maybe you'll learn to string more than two words together for the next time we meet. Wouldn't that be nice?'

He glowered as he led me through the house. It was just as

tasteless on the inside as on the out. Furniture of various styles, shapes and sizes jostled for position with figurines, sculptures, assorted suits of exotic armour and a variety of plants. It looked like a storage depot for an antiques store run by a florist rather than a place someone actually lived in.

I was led through so many passages and rooms that I soon lost my way and had to depend on my guide to stop me from getting lost.

Eventually we arrived at a steel door that dominated the end of yet another long corridor. It was the kind of door that was more suited to the front of a large castle to keep invading hordes at bay rather than guarding a rich man's trinkets.

'The study,' said Gruff. 'I'll let you in once I've switched off the security system.'

He pressed some numbers on a keypad beside the door. There was a grinding noise and some sequential clunking as locks were deactivated. The door slowly slid into the wall. Lights in the room flickered on as we entered. If the rest of the house had been a monument to clutter, this room was a testament to minimalism. Apart from a large cylindrical black pedestal in the middle of the room, it was completely empty. There were no windows and the only door was the one we had just come through.

I walked towards the pedestal to have a look. It was a column of black marble that came up roughly to my chest. On top was a smaller display stand covered in black velvet, upon which, presumably, the lamp had stood. On closer inspection I could still see the imprint of the lamp's base in the cloth.

'So this is where the lamp was kept,' I said.

'Yes,' said a familiar voice behind me. 'Hi-tech security and surveillance systems and still it disappeared.'

Aladdin strode into the room and shook my trotter. 'Glad you could make it.'

'My pleasure. Exactly how hi-tech was the security here?' I asked.

'If you care to step back to the door, we can show you.'

We all walked back to the entrance and Aladdin turned to the goat.

'Mr Gruff, if you would be so kind.'

Gruff punched some more numbers on the keypad and the lights in the room dimmed again.

'Firstly,' began my employer/landlord, 'the floor is basically one giant pressure pad. Once the security system is switched on anything heavier than a spider running across the room will trigger the alarm. Observe.' Taking a very clean, very expensive and very unused silk handkerchief from his jacket pocket he lobbed it gently into the room. It floated slowly downwards and had hardly touched the floor when strident alarms rang all over the house.

'In addition,' he continued, as Gruff frantically pressed buttons to silence the ringing, 'there is a laser grid in the room which will detect anyone that might, for example, try to suspend themselves from the ceiling and lower themselves down to the pedestal.'

Another flourish of the arm, some more button-punching from Gruff and suddenly a bright red criss-cross of beams filled the room. It looked like a 3-D map of New York. A network of lasers covered every part of the space, wall to wall and floor to ceiling. Anything that might possibly get into the room certainly wouldn't get very far without breaking one of the beams. I didn't need the alarm to be triggered again to tell me that.

'Cameras?' I enquired.

'On the wall,' came the reply and he pointed to a lens that tracked back and forth across the room. 'It scans the room constantly and the output is monitored from our security centre, which you may visit shortly. The entire system is controlled via this keypad here.' He pointed to the unit on the wall. 'It is activated every night at ten and disabled again at seven each morning. All access is monitored and recorded. On the night of the . . . ah . . . disappearance none of the systems were deactivated, the cameras showed nothing else in the room and the lasers weren't triggered. It is most intriguing.'

Intriguing wasn't the word I'd have used; downright baffling was the phrase that came into my head, but I suspected Aladdin was trying to maintain an outward demeanour of cool in keeping with his image.

'Has the camera footage been examined?' I asked.

'Yes,' said Aladdin. 'But it didn't show anything. On one sweep the lamp was there, on the next it was gone.'

'Well, just to be on the safe side, I'd like to have a look. Maybe something was missed.'

From the snort of indignation behind me, I assumed Gruff didn't agree with my supposition. Good.

Aladdin led me to the security centre. The footage from the previous night was loaded by the guard on duty and the tape forwarded to when the lamp vanished. The camera scanned the room from left to right and the lamp was clearly on its pedestal. When it tracked back on its next sweep the lamp was just as clearly gone, as Aladdin had claimed.

'See,' said Gruff in a very superior tone, as if challenging me to find something he'd missed. 'Now you see it; now you don't. Any ideas?'

Not being one to refuse a challenge, I asked for the footage to be replayed and studied the screen carefully, trying to spot anything out of place. On the fifth or sixth repeat, I saw it.

'Stop,' I exclaimed and the security guard immediately paused the tape. 'Look there, right at the base of the smaller pedestal. See?' I pointed to a tiny flash of light that sparkled briefly and disappeared almost immediately afterwards. 'Any chance of getting that enhanced?'

The guard worked his voodoo and magnified the picture.

'What is it, Mr Pigg?' Aladdin's face was so close to the screen, he blocked everyone else's view. 'I can't seem to make it out.'

I moved him gently aside and examined the camera footage carefully.

'If I didn't know better, I'd say it was a micro camera, the kind they use in hospitals to have a poke around people's insides,' I said when I had the opportunity for a closer look.

'But what the hell is it doing inside the display stand? It's solid marble.'

I was obviously putting two and two together and getting four slightly faster than the others – although in Gruff's case I suspected that he was only able to get to three with great difficulty and the help of crayons. It seemed to me that if the thieves couldn't drop into the room or walk across it without setting off any alarms, there was only one other method of entry for any creative burglar – a method that demanded incredible technique and no small amount of nerve.

I looked at Aladdin. 'I think I need to have a closer look at the room,' I said.

'But of course,' replied Aladdin and we walked back to the study.

As Gruff deactivated the alarm system again I noticed something else.

'Hold it,' I said. 'Turn it on again.'

As the red beams criss-crossed the room again, I pointed to the pedestal. 'Notice how the beams don't actually cross the area where the lamp was? If the lamp was taken, it wouldn't set off the alarm.'

'That's a crock,' sneered Gruff. 'No one can actually get to the lamp without breaking a beam or standing on the floor. How do you think they entered the room – they teleported in?'

'Maybe they didn't,' I said. 'Disable the lasers again so I can have another look.'

Once the alarm was off I walked towards the pedestal. A glass dome that didn't look as if it had ever been touched, let alone lifted, covered the top of the pedestal and was firmly clamped to the base. I was obviously in top detecting mode today as, when I looked at the surface of the pedestal through the glass, I could see what looked like a few tiny grains of salt – almost invisible to the human eye; but then again, I'm not human.

'Can you disable the clamps on the glass and turn the lights on full please?' I asked.

More buttons were pressed, and the clamps disengaged loudly. The lights came up to full strength as, very carefully, I lifted the glass dome off and put it gently on the floor. As I examined the pedestal Aladdin came up behind me.

'What do you see?' he asked.

'I'm not sure,' I replied, as I leaned in towards the pedestal for a more detailed examination. 'It may be nothing but . . .'

I picked up some of the grains and put them on my tongue. They weren't salt; they were tiny grains of sand. I looked more closely at the pedestal. Ever so gently I pushed the velvet stand. It slid easily to one side, revealing a gaping hole underneath.

'What in the blazes is this?' exclaimed Aladdin.

'Clearly, when your thieves couldn't access the room from above or through the walls, they went under. They used the micro camera to check when the surveillance system on the wall was sweeping the room and stole the lamp when it was off-camera.'

'But who could have done this and where does the hole go?'

'I don't know who, but that's what you've employed me to find out,' I replied. 'As to the where, I don't know that yet, either, but I think I know someone who can help me work it out.'

4

It's Off to Work We Go!

'**Y**ou mean you want me to climb down there to see where it goes? Cool.'

Jack Horner was clearly excited by his new Apprentice Gumshoe role as he gazed into the hole. As Tom Thumb was out of town on a small vacation (sorry!), he was my next and only other choice, seeing as the hole was too small to allow anyone else to climb into it. After assuring an understandably concerned mother that he would come to no harm, she had reluctantly allowed him to come with me.

'No heroics, Jack,' I told him. 'Just follow the tunnel until we can find out where it comes out.' I pointed to the equipment he was wearing. 'The rope is for safety, the torch will light your way and the little gadget on your belt is a tracker. We can follow you wherever you go. You can talk to us with this.' I handed him a walkie-talkie.

'Will there be monsters down there?' he asked.

'I doubt that very much,' I said, as I checked the rope one more time and lifted him up onto the pedestal. He seemed disappointed at my response.

'Ready?' I asked. He nodded in reply.

'OK then, here we go.'

He stood on the pedestal, looked into the hole again and prepared for his descent. Slowly, he made his way down until he was holding on to the edge by his fingertips. He glanced at me, nodded that he was ready and then let go. I took the strain and lowered him down carefully, as much to avoid any back injury on my part as for his own safety. It didn't take long for him to reach the bottom.

'There's a passage leading away but I don't see any daylight.' His voice came through clearly on my walkie-talkie. 'I'm walking along it now.'

'OK Jack,' I said. 'Follow it slowly but be careful.'

After a few minutes I could hear a strange noise on the walkie-talkie.

'Jack? Are you OK?'

'Yeah, why?'

'I'm hearing some odd noises on the walkie-talkie.'

'Oh, that's just me singing,' Jack replied. 'I do it sometimes to pass the time when I'm walking.'

'Uh, right.' Was this kid afraid of anything?

'I've come to a turn in the tunnel,' he said after a few more minutes. 'It bends to the left.'

From the signal on the tracker screen, he looked to be outside the house now.

'OK Jack,' I said. 'Keep going. Can you see daylight now?'

'Yeah,' he replied. 'The entrance is just up ahead.'

'Stop when you get there. We'll come to meet you.'

'Roger wilco. Over and out.' He'd obviously been watching too many war films.

Guided by Aladdin and Gruff, I walked back through the maze that was the inside of the house and made my way outside. As I walked across the lawn, I heard Jack's voice advising that he had reached the entrance to the tunnel. I told him to stick his head out and describe what he saw.

'It's a hole in the ground, surrounded by trees. I can hear cars so there must be a road nearby but I can't see it from where I'm standing.'

And, by extension, no one could see the hole from the road either.

I turned to Aladdin.

'From the signal, it looks as though the tunnel comes up just outside that wall there.' I pointed to the high wall running along the side of his estate. 'What's on the other side?'

Aladdin thought for a minute, and then for a few more. It was obvious he hadn't the faintest idea. He'd most likely never even noticed what was out there as he went in and out of his house every day – probably in a large limo with tinted windows.

I turned to Gruff. As chief of security I imagined he should know.

'It's a small open area between this house and the next. It's used occasionally by the local residents for walking their dogs, or at least those residents that, from time to time, actually venture out of their houses by means of their feet,' he said, glancing meaningfully at his boss. 'There are a few clumps of trees there. Most likely that's where your minion will be.'

We made our way out the main gate and along by those very imposing walls around Aladdin's house. It was easy to see why the thieves had gone under. The walls were very high with barbed wire on top and, as Gruff explained while we walked, equipped with more pressure sensors. If anything heavier than a sparrow landed on them, the alarms would go off. Even if an intruder was able to get over the walls without setting off the alarms (maybe he was a good pole-vaulter, I don't know) the grounds were full of heat sensors and more cameras. If he managed to get past those minor inconveniences, Ogre 'Not On Our Watch' Security would probably have fun using him as a volleyball. Your common or garden thief didn't stand a chance. It made me even more curious as to what type of thief I was dealing with.

We arrived at the open ground and could see Jack waving at us from a clump of trees about fifty feet from the wall.

'Over here,' he shouted.

When we got to him he was only too eager to show us where he had come out. We pushed through the trees with difficulty as they were very close together, and examined the tunnel. It looked like a very professional job: perfectly circular, level floor and smooth walls with supports to prevent accidental collapse. From its size, the diggers were also apparently quite small. I would have had problems had I been obliged to navigate it.

As I looked at the area around the tunnel entrance, something hanging off one of the branches caught my eye. Closer inspection revealed a bright green thread blowing gently in the wind. One of the thieves must have snagged an exceedingly loud item of clothing on the tree as he made his escape.

At this stage my brain, which, for obvious reasons, had understandably been functioning below par for most of the day, began to power itself up and began asking key questions (although not aloud). More to the point it also began to answer them. Perhaps my assailant wasn't quite as mysterious as I had thought. Putting the information about the tunnel together with the thread and my strange encounter of the previous night, a pattern began to emerge. I needed to get an expert opinion about tunnels and the creatures that dug them. It was time for a trip to the enchanted forest.

I turned to my client.

'Mr Aladdin,' I said, 'I believe, based on what we've just seen, that I am beginning to make some progress in the matter of your missing lamp. I need to make some calls and meet some people. I should have an update for you by tonight. May I contact you then?'

He whipped a card out of his inside pocket.

'My direct number; I am always available. Is there anything you'd care to share now?'

Of course there wasn't. All I had were a few ideas and a bizarre theory that was slowly taking shape but I wasn't going to tell him that.

'Not at this time. I will provide a full update later.'

He grunted, which I assumed was an acknowledgement, and we walked back to the house.

'Until later, then,' he said as Jack and I got into my car.

'Later,' I agreed and drove away. As the huge walls disappeared from view behind us, I told Jack where we were going.

'Are we really going into the enchanted forest?' he asked. 'I've never been.'

It should be pointed out right here that no self-respecting fairy tale town like ours would be without an enchanted forest. It was the location of choice for any laboratory, workshop or secret lair for magicians, wizards, warlocks, witches, alchemists, thaumaturges, vampires and the obligatory mad scientist. There is usually at least one mountain smack in the middle guarded by a horrible monster (usually a dragon) and reputed to be the location of a hoard of treasure.

If truth be known, however, most of the mountains were now just tourist attractions, the treasure having been plundered centuries before and the dragon killed in the process (and replaced by a very realistic animatronic duplicate to keep the punters happy). If you were looking for magic trees (of wood as opposed to those car air freshners that smell nice), cottages made of confectionery, any sword embedded in a stone, unofficial spell-casters, illegal potion sellers or two-headed birds, the enchanted forest was the place to go. Grimmtown's forest had an additional attraction for me, however, one that might go a long way towards solving this case.

We made our way back down from the lofty plateau of Frog Prince Heights, drove across town and into the forest. Fortunately, our destination wasn't too far in. There were far too many unpleasant things lying in wait deep in the forest for unsuspecting adventurers or unaccompanied tour parties and I had no urge to encounter any of them again (yes, I've been there before). After a short drive along a dark, tree-lined road, I pulled up to yet another large gate with yet another anonymous security system.

'The Heigh Ho Diamond Mining Company,' said Jack, reading the ornate sign over the gate. 'Why are we coming here?'

'Because if anyone can tell me anything about who built that tunnel,' I said, leaning out of the car to activate the speaker beside the gate, 'it's the chaps who run this place.'

'Name?' crackled a voice from the speaker. If I didn't know better, I'd swear it was the same voice as the one at Aladdin's.

'Just tell the lads it's Harry and I'd appreciate a moment of their time.'

Almost as soon as I'd finished speaking, the gates swung open – a lot slower and with a lot more gravitas than those at Aladdin's. There was no drive up to the building though; the offices were right beside the gate. There were seven parking spaces marked 'Director', all occupied by very fast, very sleek and very expensive cars. I was almost embarrassed to park my heap of junk beside them. Almost, but not quite – I'm unusually thick-skinned for a pig. We got out of the car and entered the office. As I opened the door, I turned to Jack.

'Not a word, kid,' I warned. 'Just let me do the talking. Some of these guys can be a bit difficult to deal with so stay shtum.'

'Yes sir,' said Jack, giving me a very official-looking salute that I hoped was tongue in cheek.

The reception area consisted of a few garish plastic chairs grouped around a battered coffee table, which was stacked with the inevitable dog-eared three-year-old magazines. Behind a desk and facing the entrance a sour-looking receptionist glowered at me, as if my arrival was a personal affront to him and had somehow ruined his day. Behind him, running the length of the wall, were seven portraits – one for each of the company's directors.

'Take a seat,' he snapped. 'One of the Seven will meet you shortly.'

'Who are "the Seven"?' whispered Jack, as we sat down. 'Are they some kind of secret society with blood oaths, strange pass-words and funny handshakes?'

'Nah,' I replied nonchalantly, picking up a well-thumbed copy of *Miner's Monthly*. 'Nothing so mysterious. They're seven dwarves, all brothers, who set up a diamond mining company here years ago. It's been very profitable. They've cornered the diamond market locally. If anyone knows about digging tunnels, these guys do; they're experts in their chosen field – or under their chosen field even.'

Fortunately we weren't kept waiting too long. A door in the wall facing us opened and a large, red, bulbous nose appeared followed – it seemed like hours later – by the rest of the dwarf. Unfortunately it was Grumpy, my least favourite.

'Well Pigg, whaddya want?' he growled. His interpersonal skills tended to leave a lot to be desired – most noticeably anything remotely resembling good manners. As a rule his brothers tended not to let him do press conferences when they announced their yearly results.

I, of course, knew exactly which buttons to press.

'I'm looking for some assistance please, Mr . . . ah . . . it's Dopey, isn't it?' I replied, knowing full well how much it would aggravate him.

His nose turned even redder and the flush spread to the rest of his face. He glowered at me. 'It's Grumpy,' he said. 'G-R-U-M-P-Y!'

'By name and by nature,' I said under my breath to Jack. He looked down and I could see his cheeks bulge as he tried not to laugh. It's tough being a detective's assistant; you must maintain a calm demeanour at all times, especially when confronted with stressful situations.

He took up the magazine I'd been reading and developed an intense interest in an article on new methods of extracting metals from abandoned mines.

'Apologies, Mr Grumpy. I tend to confuse you and your brothers,' I lied. 'I'm looking for information about tunnels and those who dig them. As you have an undoubted expertise in this area, I figure that if anyone can help me it will be you.'

Flattery will obviously get you everywhere as Grumpy positively preened when he heard me compliment him. He puffed up his chest and strutted across the room. I could see his face gradually assume a less aggressive shade of red as he came towards me.

'What kind of information?' he asked.

I gave him the details of the tunnel I'd found without revealing where it had been dug or why. He considered what I'd said.

'Definitely made by experts from the sound of it, which does narrow it down. The best in the business are Little People. It's almost genetic with us. We have an affinity with stone; we love being underground and have an innate skill in burrowing, digging and making holes.'

'What kind of Little People are we talking about?' I asked.

'Well, apart from my brothers and me – and you know it isn't us,' he said, 'you've got other dwarves, who usually dig in rock;

Halflings, who are good with earth, and fairies, good for small and very basic holes only and purely for sleeping in.'

I wasn't aware of any of these operating illegally in or around Grimmtown and neither was Mr Grumpy. As his company tended to employ all the expert diggers in the region, he would know of any newcomers – particularly as he would probably end up giving them a job, especially if they showed any kind of talent for tunnelling.

'Anyone else?' I asked.

'There are a few others that have shown tunnelling tendencies in the past. Kobolds, leprechauns, gnomes, the occasional Orc and, on very rare occasions, elves, although they've got soft hands so they tend to lotion a lot afterwards.'

I could tell he didn't hold elves in high esteem. I shared his opinion. They tended to stand around looking mysteriously into the middle distance declaiming loudly and pompously such phrases as 'The saucer is broken; milk will be spilled this night.' They never got invited to parties as they usually drank all the beer and, most annoyingly, never seemed to get drunk – apart from a tingling sensation in their fingers.

I figured that this was about as much information as I was going to get. It wasn't a lot but it did give me an inkling of where I should go next. I thanked Grumpy, dragged Jack away from his magazine and headed back to the car.

5

If You Go Down to the Woods Today

A s I drove back through the forest I kept going over the
events of the past two days. Things were starting to make
a little sense – although not much. As I mulled over the
case Jack nudged me in the side with a very bony elbow.

'Mr Pigg,' he said, 'don't look now, but I think we're being
followed.'

'What makes you say that?' I asked.

'Well, the car behind us doesn't appear to have a driver and it's
been tailing us since we left the dwarves' place.'

I looked in the mirror. He was right. Directly behind us was a
very large, very black and very battered car with no driver obviously behind the wheel. As I looked it began to speed up. I could
see the steering wheel rotate but it seemed to be doing so of its
own accord. Maybe the Invisible Man was driving the car but,
frankly, I doubted it – he had been advised to take taxis, as, every
time he got behind the wheel, he tended to cause a small panic.

This was now getting beyond a joke and I wasn't the one who

was laughing. Suddenly, the car accelerated again and rammed us from behind. The impact jolted us forward. Fortunately, apart from being winded, we didn't suffer any injuries, our seatbelts preventing any major harm.

'Whee!' shouted Jack. 'This is just like a roller coaster. Does this always happen when you drive?'

'No,' I said, trying to keep one eye on the road ahead and one on the car behind (not an easy task). 'Only on good days.'

Of course, car chases never take place on straight wide roads that run for miles with no sharp turns or oncoming traffic. Oh no, apparently convention dictates that they must take place through a busy metropolis with lots of hills, a narrow dirt track running along a sheer drop into the ocean or, as in my case, through a dark forest with a twisty road, lots of sharp bends and (being an enchanted forest) trees that might take exception to being woken up and take a swipe at whatever vehicle had done the waking. The bigger the tree, the more likely your car was to suddenly develop the art of flight when one of its branches made contact. Typically it wasn't the flying that one needed to be worried about; usually it was the landing – which tended to be uncontrolled, totally lacking in technique and, almost inevitably, resulted in your vehicle being embedded up to its rear doors in the ground. Most cars tended never to get back on the road after contact with one of our magic trees.

As I swerved to avoid hitting one of these trees and to try to ensure that my pursuer didn't, I had another of my really bright ideas.

'Hold tight,' I roared at Jack as I pressed hard on the accelerator. 'This could get scary.'

'You mean it gets better?' he shouted back, grinning from ear to ear. 'This is the coolest ride I've ever been on. Go Harry!' He stretched both arms up over his head, as people do just as they get their photograph taken on the scary part of a roller coaster ride, and yelled at the top of his voice. Truly this child had no fear.

The sudden burst of acceleration had, for a few seconds, taken me away from my pursuer. Rather than head towards the forest's edge, however, I took one of the trails deeper into the trees. I had a very specific destination in mind and one that might, if my timing was right, get this particular pursuer permanently off our backs.

As we drove further into the forest, the trees grew closer together and, eventually, their branches became so entwined over the road they formed a natural tunnel, shutting out daylight completely. I flicked on the headlights and they gave just enough illumination to prevent me driving off the road. On either side, gnarled branches were trying to grab at the car as we passed but I was going so fast they only scraped off the sides. They might be ruining the body-work, but at least the bodies inside the car were undamaged – for now.

I recklessly navigated turn after turn (by the skin of my teeth in most cases), the road getting narrower and windier as we drove. I wasn't particularly scared of the forest; being chased by an invisible maniac tended to force all other thoughts of being frightened from one's mind. Our pursuer wasn't quite as reckless though, preferring to drive fast enough to keep us in his sights but not so fast as to spin off the road. We would hardly have been that lucky but that wasn't my main objective. It would, however, have made what I was about to do much less of a risk – especially to Jack and me – if he'd managed to hit something other than us in the interim.

A fork in the road came up so fast that, even though I was expecting it, I still nearly ploughed straight into the tree that stood right where the road split in two. I swung the steering wheel in an effort to keep the car on track. It screeched around the right-hand turn, leaving a liberal helping of rubber on the road. I was hoping my pursuer might not be so lucky but as I looked in the mirror I saw him take the fork a little less dramatically than I had and continue his relentless pursuit. We were now driving in total darkness such was the tree cover all around us. Even the car's headlamps didn't do much to light the way.

I was now driving purely on instinct. Bends came and went in a blur and all the while I could see the lights of the other car behind us, never closing the gap but never losing any ground either. Well, if things went according to plan, there would soon be a fair, and somewhat unexpected, distance between us. I turned to Jack.

'Hold on tight. Things might get a little bumpier.'

His face lit up like a searchlight. 'You mean it gets better?'

'Oh yeah, much better,' I replied grimly. 'Just make sure you're well strapped in.'

At last we were arriving at our destination. In front of us the road narrowed and curved around sharply to the left. Right on the bend stood a large and very old ash tree. Its gnarled branches hung down over the road, trailing long green strands of moss. As we approached they began to twitch as if anticipating our imminent arrival. I stood on the brakes and the car stopped abruptly just in front of the tree, jerking both of us forward. Moss draped across the windscreen, obscuring our visibility, but I was only interested in what I could see out of my side window. Jack was looking over his shoulder to see where our pursuer was and was finally starting to panic.

'Why have you stopped, Harry? He's getting closer.'

'I know. Just another few seconds.' I began to rev up the car.

'We don't have a few seconds. He's right on us.' Jack was really panicking now.

There was a blurred movement of something grey and gnarled coming towards us from the side and I instantly accelerated. The car shot forward as if it had been fired from a cannon. Our pursuer, who had sped into the space we'd just vacated, was suddenly swept sideways by a large and very fast-moving branch. There was a loud wail from inside the car as it was catapulted across the road and smashed through the undergrowth on the opposite side, leaving a large and impressive vehicle-shaped hole in the bushes. Where the car had been on the road, a few leaves floated gently to the ground.

'Now that's what I call a flying car,' I muttered with satisfaction. 'James Bond, eat your heart out.'

Before I could take too much pleasure in the somewhat premature end to the chase, I had to drive my own car out of reach of the ash tree's branches before it had a second swipe. Better safe than even more damaged, I always say.

'Well, let's take a look at the incredible flying car,' I said, as I opened the door and got out. 'From the noise that it made as it flew through the air with the greatest of ease, I very much doubt that it was driverless.'

As Jack joined me and we began to make our way across to where the other car had landed I turned to the ash tree. 'Thanks Leslie,' I said. 'I can always depend on you to miss me.'

The tree shook its branches violently and sprayed moss in all directions.

'Maybe next time, Pigg,' it said in a voice that made Treebeard sound like a soprano. 'You can't be lucky forever.'

'What's his problem?' asked Jack.

'Some other time,' I replied. 'It's a long story. Suffice to say that, ever since my last encounter with him, he's had a deep longing to play baseball with me – using me as the ball.'

We made our way through the undergrowth. It wasn't too difficult as the flying car had cleared a wide path for us. We found it in a tree, jammed into the junction of two large branches. On the driver's side the door was open. Fortunately for me it was within climbing distance. Very carefully, I climbed up to the car and peered inside. Whoever – or whatever – had been driving had clearly done a runner, leaving nothing in the way of clues behind. Apart from the glass all over the floor, the inside of the car was spotlessly clean. I was now convinced that, despite initial appearances to the contrary, there had been a driver. Something had been screaming in terror as the car took flight and that same something had managed to open the door and disappear before we got there. All I had to do now was figure out what that something was, and if there's one thing I'm good at (actually, there are lots of things I'm good at) it's figuring things out. I hadn't actually expected to find anything in the car – that was a long shot. I was more interested in what may have been on the front. I swung around to the remains of the hood. Steam hissed from the mangled engine but there was no obvious smell of gasoline so I figured I was safe. I ran my trotters carefully over the front grille and felt something jammed in.

'Let's see what we've got here,' I muttered, pulling at the mysterious object.

There was a sudden screech of metal as the object I was investigating came off in my hand. With a loud shout, I fell back off the branch and plummeted to the ground. Fortunately for Jack I missed him when I landed. Unfortunately for me I also managed to miss anything remotely resembling a soft landing and hit the ground with a very unsatisfactory (from my viewpoint, at any rate) thud. As I groaned in pain and checked all extremities for damage for the second time in a day, I swore I could hear the ash tree sniggering in tones so low I could feel my fillings vibrate. He was obviously enjoying a minor victory at my expense. As I'm not a petty pig – but more because there was a small boy in the vicinity – I refrained from making an obscene gesture at him, although someone had once pointed out to me that it was very hard to make obscene gestures when you didn't have any fingers.

I was, by now, mastering the art of getting gingerly to my trotters so I managed it much better this time. Once I had dusted off the leaves and other debris, I examined the object, the removal of which had caused me to fall in the first place.

'What is it, Harry?' asked Jack.

'Exactly what I'd expected,' I replied. 'It's a very small but very powerful camera.'

'What was it doing on the front of the car?'

'Well, think of it like this, if you were really small and had to drive a car, how would you be able to see where you were going if you couldn't see over the front dash?'

I had now dismissed the idea of being beaten up by an invisible superhero. All the evidence I'd gathered during the course of the day had led me to a different, less super and far more irritating solution. The camera had now confirmed my suspicions. I now needed to pay a visit to someone very annoying. This someone would not appreciate me visiting him, so, in order to prevent a recurrence of the previous night's unfortunate incident, I needed some additional protection.

'OK Jack, let's head back to the ranch. There's nothing more to see here.'

As we walked back to the car, being very careful to avoid any aggressive branches, I reached for my shiny new phone and made a quick call. For my next trick I would definitely require a very specific type of assistance, and I knew exactly who could provide it.

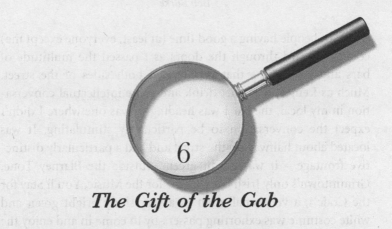

6

The Gift of the Gab

I t was early evening when we got back into town. After dropping Jack at home with a promise I'd call him again if I needed him, I drove back to the office, parked the car and headed back towards the main street. After the previous night's experience I kept a regular look over both shoulders and avoided any dark, or even not that brightly lit, alleyways. If there weren't at least twenty people in the same street as me then it wasn't going to be one I was going to walk down, across or through. Once bitten – or once punched, threatened and deposited in garbage – had made me very careful and I was also concerned about the impact that constantly being decorated with rotten vegetables was having on my laundry bill – not to mention my personal grooming.

After navigating the side streets of Grimmtown without attracting any undue attention, I turned onto Hans Christian Andersen Street. Dusk had made way for night and the city's bright young things were all out in their vampire-look finery again. On every corner a girl from Little Matchgirls Inc. was hawking hot dogs, burgers and fried chicken – the company had diversified over the years, especially after smoking fell out of favour. The sound of people having a good time (at least, everyone except me) could be heard through the doors as I passed the multitude of bars and restaurants that proliferated both sides of the street. Much as I enjoyed a quiet drink and some intellectual conversation in my local, the bar I was heading to was one where I didn't expect the conversation to be particularly stimulating. It was located about halfway up the street and had a particularly distinctive frontage – it was bright green. Outside the Blarney Tone, Grimmtown's only Irish bar ('Come for the Music, You'll Stay for the Craic'), a very small man in a very shiny bright green and white costume was exhorting passers-by to come in and enjoy the fun inside. Benny was a gnome and Grimmtown's worst leprechaun impersonator. I stopped behind him to listen to his patter. He had the worst Irish accent I'd ever heard; yes, even worse than Tom Cruise's in *Far and Away* – and I should know, my grandfather was prime Irish bacon.

'Ah sure now, will ye not come in and try a Guinness. 'Tis only the best in the town, brought in specially, direct from the brewery in Dublin. There's a free plate of crubeens thrown in for good measure. You won't see the like anywhere else.' As he spoke he did a little jig that caused the rather large silver buckles on his black shoes to clang like a set of enormous bells.

The rest of his outfit was just as subtle as his shoes. Bright white socks stretched up to just below the knees, where they were met by bright green plus fours that were kept up by a large black belt. White frills that seemed to explode from a shirt so white it hurt to look at it fronted an equally lurid green jacket. An obviously fake ginger beard and curly wig covered most of his grey-skinned face like a bright orange fungus. On his head he wore a long black hat with yet another shiny buckle. It looked like someone had rammed a bucket upside-down on his head.

He was possibly the least convincing leprechaun in history but he was also just the man I needed to talk to. Despite the ludicrous outfit he was very sturdily built. In fact, he was the type of guy who could deliver a hefty punch to your midriff while, owing to his size, every attempt you made to hit him back just went over his head.

He still hadn't noticed me as I approached him carefully and tapped him on the shoulder.

'Evening Benny,' I said cheerfully.

He spun around and for a split second his face dropped as he recognised me. Like the true pro he vainly aspired to be, he immediately recovered and began his Irish shtick again but his first reaction had given him away.

'Begorrah Mr Pigg, is it yourself that's in it. And out on a fine night like this too. Sure why not drop in and try a pint of the black stuff. 'Tis the best in town.' As he spoke he made to move towards me. This time I was somewhat better prepared and, as I quickly stepped back, I nodded to two large shapes that had just as quickly, but a lot more silently, moved up behind him. As he tried to land a punch on me a large hand grabbed his neck from behind and suddenly jerked him backwards and upwards. He dangled in mid-air, legs kicking so fast he looked like he was pedalling an invisible bicycle. The hand held his head level with my eyes and squeezed ever so slightly. Benny's face began to turn an interesting shade of bright red as his neck began to constrict under the pressure.

'Now, Benny,' I said cheerfully, 'perhaps we can discuss your recent forays into robbery and GBH.'

'I . . . don't . . . know . . . what . . . you . . . mean,' he managed to choke out. By now his face was turning from red to purple and I watched with fascination (and no small degree of pleasure I must shamefully admit).

'Ah, but how remiss of me,' I said. 'I'm forgetting my manners. Before we start, allow me to introduce my colleagues, Mr Lewis and Mr Carroll. They're ogres.' Considering their size, strength and skin colour it was probably stating the obvious, but I wanted to see Benny sweat and show him that I meant business. My 'colleagues' were each over eight feet tall with skin that almost matched Benny's jacket in hue. Their impressively muscular frames were barely contained by the immaculate evening suits they had squeezed into. They were definitely the type of guys (or creatures) that you needed when there was a possibility of any unpleasantness, as they tended to be a very effective deterrent – as they were now proving.

'Now that the introductions are over, perhaps we can get down to business,' I said to Benny. 'Let me put some perspective on this for you, just in case you're confused.'

As Benny wasn't the sharpest tack in the box I figured I'd better spell it out for him. Before I could start, however, I noticed that his face was now bright blue. Perhaps the ogres were being a trifle too eager.

'Mr Lewis, perhaps a little less pressure.'

Lewis grunted and relaxed his hand slightly. Benny's face returned to its previous shade of purple.

'OK, Benny,' I said, 'let's begin. Once upon a time there was a gnome named Benny. Not too bright but always on the lookout for an opportunity, he made a living as a dodgy leprechaun impersonator trying to get gullible customers into the local Irish bar. And, by the way, you need to work on that accent. Are you with me so far?'

He nodded, his head barely moving.

'Good. Now, our friend Benny probably got an offer from someone to help him acquire a valuable antique from a local businessman. It certainly wasn't Benny's idea, what with him not being too bright and all, but the offer was impressive enough to encourage him. How am I doing so far?'

Benny gave another little nod.

'This is called detecting, Benny. It's what I do. I examine the clues and determine what's going on. This then allows me to follow a specific line of inquiry. This specific line of inquiry has, most fortuitously, brought me to you.

'In this instance, your mysterious client clearly needed someone with some subterranean delving skills and who would also do what he was told, no questions asked, as long as the price was right.

'Unfortunately he picked you,' I continued. 'You may be a great digger, which of course pointed me in the right direction, but you were a trifle careless at the scene of the crime.' I reached into my pocket and removed a small envelope. Inside was the green thread I'd found on the tree outside Aladdin's. 'You appear to have picked up a minor tear on your sleeve and, look, the thread I happen to have here matches almost perfectly. What a coincidence, eh?'

There was another gurgle that could have meant anything from 'What great detective work. You've certainly rumbled me. I confess' to 'I'm slowly choking to death here, could you ask your moron to reduce the pressure on my neck somewhat.'

I chose to interpret it as the latter, although I certainly wouldn't describe Lewis as a moron – at least not to his face. Another nod and Lewis eased his grip slightly more.

'Now I know that you aren't working alone, not only because you haven't got the smarts to pull this off on your own, but even you couldn't drive a car into the enchanted forest, crash it rather spectacularly and then get back here to play little green man with the tourists so quickly. Nice trick by the way, getting one of your idiot cronies to use the camera to see where he was going because he was too small to look over the wheel. I take it you didn't come up with that idea either?' The response was another faint shake of the head.

'Now I know that, as a rule, when goblins get together, rather than the total being greater than the sum of the parts, the collective IQ tends drop to well below that of the dumbest member – a kind of anti-synergy. I suspect, therefore, that you were the mere executors of this cunning plan that, in all likelihood, was probably written out in very small words and very short sentences so you and your cronies could follow it without screwing up – which you failed miserably to do. So here's what I'm going to do.' I looked Benny straight in the eye to let him know that I still meant business. 'I'm going to instruct Mr Lewis here to let you go. When he does so you will make no attempt to do anything other than answer whatever questions I may put to you. Should you attempt to assault either of the ogres (which would be rather foolish) or me or even try to make a break for it, the only break you will experience will be a random assortment of your limbs. Understood?'

Benny nodded ever so slightly. I looked at Lewis and he dropped the goblin with such force that he lay on the ground groaning pitifully. I nudged him with my shoe.

'C'mon Benny, up you get. If you need some help you only have to ask. Either Mr Lewis or Mr Carroll will be only too delighted to assist you.'

This suggestion seemed to give Benny some incentive as he struggled to his feet slowly and, I have to add, with a lot less style than I had shown previously. Maybe he just didn't have as much practice at getting up as me.

'OK, Benny, your starter for ten: where's the lamp?'

Benny looked up at me with an expression that would have made his mother clutch him to her chest and console him with lots of 'there, theres'. Fortunately for both of us I wasn't his mother so he didn't get the sympathy vote from me. He also spared me the 'what lamp?' routine, presumably as even he could figure out exactly how much I already knew and that I wasn't prepared to tolerate being messed around any more – or maybe it was just the large and very obvious presence of my two companions. Despite this, however, his reply was only marginally more helpful (which wasn't saying a lot).

'I don't have it,' he gasped.

'Not a good answer, Benny,' I said. 'I'd have thought that by now you'd realise there is no point in playing dumb – or, in your case, even more dumb than usual – with us. We're really not in the mood.'

'No, really, I don't have it. Honest.' From the fearful look on his face I suspected that he was finally telling the truth. Now all I had to do was find out what he had done with the lamp, get it back to Aladdin, pocket a large pay packet and wallow in the satisfaction of a job well done. Smiling with anticipation, I asked the obvious question again and received a not-so-obvious answer that wiped the smirk off my face and plummeted me even deeper into the murk that was Grimmtown's underworld.

'One last time, where's the lamp, Benny?'

'Edna has it,' he answered.

I looked at him, dumbfounded. 'Edna?' I repeated.

He nodded his head gingerly. 'Edna,' he said with more conviction.

'Edna, as in Edna?'

He nodded again. 'Yep, that's her.'

'Please tell me you're joking and this is just another idiotic attempt to throw me off the track,' I begged, but I knew Benny was telling the truth, I just didn't want to believe it. I just wanted him to suddenly spring to his feet and yell, 'Gotcha! I had it in me rucksack all the time.' I knew this wouldn't happen. Quite apart from the fact that he could barely stand anyway, his entire demeanour suggested he was being truthful – and without being coerced any further, either.

If Edna was involved, I needed to tread very carefully indeed.

In actual fact I needed to run very quickly in the opposite direction if I wished to retain the use of all my limbs. This was more like a Harry Pigg case: lots of different people vying to be the next to hurt me in new and interesting ways while I manfully (or pigfully) tried to represent my client to the best of my ability (and he was one of those people threatening to hurt me). I figured I'd get whatever information Benny hadn't yet imparted and then decide whether it would be more advisable to get the next bus out of town or stay and get beaten up at least one more time.

'OK Benny, let's take it from the top – and don't leave anything out.'

7

In the White Room

'Emerald Isle of Adventure? Are you serious?'

Benny nodded glumly. 'Emerald Isle of Adventure,' he repeated. Repetition tended to happen a lot when you talked to Benny. It helped him focus.

'You really were going to call the theme park that?' This beggared belief. I knew Benny was as dumb as a bucket of shrimp, I just didn't realise the extent of his stupidity. This master plan of his plumbed new depths of imbecility.

Benny and his 'Brains' Trust' of gnomish friends had decided that, with the proliferation of successful and highly profitable theme parks based on our illustrious history that had sprung up all around Grimmtown, it might be a rather splendid idea to develop one based around Ireland and its past, him and his buddies being leprechaun impersonators and all. 'A sure fire hit' was how he'd described it. So far I had been regaled with how it would include Finn McCool's Rollercoaster of Terror, the Lucky Leprechaun Log Flume and the Find the Crock o' Gold Hall of Mirrors. When you eventually grew tired of all the excitement you could then relax in Mother Ireland's Bacon and Cabbage Emporium with a nice Guinness.

Now I like my thrills as much as the next man – except in this case seeing as the next man was Benny – but I just didn't think this particular wonderland had the necessary pizzazz. In fact, if it managed to draw more than twenty gullible tourists on the day it opened (if it ever did), I'd eat my own head.

To cut a long, very rambling and disjointed story short (and to spare you many tedious digressions, pauses and nonsensical musings, because I know even your patience would wear very thin), Benny had put an ad in the local press describing the concept and seeking investors for this sure-fire hit. To his – and no one else's – surprise, the take-up on the proposal was less than stellar but, just as he was about to abandon his plan, he received an email (and yes the address was evilgenius@criminalmasterminds.com) promising him a very large investment in the scheme in return for a very small favour. This favour (and I'm sure *you* can see what's coming, even if Benny couldn't) involved Benny and the boys using their burrowing skills to recover an artifact that had allegedly been stolen from this mysterious benefactor many years previously. The story was embellished by references to family heirlooms, dastardly thieves, a poor granny pining for her long-lost lamp and, of course, the dangling of the incentive of part of the investment up front with the rest to follow upon successful delivery of the lamp. Benny had swallowed it hook, line, sinker, fishing rod and angler.

The down payment had arrived and Benny had acquired the lamp – which considering his track record had to qualify as a spectacular success. All he then had to do was deliver it and the Emerald Isle of Adventure would be a reality. As you can imagine, the delivery hadn't gone according to plan – hardly surprising when you consider who the delivery boys were.

Benny and his band of idiots had begun making their way to the drop-off point. If the sight of a band of gnomes trying to look furtive while walking through the busiest part of town dressed in lurid green outfits didn't grab attention, the same group babbling on loudly about how they were going to spend their newly-acquired fortune surely would. Unfortunately for them, it grabbed the attention of two of Edna's henchmen.

Now I need to digress slightly here, as I'm sure you're asking, 'Who is Edna?' and 'Why does she want to divest those poor unfortunate gnomes of their one chance of a happy ending?' The answer to the second question is easy once you understand the first. Edna is one of a group of four witches who basically run all of Grimmtown's organised crime – a kind of Mezzo-sopranos or Contraltos, if you will. They've unofficially divided the town up into four districts and Edna runs the West Side – hence her title: the Wicked Witch of the West Side. Their control of all criminal activity is total. Nothing illegal moves without them knowing about it or profiting from it to some extent. They are a family I had kept well clear of over the years and I had no wish to alter that status any time soon. If, however, Edna did have the lamp, then that was a wish that was evidently about to come true, despite my best efforts to the contrary.

'So,' I said to Benny, 'to summarise the plan: there you were, a band of gnomes heading to a drop-off point in the middle of town, babbling on heedlessly about how you were going to be fabulously rich once you passed the lamp over to your mysterious benefactor, a lamp, incidentally, which one of you was actually carrying in a bright red shopping bag. Where in this cunning strategy do you think the obvious flaw was?'

Benny dropped his head in a semblance of shame and chose not to answer.

'So. On your way to the drop-off point – ah, where was this place, anyway?' I asked.

'Litter bin on the south corner of Wilde Park,' mumbled Benny.

'Of course it was. Instead of somewhere quiet and secluded, you picked one of the busiest intersections in the city. Could you have been any more obvious?' I laughed. Benny's story was becoming more nonsensical by the minute.

'So, as I say, you were on your way to the drop-off point when someone from Edna's gang grabbed the bag. Now, what I can't figure out is this: you guys are thick but can certainly pack a punch.' I rubbed my stomach at the memory of just how packed the punch was. 'How come they got the lamp so easily?'

Benny mumbled again.

'Speak up, Benny,' I asked. 'I can't make out a word you're saying.'

'Otto took it,' said Benny, a little more articulate this time. 'He just flew down out of nowhere, grabbed the bag in his claws and scrammed again.'

Otto the Owl was one of Edna's henchbirds and I suppose that a bright red bag wasn't too hard to miss if you had spent your formative years flying around a forest hunting tiny rodents in total darkness.

To put it mildly, this new development presented me with a problem: my client's lamp was now in the possession of one of Grimmtown's most ruthless criminal families; a family who would have no compunction about rearranging my anatomy should I even hint that it might be a good idea for them to return it. My client would also, in all likelihood, rearrange my anatomy if I failed to return his lamp – and probably evict me to boot. Either way it seemed that anatomy rearranging was about to become my newest pastime and one I didn't particularly feel like taking up, especially as we were talking about my anatomy and its capacity to be rearranged. In the faint hope that I might get something else out of him, I turned back to Benny.

'Apart from emails,' I asked, 'I don't suppose you ever got to meet this investor of yours?'

'Not as such, no,' Benny said. 'But I came close one night or, at least, I think I did.'

'What do you mean?'

'Well, the night we were due to receive our down payment my instructions were to go into the men's rest room in the Blarney Tone, make sure I was alone, send a text message to a particular number that I was ready, and wait for further instructions. When I got in there, I waited until it was empty, did as I was asked and stood there. Suddenly there was a loud bang, everything went white and next thing I knew I was in a room with funny walls, lots of rugs and carpets and stuff like that. I couldn't see anyone in the room but a voice told me to pick up a bag that was on a table beside me. As soon as I did, I was suddenly back in the rest room again with my down payment.' He looked at me. 'I know how it sounds, but it's the truth, Mr Pigg. Honest.'

I was just about to tell him how ludicrous his story was and did he really expect me to swallow something so ridiculous when there was a loud bang, everything went white and I was suddenly in a room with funny walls, lots of rugs and carpets and stuff like that.

As you can imagine, it took a few seconds to get my bearings seeing as I had suddenly been transported from Point A to Point B without any knowledge of where Point B actually was, how far it was from Point A, or exactly how precarious my situation now was as a result. At first glance, fortunately, precarious didn't seem to figure high on the agenda. I was in a long oval-shaped room with no windows or obvious doors. Bright white walls curved inwards from an equally white floor to an oval ceiling. Lamps ran along the walls illuminating the room with a soothing white light. It was, in fact, a very white room.

The only sop to an alternative colour scheme were the very expensive-looking rugs (expensive to my unsophisticated eyes at any rate) that were casually flung on the floor in a feng-shui kind of way and the colourful tapestries that hung from the walls. The décor suggested the Orient, which, considering my current assignment, hardly seemed like a coincidence. Whoever had summoned me here was clearly connected to Aladdin in some way – if only by culture. My suspicion, however, based on Benny's tale was that I was in the presence of this mysterious stranger, although the room was currently devoid of any presence other than me. As most of the people I'd encountered in this case so far seemed intent on doing me harm, this was a small mercy for which I was incredibly thankful.

As I stood there I became aware of a faint whirring behind me. I turned around – ever so slowly – to see if some strange mechanical torture device was about to dismember me. To my relief, I found myself gazing at a not-so-sinister, large and very hi-tech-looking computer. There were so many wires, cables and other devices hanging from it, it looked like it was in an intensive care unit. With all the printers, modems, scanners, microphones and assorted paraphernalia – that even I couldn't figure out the use of – there seemed to be enough hardware to run a small country and still have enough processing power for a quick game of Half-Life while affairs of state were being mulled over.

It also occurred to me that the computer might shed some light on the identity of the thief and maybe even some clue as to their motive. As I surreptitiously reached for the keyboard a voice erupted from the walls around the room.

'Naughty, naughty, Mr Pigg,' it boomed. 'Please step away from my machine.'

I raised my trotters over my head and took three steps back from the hardware. Looking around, I tried to see where the voice was coming from. Best I could figure was that there were speakers hidden behind the wall hangings and, from the quality of the sound, they were clearly very expensive.

'Please forgive both my brusque manner and the somewhat unorthodox kidnapping,' the voice continued. 'I hadn't meant for us to meet in quite these circumstances. In fact, I hadn't intended for us to meet at all but I suspect that my original choice of miners left much to be desired when it came to not leaving obvious, or indeed any, clues behind. Clearly I should have been more discriminating in my selection.'

'If you pay peanuts, you get monkeys,' I said. I enjoy a cliché every now and again and it was the only thing I could come up with while I tried to figure out what to do next. I'm not always witty and quick with the rapier-like repartee – hard, as I'm sure it is, for you to believe.

'Indeed,' said the voice. 'And while you're trying, no doubt, to figure out where you are, who I am and what you should do next, allow me to recommend that you make yourself comfortable while I make some suggestions.'

I slowly sank onto a very ornate and very comfortable ottoman and waited.

'As you have probably already deduced, the gnomes were clearly not a good investment. In less than twenty-four hours they stole the lamp but left clues so blatant that a corpse could have followed them. They then managed, with an incredible lack of subtlety, to make Grimmtown's organised crime fraternity aware that they had an object of immense value and then, while bringing it to me, succeeded in handing it over to one of our more illustrious criminal masterminds in the process. Do I summarise the situation accurately?'

I nodded weakly as I could see where this was going and I didn't need a map to give me directions.

'I think I now need to utilise the resources of a more accomplished craftsman to reacquire the lamp and you will probably not be surprised when I tell you that I have chosen you, Mr Pigg.'

I opened my mouth to object with whatever reasons I could think of but before I could even come up with 'Scintillating Excuse Number One to Avoid Locating a Stolen Lamp', I was interrupted.

'I will, of course, not tolerate any refusal on your part,' said the voice with an uncanny sense of anticipation. 'My need for this lamp is far greater than your need to refuse and I can change you into anything I choose should you prove to be difficult.'

Now I was getting paranoid. There was a definite trend here and it wasn't one I was particularly enamoured with. Why was everyone suddenly so intent on hiring me and, when I expressed any kind of reluctance, quite prepared to use very effective threats of bodily harm to compel me to agree to work for them? Was I really that good, or was I just that unlucky? Was it possible for anyone to be that unlucky? Maybe I just had that kind of face.

Whatever the reason, it now looked like I had two clients, both of whom wanted the same thing and one of them was now telling me I had to steal back an already stolen lamp from one of our most ruthless criminals or face an unpleasant, but as yet undefined, alternative. With my imagination, however, I could think of quite a few 'alternatives', none of which were remotely attractive and none of which I particularly wanted to face. It looked like I was about to add breaking and entering to my already extensive set of skills.

'OK,' I said, resigning myself to the inevitable. 'What do I have to do?'

The whirring sound increased in volume and a large amount of paper was ejected from one of the printers at the high-tech end of the room. From what I could see, it was building plans of some kind.

'Blueprints of Madame Edna's building,' confirmed the voice. 'My understanding is that the lamp is in a room on the third floor,

70

securely under lock and key. Unfortunately, security in the building is, by definition, rather tight. This means, of course, that it will be difficult to find a means of access that won't be guarded in some way. I, however, have a high degree of confidence that, if undetected access can be found, then you are just the pig to find it. I would suggest that, if you are successful, you should reflect on the options available to you and, perhaps, the recovery of the lamp may not be as difficult as it first appears.'

Great, now he was talking in riddles as well. I grabbed the sheaf of papers and looked at the ceiling.

'On the off chance that I do manage to get the lamp back, how do I contact you again?'

'You don't,' came the reply. 'I shall contact you.'

'Great,' I said, with a considerable lack of enthusiasm. 'Can I go now?'

There was another loud bang and associated white light. When my head cleared I found myself back outside the Blarney Tone, staring into Benny's ugly mug. As Messrs Lewis and Carroll were still in close proximity it mitigated against his taking advantage of my disorientation. When asked, they confirmed that I had disappeared from right in front of their eyes, had been absent for about ten minutes, and then reappeared in exactly the same spot.

This had been one of the strangest days of my life and I should know; I've had quite a few. I decided it was time to cut my losses and plan for tomorrow before things got any weirder.

I turned to Benny. 'Benny, stick to the day job and give up burglary.' I paused for a moment and reconsidered. 'On second thoughts give up the day job as well. You suck at it. And while we're on the subject, please don't ever let me see you within a mile of me, or my associates here may play with your neck again.'

Benny went pale but nodded in agreement.

'Very good, Benny; you're a quick study.'

He disappeared up the street so fast I was impressed with his powers of recovery.

Satisfied that they were no longer required, Lewis and Carroll disappeared back into the darkness.

Clutching the plans I'd been given, I trudged slowly home to formulate some way that would allow me to enter Edna's base of operations, steal back the lamp from under her very prominent witch's nose, escape undetected and return it to one of its alleged owners, while trying to keep the other alleged owner from doing something unpleasant to me.

Easy!

72

8

A Brief Interlude in which Harry Doesn't Get Threatened or Beaten up by Anyone

In the relative safety of my apartment I finally managed to find some time to consider the case.

None of it seemed to make any sense. The original theft was clearly an inside job because of the in-depth knowledge of the security systems, but I didn't figure either of the two possible suspects (Gruff or Aladdin) for it. Aladdin had no obvious need to steal his own lamp and was wealthy enough to suggest that an insurance scam wasn't high on his list of priorities. Gruff seemed to be too loyal to his employer to consider stealing the lamp and was probably only too aware of the likely consequences if he was found to have been responsible. There was nobody else in Aladdin's employ that had either the smarts or the access, so where did that leave me?

Well, I'd (sort of) met someone who claimed to have masterminded the job even if I didn't have the faintest idea who he was either. He seemed to fall into the criminal megalomaniac category

Boy Blue had referred to, as he had all the tricks of the trade: deep dramatic voice, an impressive HQ – at least what I saw of it – and a strong desire to show off. All he needed to complete the effect was a white Persian cat to sit in his lap and be petted constantly – assuming he actually had a lap.

Mind you, having used Benny as the actual thief also demonstrated a certain fallibility on his part. Maybe he wasn't as all-powerful as he thought. Of course, he was powerful enough to compel me into reacquiring the lamp for him – a task I had to take somewhat seriously or suffer embarrassing, if not downright unpleasant, consequences.

Heaving a sigh of such resignation that it would have evoked sympathy from a zombie, I resigned myself to my lot, rolled out the plans and studied them as best I could. I didn't know how Mr Big (I know, I know, tremendously clichéd but I couldn't keep calling him by the more pretentious and even more unoriginal 'mysterious stranger' moniker now, could I?) had gotten the plans but they were incredibly detailed. Were there any premises in Grimmtown he didn't have an in-depth knowledge of?

The plans, however, confirmed what I had already suspected: all access to Edna's residence was controlled by yet more sophisticated and, no doubt, very effective security systems. Complementing these were somewhat less sophisticated – but no less effective – guards who were, in all probability, armed with a variety of interesting instruments of pain. The only way I was going in the front door was as the main ingredient in a Chinese takeaway – and that was a step that I was, understandably, very reluctant to take.

The more I studied the plans, the more unlikely the prospect of recovering the lamp became. I could see no way in that avoided me being detected and if I couldn't get in then my career as Grimmtown's foremost detective would come to a premature end.

I was about to ball the plans up and fling them in the garbage when I noticed a small tunnel I hadn't seen before. At first glance, it looked like it led into one of the lower levels of the house from under the street. Upon closer examination, it became clear that it didn't lead into the house as such. Rather, its primary function was to take some unpleasant material away from the house. Yes, you've guessed it; if I was to successfully enter the house unde-tected, I was going to have to do it via the sewage outlet. Yet another lucky break for me, eh? And if I actually managed to get into the building, I still had to navigate my way to where the lamp was kept, find some way of taking it and make my way back out again – all without alerting anybody. No problem!

Ah well, may as well be hung for a boar as for a piglet. All it needed was a little bit of careful preparation, a massive slice of good luck, no one to flush suddenly and I might yet get out of this smelling of roses (or possibly not, bearing in mind what I was going to have to crawl through).

I reached for the phone as, once more, I was going to have to utilise the resources of another of my many contacts – and I was well connected. There may have been a thinness on the ground when it came to my informants but, when I needed to lay my hands on 'stuff', I knew some people who knew some people who could source anything: from doorknobs to a tactical nuclear warhead.

Ezekiel Clubfoote was the man to go to for all your gumshoe shopping requirements. If he didn't have it, or couldn't get his hands on it, then chances were it didn't exist or you never really needed it in the first place. He had been an exceedingly poor shoemaker (from both a finance and quality perspective) some years back. Business had, consequently, been pretty bad but, on the brink of total ruin, he had allegedly made some deal with elves that rescued his career. Apparently, whatever raw material he left in the shop at close of business each day would have been transformed into high-quality footwear by the next morning. Suddenly his shoes and, by extension, his services were in popular demand and in Grimmtown being in popular demand made you a very wealthy person indeed.

Not one to miss an opportunity, he experimented with leaving other materials out for the elves each night. No matter what he left out, the next morning he'd be presented with a finished product of some description. Put out some clay – get high-class porcelain. Leave some wood: an antique chair. From such small beginnings are large warehouses of equipment – and a thriving distribution company – made.

I dialled and waited. I didn't have to wait long.

'Yes?' came a very cultured voice from the other end of the phone.

'Zeke, it's Harry. I need something from your elves.'

'Of course you do. Big or small?'

'Not too big this time; I only need a lock pick, a wetsuit and an Orc costume.'

Considering the last time I had contacted him, I had looked for infrared glasses, four kangaroos, a machete and a rocket launcher (remind me to tell you sometime), a lock pick wasn't too excessive a demand.

'An Orc costume?' I imagined his eyes opening wide in surprise. 'There isn't really any such thing. It's more of a collection of smelly furs and skins held together by dirt and an occasional chain. You don't so much acquire one as have bits of one stick to you after rolling around in a rubbish tip.'

Considering what happened during my initial encounter with Benny, I knew what he meant.

'And what kind of lock will you be picking? And, no, I don't want to know the personal details – just the technical ones,' said Zeke.

'Well, there's the problem,' I replied. 'You see, I'm not really sure. I suspect that the door I have to open will more than likely be locked, but I have no idea how sophisticated this lock may be.'

'Hmmm, without knowing the details, I suspect that you'll need the Masterblaster. It's so good, a man, or indeed a pig, with no fingers could open any lock with it. It's a "Choice of the Month" in *Lock Pickers Illustrated* and it doesn't come more highly recommended than that, let me tell you.'

I rolled my eyes upwards. He did so like his little sales pitches.

'Fine, fine. How soon can I have them?'

'Give me an hour. I need to make sure it's in my next run so I'll organise to have them dropped off to you as soon as I get them.'

'Thanks, Zeke. I owe you.'

'Yes, you do. And I'll collect.' Zeke hung up, leaving me with the dial tone for company.

While I waited for the equipment, I studied the plans some more. Edna's outlet (if you'll forgive the phrase) connected to a main sewer that serviced the entire block where her headquarters was located. Access to this larger sewer could be gained via a number of manholes; I just needed to find one that wasn't too public and just far enough away to avoid being seen by whatever surveillance systems she had in operation. Mind you, that was the easy part. After that I had to make my way up a very narrow tunnel and hope that the exit at the other end was a little larger than a U-bend.

In the short term, personal hygiene would be a thing of the past and a shower very much an aspirational goal until I had what I came for – assuming I managed to get that far in the first place.

I can't say I was particularly looking forward to the next few hours.

9

Flushed with Success

O f course, no matter how well I plan these jobs, there's always something. Well, have you ever tried to open a manhole using trotters? Let me tell you, it's not easy. For one thing, it's hard to get a grip on the rim. For another, manhole covers are heavy and, thirdly, I was on my own. Lastly, I was wearing a bright blue wetsuit (although it was so worn and full of holes it could be more accurately described as a dampsuit) under a foul-smelling collection of rags that could probably have represented the height of fashion from an Orc's perspective. All this, and I had to try not to appear too conspicuous as well. As a result, by the time I finally got the drain open (with the help of a tyre iron), my wetsuit had even more holes, my back hurt, and my skin was a darker shade of pink than usual from my exertions.

As I levered the manhole cover off, I lost my grip on it but, thanks to my quick reflexes and uncanny sense of self-preservation, I didn't lose any body parts as it fell heavily (and with a very loud clang) to the ground. Fortunately, as Edna's stronghold was in an area where the occasional loud noise wasn't an undue cause for concern, it didn't appear to have attracted any attention.

I shone my torch down the manhole and looked in carefully. At first glance, the sewers didn't look (or smell) too unpleasant. In actual fact they smelled better than me. This, I suspected, was largely because of the recent heavy rains, which had run off via storm drains and into the sewage system, effectively washing most of the unpleasant stuff away.

Now that was something to be thankful for.

Grabbing the top rung of a metal ladder that led from the street down into the sewers, I slowly and carefully made my descent. Arriving safely at the bottom I took my bearings with the help of the plans.

I was in a large tunnel that stretched off into the darkness in both directions. Smaller tunnels opened out from the walls as far as I could see but none, I was glad to note, seemed to be active. The only evidence of any discharge other than rainwater from these tunnels was a trail of green scum that dripped downwards towards the floor of the main sewer. Although I was ankle deep in liquid, it appeared to be mostly water. Then again, I had no intention of examining it too closely. What I didn't know, wouldn't hurt me.

I had a quick look at the plans, figured I had to go right and slowly made my way up the tunnel trying to keep the sloshing to a minimum – just in case. Although I wasn't entirely sure which of the smaller outlets led into Edna's HQ, it didn't take me long to figure it out. Not surprisingly, it was the one with the large securely-padlocked grille that covered the entire tunnel entrance. After a few pulls it was evident that this grille wasn't going to come away from the wall that easily.

'OK Harry,' I said to myself as I reached for the lock pick. 'Let's see how good the Masterblaster is.'

In fairness, I haven't had much cause to pick locks in the past. Any time I've had to 'enter' a residence without legally coming in via the front door, I've found that the old credit card trick so beloved of TV detectives actually worked. It was, therefore, no surprise that jiggling little iron pins in a keyhole wasn't quite as simple as it first appeared. No matter how I tweaked, twisted and pulled at the lock, it stubbornly refused to open. Even reverting to Plan B – swearing at the grille – didn't appear to have any effect either.

In total frustration I hit out at the lock with my torch. To my surprise the lock broke and fell to the ground in pieces. Years of rust and an application of brute strength had succeeded where subtlety and bad language had failed.

Of course, it wouldn't be a Harry Pigg case without something bad happening as well. In this instance, the breaking of the lock had also resulted in the unfortunate breaking of the torch. I now had to navigate my way through a sewage outlet and into Edna's lair in total darkness, using only my sense of touch (and possibly smell).

I felt for the grille and dragged it away from the entrance. Aware that I was now possibly within earshot of one of Edna's more alert henchbeasts, I struggled to keep it from falling to the ground – which I managed to do at the expense of a large tear in my wetsuit and a pulled muscle in my shoulder. As if my job wasn't difficult enough already!

At least I was able to use the bars of the grille as a mini-ladder to lift myself into the smaller outlet. My shoulder objected strongly to being forced to help in dragging me up and into the tunnel but I managed to pull myself up without doing any additional damage.

This new tunnel was a tight squeeze and I was forced to crawl along, rubbing against the walls and roof as I did so. It was much narrower, much smellier and showed very distinct signs of much more frequent usage. Unpleasant substances stuck to my back and legs and I had no great urge to investigate what they actually were. In an effort to take my mind off my current situation, I pictured myself in a hot shower liberally applying sweet-smelling soap to my body. This seemed to work and I was wallowing in the imaginary sensation until my reverie was broken by a gurgling noise from somewhere up ahead.

'Oh no,' I said anxiously. 'Please don't let it be someone flushing. Anything but that.'

The gurgling grew noisier and it was joined by a loud flowing sound as something large and liquid made its way down towards me.

Frantically, I tried to reverse back down but in my panic I only succeeded in wedging myself tightly into the tunnel. Firmly stuck and unable to move, I could only close my eyes and mouth as a noxious brown liquid washed over (and under and around) me, covering me liberally in a foul-smelling residue.

Coughing and spluttering (and now smelling even worse than before), I tried to wipe my face clean but only succeeded in spreading the vile substance around even more. As there was no point in going back now, I slowly twisted and turned until I had forced myself free and gradually made my way up the tunnel again. Some things just shouldn't happen to a hard-working detective and getting liberally covered in raw sewage was most certainly one of them.

As I crawled slowly forward I saw a thin crack of light shining faintly through the roof ahead. Eager for any way of getting out of the tunnel, I struggled on. To my intense relief, the light came from where the side of a square metal drain cover wasn't flush (no pun intended) to the edge of a manhole. Hoping that I could push the cover off, I wedged my back underneath it and pushed upwards with all that was left of my strength. Slowly but surely it lifted away and slid off my back gently onto the floor above.

Muscles howling in pain, I hauled myself up and carefully peered over the edge. I was looking at a dimly lit corridor. From the dust on the floor, it wasn't one that was used too often so, thankful for one lucky break, I heaved myself out of the sewer and lay on the ground panting heavily, stretching my knotted muscles and trying to get my breath back. Now all I had to do was find the room where the lamp was kept, if the plans were to be believed, and steal it back.

I took the building plans from inside my wetsuit where I had stored them for safekeeping. Although stained with sweat and effluent they had escaped the worst of the deluge so I was able to work out where I was without too much difficulty.

If I was reading the plans correctly, I appeared to be in a basement. I just needed to make my way to the stairs at the end of the passageway, go up four levels, find the room halfway down a long corridor and take the lamp. Of course, I had no idea exactly how well protected the room was but at least I now knew how to get there. Limping slightly, smelling heavily of unmentionable substances and groaning as quietly as I could, I struggled towards the stairs.

If walking caused some discomfort then climbing the stairs was an exercise in agony. Every step upwards jarred another aching limb or my torn muscle. I felt as though I'd been skinned and roasted over a roaring fire. Everything burned or stung in some respect after my tunnel experience and, with my luck, there was no obvious hope of easing this agony in the near future.

When I eventually dragged myself to the top of the stairs, all I wanted to do was lie down and be mothered. As there wasn't a mother to be seen in the vicinity and as lying down would probably result in me not getting back up again for probably quite a few months, I willed myself to go on and through the door.

Fortunately, the door wasn't locked, as I probably wouldn't have been able to bend down to try my luck at another lock-picking attempt. Opening the door slightly as quietly as I could, I peered down the corridor. It looked more used than the one I'd just left but there didn't appear to be anyone on guard that I could see. Pushing the door open just enough to squeeze through I squelched carefully down the corridor towards the next flight of stairs.

I managed to climb three flights before meeting anyone. On the third-floor landing two henchOrcs were standing guard. Now the reason for my cunning disguise could be revealed. Most of Edna's troops were Orcs – not too smart and not too alert but very handy in a fight. Looking like them, although a trifle larger, I might be able to make my way around the building without being too obvious.

I was about to find out how convincing my costume was. Keeping my head down, I shuffled towards the guards. As I got close, they recoiled at the smell. Good, at least they wouldn't look too closely. It also appeared as though I actually smelled worse than they did – which in itself was quite an achievement and something that, in other circumstances, I might have taken some (but not a lot of) pride in.

I knew some very basic Orcish – which to all intents and purposes sounds like a flu-ridden gorilla strangling a hyena – so when they hailed me I muttered something along the lines of being required on the third floor in order to relieve a sentry there. At least that's what I think I said; I could have just as easily asked the sentries for some hot, buttered toast and a glass of dragon's blood. Sometimes it was difficult to get those choking sounds just right. I must have been convincing (or smelly) enough, as they let me pass without examining me too carefully. Can't say I blame them. If I had been on sentry duty, I wouldn't have been too eager to examine me either.

I made my way up another, and hopefully last, flight of stairs. At the top I paused for breath and to give my long-suffering body some respite. A long corridor, covered in a luxurious red carpet, stretched out in front of me. Suits of armour lined the corridor, one beside each door. With one exception, all the doors were made of very ornate patterned wood. The exception was the door behind which, presumably, all Edna's interesting stuff was kept.

I walked up to it. It looked like a standard metal security door:

grey, impregnable and securely locked. Heaving yet another of my many sighs of resignation, I took the lock pick from my pocket, cleaned it as best I could and began to jiggle the levers in the keyhole.

After ten minutes or so it had become clear that I was never going to add breaking and entering to my long list of skills. My efforts to pick the lock had resulted in very sore trotters, a rising sense of frustration and a door that steadfastly refused to be unlocked. Maybe I was doing something wrong or maybe it was just that the Masterblaster wasn't actually the state-of-the-art tool I had been promised. In any event, I suspected that hitting the door with whatever implement was to hand wouldn't be quite as successful as it had been down in the sewer. As I sweated and struggled, I became aware of a conversation from behind the door.

'How's he doing?' said a rough-sounding male voice.

'Not too good,' came the reply. 'He's been out there for quite a while now and he still hasn't managed it.'

'How long do you think we should give him?' said the first voice again.

'I dunno,' replied the second. 'But I know I'm getting bored just waiting here. The fun is going out of it.'

'Let's not wait any more,' said the first voice again. 'Let's just do it now.'

'OK. On a count of three: one . . . two . . . three.'

Before I had a chance to make any kind of sense of the conversation, the door swung open and two pairs of hands reached out and grabbed me. Hauling me into the room, they threw me unceremoniously to the floor where I lay panting, aching, smelling and trying to get my bearings.

'Well, paint my backside green and call me a goblin,' said a loud and very familiar voice from right in front of me. 'If it isn't Harry Pigg, crap detective and failed burglar. I don't think I've ever seen anyone take so long to pick a lock. What kept you?'

85

My eyes ran slowly up past two legs so fat they were doing GBH to a pair of green stretch trousers. They traversed a torso that suggested its owner enjoyed several square meals a day (quite possibly a few circular, triangular and oval ones as well) and up to a face that defined new levels of ugliness, even for a witch. Imagine Jabba the Hutt with bright red lipstick and a long off-blonde straggly wig and you may get some idea of just how repulsive Edna – for it was she – actually was.

She grinned at me, which was a particularly unpleasant experience as it showed off a mouth with teeth that varied in shades of yellow and green, and that gave off a breath so unpleasant that I almost smelled good in comparison.

'There I was, wondering exactly what was so special about that lamp I took from Benny when suddenly you appear, stinking to high heaven and apparently eager to take it back.' She looked me straight in the eye – or at least as straight as someone whose eyeballs rotated in two different directions could – and leaned forward so our faces were almost touching. 'Looks like you're the man who can answer this most intriguing of questions. What a timely arrival, eh?'

She was about to slap me enthusiastically on the shoulder but quickly reconsidered when she saw what I was coated in.

She turned to the two henchOrcs who had dragged me into the room. They were small but very mean-looking.

'Tie him to a chair and hose him down,' she ordered. 'I'm not asking him questions until he smells better than he does now.'

She walked towards the door and, as she opened it, she appeared to have an afterthought.

'Oh and I'm going for a bath, boys,' she said with a malicious gleam in the eye that was currently looking at me. 'So no need to use up all the hot water on him, is there?' And with a long, loud and unpleasantly mocking laugh, she left the room.

10

Anyone for Pizza?

As you can imagine, it doesn't take too long for two very burly henchOrcs to tie a relatively defenceless pig securely to a chair – even a pig that they had to keep at arm's length owing to the smell. And there was going to be none of that slowly working the trotters free while being interrogated either. These guys were pros in the tying-up game. My trotters had been tied to each other, then to my body and then to the chair. I felt my extremities begin to go numb as the ropes constricted the flow of blood. The only way I was going to free myself was by diligent use of a chainsaw and there didn't appear to be one conveniently to hand. I had been trussed up more securely than Hannibal Lecter; all I was missing was the hockey mask.

While the goons located a long hose and began running it out of the room and down to the nearest bathroom, I took the opportunity to have a closer look at my surroundings. As I expected, bearing in mind what had just happened to me, the lamp was nowhere to be seen. The room itself was relatively bare. All it contained were a few chairs, a long table and what looked like a drinks cabinet. Considering where Aladdin had kept the lamp, this room was a bit of a surprise. I had expected more hi-tech surveillance and security systems.

A large oval mirror hung from the wall directly opposite me (presumably deliberately, so I could see just how bad I looked). Without going into too much detail, my skin was no longer a fetching shade of pink and the new colouration wasn't entirely due to bruising. What was left of my Orc costume was sodden and covered in a variety of strange substances that didn't warrant a more detailed forensic examination.

It looked as though whoever had supplied the plans to Mr Big had led him up the garden path (and into the garden shed where-upon they had hit him across the back of the head with a shovel), as there certainly wasn't any sign of a lamp here.

Even I couldn't figure out how to rescue myself from this particular predicament. Apart from the unpleasant experience of being hosed down with cold water, I also had the pleasure of Edna's interrogation to look forward to – and I was assuming this was going to be a little bit more intense than just having a bright light shone in my eyes while she shouted 'you will answer the questions' at me.

I was still looking around the room when the Orcs came back in. From the expression on their faces, it appeared as though they were relishing the thought of hosing me down. Can't say I blamed them; I was looking forward to a shower myself – albeit a some-what hotter one than the one I was about to receive.

Grinning at each other, the two henchOrcs lifted the hose, aimed it at me and began to twist the nozzle. I turned away to shield my face and braced myself for the freezing deluge. There was silence, then two loud clangs in quick succession and the sound of the nozzle hitting the ground. After another brief pause this was followed by two more thuds – this time slightly further apart and much heavier. More importantly, I didn't seem to be getting wet.

I looked around very slowly and not without some trepidation as I had no idea what had just happened. To my utter amazement, both Orcs were lying unconscious on the ground. Standing over them, wielding a large metal leg – presumably borrowed from one of the suits of armour outside – was a very satisfied-looking Jack Horner.

'Jack,' I asked, somewhat stunned at this unexpected turn of events, 'what are you doing here?'

'Hey Mr Pigg,' he said cheerfully, 'I'm rescuing you. I told you you'd need my help.'

'But how did you find me?' I asked weakly.

'C'mon Mr Pigg,' he replied. 'You smell very strongly of shi . . . I mean poo. How difficult do you think it was to find you? I just had to follow my nose. Anyway, you left a trail of muddy footprints all over the building. It was easy.'

'And you got in how exactly?'

'Almost as easy. After I followed you here, I just bought a pizza from the takeaway around the corner, stuck a red hat on my head, called to the front door and said I was delivering a super pepperoni to Grazgkh. There's always a Grazgkh around, it's the Orc version of Joe.'

And I was supposed to be the detective!

'Then I just made my way up through the building, following your trail,' he continued, obviously enjoying himself. 'These Orcs aren't too observant, are they? Not one noticed me all the way up. Then I crept up behind those two guys and hit them over the head with this leg.' He swung it around with some relish. 'They were so busy with the hose they never heard me.'

'Good work, Jack,' I said. 'Now, can you untie me and we can get the hell out of here before someone discovers I've escaped.'

'Righty-o,' he replied and went behind me to untangle the spaghetti of knots that bound me to the chair.

After a few minutes I still hadn't noticed any relieving flow of blood coursing back into my numb trotters.

'How are things going back there, Jack?' I asked.

'Not too good, Mr Pigg,' Jack replied. 'I can't seem to get these knots undone.'

'Well, try to find something that you can use to cut the ropes,' I said, scanning the room for anything that might have a sharp edge. 'But hurry. I'm sure Edna will be back soon, suitably refreshed, smelling very nice and eager to inflict pain.'

Jack began searching the room frantically, shifting bits of furniture aside as he looked for anything that might be used to set me free. As he searched I struggled to loosen the knots but my efforts were as fruitless as his. I could see that he was beginning to panic so I tried to calm him down.

'Take it easy, Jack. You need to calm down and focus. There must be something here we can use.'

'But I can't see anything, Mr Pigg.'

As I looked around the room yet again, I caught my reflection in the mirror. Inspiration struck me – and it was probably the only thing that had struck me recently that hadn't hurt me in some form or another.

'Jack,' I said urgently, 'take that thing you hit the goblins with and throw it at the mirror. Cover your eyes as you do.'

After a moment's incomprehension, Jack suddenly understood and, grabbing the metal leg, he flung it at his reflection. There was a loud crash and shards of glass flew in all directions. When the noise died down, Jack slowly brought his arm away from his eyes and scanned the floor for a suitable piece of glass. He picked up a shard so big and sharp it looked like it could have beheaded an elephant and, with great care, began sawing at the ropes. As they began to fall to the ground, I could hear what sounded like a small army pounding across the floor overhead. Someone (or lots of someones) was coming to investigate the noise and I really didn't fancy being here when they arrived.

'Come on, Jack,' I muttered. 'Speed it up, speed it up.'

'I'm going as fast as I can,' he replied, panting from the effort. 'I don't want to cut my hands.'

'Cut hands will be the least of your worries if we don't get out of here soon.' As I spoke, the ropes binding my trotters fell to the floor. Despite the pain as the blood rushed back in, I grabbed the glass off Jack and attacked the other ropes binding me. The sharp edge cut cleanly through them and I stood up – a little bit unsteady but ready to accelerate out of the room as fast as I could.

'Good work, Jack. Now let's not be here.' I grabbed his hand and pulled him towards the door. As we were halfway across the room he stopped unexpectedly, almost pulling me off balance. I turned to him. He was looking at the broken mirror in fascination.

'Jack, what are you doing? We don't have time for admiring our reflections.' I was on the point of lifting him onto my shoulders and carrying him out when I saw what he was looking at. What he had broken wasn't a mirror; it was a door cleverly disguised as a mirror. With the glass surface now all over the floor we could see into the room beyond and sitting on a shelf (along with what I suspected was a lot of very expensive and probably very stolen artifacts) was what looked like Aladdin's lamp. It certainly looked battered enough.

'Nice one, Jack, I take it back. Get to the door and tell me when the ravening hordes charge down the corridor. If I'm quick enough we may be able to grab the lamp before they get here.'

Jack peered cautiously around the door.

'Nothing out there yet,' he reported, 'but there's definitely someone coming. I can hear lots of grunting, stomping and shouting. Hurry up.'

Very cautiously, so as not to cut myself on the jagged edges that were still embedded in the rim, I sidled through the doorway and into the storeroom beyond. Not even pausing to look at what other goodies might be on the shelves, I grabbed the lamp, stuffed it into my wetsuit and reversed just as carefully back out again. Once I was safely back out of the storeroom, I ran out the door, dragging Jack by the scruff of the neck as I went. Together we ran back down the corridor towards the stairs. As we did so, a horde of Orcs brandishing an interesting array of sharp and pointy objects came around the corner at the opposite end. Immediately spotting us (not that it was too difficult) they roared angrily and gave chase.

Fortunately for us, there were so many of them and the corridor was so narrow that they fell over each other in their eagerness to catch us. This slowed them down enough that we were able to get to the stairs. The two Orcs that manned the guard post on the landing tried to block our way but my impetus, speed and bulk bowled them easily aside and they tumbled down the stairs in front of us.

Tucking Jack under one arm, I threw a leg over the banister and slid down, trying to maintain what was a very precarious balance. For once, Jack didn't treat it as a theme park ride; presumably he was as scared as I was. The banister itself spiralled down in wide arcs all the way to the ground floor so I had no hairpin bends to navigate, which was probably just as well because with the rate we were accelerating, any sudden departure from the stairs would probably have resulted in us splattering against the wall at the far side of the room. Spotting a number of Orcs running up the stairs towards us I yelled at Jack to hold out his metal leg (which he'd shown the good foresight to hold on to) and he cut a swathe through them as we passed, their bodies cascading down the stairs like ugly skittles.

We reached the ground floor and flew off the end of the banister.

Fortunately, the thick carpet broke our fall and we avoided a collision with any of the furniture. Dizzy but otherwise unhurt, we staggered to our feet and ran through the door to the basement. Grabbing the leg from Jack, I placed one end on the ground and wedged the other under the door handle. It wasn't going to hold our pursuers at bay for long but might give us enough of a lead to enable us to get to the drain safely.

As we charged recklessly down another flight of stairs there was a very satisfactory thump as the first of our pursuers hit the door, followed by more thumps and much shouting as the rest of the pack hit it (and the leading Orcs) with equal force.

'Quickly, Jack, let's go,' I urged. 'It won't hold them up for long.'

Jack nodded and picked up speed. Now he was beginning to leave me behind. Willing my body to one last effort, I caught up with him and we ran for the manhole. As we reached it, there was a loud splintering from behind us as the door finally gave way. We only had minutes before the Orcs reached us. Grabbing Jack, I threw him into the tunnel and dropped down behind him.

'Go, go, go,' I roared.

Jack disappeared down the tunnel and I followed as fast as I could. Thankfully, someone – most probably Edna – had taken a bath since my last passage through the drain, as it wasn't quite as unpleasant as previously, making our progress relatively more comfortable than before. In front of me, Jack was sliding away down the tunnel and I tried pigfully to keep up with him. Behind me I could hear voices raised in argument as the Orcs decided whether or not to follow us.

'You go first,' said one.

'Me? I'm not going in there,' said another in reply.

'Ma'am will be very angry.'

'Well you go, then.'

'I'll go if you go first.'

As is usual with Orcs in these situations, they then started squabbling and this soon erupted into a fully blown brawl. Orcs are good like that – low attention spans but high animosity. By the time we reached the main sewer, they'd probably have either all killed each other or forgotten all about who they were chasing in the first place. We made our way through the water back to the ladder and climbed up to the street.

As we headed back to the car, it struck me that Edna would be somewhat miffed that I had stolen back the lamp. She would be probably even more annoyed that she hadn't had the chance to slap me around a bit. I figured it wouldn't take her too long to track me down – especially as both my apartment and office were in the phone book.

I was going to have to come up with a plan to resolve this dilemma and this had to be the plan to beat all plans. In fact, this one had to be a doozy or I was quite possibly going to end up revisiting the sewers – this time face down and probably not breathing.

11

I Have a Cunning Plan!

With Jack safely dropped off home, I decided to lie low to try to avoid detection by all the various factions that were by now, presumably, scouring the town for me – and that didn't come any lower than the Humpty Inn chain of hotels. It was the cheapest and least reputable hotel chain in town. If they were any seedier you could have used them to feed birds. Fortunately, their very seediness meant that they were the perfect place to hide out as no one noticed, or even cared about, who was in the rooms.

Comfort wasn't high on the list of facilities offered by the hotel. The bed felt like it was made of rocks, there was a strange fungus growing on one of the walls and, yes, the room was lit up by the garish purple light from the neon sign that ran vertically along the front of the building and flashed on and off at regular intervals. The curtains didn't do much to block this light out as they looked to be made out of tissue paper.

The room had one very important feature, however – a working bathroom. Despite the imminent threat to my person, the first order of business was a long, hot, luxurious shower. I have to say

I wallowed. If someone had broken in and pointed a gun at me, I'd have told them to get on with it and died a happy pig. Of such little pleasures is life made.

After my shower, and smelling a lot better, I sat at the wobbly dresser and studied the lamp carefully. It was as battered as its photograph suggested. The amount of dents in the metal suggested it had had a long and interesting history – quite a bit of which seemed to involve it being used as a football. It was so tarnished it was hard to make out what its original colour was. Try as I might, I couldn't open the lid. Although it didn't look to be sealed shut in any way, it just would not lift. I tried using a knife but it wouldn't budge. It was one stubborn lid.

There were no markings of any type on the surface, or at least none that I could see. I did contemplate dropping it in a fire to see if the flames revealed any mysterious writings but I didn't actually have a fireplace and I figured that a match wouldn't be quite as effective. In all probability, the room was so flammable even lighting a match would have caused it to catch fire.

I put the lamp on the dresser and stared at it. Then I stared at it some more and, just as I was about to give up, I stared at it especially hard. It didn't make any difference; it still sat there mocking me with its dullness and downright shabbiness.

Then I had a really outrageous idea: what if I rubbed it? What was there to lose? There was certainly a lot to gain, assuming the rumours were true. If all went according to legend then I was on the point of leaving all my troubles behind. Wealth beyond my wildest dreams was within my grasp. No more worries; no more Aladdin, mysterious stranger or Edna. And that could be a real result rather than just a turn of phrase.

The more I thought about it, the more it appealed to me. What could possibly go wrong? I figured that the more I thought about it the more likely I was to talk myself out of it. Best be decisive and take immediate action.

I grabbed the lamp with my left trotter. It wasn't easy but I managed it. Holding it level with my eyes I contemplated it one last time; it was still as dingy and battered as before. I slowly raised my right arm and, taking a deep breath, I brought the lamp towards my trotter and when they touched, I rubbed the surface furiously.

There was a . . . well . . . nothing actually. No sudden clap of thunder. No flash of light. No puff of smoke. No intimidating eastern gentleman with a trail of vapour where his lower legs should be. No deep and terrifying voice shouting: 'I am the Genie of the Lamp. What are your wishes, my Lord?'

Nothing!

The lamp still sat there silently mocking both my efforts and me. Either that or it wasn't as highly positioned on the alchemical plane as had previously been speculated. With a grunt, I flung it back on the dresser and headed for the bed. As I prepared for what looked like a very uncomfortable night's sleep, I took one last look back. Something about the shape of the lamp tried to trigger a thought at the back of my mind. My mind, however, was refusing to play ball and the door marked 'Free Association' stayed resolutely shut. On the off chance that my subconscious would do what my waking mind couldn't, I stumbled into the bed, pulled the flimsy blankets over me and was asleep in seconds.

I was also awake within seconds as the synapses in my brain – that had steadfastly refused to work earlier – set off a chain reaction that jolted me back to full consciousness. I sat bolt upright in the bed with a large grin on my face.

'You are so clever,' I shouted gleefully. 'No wonder you wanted to steal the lamp. If it was me, I'd probably have done the same. Any wonder it didn't work when I rubbed it.'

The beginnings of a really dastardly plan began to form in my mind as I tried to figure out where the nearest Internet café was. As I dressed, I thought I heard a noise from the corridor outside my room. I padded carefully to the door and put my ear against the wood. Fortunately, the quality of the workmanship was as poor as everything else in the hotel. The door was so thin I could hear clearly what was happening on the other side. As per usual, it didn't bode well for me.

'Is this the room?' whispered a voice – very low and very guttural; very Orcish, in fact.

'Yeah, he only checked in an hour ago,' replied a second voice I recognised as the concierge from downstairs. So much for anonymity. Obviously Edna's grapevine was very efficient. Once he'd heard she was looking for a pig, it didn't take the concierge too long to make both the obvious connection and the inevitable phone call and no doubt pocket the reward.

As I was only seconds from having a horde of Orcs explode into my room I had to think very fast. I grabbed the dresser and pulled it in front of the door. It wouldn't be a barricade – more a minor hindrance – but it might give me a few seconds' head start. Grabbing the lamp, I ran to the window, forced it open and prepared to drop onto the fire escape that I realised at the last minute wasn't there. Well, I did say it was a seedy hotel and safety regulations obviously weren't high on management's list of priorities. As I quickly tried to formulate a Plan B, there was a splintering noise from the opposite side of the room and the door was reduced to matchwood under the onslaught of a variety of crude swords and axes although, in fairness, you could probably have broken it down with a rubber knife without too much effort.

The horde swarmed into the room – or at least would have if

they hadn't, yet again, fallen over each other in their eagerness to get me. It appeared that Madame Edna had placed a very high bounty on my head.

'There he is,' growled one, stating the very obvious as they could hardly have missed me sitting on the window ledge. 'Get him.'

There was only one thing for it. Taking a deep breath, I swung my legs over the ledge and threw myself at the neon sign. My luck was in and I managed to grab the crossbar of the letter 'T' in Humpty. My luck wasn't in for long, however, as, with a screech of metal, the whole letter detached from the wall and slowly fell outwards and downwards. Like a demented stuntman, with my skin glowing purple, I clung on for dear life wondering if the rest of the letters would stay fixed to the wall. My question was quickly answered as, to my total lack of surprise, the other letters advertising the hotel slowly peeled away from the hotel wall and down towards the ground in a gigantic neon arc.

On the street below, three Orcs that had obviously been asked to guard the hotel entrance looked up vacantly as I fell towards them. Taken completely by surprise, they didn't have time to get out of the way as a large glowing 'TY INN' and a purple-hued pig landed on them. For once I got lucky as I dropped on the largest and fattest of the Orcs and was exceedingly grateful for the soft landing. Unfortunately I didn't have the time to express my gratitude properly, seeing as the rest of his buddies were about to come charging out of the hotel in hot pursuit of my blood. In any event the poor guy was unconscious and I didn't have the luxury of enough time to even write a thank-you note; not that I would have anyway – I wasn't that grateful!

Checking to ensure I still had the lamp, I slowly got to my feet and raced – well, staggered actually – down the street. Seconds later, what was left of the Orc posse charged from the hotel and, spotting me limping towards the next intersection, howled in triumph as they ran after me.

I now had two objectives: evade my pursuers any way I possibly could and, assuming I was successful and didn't end up skewered by a large and rusty spear, get to an Internet café so I could send the most important email of my life.

I made the intersection and ran up the next street looking for something – anything – that might get the Orcs off my back. All I could see was the usual collection of seedy bars, dodgy clubs and occasional pawnshop that seemed to proliferate in the more disreputable parts of town. Despite my vain hope, there didn't appear to be any obvious cavalry-coming-over-the-hill-type rescue operation waiting for me. I had to admit it was looking grim. I could hear the grunts and shouts of the Orcs as they gained on me. Surely it was only a matter of seconds before I became a pork kebab.

Then I spotted it: a possible way out of my current predicament. Limping across the street, I staggered through the doors of the Tingling Finger Bar and Grill, hoping that the name reflected the nature of its clientele. I almost fell to my knees in relief (and pain and exhaustion) as every elf in the bar stopped what he was doing and stared at me in surprise.

Hanging on to the door for support with one arm, I indicated back over my shoulder with the other.

'Orcs,' I gasped. 'Following . . . me, trying . . . to . . . kill . . .'

I couldn't get any more out and clutched the door, trying to catch my breath.

Despite my semi-coherent gasping, they got the thrust of my message quickly enough. Then again, all they really needed to hear was 'Orc', as it tended to provoke an almost Pavlovian response when uttered in the presence of an elf. All the rest of the message was just supplemental information.

As any reader of fantasy fiction will tell you, Orcs and elves are sworn enemies. All it takes is for one to unexpectedly bump into the other at, say, a movie premiere for a small-scale war to break out. As a rule, hostilities usually only cease when one of the two opposing sides has been rendered totally unconscious – or worse.

It was no surprise, therefore, when my arrival resulted in the entire bar suddenly changing from a bunch of happy-go-lucky elves (if elves could ever be described as happy-go-lucky) trying unsuccessfully to get drunk to an efficient and very hostile fighting machine waiting for their enemy to burst through the door.

They didn't have long to wait, as the leading Orc pushed his way in, to be met by the heavily moisturised fist of the lead elf, the impact of which drove him back out again and into the arms of his colleagues.

'Orcs in the pub; blood will be spilled this night,' shouted one of the elves as he followed his leader outside to give both moral and physical support. Within seconds the bar was empty, apart from the barman and me. Like barmen the world over, he nodded at me and continued to clean glasses with a pristine white cloth as if nothing untoward had actually happened. Maybe his customers poured out of the bar every night in search of a row but I doubted it; elves usually preferred a quiet drink as opposed to a full-blooded brawl – except, that is, where Orcs were involved.

Still hurting, I staggered to the bar and looked up at the barman.

'Back . . . door?' I asked him.

He indicated a door at the back of the room with a brief twist of his head.

'Nearest... Internet... café?' Barmen usually knew everything about the locality; I just hoped this chap was one of them.

'Out the door; turn right; two blocks down. It's called the Cyber Punk. You can't miss it.'

I thanked him and struggled onwards out of the bar and down the street. The Cyber Punk was exactly where he described it.

Looking around to confirm I was no longer being followed, I pushed the door open and made my way to the counter. A geeky goblin (the actual Cyber Punk presumably) sat behind it, glancing through a magazine. I waved a twenty under his nose to get his attention. He looked down at me over glasses that were so thick they could have been used as bullet-proof windows.

'I need to access the web,' I said to him and waved the twenty from side to side. His head moved back and forth tracking every movement, his eyes never leaving the money.

'Pick any one you want,' he said slowly reaching for the bill.

Picking a terminal at the back of the room, where I was less likely to be seen from the street, I accessed one of my many email accounts. I began to carefully compose the most important email I was probably ever going to send. After typing furiously for a few minutes, I reviewed what I had written. I hoped it was enough to get the attention of the recipient without giving too much away to anyone else that might intercept it.

Dear Criminal Mastermind,

I know who you are and why you stole the lamp. I understand your need for complete secrecy, although transporting me to your hideout ultimately gave the game away (and employing Benny certainly didn't help your cause, either). To prove I know what's going on, I offer you this: he who controls the third option controls the power. It may be cryptic but I think you'll understand what I mean.

I think I can help you. Be prepared to be present at the original drop point early tomorrow morning and take your cue from me. If all goes to plan we may both find ourselves out of this sorry mess for once and for all.

Best regards,
Harry Pigg

After a moment's panic when I couldn't remember it, I typed in the address Benny had used previously (evilgenius@criminal-masterminds.com), hit the send button and my email disappeared from the screen. All I needed to do now was to get the other two players in this dangerous game to meet me tomorrow, and hope I could pull off a very elaborate stunt.

If I was successful, then I would be free of any unpleasant entanglements forever. If not, then I was likely to be caught in a very unsavoury Aladdin and Edna sandwich – with me as the filling.

I borrowed a phone from the Cyber Punk and, with a certain degree of trepidation, I made two very nervous calls. With nowhere else to go, I spent the rest of the night in the Cyber Punk, alternately surfing the web and playing World of Warcraft.

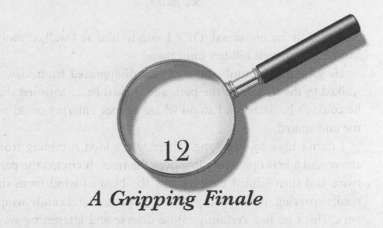

12

A Gripping Finale

E ven early in the morning, Wilde Park was busy.
The Three Blind Mice were begging as usual at the
main gate. Fairy godmothers fussed around their charges,
making sure they were well wrapped up against the morning chill
as they played on the swings. An occasional elf jogger in pastel
Lycra running gear panted along the pathways. Show-offs – always
more concerned with looking good than actually keeping fit.

I had picked the most public area I could find for my dangerous
rendezvous: a large open area with a small clump of trees to one
side. Hidden in the trees was a very nervous Jack.

I had called him first thing and briefed him on the plan. He
wasn't going to be in any danger but his role was critical. Precise
timing was essential so I drilled him over and over on his instructions.

'You sure you know what to do?' I asked him as we walked
towards the bushes.

'For goodness sake, Mr Pigg, we've gone over it twenty times.
Just give me the lamp.' Grabbing it from my hands he forced his
way into the bushes and crouched down.

'Just wait for my signal, OK?' I said to him as I walked away. 'And keep yourself hidden until then.'

He gave me a thumbs-up sign and disappeared from view. I walked to the middle of the park and looked back. Satisfied that he couldn't be detected, I stood where anyone entering could see me and waited.

I didn't have to wait long. There was a loud rumbling from above and a helicopter flew low over the trees. It circled the park twice and then landed close to me, the blast of wind from the rotors covering me in dust, potato chip packets and candy wrappers. This case had certainly found diverse and interesting ways of getting me dirty.

Peeling away a potato chip packet that had stuck to my forehead, I watched as Aladdin and my good friend Gruff alighted from the 'copter. The wind from the rotors didn't appear to affect Aladdin in the slightest. Nothing stuck to his suit, and his hair moved so little it must have been glued to his head. If nothing else, the man had style in spades.

'Mr Aladdin.' I stretched out my trotter. 'Glad you could make it at such short notice.' I didn't acknowledge Gruff and, strangely, he didn't offer to shake my trotter either.

Aladdin gave my trotter a perfunctory shake. 'Mr Pigg, I assume from your call that you have my lamp.'

'It's nearby and very safe,' I replied. 'Please be patient and you'll have it back shortly.'

From the look he gave me, patience clearly wasn't going to be top of Aladdin's order of business for the day. I hoped that Edna was going to arrive soon as I didn't know how long Aladdin's fuse was.

Fortunately, the Wicked Witch of the West Side was as anxious to recover the lamp as everyone else. A long line of stretch limos snaked from the main entrance of the park to where we waited.

A small army (in both size and number) of henchOrcs disgorged from the cars and took up positions around us.

Two very large minders in black tuxedos and sunglasses squeezed themselves out of a large black Merc and stood beside the rear door as Edna made her entrance. These bodyguards exuded menace and were the kind of muscle that would still look intimidating dressed in pink tutus. They stood at either side of Edna as she walked towards us, their faces (at least what I could see of them behind the shades) expressionless. When they got closer I could see they were actually gorillas (as in silverbacks and mutual grooming). Clearly Edna relied on minders that were a little bit more effective than Ogre Security (Not On Our Watch). Her gorillas were the genuine article.

Aladdin and Edna both eyed each other warily. Clearly both wanted to know what the other was doing here, but neither was going to be the first to ask. They had their pride. I let them posture and sweat for a bit longer just to show who was nominally in charge, but primarily because I was thinking of a thousand ways how my plan (which seemed so foolproof last night) might, in the light of day, actually blow up in my face now that all the key players were here.

Edna broke the silence first.

'Harry Pigg again,' she sneered. 'And smelling so much nicer than when we last met. Care to tell me what we're all doing here?'

'A very good question, Mr Pigg.' Aladdin looked at me steadily. 'More to the point, do you have my lamp?'

'*Your* lamp?' exclaimed Edna, turning her attention to Aladdin. 'No way, pal. It's my lamp.'

Aladdin took a step towards her and the two bouncers suddenly appeared in front of him, blocking his way. I was interested to see that Gruff was keeping himself a safe distance away from his master, which was quite understandable, considering the size of Edna's minders, but hardly a career-enhancing move. Unless he backed up his employer, it was quite possible his next job could be propping up a bridge – from inside the concrete support. Mr Aladdin had certain expectations of his employees.

'Ma'am,' said Aladdin, raising his hands in a conciliatory gesture, 'I assure you the lamp is mine. In fact, I employed Mr Pigg here,' and he waved an arm in my direction, 'to locate it for me.' He looked at me again. 'And you have found it, haven't you?' he said levelly. 'Because I really hope you didn't bring me to this accursed place at this unearthly hour of the day for any other reason.'

Despite my best effort I was now the centre of attention and that was the last place I wanted to be. Beads of sweat formed on my brow.

Edna took a few steps towards me. 'Well, Pigg, is this true? Is it his lamp?'

I coughed nervously and cleared my throat.

'OK folks,' I stammered. 'Let me explain. Now if you could all step back a small bit and give me some room, I'll begin.'

I didn't really need the room; I just wanted to be able to see where Jack was hiding.

Everyone shuffled back slowly, muttering and giving me foul looks. If this didn't work, chances were I'd become the booby prize in a turf-war between Aladdin and Edna and I really didn't fancy my head being mounted over the fireplace of the winner.

'Ladies, gentlemen, foul-smelling Orcs, very muscular simian bodyguards and offensive goat,' I began. 'Let me tell you a little story.

'Once upon a time, a very rich man had a magic lamp that he treasured above all else. One night the lamp was stolen by person or persons unknown and, through a series of bizarre circumstances, ended up in the hands of another of our foremost citizens.' I nodded towards Edna, who just continued to scowl at me.

I know, I know; I was piling it on with a trowel but I had to keep both of them sweet for a little while longer.

'Now this lady,' I nodded at Edna, the word 'lady' sticking in my throat, 'assumed that the lamp was now her property, possession being nine-tenths of the law and all that.

'Unfortunately, the original owner of the lamp employed the town's foremost detective to track it down and return it.' For some reason there was much coughing, clearing of throats and disbelieving glances at this statement – I can't imagine why.

'Through prodigious feats of deduction,' more coughing, 'he tracked down and recovered the missing lamp and can now return it to its rightful owner.'

I looked straight at where Jack was hiding and nodded my head. I caught a glimpse of him as he bent down and began to cover the lamp in mud. When the lamp was liberally smeared, he cautiously made his way towards me, holding it carefully in both hands.

'Tell me, Mr Aladdin,' I asked, 'what do you most wish for right now?'

As I waited for his reply, I took the lamp from Jack and handed it to him. He looked at it aghast.

'For goodness sake, Pigg. Could you not have cleaned it before you handed it back?'

Reaching into his pocket, he grabbed a handkerchief and began cleaning the lamp.

I was sweating profusely now – like a pig, in fact. The success of my plan depended on the next few minutes.

'I'm sorry, Mr Aladdin, I just hadn't time. I wanted to get it back to you as soon as I could. But you haven't answered my question.'

He continued rubbing the lamp furiously, oblivious to the plume of white smoke that was beginning to pour from the nozzle.

'Oh yes, your question,' he said. 'What I really wish for most right now is to find out who stole my lamp and why.'

There was a loud crack and the white smoke solidified into a very large and very happy-looking genie – all turban, silk trousers and a cone of smoke where his feet should have been.

'BEHOLD, I AM THE GENIE OF THE LAMP,' he bellowed. 'AND YOUR THIRD WISH SHALL BE GRANTED. IT WAS I WHO STOLE YOUR LAMP.'

Aladdin looked at him in horror and with dawning comprehension. He'd been had.

I turned quickly to Jack while everyone was looking in astonishment at the genie.

'Jack, now!' I roared.

Quickly, Jack ran to Aladdin and, before he could react, had grabbed the lamp and flung it at me. Catching it skilfully, I quickly rubbed it again.

The genie looked at me and his smile grew even broader.

'I AM THE GENIE OF THE LAMP. YOU HAVE THREE WISHES. WHAT IS YOUR BIDDING, MY MASTER?'

I took a deep breath and in a very loud voice – to ensure everyone could hear – outlined my first wish.

'I wish that if, as a result of this case, any harm should come to me or any of my associates at the hands of either Aladdin or Edna, or anyone connected with them for that matter, both will suffer cruel and unusual punishment – such punishment at the genie's discretion.' Granted, it was a mouthful but I needed to cover all the bases.

The genie bowed deeply.

'YOUR WISH IS GRANTED.'

From the horrified look on their faces, I could see that both Edna and Aladdin clearly understood what had happened. I was safe from any retaliation by either of them and, in the context of what had happened in this case, that had understandably been my first priority. I was untouchable – at least by them – and was savouring the moment. But I wasn't finished yet.

'My second wish is that, after thousands of years of imprison-
ment at the hands of selfish masters, the genie is to set himself
free.'

The genie bowed even more deeply and waved his arms theat-
rically – obviously playing to his audience.

'YOUR WISH IS GRANTED.'

As he said this, the smoke began to drift away on the wind and,
from his knees down, the rest of his legs began to materialise.
Slowly he descended to the ground and landed carefully, testing
his balance. Satisfied that he could at least stand without falling
over (if not actually walk) he smiled at me and nodded his gratitude.

'I thank you, sir, from the bottom of my heart. For too long
have I been in thrall to masters who have used me for their own
devices with no thought for my wishes. Now I am free and shall
be no man's slave from here on in.'

I didn't want to point out to him that now that he was free
he'd have to get a job. I wondered what skills he did have but
imagined that being an ex-genie wouldn't necessarily endear him
to potential employers. I also noticed that he wasn't shouting in
block capitals any more – presumably another advantage of being
a free man, and one that wasn't quite as hard on the ears of anyone
within a ten-mile radius.

As he spoke I noticed Edna nod to her gorillas. They surreptitiously made their way towards me, trying (not very successfully
it has to be said) to be unobtrusive. As they advanced I began to
back away ever so slowly. As I did so, the genie shook his head
and, with a slight wave of his hand, motioned for me to stop.

I gave him a 'you must be joking; have you seen who's coming
after me' look but he nodded more emphatically. As he did so I
noticed that as the heavies got to about ten feet from me, they
suddenly shrank to the size of garden gnomes. I suddenly became

very brave and raised my foot to stomp down on them. Squealing in fear they ran back towards Edna and, as they did so, they quickly grew back to their original height. My enthusiasm for squashing them evaporated, primarily because they were now more than capable of squashing me first.

I looked at the genie in confusion.

'It's very simple,' he said. 'Even though I'm free and no longer capable of magic, any spell I've already cast remains in force. If either of them,' he nodded at Edna and Aladdin, 'tries to harm you, or employs someone to do so, they will suffer most unpleasant consequences indeed.'

I smiled at my sudden invulnerability.

'Of course,' he continued, 'that won't stop you from being harmed by anyone else.'

The smile disappeared as fast as it had arrived. Typical, I thought – there's always a downside. Mind you, at least I was safe from the two people currently most likely to do me harm – both of whom, along with their respective entourages, were backing away quietly from me so as not to incur any further pain or humiliation.

I couldn't resist it; I ran quickly towards them. It was one of the finest moments of my life. Imagine, if you will, one very fat oriental gentleman, a goat, two large gorillas in tuxedos, a disorganised swarm of Orcs, and Edna (who had trouble walking let alone moving any faster) all desperately clambering backwards over each other in a frantic effort to get as far away from me as they could. The resulting scrum made me laugh out loud for the first time in quite a while.

I think it was at that point I realised that the case was more or less over. All I needed to do was tie up a few loose ends and explain to Jack what had happened.

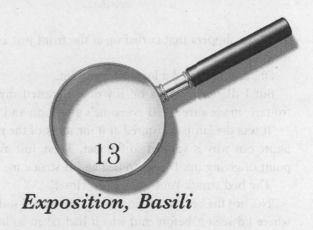

13

Exposition, Basili

'**B**ut how did you know it was the genie?' Jack asked.

The three of us – Jack, the genie and I – were in my office, sitting around my desk drinking coffee. Much as I'd like to take all the credit for solving the case – being a famous detective and all – if Jack hadn't turned up at Edna's wielding the leg from a suit of armour, chances are I'd have ended up a permanent face-down resident in the sewers I'd come to love so much. The least he deserved was an explanation.

The genie, on the other hand, was just hanging around. Now that he was homeless, seeing as he couldn't fit into his lamp any more, he had latched on to me – and it was placing me in a very difficult position.

In my job, I needed to be discreet, and discretion was going to be very difficult when you were being shadowed by a large dark-skinned ex-genie whose idea of sartorial elegance was a bright yellow turban, a yellow and red patterned waistcoat that seemed twenty sizes too small and a pair of baggy yellow silk trousers that ended just above the ankles and looked like someone had inflated a large hot-air balloon in each leg. On his feet a pair of yellow slippers that curled up at the front just added the final lurid touch.

Oh, and he farted a lot – an awful lot.

But I digress. Elbows on my desk, I rested my head on my trotters, made sure I had everyone's attention and began.

'It was the lamp. I'd stared at it for most of the night trying to figure out why it seemed so familiar. Then, just as I was on the point of giving up, I went to bed and it struck me.'

'The bed struck you?' said Jack. 'How?'

'No, not the bed,' I replied wearily. 'An idea. I suddenly realised where I'd seen it before and why it had taken so long to work it out. I'd seen it from the inside.'

'Huh?' The look on Jack's face said it all.

'It was when I was in that white room. The curved walls were the same shape as the body of the lamp. I'd been pulled into it by our friend Basili here,' I said, nodding at the genie. 'Of course, I didn't know it at the time; I just thought I'd been taken prisoner by an insane interior decorator.

'Once I figured that the genie was looking for his own lamp, it all began to fall into place.'

I could see the confusion on Jack's face and held up a warning trotter before he could ask another 'why' or 'how' question.

'When I rubbed the lamp, nothing happened,' I continued. 'My first reaction was that it was all a hoax and the lamp was exactly that: a lamp; with no magic, no three wishes and no genie. No offence.' I looked across the table at the genie.

'None taken,' he replied calmly.

'Then I figured that if the last owner hadn't used up all his wishes yet, then rubbing the lamp would probably have no effect. However, once the three wishes had been granted then the lamp was up for grabs again, making it a very valuable antique indeed.'

The genie nodded his agreement.

'This would explain why Aladdin had kept the lamp so securely under lock and key. As long as he had it, he still had a last wish, but it was useless to anyone else unless they could get him to use up that last wish.

'Now, if you were the genie that provided this somewhat unique service, I imagine that it would get quite tedious, if not downright frustrating, being stuck in a lamp with no way of getting out, just sitting there waiting for that last rub to happen.'

I turned to Basili. 'How long were you waiting after Aladdin's second wish?'

The genie heaved a deep sigh. 'Forty years.'

'Wow!' exclaimed Jack. 'You were stuck in there for forty years? What did you do to pass the time?'

'Initially, I read, watched TV and ate a lot,' said Basili. From his size, it didn't need a detective to work that out. 'Then with the arrival of the computer age and the information superhighway, I learned everything about PCs and used them to interface with the outside world, looking for an opportunity to set myself free.'

'Which is how he met Benny,' I said.

'Poor Benny,' said Basili with a sympathetic shake of the head and a loud fart. 'I'm sorry about that but he was my only option.'

'Don't worry, he's probably already forgotten about it. Gnomes have a very short attention span.' I looked at the genie. 'What I want to know is how you managed to find out so much about security systems?'

Basili's grin was so wide his head looked like it was split in two. In fact, I don't believe he'd actually stopped smiling since he'd been freed. 'Hacking.'

'Hacking?' I repeated stupidly.

'Yes, hacking. With twenty years of computer experience, I was at the cutting edge of cyber crime from the word go. There isn't a system out there I can't crack. Aladdin's just needed a bit of time. Once I had access, it was easy to figure out where the weaknesses were. I just wish I'd picked someone brighter to actually steal the lamp.' There was another loud rumble from his side of the desk, which I hoped was his stomach telling him it was hungry. A few moments later that hope was cruelly dashed and I walked over to the window to let some fresher air in. Basili gave me another apologetic look.

I figured it was about time I took back control of the conversation and make myself the centre of attention once more. I walked back to the desk and looked at the other two.

'Once I figured that the genie was the one who was calling the shots, or at least one of the three calling the shots, I thought that if I could strike a deal with him I might get the other two off my back – assuming he was willing to play ball.'

'And I was,' grinned Basili. Paarp! Phut-phut-phut-phut! 'All I wanted was someone to help me gain my freedom and Mr Harry here was most anxious to help me, as well as himself.'

I nodded furiously. 'Using the same email address Benny had used, I told him that I knew who he was and proved it by cryptically suggesting that the person who controlled the third wish effectively controlled the genie. If the message was understood then all he had to do was follow my lead at Wilde Park when I was hopefully going to make him appear.' I smiled at the memory of the look on Aladdin's face when he realised he'd been duped. 'Fortunately for us all, everything went more or less according to plan. Basili was set free and I got Aladdin and Edna off my back. Unfortunately, as I was no longer flavour of the month with Aladdin, he declined to pay me for my services.'

As usual things hadn't panned out yet again for the proprietor of the Third Pig Detective Agency. Then again, I was getting used to it. This time, however, I had also picked up a stray – a very large, yellow stray that, partly thanks to me, no longer had a home.

To my surprise (and embarrassment) Basili stood up, walked around the desk to me and gave me a big hug. It was the kind of hug that large bears used to crush their prey but he managed to break off before any major organs were ruptured. Struggling for breath, I dropped back into my chair.

'It is not so big a problem, Mr Harry.' His smile was even broader. I suspected that both ends met at the back of his head. 'While I waited in my lamp for all those years, I also used my computer to play the market. I have been very successful and have built up a most valuable and highly diverse portfolio. Perhaps I can recompense you somewhat for your efforts in this matter.'

If this had been a cartoon, my jaw would have bounced off the ground in surprise. I struggled to get words out. 'You mean, you're rich?' I gasped.

'But of course,' Basili replied. 'How else would I have been able to help Benny with his most audacious plans for the theme park? I insist that you be paid for the most successful resolution of this case.' He thought for a moment. 'Hey, maybe I can become your backer – like Charlie in *Charlie's Angels*.'

I was about to point out that I looked nothing like any of Charlie's Angels when I became aware of a commotion from reception. Two voices were raised in argument. One was clearly Gloria's but the other was unfamiliar and very loud, very female and very commanding. For one awful minute I thought Edna or one of her sisters had come to 'pay me a visit', but the voice sounded a little more cultured than those of the Wicked Witch sisters so I relaxed a little – but not too much.

'But you don't have an appointment,' I could hear Gloria say.

'Nevertheless, I must see him,' said the other voice, in a tone that suggested she wasn't used to being obstructed. She didn't realise that she was being obstructed by the best. If she managed to get past Gloria, she deserved an appointment.

117

'No appointment, no meeting,' said Gloria emphatically. 'Mr Pigg is a very busy detective and can't afford to have his time wasted. If you care to make an appointment, I can organise a suitable time.'

'No way, lady,' came the reply. 'I know he's in that office and I am going in to see him now. Please do not get in my way.'

Now I was starting to get scared. What kind of monster was in my reception area and why did she want to see me? More to the point, did I really want to see her?

I could see that Jack and Basili were giving me anxious looks as well. We all started to back away from the door slowly and quietly. In hindsight there wasn't really any point. The only thing behind us was the window; we were on the third floor and there was no fire escape.

Note to self: speak to new landlord about fire safety regulations.

Through the frosted glass I could see a large red shape move towards the door.

'Do not go in there,' shouted Gloria.

'Try and stop me, lady.' There was a sound of scuffling and then the door burst open, banging off the wall with a loud crash.

A very large lady dressed in black boots, bright red trousers and a hooded red jacket stood there. Gloria was clinging on to one of her legs. She had clearly been dragged across the room in her efforts to keep this person out.

'Sorry, Harry,' she gasped. 'She got by me when I wasn't looking.'

'It's OK, Gloria,' I said and walked over to her to help her up. 'Let's see what this lady wants that's so urgent.'

I looked at the new arrival. Her face was as red as the clothing she was wearing – presumably from her altercation with Gloria. White fur lined the cuffs of her jacket and rimmed her hood. For some reason her appearance suggested Christmas.

I indicated one of the seats recently vacated by my colleagues.
'Ma'am,' I said, turning on the charm, 'if you'd care to sit down.'

As she sat I turned to the others. 'If I could perhaps speak to this fine lady alone,' I suggested. Gloria nodded and, grabbing the other two by the arm, dragged them both out of the office before they could protest.

I nodded towards the door as they left. 'My partners. They may not look like much but they've got it where it counts.'

As I spoke, I realised that they had indeed become partners, either by virtue of the help one had given or the financial backing the other was offering. Looked like the Third Pig Detective Agency was expanding.

I turned to my newest prospective client.

'Now then,' I said. 'How may the Third Pig Detective Agency be of help, Miss, Mrs, Ms . . .?'

'Claus. It's Mrs Claus and I need you to find my husband. He's been kidnapped and it's only two days to 25th December. If he's not found soon we may have to cancel Christmas.'

The End

Acknowledgements

This book's formative years were spent on the web so huge thanks go to all at Writelink for the initial encouragement and those at YouWriteOn – especially Edward Smith and Michael Legat – whose critiques (good, bad and otherwise – but always constructive) helped shape the opening chapters into something approaching legibility.

I owe a lot to the good people at the Friday Project: especially Scott, whose unflagging belief in Harry's adventures and championing of the cause kept the book alive when things didn't look so good.

Thanks to Dooradoyle and Adare Libraries for providing a quiet corner to write in and to Carol Anderson for a wonderful copy-edit.

I also owe a debt of gratitude to my parents who instilled a love of reading in me at a very young age. This is all your fault!

Above all, huge thanks go to my wife Gemma and my three boys, Ian, Adam and Stephen, whose support, belief, encouragement and the occasional 'get back in there and write another chapter now' made all this worthwhile.

No, Ian, we won't be getting a Gulfstream jet with the proceeds. Yes, Adam, the book will be in the shops. No, Stephen, you can't have your tea – you only had your dinner an hour ago.

Harry would like to thank the Big Bad Wolf, for giving him that first big break; Little Red Riding Hood, for not appearing in this book and making a show of herself; Jack Horner, for the pizza (you know what I'm talking about!) and his legions of fans – he knows you're out there somewhere, you just haven't made yourself known to him yet.

THE HO HO HO MYSTERY

To Ian, Adam and Stephen

For the inspiration
(and for keeping me grounded)

Contents

Contents

1

Lady in Red

The woman claiming to be Mrs Claus glowered at me, her face turning as red as her very Christmassy jacket. 'Well,' she demanded, 'is there a problem?'

I considered the question carefully. There were a number of problems actually, but I wasn't about to list them out – at least not to a very angry woman who seemed capable of doing me serious physical harm. I'd received enough punishment during my last case and I wanted this one – if, in fact, it turned out to be a case at all – to be as pain-free as possible. Diplomacy was clearly the order of the day.

'Mrs Claus, please make yourself at home.' She squeezed herself into the offered chair, which protested loudly at the intrusion. It looked like someone had tried to stuff a red pillow into a flowerpot. When she was comfortable (or at least not too uncomfortable), I asked her to tell me the story from the beginning; if nothing else, it would give me a chance to get my thoughts together – and these thoughts were currently so far apart they couldn't even be seen with the help of the Hubble telescope.

'It's my husband, you see,' she said, fidgeting with her cuffs. 'He's disappeared.'

'And your husband would be . . .?' I knew what she was going to say; I just wanted to hear her say it. This was obviously a very poor attempt at a practical joke and I needed to stay sharp to find out who the culprit was, although the finger of suspicion was pointing firmly at Red Riding Hood. This was just the kind of stunt she'd pull. More importantly, once I knew who it was, I could figure out a way to get back at them. No one got the better of Harry Pigg in the practical jokes department.

'He's Santa Claus, of course.' Her face got redder with indignation. 'Who did you think I was married to dressed like this?'

I had to admit she did look the part. If I had to buy an outfit for Santa's wife, it was exactly what I'd have picked: fashionable red trouser suit with white fur lining and a very trendy pair of black high-heeled boots. Well, I'd have picked something red anyway.

'OK, let me get this clear,' I said, trying hard not to snigger. 'You are married to Santa?'

'Yes,' she replied.

'As in the jolly fellow with the white beard who says, "Ho ho ho" a lot and flies around dropping off presents to children all over the world on Christmas Eve?'

'Is there another?' she demanded.

'Not that I'm aware of.' I was now biting the inside of my cheek so as not to laugh hysterically in her face. 'And he's missing?'

'Yes, as I've already pointed out to you.'

'You're sure he's missing and not just away on a boys' weekend with the Easter Bunny and the Tooth Fairy?' I couldn't contain myself any longer and burst into howls of laughter.

Seconds later I was pinned to the wall behind my desk with Mrs Claus's forearm rammed firmly up against my neck. I felt my

130

eyes bulge from the pressure on my throat and I was distinctly short of breath.

'Do you think this is funny?' she demanded. 'My husband has disappeared; children all over the world are facing huge disappointment when they wake up on Christmas Day and find nothing under their trees except bare carpet and some pine needles, and you see fit to sit there making jokes at my expense?' She pulled her arm away and I dropped to the floor gasping for air. I noticed that my two new 'partners', Jack Horner and the genie, had beaten a hasty retreat into the main reception area outside. Cowards! I might have to revisit this new working arrangement if this was going to be their attitude at the slightest hint of trouble.

'Clearly I'm wasting both my time and yours, Mr Pigg,' she said, with what I must admit was a certain degree of righteous indignation. 'I shall take my business to someone who is prepared to take my problem somewhat more seriously. Good day to you.'

As she stomped to the door and made to leave, it occurred to me that she might actually be telling the truth; she was pushing it a bit for someone playing a joke. More to the point, if she was being truthful, taking her business elsewhere meant Red Riding Hood would get the case and the only way she was getting any case at my expense was over my cold and lifeless body. Then again, with my luck, that mightn't be beyond the bounds of possibility either – I'd come close a few times on my last case, why would this be any different?

It was time for eating some pie of the humbly flavoured sort.

'Mrs Claus, please accept my apologies for my behaviour.' I walked after her and extended my trotter. 'My last case has left me the worse for wear and I'm not quite myself at the moment.' If you've been keeping up with my career, you'll know this wasn't entirely untrue. 'Please make yourself comfortable and I will give you my complete and undivided attention and will personally guarantee the quality of service for which this agency is renowned.'

I was piling it on a bit, but, in my defence, I was getting desperate. I needed to keep this client. Apparently mollified, she turned and sat back down in the chair – which once more protested loudly at the strain.

I breathed a sigh of relief. 'Thank you,' I said. 'It won't happen again.'

'Make sure it doesn't,' Mrs Claus replied. 'I haven't got time for amateurs and I need to find my husband before it's too late.' Her tough veneer finally cracked and she began to cry gently.

'You mean they might kill him?'

'No,' she blubbed. 'I mean too late for Christmas.' Obviously the thought of her husband being killed hadn't crossed her mind and the tears came even more quickly when she realised what I'd said.

Nice one, Harry, I thought. *Make the client feel worse.*

I handed her a tissue from a box in my drawer and she dabbed her eyes. While she did so, I quickly checked the box to make sure I had enough tissues. I figured she could be crying for quite some time.

'Mrs Claus, perhaps you could start from the beginning so we can decide on a proper course of action. How long has he been gone?'

'Since yesterday morning,' she replied. 'He left the previous night for our northern base and was due to arrive first thing yesterday. According to the elves, he never showed. We've checked with air-traffic control and they've had no reports of any accidents. The last thing we heard was when he gave us an update an hour out of Grimmtown. Since then, nothing. It's as if he just disappeared into thin air. I may never see him again.' This brought on a fresh deluge of tears. Now I was really concerned; if she didn't stop soon there was the distinct possibility my office would be flooded and I wasn't sure that my insurance would cover the cost of the damage.

'OK, OK.' I whipped out my notebook and began to scribble down what she was saying. 'How was he getting to your base? Grimmair?'

'Oh goodness, no. He always flew himself. He's quite an accomplished sleigh pilot, you know. He doesn't like travelling by commercial airlines.'

I didn't blame him. I didn't fancy it too much either. I always seemed to end up squashed between the two smelliest, loudest and most unpleasant Orcs on the flight – and they always took my peanuts.

'So, he left on his sleigh. Was this some sort of motorised craft or . . .?'

'Goodness, Mr Pigg, do you know nothing about my husband? It was reindeer powered. All his sleighs are propelled by a team of reindeer. Of course this wasn't the elite team; they're saved for the Christmas run. These were just economy reindeer, but certainly capable enough of getting him to the North Pole without incident. But he never arrived.' More tears.

'And you've received no communication of any sort, either from him or anyone who may have taken him?'

'Nothing and I'm so worried something might have happened to him. Please, Mr Pigg, I need your help; the children need your help.'

I thought of Jack Horner waiting outside. What would he think of me if I didn't find Santa Claus – especially if I didn't do so before December 25th?

'OK, let's go through some of the more obvious questions. Does he have any enemies?'

A shake of the head.

'Have you noticed anyone suspicious hanging around the house over the past few days?'

Another shake.

'Do you know of any reason why anyone would want to kidnap him? Are you rich?'

'We have some money put aside, but we reinvest most of what we make back into the company. Every year there are new toys added to the children's lists, so we're constantly developing new products and this puts quite a drain on our finances. We're not in it for the money, you know. If whoever did this did it because they think we're wealthy, they'll be sorely disappointed.'

That left one obvious question. 'So if he wasn't kidnapped for the money, then why was he kidnapped?'

Mrs Claus shrugged and said, 'I don't know; I just want you to find him, whatever it takes.' But as she said it, I thought I detected the faintest hint of evasion in the glance she gave me. She knew more than she was saying. There was obviously something else going on here and, with my luck, it would almost certainly result in something unpleasant happening to me while I tried to work out what it was.

Super!

'Is there anything else you can tell me that might be important?' I pressed. 'Did your husband appear any different before he left? Did he seem tense, out of sorts? Any little detail, anything you might have noticed, no matter how insignificant, might be important.'

Mrs Claus thought for a second and shook her head. 'No, nothing. It was just another trip. He was as happy as always. Lots of "Ho, ho, ho's" and "Merry Christmas, everyone's". He did like to get into the spirit of things early. And now he's gone.'

Just when I thought the waterworks had finished, they started up again. She was a one-woman reservoir. She appeared to be storing enough water inside her to supply an entire town for a year. Where did she keep it all? I was hoping she'd stop soon – I was running out of tissues.

'Mrs Claus, let me assure you that the Third Pig Detective Agency is on the job. Our skilled operatives will be working on the case to the exclusion of everything else and we will do our utmost to ensure your husband is returned safe and sound.'

I know, I know: 'skilled operatives' was stretching it a little, but I was hoping she hadn't noticed that, apart from me, they consisted of a small boy and a fat ex-genie dressed in bright yellow silk trousers.

She seemed reassured by my charm (in fairness, who wouldn't be) and got up to leave. As she walked to the door, something struck me – and it wasn't her forearm this time.

'Just one last question: have you talked to the police about this?'

'I reported it as soon as I found out he was missing, but they don't seem to be taking it too seriously. As there wasn't a ransom note and he's only been gone for a day, they're suggesting he might have just run off with someone else.' She hauled herself to her full height and bristled with indignation. 'As if!'

Frankly, if I was him, I'd be breaking all land-speed records to get as far away from this woman as was humanly (or porcinely) possible: she terrified me. 'Just out of curiosity, how long have you been married?'

She smiled proudly. 'Two hundred and thirty-seven years of wedded bliss last October.'

That stopped me in my tracks. 'He must be quite a man.' I couldn't think of anything else to say.

She nodded. 'And I, Mr Pigg, am quite a woman. I quickly put the police right on that particular theory of theirs, let me assure you, but I don't expect them to give it their full and undivided attention just yet – despite my best efforts to persuade them otherwise.'

I didn't have any doubts as to the effectiveness of her powers of persuasion; she'd already convinced me to take on her case – and against my better judgement too. It looked like I had a new client.

'OK, Mrs Claus, we'll probably need to check out your house and wherever your husband left from on the off chance there might be a clue as to what happened. Is there anyone else in the house at the moment – housekeeper, gardener, someone else who might know where your husband has gone?'

'Goodness no, apart from the local flight-control team and reindeer wranglers, there's just the two of us. All the rest of our employees are at our headquarters at the North Pole.'

'How many employees do you have up there?'

'Apart from the reindeer, we've got our admin staff and about one hundred elves. They're very diligent, you know.'

Elves! I'd probably have to talk to them as well; there was always the possibility that if this did turn out to be a kidnapping, someone there might be involved. Great! A trip to the North Pole in December: ice, snow, freezing temperatures and elves – and you know how much I dislike elves. They're pompous, arrogant, over-bearing and talk in riddles – and that's just their good points.

'We'll need to interview everyone,' I said to her. 'Where's the nearest airport?'

'Let me take care of that,' she said. 'We have our own fleet of reindeer-powered luxury private sleighs that will take you straight to the facility.'

I wasn't sure how comfortable a private sleigh flight would be, but I imagined there wouldn't be much chance of an in-flight movie – or in-flight catering either. On a brighter note, I probably wouldn't be forced to sit between two Orcs and watch them fight over my peanuts. Every cloud, eh?

'I'll contact you when we need to go north, then,' I said to Mrs Claus.

She nodded in reply and turned to me as she went out of the door. 'Please don't let me down, Mr Pigg. Time is short and I don't have much of it to waste.' Although her tone was abrupt, I couldn't fail to notice the look of relief that skated quickly across her face before disappearing behind that stern mask once more. Maybe this wasn't a con job after all.

'We're on it,' I reassured her as she left the office.

2

Shop Till You Drop

Seconds later – once they were sure she was gone – my two partners peered around the door. For those of you who don't know them, Basili was an ex-genie (don't ask) who I'd inherited after my last case and Jack Horner was an annoying small boy and wannabe detective with a tendency to be always right and who had gotten me out of a tight spot or two recently. I hadn't the heart to sack either of them (yet).

'Is it OK to come in?' asked Jack nervously. I waved for them to enter and sit down.

'You two were a great help,' I said to them. 'Where were you when she had me pinned to the wall?'

Basili looked at me apologetically. 'Well, Mr Harry, you did seem to be having the situation under control and we were thinking it would be better if you perhaps spoke to the red woman on your own.'

For a moment I considered how dangling in the air while an angry woman used my throat as a resting place for her forearm could possibly constitute having the situation under control and then realised that my partners were cowards – yes, even more cowardly than me. They were just the kind of guys I could rely on when we were in a tight spot – rely on to beat a hasty retreat and leave me to face the music. A consensus of cowards – what a team.

'Well, it looks like we've got ourselves another case, so it's time to get to work. Jack, you need to start talking to other kids. Try to find out everything you can about Santa Claus. If anyone knows, kids will.' Jack nodded and raced out of the office, eager to be of assistance.

When Jack had disappeared down the stairs, Basili looked at me curiously. 'Why did you ask young Mr Jack to do this investigating? Surely he will return with the information that this Santa Claus is a jolly old man who is dressing in red, is being very happy and is bringing lots of nice things to them. This every child knows.'

'Exactly,' I replied. 'I just wanted him out of the way while I talked this case over with you. I didn't want him to hear what we were going to say.'

'With me? How can I be of assistance?'

'Because surely that story can't be true, can it? Think about it: how can one old man possibly deliver that many presents to that many houses all over the world in one night? It's not physically possible. At the very least it would take an army of Santas – and a fairly big army at that. If he was on his own and could get his sleigh to move fast enough to do the run in one night, both he and his reindeer would be vaporised in an instant. He'd never even get out of the hangar. He wouldn't be delivering too many toys then would he? Of course,' and I began to have that sinking feeling I knew only too well, 'there's always magic. As an ex-genie, and with your knowledge of things magical, is it possible that someone would be powerful enough to generate enough magic to actually allow him to do it?'

Basili thought for a moment and then shook his head. 'Even I

140

would not have been capable of it. Such a power would go beyond the realms of magic. I have never heard of such a thing.'

'Exactly my thinking; now you can see why I didn't want Jack to hear. It would have destroyed his fantasy about Santa Claus and destroyed his Christmas. I certainly wouldn't want that on my conscience.'

'But, Mr Harry, it still begs the question: why did that red woman come to you? Even if what she has said is untrue, maybe her husband has still been kidnapped. She seemed to be most persuasive in that regard.'

I touched my neck gingerly. He had a point. 'Well, I suppose there's no harm in popping out to see the scene of the alleged crime, is there? It might give us a clue as to what's going on.'

Basili clapped his hands in excitement. 'A clue, a clue. Yes, that is what detectives do. We are finding clues and solving the mystery.'

He probably had an image of us arriving at the scene, walking around with a magnifying glass, picking up clues casually off the ground like we were picking fruit and having the mystery solved before lunch. I tried to bring him down gently. 'I don't think it's going to be that easy: there's still the possibility that Santa did a runner and will turn up later today looking embarrassed and begging for forgiveness – and if I was him I'd be doing some quality grovelling.' I stood up and put on my jacket. 'But before we do anything else, we need to go shopping.'

The ex-genie looked at me with a puzzled expression. 'Shopping, Mr Harry? At a time like this?'

'Yes, Basili, shopping. It may have escaped your notice, but as an apprentice detective, partner and potential undercover operative you are hardly a model of inconspicuousness at the present time.'

He carefully considered what he was wearing and acknowledged that I had a point. Flouncy yellow silk trousers that looked like he'd attached a pair of hot-air balloons to his legs, an ornate shiny waistcoat that barely covered his chest and left most of his ample midriff exposed, and a pair of shoes that gave the impression they'd be more comfortable being piloted down a canal by a gondolier singing 'O Sole Mio' at the top of his voice. No, Basili needed new threads and fast, otherwise he'd be indefinitely confined to desk work.

A thought struck me – desk work, now that's not a bad idea at all. It would certainly keep him out of the public eye and he could wear whatever selection of brightly coloured silks he possessed – and I probably wouldn't ever need to pay for lighting in my office again.

At the same time another more predatory thought (I have lots of those too) pointed out that if he did have as much money as he'd claimed then I needed to keep him sweet so I could use some of it to invest in the Third Pig Detective Agency like he'd promised. And don't get too upset by my seemingly mercenary attitude. The genie owed me. After all, it was me who had risked my precious hide by rescuing him from a very miffed Aladdin (and an even more miffed Edna) and making sure he wouldn't get caught up in that three wishes lark ever again. The least he could do in recompense was sub me some cash to buy some cool stuff.

I began clocking up my shopping list, all that kit I'd had to do without over the years: bugging devices, proper cameras, cool hi-tech surveillance equipment. With all that gear I could really outdo Red Riding Hood and consolidate my position as the foremost detective in town. All it was going to take was a bit of imagination and some shrewd investment at Gumshoes'R'Us and I was on my way.

'OK Basili, let's do it. Two hours from now you'll be stunningly sartorially elegant or my name's not Harry Pigg.'

*

142

Two hours from now the bottom had fallen out of my day.

'I'm sorry, sir, but that card is also being refused.' Danny Emperor, proprietor of Emperor's New Clothes Men's Emporium had run three of Basili's credit cards through the machine and all had been refused.

'Are you sure?' I asked, getting just a tad concerned. 'Can you try it one more time?'

Danny swiped the card once more and, once more, there was a high-pitched and (I thought) gleeful beeping as the system failed to validate it. I turned to the genie, who was becoming more dejected by the minute. He cut a forlorn – if somewhat conspicuous – figure, standing luminously among the racks of dark suits like a lighthouse in the middle of a bog. 'What's going on?' I asked him. 'Are you sure you were telling me the truth about all this money of yours?'

'Oh yes, Mr Harry,' he said glumly. 'As I told you, I had played the markets for many years while I was in the lamp. The return was, how shall I say, significant.'

'You could have fooled me,' I muttered to myself as Danny cut another of Basili's credit cards in two. As my dreams of a high-tech detective agency began to fade back into obscurity, a thought struck me. Reaching for my cellphone, I made a quick call to my lawyer, Sol Grundy (a man I keep very, very busy most of the time), and explained the situation to him. He told me he'd see what he could do and get back to me asap. If anyone could find out what was going on, he was the man. In the meantime all we could do was wait (and hope), surrounded by all the extra-large suits we were trying to buy.

Fortunately my lawyer works fast. Barely ten minutes had passed before he rang back.

'Sol,' I said, 'what's the story?'

'Not good, Harry,' Sol replied. 'Looks like your buddy has some

143

problems. From what I've been able to find out, it looks as though Aladdin has had all his assets frozen, claiming that as they were acquired while your man was in his employ then, legally, they're Aladdin's. As of now, Basili has nothing. I know it sounds a bit high-handed and I'm not sure as to the legality of Aladdin's actions, but it's a grey area, so the courts will have to decide.'

'See what you can do, OK?' Aladdin was probably doing this out of sheer spite because we'd gotten one up on him. 'But watch out: that Aladdin is a slick operator.'

'Yes Harry, I'm aware of that. I wasn't born yesterday, you know.' Which was true, yesterday was Thursday. 'Oh, by the way, he's repossessed the lamp too.'

'He's more than welcome to it. It's worthless now.' Even the genie couldn't use it as a home now that he had no magic. He'd already bruised his big toe trying to get back into it through the spout. It was most definitely an ex-magic lamp. Then another awful thought struck me – it was clearly my day for them: if the genie couldn't get back into the lamp and had no money, then where was he going to live?

This was a question with only one possible answer: it looked like, for the foreseeable future, I was going to have a large, farting, silk-clad genie sleeping on my couch.

3

Wondering in a
Winter Wonderland

The Claus house was so sweet and twee it made those candy cottages that dotted the Enchanted Forest look like outhouses. I could feel my teeth starting to decay and my arteries hardening just by looking at it. I'd probably die of a sugar overdose once I crossed the threshold. No matter what angle you looked at it from, it screamed Christmas in much the same way as Aladdin's mansion had screamed bad taste.

The house itself was a long, low log cabin – at least I think so. It was impossible to make out for sure, covered as it was from floor to roof in brightly coloured Christmas lights, which explained the bright glow in the sky we'd noticed as we drove over. These weren't just your usual strands of lights draped along the roof; oh no, there were rock bands that didn't have light shows as extravagant as what we were witnessing here. Rumour had it that Hubbard's Cubbard's lighting tech had spent six weeks studying these illuminations so he could get some good ideas for their next world tour. I couldn't say I blamed him; at any moment I expected a plane to land in the front garden, having mistaken the house for the approach to Grimmtown Airport. Even sunglasses wouldn't have been of any use here.

I could have sworn I even saw some people stretched out in the garden getting themselves a nice tan, but I couldn't be sure such was the assault on my eyes.

Seasonal ornaments covered the lawns. Reindeer jostled with Christmas gnomes; trees and snowmen seemed to be fighting for space with models of sleighs and Santas. It looked like a Christmas civil war had broken out and I had no idea who was actually winning. Even the corner of the swimming pool that I could see around the back of the house looked to have been covered with some sort of plastic ice on which mechanical rabbits, reindeer and snowmen skated happily away.

Snow covered the entire scene, giving it a little extra seasonal ambience – as if it really needed it. As we hadn't seen snow in Grimmtown for over five years, I used my powers of deduction to work out that it too, like everything else, was clearly fake.

Gingerly stepping around sunbathers and giant ornaments, I made my way to the door, pausing only to flick my fingers against a giant stalactite that hung from the eaves in front of me. Plastic too! I hammered on the reindeer-head door knocker, which lit up when I grabbed it and began singing 'Rudolph, the Red-nosed Reindeer'. It had gotten as far as 'Then one foggy Christmas Eve' before, to our relief, the door finally opened and Mrs Claus's familiar imposing figure peeked out. Just in case she wanted to exercise her forearm again I took a careful step back, but this time she seemed happier to see me – thankfully.

'Mr Pigg.' Then she saw Basili standing behind me. 'And your comedic sidekick, how nice.' There was an indignant snort from just over my left shoulder. 'It's good of you to come so soon. Please, come in.' She held the door open so we could enter.

Inside was just as tastefully decorated as outside. It seemed to be going for that ever-trendy neo-Lapland Rustic Charm look – as in pine everywhere. A mouth-watering aroma of mince pies emanated from a nearby kitchen. If the effect was to lull visitors into that warm Christmassy mood and leave them feeling good about themselves and everyone else, then it was very effective – until it came up against a cynical gumshoe like me. I was more of a 'Bah humbug' merchant when it came to Christmas.

Mrs Claus led us into a large living room dominated by a roaring fire. Gaudy red-and-white patterned socks hung from the pine mantelpiece and an enormous Christmas tree towered in one corner of the room. She indicated that we should sit in the comfortable-looking armchairs facing into the blazing inferno.

Once we were settled, I began. 'Has your husband contacted you?'

A quick shake of her head was the only response.

'Anyone else been in contact? A phone call or ransom note?'

Another shake of the head. Her lower lip began to tremble.

Please, no more waterworks, I thought to myself. *I didn't bring any wet gear.*

'Very odd,' I mused. 'I would have thought by now someone would have gotten in touch.' Of course, the fact that no one had contacted her gave credence to the police theory that Santa had done a runner – but I wasn't going to say that in front of the lady with the strongest forearms I'd ever seen. On the other hand, I had to be seen doing something to justify whatever fee I might get out of this case.

'Mrs Claus, do you mind if we have a look around? I'd particularly like to see where your husband left from yesterday. We might just spot something.' I have to confess that I couldn't see how it was possible for a sleigh and team of reindeer (whether they could fly or not) to actually leave the property; there just didn't seem to be any space available in the grounds to do so. Chances were that any vehicle trying to depart would end up colliding with a giant plastic snowman and crashing into a hill of artificial snow trailing streams of coloured lights behind it. Now there was a traffic accident I'd love to get the police report on!

After getting her consent, we went through the house looking for anything out of place, anything that might throw some light on what had happened. Let me tell you, there was so much Christmas junk around it was hard to tell what might constitute a clue. Everywhere we looked there was another tree laden down with tinsel or a sleigh hanging from the ceiling, and effigies of the man himself seemed to have been placed strategically in every room we entered. We certainly wouldn't have any difficulty identifying him; he was just like every picture you've ever seen: large, fat, jolly, dressed in red with a long white beard. I just hoped that we wouldn't be doing that identification as he lay on a slab in the morgue. That would certainly put a damper on Christmas – and would be more than a little difficult to explain to all the kids who were waiting expectantly for their presents.

Eventually we came to the conclusion that either the house had no clues whatsoever or else they were so successfully buried under mounds of festive tat we were never going to find them anyway. Even though Santa seemed to have taken his passport, some money and a suitcase of clothes (more red outfits, I assumed) with him when he'd left, Mrs Claus had advised that that was standard practice when he went to the North Pole. In fairness, I hadn't expected to find anything out of the ordinary, I was just covering all the bases.

4

Ground Control to Harry Pigg

The only thing we hadn't seen yet was the sleigh departure area and I asked if we could be taken there. Mrs Claus took us to a metal door – somewhat incongruous amidst the pine – and pressed a button on the wall beside it. It slid silently open and we were ushered into a tiny room, barely big enough to fit us all. Inside she pressed another button on a console and, after the door had closed again, we began to descend. Cool, I thought, we're on our way to some secret underground base.

I didn't realise how right I was. Once the lift had stopped and the doors opened, we stepped out on to a balcony overlooking a brightly lit, high-tech facility that bore no relation to the house constructed above it. Mrs Claus saw my look of astonishment and nodded.

'Yes, it's a bit different, isn't it? This is where the real business of Christmas is carried out – as well as at our North Pole base, of course. What's above is only for show and to satisfy the expectations of the locals. After all, they do have certain preconceptions we must meet.'

I was tempted to tell her that these expectations could have been met with a lot more subtlety and taste, but bit my tongue before saying something I'd probably regret later. Instead I walked over to the edge of the balcony and looked down. Below me a large ramp curved up from the ground towards a flat ceiling, where it seemed to end abruptly. To one side a group of reindeer were being brushed down and led away to straw-lined stables. Over speakers that dotted the walls a loud voice was saying, 'Attention, attention, flight SCA219 has arrived safely from the North Pole. Reindeer have been unhitched and are being refuelled for the return flight, which will depart in approximately two hours. Please ensure all cargo has been loaded and safely strapped down. We do not want a repeat of the frisbee incident.'

I looked over at Mrs Claus and raised an inquisitive eyebrow.

She sighed heavily. 'One of our more infamous accidents. During a Christmas delivery back in the fifties a number of frisbees fell off the sleigh as we flew over a place called Roswell. We managed to gather them all back up before they could do too much damage, but unfortunately some of the larger ones – the ultra-giant luminous ones – were seen by a number of the locals. They caused quite a stir, you know.'

Now there was a perfect definition of the word 'understatement' – and she'd said the whole thing without any suggestion of irony.

'Ever since then we've made sure to keep all cargo securely fastened to avoid any further unpleasantness,' she concluded.

'I'm sure you have,' I said, trying to keep a straight face. 'Did anything else happen to fall off the sleigh at the same time?'

'Yes, we did lose two inflatable toy aliens as well. We never did find them that night. I've often wondered where they got to.'

Basili nudged me sharply in the side. 'Don't even be thinking about telling her, Mr Harry,' he whispered.

I nodded and bit my lip – but I was tempted. 'Mrs Claus, is it possible to talk to the air-traffic controller who was on duty when your husband disappeared? I'd like to get a better idea of the timings.'

'Yes, of course, and please call me Clarissa; Mrs Claus seems so formal, don't you think?'

She led us to a small control room that seemed to be wall-to-wall computers and consoles showing a bewildering series of numbers, radar displays and what presumably were flight paths. Sitting in front of them, speaking urgently into a large microphone was one very stressed air-traffic controller who seemed to be talking to seven different sleighs at once.

'Yes SCA74 you are clear to land. SCA42 please keep circling at your current height until you hear otherwise. No, SCA107, I didn't get to record the Hubbard's Cubbard concert on TV last night for you. What's that, SCA92? Say again. Did I hear you correctly, you have a lame reindeer? Keep on this flight path and we'll divert you to the emergency runway. We'll have rescue teams standing by. Ground control out.' He pressed a button and sirens began to wail all around. 'Emergency, emergency; rescue teams to emergency runway. Repeat, rescue teams to emergency runway. We have a landing-gear problem on SCA92.'

There was a flurry of activity from down below as rescue teams in fire engines and ambulances raced out to the runway to await the arrival of the stricken sleigh. I turned to Mrs Claus. 'Does this kind of thing happen often?'

She shook her head. 'Not really – and, frankly, it's not much of an emergency either. All the reindeer has to do is keep his legs up when he lands and the others will bring him in safely. Our man here,' and she pointed at the harried controller, 'just likes to do things by the book.'

'Any chance I might have a quick word? I won't keep him too long.'

'Go right ahead.' She tapped the controller on the shoulder.

'Charles, this is Mr Pigg. He's investigating my husband's disappearance. He'd like to ask you some questions about the night he vanished.'

Charles nodded once but never took his eyes off the displays in front of him.

'OK, Charles. Can you tell us what happened?'

'Sure. Santa's private sleigh left here as scheduled at 21:00 hours. At 22:00 hours he contacted us to let us know that things were OK and that he was ascending to his cruising height. After that nothing, and he never arrived at Polar Central. That's all I know.'

'How long would the flight normally be?'

'About three hours, give or take.'

'And would it be unusual for Mr Claus to maintain radio silence for the duration?'

'It depends. It was a routine flight, so apart from an occasional update we might not hear from him until he was beginning his approach to Polar Central, so it wouldn't necessarily be a cause for concern. He does this run very regularly, you know.'

'I see, OK. Thanks, Charles.' He barely acknowledged me as he turned his attention back to his screens. I looked at Mrs Claus. 'Mrs Cl . . . I mean Clarissa, this is a most peculiar case. I can find no evidence of any wrongdoing here nor can I explain your husband's disappearance. Clearly he's missing, but I can't explain it. It is possible that I may be able to find out something by interviewing the staff at your North Pole base. How soon can you organise a flight for us since I'd like to start talking to them as soon as possible?'

'You can leave right now,' she said. 'We have a number of private sleighs – state of the art – that we keep on standby for any sudden or unexpected departures. They're very comfortable and should get you there in a matter of hours.' Mrs Claus turned to Charles. 'Ask the ground crew to prep *Jingle Bells* for an immediate departure to Polar Central.'

'Yes, ma'am,' he replied and issued orders into a nearby radio.

As he spoke we were shepherded downstairs into an (admittedly very comfortable) departure lounge, where we were given heavy fur coats to wear – which didn't bode too well for the journey ahead. Once we were warmly wrapped up we were taken to the sleigh.

I have to confess at this point that I was expecting an open box with a hard wooden seat and large storage area; all sitting on top of two long, curved, metal skis with a team of smelly, flea-ridden reindeer attached to the front.

The reality was so very different.

A sleek red-and-white (of course) chassis, like a giant covered bobsleigh, rested on huge, sturdy-looking skis. To my relief there was no sign of outside seats so it looked as though we'd be inside – and warm, I hoped. Naturally it wasn't all high-tech. I'd been expecting something like rocket-powered engines, so I was a tad disappointed to see a team of twelve reindeer being hooked up to the front of the sleigh, but at least they looked the part too: sleek, strong and very healthy looking. I just wasn't too sure they'd manage to get the sleigh off the ground.

Mrs Claus saw my look of uncertainty and quickly reassured me, 'They're Class Two reindeer; some low-level raw magic and power. Don't worry; they'll get us there without difficulty.'

Magic: I knew there'd be magic involved somewhere. I didn't share her confidence. Magic and me just didn't mix. If something was going to go wrong with this craft, chances were it would be when I was travelling in it.

Slowly and with a large degree of caution I approached the sleigh. As I did, a door in the side slid quietly open, revealing a luxurious interior. Large, comfortable-looking seats lined the walls and a plush carpet covered the floor. No prizes for guessing the colour scheme. Hey, maybe this wouldn't be too bad after all.

One of the ground crew approached. 'Everyone inside please, we depart in five minutes.'

We all entered and quickly strapped ourselves into the seats. I sank into mine and it surrounded me like I was in a hot bath. This was the life. If I didn't know better I'd have thought I was in someone's living room. Across from me Basili struggled with his seat belt and looked anxiously at me. I gave him a reassuring smile, but he didn't seem too convinced. Maybe he didn't like flying either – which was strange, considering he used to be a genie and spent most of the time when he popped out of his lamp hanging in the air with smoke for legs. I hoped for his sake we'd have an uneventful flight.

Behind me Mrs Claus was talking to our in-flight steward and asking him to organise drinks and something to eat as soon as we were airborne. As he walked back to the galley, there was a sudden jolt and the sleigh began to move forward along the ramp. As we began to pick up speed, I noticed – somewhat nervously – that we were racing up the ramp towards the ceiling I'd seen earlier. The sleigh got faster and faster as we approached the blank wall ahead.

'Shouldn't there be a door or something?' I shouted over my shoulder to Mrs Claus, who was lying back with her eyes closed, seemingly blissfully unaware of our imminent collision.

'Don't worry, Mr Pigg. I'm sure the pilot knows what he's doing.'

Outside, the scenery was passing by in a blur as the reindeer picked up speed, apparently oblivious to their impending doom.

The ceiling got closer and closer and I got more and more scared. 'Ohmigod, we're all gonna die; we're all gonna die; WE'RE ALL GONNA DIIIIAAAARGH.' As I screamed in terror at our imminent collision with the ceiling, it suddenly split in two and the sleigh shot out through the opening. Through the window I got a blurred glimpse of the swimming pool parting on either side as we came up through it. Seconds later we'd left the ground behind us and hurtled into the night sky.

'There,' came a sleepy voice from behind me. 'I told you he knew what he was doing.'

5

And Pigs Might Fly

I sank back in my seat, sweating . . . . well, um, like a pig actually. I was close to hyperventilating and tried to get my breathing under control before I passed out. Across the aisle Basili was studying me with interest, seemingly oblivious to what just happened.

'You are well, Mr Harry?' he asked.

'I'll live,' I gasped. 'But I don't think I'll be able to cope with any more scares like that.'

Behind me, a gentle snoring sound suggested Mrs Claus was far less worried than either of us.

'I am sure there will be no more incidents until after we are arriving at our destination.' Basili unfastened his belt – which was clearly making him uncomfortable – let his seat back and closed his eyes. Seconds later he too was snoring, but much louder than the ladylike trilling from Mrs Claus. Great: snoring in stereo for the rest of the trip! I wondered if there was an in-flight movie; I could certainly do with some distraction.

Unfortunately, it looked as though the nearest I was going to get to in-flight entertainment was looking out of the window.

Mind you, judging by the speed at which the clouds passed by it seemed that the reindeer were moving at quite a clip. Maybe there was some germ of truth in what Mrs Claus had told me. If these were Class Two animals, I wondered how fast Class One reindeer could go. Idly musing on thoughts like this (and because I had nothing else to do – the current case proving to be completely devoid of any leads), I eventually sank into a light doze.

A loud blaring brought me to my senses. The captain was shouting at us through the intercom. 'Attention, passengers. Ground control has detected another craft approaching us at speed. We have as yet been unable to make contact with them. Please return to your seats and ensure your seat belts are securely fastened while we establish what is going on. Thank you.'

Just as he finished there was a loud thud on the side of the sleigh as something made heavy contact. The impact caused the sleigh to lurch wildly and turn on its side. Before I could grab on to anything, I slid across the floor and smashed into the cabin door. Showing scant regard for safety regulations and quality construction, it swung open and I dropped out of the sleigh into the freezing night.

I felt a trotter bang off something as I fell. Using whatever innate survival instincts I possessed (I certainly wasn't doing this by design – trust me), my other trotter swung around and clung desperately to one of the sleigh's landing skis. The sleigh careened wildly as it was hit again and I just managed to keep my grip. Almost immediately, Basili's semi-conscious body fell out of the cabin above and plummeted past me. Using the same innate sense of self-preservation I'd used, his arms were stretched out trying to grab on to anything that might save him. Unfortunately for me, he wasn't quite as good at it as I was. Instead of grabbing the ski, he wrapped an arm around my legs and clutched them tightly.

I tried to look down at the ex-genie dangling from my legs.

'Basili,' I shouted, trying to be heard over the wind, 'can you climb up my body and grab on to a ski?'

'I do not think so, Mr Harry. I am barely feeling my hands. It is a most unusual and unpleasant sensation. Perhaps if I am letting go, you may be able to climb back in.'

'Not an option, Basili,' I muttered through gritted teeth. 'We need to come up with something else – and quickly.'

'Trust me, Mr Harry,' came the strained voice from below. 'I am thinking as fast as I can.'

As I gamely struggled for inspiration, there came a voice from above asking what was, in the circumstances, possibly the most idiotic question I'd ever heard.

'Are you two gentlemen OK?' asked Mrs Claus, peering down from the open door.

'Not really. Now if you would be so kind as to find something we can grab on to before we end up trying to fly of our own accord, we'd be really grateful.'

'One moment, I'll see what I can do.' Her head disappeared back into the sleigh before I could point out that we really didn't have the luxury of a moment to spare.

'Hold on, Basili,' I roared down to the genie. 'Help may be on its way.' As I did so, my trotters began to slip away from the skis. Frantically, I tried to hold on, but the strain was too much. My trotters protested at what they were being asked to do – they didn't seem to think it was fair. Inch by inch they began to slide apart. I wasn't going to manage it.

Just as I was about to give way, Mrs Claus shouted down at us again. 'Here, grab on to this.' Something snaked past my shoulder and I grabbed on to a thick rope and held on to it as if my life depended on it (which it did).

I was just thanking my lucky stars, lucky rabbit's foot, lucky anything-else-lucky-I-had-in-my-possession when the big, ugly, hob-nailed boot of fate stamped down on me one more time. The sleigh skewed wildly as our attackers hit it once again. There was a scream and I saw a blur of red as something large fell past me. There was an almighty tug on my legs as if someone had attached something heavy – like, say, a truck – to them.

Whatever chance I had of hanging on while Basili dangled from my legs had disappeared when Mrs Claus added her ample frame to the equation. Now, I could feel the rope sliding through my trotters as my arms finally gave up, shouted surrender and lay down their weapons. I didn't know how long the rope was, but from the speed I slid down along it I didn't think there was much more left to hold on to. This was it; this was the end.

6

The Soft Shoe Slingshot

Or was it?

I didn't plummet down through the inky blackness and end up an unpleasant mess on the ground below (as I'd not unreasonably expected) but landed instead on something hard and metallic. Behind me I could hear Basili crying, 'Thank the gods', and, behind him again, Mrs Claus was just crying. I didn't even bother trying to work out what had happened; I just lay where I was and breathed a heavy sigh of relief. From the speed of the wind across my face it seemed like we were on something that was moving fast – but what? When the surface underneath me lurched sharply and I saw us move towards the sleigh we'd just fallen from, I knew exactly where we were.

Were we safe? Hell, no!

Were we in a better position than before? Marginally – in the sense that we weren't hanging off each other and facing certain death.

Where exactly were we? We'd fallen on to the roof of the sleigh that had been attacking us!

Was that better? Only if it flew in a straight line.

159

I turned to my companions and broke the good news to them. From what I could see of their expressions they were less than gruntled too. Clearly they shared my opinion of our predicament.

'Is there any way we can climb down and get into this sleigh?' bellowed Mrs Claus.

'I doubt it,' I shouted back, trying to make myself heard over the howling wind. 'If we let go of what we're holding, we'll be blown off. More to the point, do you really want to climb into a sleigh full of people who have been trying to kill us for the past ten minutes?'

'Good point. So what do we do now?'

The obvious answer (if any solution to this predicament could be called obvious) would be to get back to our own sleigh and try to escape from our attackers. Yeah, easy really; all we had to do was jump from one sleigh to another while travelling at great speed thousands of feet in the air. Easy!

Of course, I had no idea where our sleigh was. If our pilot had any sense he was flying as far from our attackers as possible to preserve his hide. It's what I'd have done.

But he proved me wrong. There was a drumming sound from above and a flurry of hooves narrowly missed my head. I looked up and saw our sleigh hovering inches above me. Through the cockpit window our pilot was waving madly at us, urging us to get back in.

I didn't need a formal invitation. I grabbed the ski that was hanging above me and pulled myself up and back into the passenger section. Seconds later, the other two fell in on top of me and we lay on the floor gasping for breath.

'No time,' I urged. 'We need to get strapped in now. I don't know about you two, but I certainly wouldn't care for a repeat of that little adventure.'

For big people they could move fast when they wanted. Both of them were in their seats and buckled before I'd even stood back up. Once I was secure I grabbed the armrests and held on as if my life depended on it – which, when you think about it, it did. There was no way I was falling out of that door again. No thank you very much.

Mrs Claus spoke to the pilot and the gist of the long conversation was 'Get us the hell out of here as fast as you can.' I couldn't make out all of his reply but I did pick up the words 'faster than us' and 'reindeer getting tired'. No matter how I juggled the phrases in my head, I couldn't make them into a sentence that didn't mean bad news for us.

'Are we in trouble?' I asked.

'You mean worse trouble than we're already in? Marginally. The pilot doesn't think he can get away; the reindeer are tiring and we've taken a fair bit of damage.'

'But that other sleigh must be having problems too. Surely in all the battering it gave us, it must have taken a dent or two? What about its reindeer? They must be tired too.'

'Ah, but I'm told that their sleigh is one of those new-fangled jet-powered ones. No reindeer to tire, I'm afraid. Unless they run out of fuel soon, we don't stand a chance.'

Mrs Claus waved frantically in the direction of the still-open door. 'Brace yourselves, here they come again.'

'Sod this for a game of skittles,' I exclaimed, partly in frustration but mostly in anger. I wasn't sure if there was anything I could do but I wasn't just going to sit there and wait for us to fall out of the sky. I unbuckled my seat belt and stood up carefully – ever mindful of the gaping hole where the door used to be. Looking around the cabin, I saw another door in the rear wall. 'What's in there?' I asked.

'Just some light luggage for me, some raw materials for the toy factory and other bits and pieces. Nothing important. Why do you ask?' said Mrs Claus.

I scrambled back and pulled the door open. 'Because I'm fed up with waiting to be bumped out of the sky. I'm going to try to fight back. There might be nothing I can do but I'll feel a whole heap better.'

I examined the contents of the luggage area. Mrs Claus was right. There didn't seem to be much that I could use as a weapon. Large crates were stacked neatly and fastened to the walls. Just in front of them was a mountain of suitcases that filled the rest of room. 'Light luggage' indeed. If this was what she took for an overnight trip to the North Pole, I shuddered to think what she might need for a two-week vacation.

Nope, nothing useful here. I banged my fist against the door in frustration and, just as I was about to give up, a thought struck me.

Suitcases!

I grabbed a medium-sized one and hefted it. Heavy – but I could still carry it. Maybe . . . just maybe.

I dragged it across the floor towards the open door. Mrs Claus saw me. 'Hey, what are you doing with that suitcase? It's mine.' I chose to ignore her. At the door I clung to the frame and waited. In the distance I could see the large dark shape of the jet sleigh moving rapidly in our direction once more.

I lifted the case and swung it gently once or twice to get the balance right. The sleigh grew bigger as it neared our ailing craft. 'Strap yourselves in guys; we're in for some chop,' came the captain's voice over the intercom. I ignored him; I was through with strapping myself in.

The dark outline of the approaching sleigh was completely blocking out what little starlight there was. I waited for my opportunity and, with what little strength I had left, I flung the suitcase out of the door and straight at it. It made a satisfying contact and I heard the engine tone change from a low growl to a high-pitched and strangled whine – the kind of sound that suggested I had done some damage. I watched the sleigh begin to spin wildly over and over like a nuclear-powered spinning top. Whoever was in it was going to be very sick, very soon. Whirling madly, it careened wildly away from us, out of control and no longer a threat.

Of course, there was a knock-on effect too (there always is). As the turbine shredded the suitcase, it flung bits of shoes in all directions – like leather machine-gun bullets. There was a shriek of anguish from behind me. It sounded like Mrs Claus had been hit by the shrapnel.

How wrong I was.

'My Manolos,' she wailed. 'You've destroyed my Manolos.'

Manolos? What were Manolos? I looked at Basili. Maybe he knew what she was talking about.

'I think she is most unhappy that the suitcase you have ejected from our craft was full of her very expensive shoes.'

Oh, was that all? So it wasn't serious then, although from the sound of her you'd think someone had just died. She hadn't cried like that when we were in danger. Women!

7

Ice Station Santa

The North Pole was cold. No, that's an understatement: ice cream is cold, beer is cold; this was a whole new sensation that the word *cold* had only a passing acquaintance with. This was extremities turning blue cold, struggling to breathe cold and, most of all, impossible to walk on sheet ice with trotters cold. As soon as I stepped out of what was left of our battered sleigh, I wanted to race right back inside, huddle under a cosy blanket and wait until spring. At least now I knew why we'd been given all that warm gear back in Grimmtown.

We walked – well, slid might be more accurate – towards a small welcoming committee. Four people stood outside the arrivals area, clearly waiting for us. When we were near enough for them to approach without landing on their backsides the smallest of the group, a very pleasant and worried-looking woman, rushed forward and hugged Mrs Claus tightly.

'Oh, Clarissa,' she wept. 'I'm so glad you're safe. When we heard the news we feared the worst.'

Mrs Claus pushed her away gently. 'It's all right, Mary. It wasn't too pleasant, but we're here now and we're OK.'

'Wasn't too pleasant!' That was like saying Red Riding Hood wasn't too irritating – it made no effort to describe exactly how terrifying our experience had been. Before I could tell everyone how I had saved us all from certain death, I caught the warning look Mrs C was giving me – better not say too much until we knew exactly who was listening. I still had no idea what was going on but despite my initial doubts there was clearly a mystery to be solved here – and with my usual magnetic attraction to such mysteries, it was one of those that was hell-bent on putting my delicate hide in as much danger as possible.

No change there, then.

As I mused on how consistently unlucky I was in my choice of clients, I became aware that Mrs C (that's what I was calling her now – it seemed catchier than Mrs Claus and I was still nervous about calling her Clarissa) was trying to make introductions. She waved at the woman first. 'This is Mary; she runs the show at the North Pole while we're in Grimmtown. You'll find she is a most capable administrator and can probably tell you anything you want to know about what goes on here.'

Mary grasped my trotter in a firm, welcoming handshake. 'Very pleased to meet you, Mr Pigg. I've heard a lot about you.'

'Glad to meet you too, Mary. Mary um . . .?' I replied, trying to get her surname.

'Mary,' she said.

'Mary?' Once more with feeling.

'Mary.' And again.

'Ah,' Mrs C interrupted. 'There seems to be some confusion here.'

You have no idea, I thought.

'This is Mary Mary. She's a bit contrary, hence the difficulty. We originally hired her to look after our gardens here, but she was so good she eventually became our facility manager.'

They had gardens here? What grew in them? Icicles?

'Ah,' I said, 'I see.' Although I wasn't sure I saw at all.

'And these are our heads of toy manufacturing.' She indicated the three elves who had accompanied Mary. 'This is Carigrant, head of Trad Toys.' The first of the elves gave me a weak, dismissive half-wave. 'And this is Gladaerial, head of Tech Toys.' Again, another superior, flippant acknowledgement. 'And finally, this is Gilgrisum, head of R&D.' Gilgrisum raised an eyebrow a fraction of an inch, which I assumed was the elven equivalent of rushing over to me, hugging me tightly and roaring 'Great to meet you' in my ear.

Mrs Claus continued, 'They will arrange for any interviews you might want to have with the workers.'

In truth, I didn't *want* to interview any elves; it was more a case of having to. For reasons outlined before, I disliked elves intensely. It was hard to trust a race who spent most of their time being obsessed with personal hygiene and looking at themselves in mirrors. And I wasn't too enamoured with the way they spoke either.

As if he could read my thoughts, 'A detective arrives; mysteries will be solved this night,' said Carigrant, right on cue.

See what I mean. Why not just say it plainly: Harry Pigg is here; all our problems are over. This genius detective will have things wrapped up before you can say something long-winded and pretentious.

'How many elves do you have working here?'

'One hundred,' said Mary Mary promptly.

Great – one hundred gibberish interviews. I wondered if it was possible to get an elvish interpreter – although I imagined after two days in the job they'd be quite insane. As jobs go, I'd rate it up there with Orc etiquette coach and wolf dentistry. Still, this is why I get paid the big bucks (or, as is more usual, small bucks paid in instalments or replaced by a basket of fruit or an IOU – usually the last).

It was time to get down to business. I addressed everyone, 'Right, we're not sure what has happened to Mr Claus – I mean, Santa. It's quite likely he's been kidnapped, so someone here may know something about it. I'll be talking to everyone so please make sure your teams know this. I'd also appreciate it if you would ask them to be as candid as possible. The more information we have, the better. It may be just one small detail that they might even consider unimportant, but it could be crucial.'

From the looks on their faces, they seemed to take my statement with a degree of disbelief, as if I was impugning the integrity of their workforce. Who, me?

I continued, 'We'll also need some place to work out of for the duration.'

Mrs C nodded. 'I'll make sure you have somewhere suitable. Mary, please organise a room for Mr Pigg.' Mary nodded and scurried off, followed a few moments later by the elves – who didn't scurry, they were far too dignified. They moved gracefully over the frozen surface as if it was made of asphalt. Typical – even on ice they looked elegant.

Behind me I heard a strange rattling noise. Too cold for snakes, I thought as I turned to investigate. It was Basili's teeth hammering out a very impressive drum solo he was so cold. 'P . . . p . . . perhaps we g . . .g . . . go inside now, p . . . p . . . please. It is m . . . m . . . m . . . most c . . . c . . . cold out here.' He wasn't used to temperatures like this. When he was attached to his lamp, he probably spent his time being washed up on warm sunny beaches and being summoned into bright sunlight to do as his latest master might bid – or at least that's how I imagined it. Poor beggar probably only saw ice when he added it to his margarita after settling down in his lamp of an evening after a hard day's magic.

The Ho Ho Ho Mystery

'A good idea,' I said. 'It is a bit chilly out here.' My talent for understatement is unsurpassed.

Minutes later we were in – oh joy – a warm and welcoming reception area. A Christmas theme was (inevitably) the order of the day, except that here large images of the main man dominated. A huge picture that stretched from floor to ceiling hung behind the reception desk and large red statues of Santa dotted around the room were hard to miss. I wondered if there might be some over-compensation issues here – on top of everything else – but I was smart enough to just nod my head maniacally and comment on how tasteful the décor was. Basili gave me an incredulous look, but I managed to nudge him sharply in the side before he could say anything that might reflect badly on me.

Mary Mary approached us and ushered us into a slightly more tastefully decorated meeting room. A tinny 'Santa Claus Is Coming to Town' was being piped in to set the atmosphere. Not this year, I thought, unless I suddenly had a major breakthrough in the case.

'You can use this room for the duration of your stay,' said Mary Mary. 'Everyone has been instructed to cooperate fully with your investigation. If you need anything else, don't hesitate to contact me.'

'Thank you very much,' I said. 'Apart from the elves, is there anyone else here I should be talking to?'

Mary Mary thought for a moment. 'Well, there's Rudolph. He is quite close to Santa. He might be able to help.'

'Right then, we'll need to speak to him too. Can you set it up for us?'

Mary Mary shifted uncomfortably. 'Well, you don't really talk to Rudolph; you listen. He's got quite a strong personality.' By that I presumed she meant he was an arrogant, superior reindeer with an attitude problem. That was fine; it wouldn't be the first time I'd experienced that.

169

'Why don't you let me worry about that?' I said. 'I'm sure he'll talk to us. In fact, why don't we get him in here as our first interviewee?'

'Oh goodness, no,' Mary Mary exclaimed. 'He doesn't do house calls. You'll have to make an appointment to see him. He's very busy, you know.'

I wasn't having any of that. 'I doubt it very much. I imagine the only time he's busy is on Christmas Eve when he does his "Rudolph with your nose so bright" routine at the front of the sleigh. Let's go and see him now.' I strode purposefully out of the office and stopped when I realised I had no idea where I was going. Somewhat abashed, I waited for the others to join me.

'OK, where does Rudolph hang out when he's not on sleigh duty?' I asked.

'His rooms are this way.' Mary Mary pointed down a nearby corridor. 'But I don't think he'll see you.'

'Oh, I beg to differ.' Determination writ large on my face, I marched down the corridor. Seconds later I stood outside a heavy wooden door. A large sign surrounded by flashing fairy lights read: 'Rudolph. Unavailable from 24th December to 26th December. Any other time by appointment only.'

'Who does he think he is?' I muttered as I flung the door open and walked in. Inside, a very nervous gnome sat at a small desk, guarding a set of double doors at the far side of a small lobby. When he saw us, he stood up and brandished a pen angrily in our direction.

'You can't go in there,' he squeaked. 'You don't have an appointment.'

'Wrong. I can, I do and I will.' I walked past him towards the double doors.

In fairness to him he tried to stop me, but I brushed him aside, swung the doors open and stopped abruptly, jaw hitting the ground. I wasn't sure what I'd expected to see, perhaps a plush office, ornate mahogany desk, comfortable leather chairs, expensive carpet and lots of plants; I certainly didn't expect . . . well, the first thing that caught my eye was the reindeer.

Instead of a flea-ridden, hay-chomping animal resting up in a straw-lined stable getting ready for his big night, I got a sleek reindeer draped across a divan, clad in a red dressing gown and matching silk pyjamas. An elf stood on either side of him; one dropping grapes into his upturned mouth while the other waved a large feather over his head – presumably to cool him down. On a small table beside him a large cigar burned away in an ornate ashtray.

As we entered Rudolph looked up sharply, clearly annoyed at the unexpected intrusion.

'Who the hell are you and what are you doing in here uninvited? Do you know who I am?' His voice had an upper-class twang that was purely for effect. It sounded like he'd practised it every day until he got it just right and used it to intimidate people. Well, he was intimidating the wrong person here. I walked straight up to where he was lying and stuck my snout into his face.

'I'm the guy who's been asked to find out what happened to your boss. I invited myself and, yes, not only do I know who you are but I don't really care. Any more questions?' I stood there staring into his eyes, willing myself not to blink first. We continued to glare at each other, each waiting for the other to crack. He didn't realise he was up against the best; I could outstare a basilisk. This time, however, I thought I'd met my match as he glared at me, gaze unwavering, his brown eyes drilling into mine, challenging me. Just as my eyes began to water over (please don't blink, Harry; please don't blink), Rudolph capitulated, clearly realising who was boss (or maybe he just had to close his eyes) and turned his face away. When I was sure he couldn't see me I blinked furiously to relieve my aching peepers. Pig 1, reindeer 0.

'Good,' I said. 'Now that we've gotten that out of the way, I'd like to ask you some questions.'

Rudolph was still trying to gain the upper hand. 'I'm somewhat busy at the moment; if you'd care to make an appointment I'm sure I can squeeze you in early next week.'

I'd had enough. I grabbed him by the silk lapels and pulled him up so he was staring once more into my face. This time I wasn't interested in a staring contest. 'Listen, antler boy, I don't know who you think you are but I don't have time for this upper-class twit-of-the-year nonsense. Your boss's wife has asked me to find him and I'm going to do that to the best of my ability. As part of that investigation I need to talk to you and we are going to do that right now. Are you OK with that, or do I have to incentivise you in some way?' I flicked my head casually towards Basili, who was standing nervously in the door. Now I knew that, as an enforcer, Basili was about as useful as a snowman stoking a furnace but Rudolph didn't and, in fairness, Basili did look the part – up to a point.

Rudolph looked at Basili, looked back at me, looked at Basili again and made up his mind. 'OK, let's talk.' As he did so, I noticed something very strange happen to his nose: it began to glow slightly, giving off a reddish light that cast his face in shadow.

'Does that happen often?' I said, fascinated.

'Usually when I get emotional,' Rudolph replied. 'The more emotional I get, the stronger the light becomes. It's what sets me apart from the others.'

I was tempted to point out that dressing in red silk pyjamas and being fed grapes probably set him apart from the others too, but I didn't; sometimes I'm just too nice.

'So you really do lead the sleigh on Christmas Eve then?'

Rudolph nodded. 'Yes, it can get very foggy, you know. That's when I'm needed most. But they have to make me very angry if it's to be really effective.'

'What do they do, deprive you of elocution classes?'

Sarcasm was completely lost on him. 'No, they just put me in with the rest of the reindeer for a week. That really bugs me: no dress sense, bad table manners and an unhealthy fascination with reality TV. I tell you, it would make anyone mad, let alone someone of my obvious refinement.'

I almost felt for him. Maybe it would have been easier just to take his jimmies and grapes away. That'd probably do the trick without the need to inflict him upon the other unfortunate reindeer. Why should they have to suffer too? That was just cruel and unusual. And speaking of cruel and unusual, now I had to try to interview this twit.

I went through all the usual questions and received all the usual answers until I came to the 'Any reason why anyone might want to kidnap Santa?' one. Although he shook his head and said he couldn't think of any, there was that same hint of evasion I thought I'd detected with Mrs C. Now I was beginning to get the feeling that there was more going on here than I'd previously thought. Despite their denials, both Mrs C and Rudolph had given the distinct impression that they knew more than they were letting on. But what was it? And how did it relate to the case? More questions; fewer answers. Maybe the elves might be able to tell us something – although I doubted it very much.

Telling Rudolph not to make any travel plans as we'd probably need to speak to him again, we left and made our way back to our interview room.

'What a clown,' I said to Basili. 'And now we get to talk to elves.'

Despite my own reservations, Basili seemed to be looking forward to the next set of interviews (ah, the enthusiasm of the newly minted detective!).

8

I Am Not Spock

'Very well then,' Basili said, rubbing his hands – he was really getting into this – 'it is time to be talking to some elven peoples.'

'Well, that could be a bit of a misnomer; it's more like we'll look at them blankly while their mouths make noises that could perhaps be construed as talking, then we'll try to make some sense of whatever we think they've just said. And we'll have to do this one hundred times,' I replied. 'Just so as you know, this will be like pulling teeth, only more painful. I suspect that by the end of the day your ears will be bleeding and you'll wish you were back with Aladdin.'

'Oh, Mr Harry, I do not think so. Surely nothing could be worse than spending year after year stuck in that lamp waiting to grant one final wish.' He did have a point there, although it was probably a photo-finish to decide which was worse.

After the seventh interview, I suspected he was having a change of mind. I could see his eyes were glazing over and a thin trail of drool trickled from the corner of his mouth. He was rapidly losing his sanity, his grip on reality and his will to live – and we had another ninety-three elves to talk to! He buried his head in his hands and wailed mournfully. 'Oh, Mr Harry, I do not know how much more of this I am taking. I am failing to comprehend any word these elvish folk are speaking.'

I understood his plight; I was hovering on the brink of complete mental breakdown too. My grasp of what was real – already eroded by Christmas decoration overdose and my conversation with Rudolph – was now being washed away in a sea of double talk and nonsense. Just to give you an example:

Conversation One:

Question: When did you last see Mr Claus?

Answer: The gentleman in red was perambulating the environs some weeks hence but has not been in attendance at the child's plaything fabrication facility for some thirty-six planetary rotations.

Conversation Two:

Question: Are you aware of any reason why someone might want to harm Mr Claus?

Answer: Gentleness is his path; harm will not be the stone upon which he trips.

If I was to interpret what we were being told correctly, Santa hadn't been seen at the North Pole since his last visit some thirty-six days earlier and no one knew of any reason why anyone might want to do him harm. At least, that's what I think they were telling me. I wasn't sure the other ninety-three interviews would change that.

Or would they?

Candidate eighty-six set all kinds of alarm bells ringing. His story was the same as all the others, but when he'd left the room I told Basili we needed to carry out further investigations into that particular elf.

'Why so, Mr Harry?' he asked.

'Well, did you notice anything strange about him?'

'No, I was so concentrating on staying awake that I did not fully take in what he was talking about.'

'No, Basili,' I said. 'It's not what he was saying; he sounded just the same as all the others. Did you not notice anything about his personal grooming?'

Basili raised an eyebrow.

It looked like it was time for elves 101. 'Let me list them for you: he was unshaven, his hair was greasy (and not tied back in an ever so look-at-me-I'm-cool ponytail), his clothes weren't ironed and, most importantly, he had BO.'

'So?' Basili was even more confused.

'So, when have you ever seen an elf that wasn't immaculately turned out? They fancy themselves as style icons (if you like Lincoln green tights and pointy boots, that is) and are obsessed with personal hygiene. I think it's fair to say elf number eighty-six is a ringer and a badly prepared ringer at that. He really should have washed himself, or at least applied some deodorant.' I stood up, excitement building now that we had a lead at long last. 'Let's see what we can find out about him.'

'Why don't we take him down to the station, let the boys be sorting him out?' Basili was hopping up and down enthusiastically (and let me tell you it wasn't a pretty sight). I wondered what kind of TV shows he'd been watching while stuck in the lamp.

'That's not how things are done,' I said – although, it being elves, the idea did have some merit. 'Anyway, we don't want to let him know we're on to him. The best thing to do is keep a discreet eye on him and see what he does; or maybe,' a thought had just struck me, 'we can try to get close to him and see if he'll let anything slip. He certainly doesn't strike me as being too bright.'

'Yes, but how? We are much too big and, anyway, you are a pig. Even he would be spotting the attempt at deception.' Basili was right. Apart from the three elves we'd met when we arrived, all the others were northern elves and much smaller than their southern cousins. In fact, they were just like the elves you've seen depicted in those cheerful Christmas cards showing Santa's workshop – just a lot less cheerful and a lot more pompous in reality. Even the dimmest of elves would have no difficulty seeing through whatever disguise we might adopt. No, we needed someone else; someone smaller; someone with the brass neck to be able to pull a deception like this off.

I smiled broadly. 'Basili, I think I have a plan.'

'No way! There is no way on this planet that I'm wearing those things.' Jack Horner was indignant. He flung the fake ears we'd given him on the ground. 'They're the most idiotic things I've ever seen. They look like they were made out of a cereal box.'

There's ingratitude for you. With Mrs C's help, we'd managed to fly him at inordinate expense to a place most children would give both arms to visit and all he had to do in return was dress up as an elf for a few minutes. Sometimes I just don't understand children.

I tried to placate him. 'Jack, Jack, take it easy. We need someone to mingle with the elves and find out what number eighty-six is up to. That someone has to be fearless, able to think on his feet and be brave in the face of certain danger.' OK, I was laying it on with a trowel, but I knew how to get to him. 'When I started to draw up a list of suitable candidates only one name sprang to mind. I still remember how you risked certain death to rescue me from Edna's.'

Jack preened himself. I could see my hyperbole was working. 'You know, I might just be the answer to your prayers,' he said.

'But there's still no way I'm wearing those stupid cardboard ears. Get me something that looks real and I'll think about it.'

Result!

I grinned happily. 'Looks like the team are all together and hot on the trail once more.'

'Yep,' replied Jack. 'Now we just need to find some fake ears.'

'We're in the biggest toy-manufacturing facility in the world; just how difficult do you think it's going to be?'

Very, as it turned out.

Play-Elf outfits were so last year that no one wanted them any more. All available stock had been recycled as Robin Hood costumes, but as Sherwood Forest's most famous inhabitant wasn't noted for having pointy ears, they had all been melted down and remoulded into Hubbard's Cubbard action figures (and they weren't selling too well either; rock bands aren't in great demand as toys). We had scoured workshops, storage bins and were rummaging through a disused warehouse full of obsolete toys when Jack shouted, 'Would this work?' and waved a large, if somewhat battered crate at us. We gathered around to see what he'd found.

I blew years of accumulated dust off the top of the box and read the contents. 'Yes, this might just do the trick.' Opening it, I took out a pair of black pants and a dark blue top. Throwing them to one side, I continued to search. 'So far, so good,' I murmured. 'Now somewhere in here there should be . . . aha, got you.'

Very carefully, I removed what looked like two dead pink slugs and carefully unrolled them in my hand. 'I haven't seen one of these in years. They were all the rage in the sixties.'

Beside me, Jack picked up the cover of the box and studied it.

'What's logic?' he asked. Before I could answer he continued, 'What's a phaser?' and, barely pausing for breath, 'Who's Mr Spock? He looks kinda weird.' He handed me the box and I read it:

179

Now you too can be a master of logic.
Be the envy of your friends as you stun them with
your Vulcan nerve pinch.
Beam up this box and be Mr Spock.
Note: the phaser is a toy and will not disintegrate either
humans or aliens (batteries not included).

A picture of one of science fiction's most famous pointy-eared non-humans adorned the cover.

'This guy was one of the most famous TV aliens of all time but, most importantly,' I held up the two unrolled pink things, 'he had pointy ears. Let's try them on, but be careful, they're old so they might be a bit delicate.'

Ever so gently, I attached them over Jack's ears. They snapped on easily and when I took my hands away they stayed upright.

'Live long and prosper,' I said to him. He looked at me blankly. 'Before your time, never mind. Now we just need to borrow one of those Robin Hood suits and you'll be good to go.'

Once we'd dressed him up he looked just like any of the Santa's little helpers who swarmed around the workshops building, packing and shipping millions of toys.

'Are you sure this is going to work?' Jack asked anxiously as he attached a small microphone to his vest (we'd 'borrowed' it from an old James Bond Junior Spy Kit).

'Nope,' I said, 'but I don't think you're in any danger, if that's what you're worried about.'

'It isn't. I'm just wondering how long I'm going to have to wear this stupid costume – it itches.' He scratched his back furiously – mostly for effect.

'You'll be fine. Just talk to our suspect as if you're his best friend. Judging by his personal hygiene I suspect no one else will so he'll probably be glad of the company. Don't be too pushy' – which, of course, was like asking water not to be too wet – 'don't bombard him with questions. Just play the "I'm new here too" routine and see if he responds.' I patted him reassuringly on the shoulder. 'Remember, we'll be listening in. If there's any hint of trouble, we'll pull you out of there faster than blackbirds out of a pie, OK?'

Jack nodded once. 'Right, let's do it.'

'Good man. Remember, we're counting on you.'

'So no pressure then.'

'Absolutely not,' I said.

'Good. Now where do I go?'

'You see all those elves over there building toy robots?'

Jack nodded. 'Yep.'

'See the way they're all studiously avoiding that one guy who's attaching the legs?' There was a large elf-free space around our suspect (which didn't seem to bother him in the slightest).

'Yep.'

'Well, he's your guy. Just try not to mention the smell.'

'What smell? Hey, you never told me the guy smelled. How close will I have to get to him?'

'It's not too bad and after a few minutes you won't even notice it. Now get to work.' I pushed him away and into the workshop. Within seconds he'd disappeared into a sea of bright-green elves. I spoke into the microphone that was taped to my jaw. 'Jack, can you hear me OK?'

'Messages are clear; communication will be unbroken this day.' Well at least he was getting into the spirit of things. Maybe he was suited to undercover work; two minutes in and he already sounded like an elf. I just prayed he wouldn't stay like that as I didn't fancy having to listen to elfspeak twenty-four seven; I didn't think my head could take it.

As Jack tried to ingratiate himself with the world's most slovenly elf, I mulled over the case and our progress to date – or, more accurately, our lack of progress. We hadn't really got very far other than establishing that something fishy was going on and the two people closest to Santa were not telling me the entire truth. Santa had clearly been abducted, otherwise why would someone have tried to kill us? But the big questions were why? And indeed who? In terms of the case itself, we still had very little to go on – elf impostor aside. I suspected he was planted purely to keep an eye on things and wasn't a big player in whatever was going on, but he might know something.

There were a few things that we might be able to follow up on though: we'd been attacked by a jet-powered sleigh. It was most definitely a luxury item, so who might have bought one? Surely there couldn't be too many winging their way through the skies – and, after our little adventure, there was probably one less. Mrs C might be able to point me in the direction of flying-sleigh vendors; after all, she had enough of them.

Who dropped the pseudo-elf into the workshop – and why? That one was a long shot, but you never know.

Why were Mrs Claus and Rudolph not telling me the whole story? Although I didn't think they had anything to do with Santa's disappearance, they'd been evasive when I'd asked them about it. They knew something they were unwilling to tell me; but what – and how did it tie into the case?

I sighed in frustration. There was something strange about this case; something I couldn't quite figure out, but I knew I'd get there eventually – as long as I didn't get beaten to a pulp first.

9

Dashing Through the Snow

Wow, electronic surveillance was boring. For an elf-alike, Mr Scruffy was positively taciturn. Not only did he fail to spout the usual meaningless waffle, he barely acknowledged Jack and his replies to the questions put to him were variations on the monosyllabic grunt. If I'd any suspicions that the guy was an impostor, his lack of verbals confirmed it. Through my earpiece, I could hear Jack valiantly – and none too subtly – trying to find out whatever he could without making it too obvious.

'Have you been working here long?'

'Unh-unh.' Which I took to mean no, seeing as he was shaking his head at the same time.

'Where did you work before here? I was in snow globes.' Uh-oh, now he was laying it on with a trowel. Maybe he was getting into character a little too much.

'Unh.' Nope, I have no idea either.

Jack was persisting though. 'No, I mean really. Where did you come from?'

Mr Scruffy evidently found this particular line of questioning a little too direct by elf standards and began to smell an unsavoury rodent of some type. In an instant, he'd pushed Jack away and was running for the door. Seconds later I was after him. Seconds after that Basili was lumbering after me, followed by an indignant Jack. 'Did you see that? He pushed me. I'm not letting him get away with it.'

Privately, I hoped I'd get to him first. An angry Jack Horner was not someone to be trifled with.

Mr Scruffy had raced out of the workshop and across the lobby towards the exit.

'Is he nuts?' I said. 'It's freezing out there.' My question was promptly answered when he grabbed an unsuspecting elf who had just come in and ripped his furs off him. The dazed elf was still standing at the door trying to figure out where his furs had gone as our quarry raced out through the entrance and into the snowy wastes outside.

I skidded to a stop. 'Whoa, let's think about this for a minute, guys.'

'We can't let him get away,' shouted Jack. 'He knows something; I know he does. He might be our only chance.'

Now don't ever say this back to him, but, in this instance, Jack was right. We had little enough to go on – and what little we did have was disappearing into the wilderness outside. Cold or no cold, we had to follow. I rolled my eyes upwards, nodded to Jack and said, 'OK, let's go get him.'

I pushed the door open and stepped out on to the ice – and promptly slid twenty feet along the ground, legs spinning, like a crazy cartwheel, before landing painfully on my rear. There were hoots of hysterical laughter from behind as my – obviously highly amused – partners took pleasure in my pain. Seconds later I was laughing as well, as they too slid on the slippery surface, tried to grab on to each other for support in a flailing mass of arms and pulled each other down on to the ice – although I did feel a tad sorry for Jack, Basili landed on him.

With as much dignity as I could muster, I carefully stood back up and leaned on a nearby snowdrift for support. As I did so, there was a low humming sound from beyond the drift. I peeped carefully over the edge and almost had my head taken off as a bright red jet ski careened wildly towards me. I barely had time to pull my head back down before it crashed into the edge of the drift above me, covering me in a mini-avalanche of snow, and flew through the air on to the ice beyond. It slid wildly from side to side before the driver eventually recovered control and headed away from me at high velocity.

'He's getting away,' Jack yelled.

I saw my fat fee disappearing in the flurry of slush that was being forced up by the passage of the jet ski – no way; not on my watch; especially not where money was concerned. 'No he's not. We're going to follow him.'

Jack and Basili looked at me as if I was quite mad – which was a distinct possibility.

'What do you suggest we do, run fast? Harry, we'll freeze without proper outdoor gear.' Jack was clearly concerned.

'We'll have to take that chance. We can't afford to let him get away.'

There was a loud roaring from behind us and a familiar voice said, 'Hopefully you won't have to.' Two jet skis pulled up beside us; one piloted by Mrs C, the other by Mary Mary. Slung across the back of both was a heap of furs. The ladies flung the furs at us.

'Get 'em on you, we've no time to waste,' bellowed Mrs C, trying to be heard over the noise of the engines.

I didn't need a second invitation. I quickly donned the furs, threw myself up on the jet ski behind Mrs C and hung on tightly

– praying that I wouldn't fall off. Beside me, Basili had joined Mary Mary on hers. A look of disappointment crossed Jack's face. 'What about me?'

Mrs C gave him an affectionate hug. 'Too dangerous, Jack. Your mother would never forgive me if something happened to you. Just keep an eye on things here while we're gone. If we don't make it back, it'll be up to you to break the case. We're counting on you.' It was certainly dramatic, but it had the desired effect. Jack cheered up instantly with his new-found sense of responsibility and gave an elaborate salute.

'Yes, ma'am,' he said proudly. 'This case is in safe hands with me.'

Before I could say anything else, there was a sudden jolt as the jet ski lurched forward. I just about managed to stay on by grabbing Mrs C tightly and holding on to her for dear life. If this was what it was like while we were starting, what would it be like when we were racing across the snow? One of those 'This isn't such a good idea' thoughts marched into my mind and demanded my attention. I chose to ignore it, although I knew it was right. If I'd really thought about it, I'd have realised how ridiculous the whole thing was: a city pig like me at the North Pole, risking near death from exposure in pursuit of someone with bad personal hygiene who might (and it was a long shot) just provide a breakthrough in the case, riding across freezing wastes on a jet ski piloted by a woman who claimed to be the wife of a mythical character who brought toys to millions of children once a year. Had I missed anything?

I was bumped, jostled and swung from side to side as we lurched after our quarry. But for the fact that I was gamely trying not to be flung off the violently bucking machine, it didn't feel like we were moving at all. The only things that weren't white were the red dot in the distance that we were just about keeping up with and the four of us. With the furs on, we looked like grizzly bears out for a jaunt on the snow. Grizzlies on ice! That would make their polar cousins turn their heads and stare in amazement.

'Faster, faster, we're gaining on him,' I roared in Mrs C's ear, hoping she could hear me over the noise of the engine and howling wind. She nodded and gunned the accelerator, trying to squeeze out every last particle of speed we could muster.

Now the jet ski ahead was definitely getting closer. I could make out Mr Scruffy giving an occasional panicked glance behind to see where we were. Not too far was the answer. Only a few more minutes and we'd be right on top of him.

And then what?

How were we going to stop him? He was hardly going to pull over and come quietly. At the speed we were going at, any attempt to force him to stop would probably only end in disaster – more than likely ours. Then I had my brainwave; my gloriously insane, probably-ending-in-certain-death brainwave. I can only claim that the cold had somehow suppressed my cowardice gene and made me temporarily prone to insane acts of bravery.

'Try to get beside him,' I roared at Mrs C. She nodded and gradually drew alongside the red jet ski.

'Keep it as steady as you can,' I shouted as I stood up, blissfully ignorant of the stupidity of what I was about to attempt. I fixed my eyes on Mr Scruffy's jet ski, watching it get closer and closer. Nearly there, I thought. Just a few more seconds.

Now!

I threw myself off our jet ski and made to grab him. As if anticipating my actions – actually, with hindsight, he was definitely anticipating my actions – as soon as I jumped Mr Scruffy hit the accelerator and his craft leaped forward. I sailed through the air and completely missed him. It wasn't a total disaster though, as I did manage to grab on to Basili, whose jet ski had just pulled up parallel to us on the far side. This of course wasn't part of the plan and, since it was entirely unexpected, it caused the jet ski to skew off the ice and up a small slope while Mary Mary vainly tried to wrest it back on course. We crested the top and rocketed into the air while Basili tried to hold on to the back and I tried to hold on to him.

'Mr Harry, what were you thinking?'

'Trust me, Basili,' I roared back. 'It wasn't planned. I was rather hoping to land on the elf's jet ski, not this one.'

'Ah, I am seeing now. Perhaps if I am dropping you, you might be achieving your original aim,' and before I could object he'd grabbed me and flung (*note*: not dropped) me towards the fleeing elf. I closed my eyes and there was a satisfying thump as I made contact with something softish. Seconds later I was lying on the snow gasping for air and thanking whatever gods of fortune had been watching over me that I was still alive, while a muffled voice from somewhere under me shouted, 'Get off, I can't breathe.'

Slowly (I wasn't really too keen to oblige) I rolled off the semi-flattened elf impostor and grabbed him before he could escape again.

'Now wasn't that fun?' I roared in his ear. 'We really must do it again sometime. I do so love winter sports, don't you?'

He snarled in reply. I guess he wasn't as big a fan of snow as I'd thought.

'Now that we're all nice and cosy, I'm going to ask a few questions. If I don't like the answers I get, I'll set my friend on you.' I was quite getting used to the idea of using Basili (as mild-mannered an ex-genie as you're likely to see) as an intimidating threat. What they don't know won't hurt them – especially in this case as Basili wasn't capable of hurting anything. Of course the pseudo-elf didn't know that: the threat was sufficient to transform him into a remarkably talkative subject indeed.

'What's your name?' I asked.

'Porgie,' came the sullen reply. 'Georgie Porgie.'

'Who sent you? Who are you working for?' At last I was finally getting somewhere – or at least that's what I thought. Just as he was answering, there was a loud neighing and snorting noise from above. Something snaked down and grabbed on to Georgie by the chest – a grappling hook. As I watched he was snatched up and away from me. Instinctively, I grabbed his legs and held on tightly. Once again I found myself flying through the air, hanging on to something and grimly willing myself not to lose my grip.

This time, however, my aerial jaunt came to a sudden halt. There was an explosion of white around me as I ploughed into a snowdrift. Unable to maintain my hold, I felt Georgie Porgie's feet slip through my arms as he was lifted away. Coughing up snow, I managed to extricate myself from the drift just in time to see him get pulled into a sleigh – reindeer-powered this time – which then accelerated away, leaving me to punch the ground in frustration – which hurt as it was a solid sheet of ice with a thin covering of snow.

Ouch!

What was it he'd said as he was pulled away? I tried to make sense of the snatch of speech I'd heard. It sounded like 'ken' or 'king' or 'khan'. At least that's what I thought he'd said. I didn't even know if I'd heard him correctly. It could just as easily have been 'cake' or 'keg'. Either way, it made no sense whatsoever.

As I sat there, freezing and coughing up snow, the other two jet skis arrived – fashionably late. After establishing that nothing other than my pride was hurt, I was bundled on to the seat behind Mrs C and we made our way back to base. I clung on to her solid frame, becoming increasingly despondent. Would I ever get a break in this case?

It seemed like someone up there – other than those who flew

around in jet-propelled sleighs – was listening and took pity on me in my hour of need. We had no sooner arrived back at Santa's workshop when Jack rushed out to meet us, waving frantically, clearly excited.

'Harry, Harry,' he gasped, 'it's the Grimmtown police. They called while you were away. They've discovered Santa's sleigh.'

10

CSI: Grimmtown

'A s you can see,' said Detective Inspector Jill of Grimmtown PD, 'the sleigh doesn't appear to have crashed. From the impact marks on either side, it does look as if it was forced to land by a person or persons unknown, but they seem to have taken care to ensure that the landing was relatively safe. There is no indication as to what happened to any of the occupants afterwards, but we have found no evidence to suggest that they were injured when the craft went down.'

I could see the relief on Mrs C's face. Now, at least, she had some hope that her husband might still be alive. I walked over to the yellow tape that cordoned off the area around the sleigh and had a good look. It was just as DI Jill had said: the sleigh itself didn't look in too bad a condition, the tracks in the ground behind indicated a clean landing, but of the reindeer or Santa there was no sign. I called DI Jill over.

'Did your forensics guys find anything?'

'C'mon Harry, you know better than that,' she said. 'This is police business. I can't just pass on confidential information to any Tom, Dick or Harry now, can I?'

191

'Maybe not,' I said, 'but you owe me one. Who gave you the info that let you break the Little Red Hen case? Me. If it hadn't been for me, she'd still be out there.'

DI Jill looked at me for a second, considered her options and rolled her eyes skywards. 'OK, Harry, you win. Forensics haven't found too much. No fingerprints; nothing we might get a DNA sample from; very little trace evidence. Whoever did this went to inordinate lengths to cover up their tracks.'

I immediately picked up 'very little trace evidence'. 'But they did find something?'

Jill said nothing. I could understand that, she could only say so much to me without getting into trouble. On the other hand, the techs might be a different story.

'Mind if I talk to them?' I asked Jill.

She sighed heavily – a do-I-really-have-a-choice kind of a sigh – and lifted the tape to allow me under. 'Why not? They're nearly done, but they were pretty thorough,' she said as I passed by.

'Who's the lead tech?' I asked.

'Crane.'

'As in he of the bright orange head feathers and meaningful silences?' In fact, Crane was so predictably enigmatic that the cops used to play a game when he was working on a crime scene: try to guess which expression he'll use next. The scoring was complicated but could be summarised as: sunglasses on or off = one point, meaningful pause = two points, withering stare = three points, and enigmatic quip = four points. All four at once got a bonus of ten points. The current record stood at thirty-four and I was determined to beat it.

'The same, but you have to admit he knows his stuff,' said Jill.

I didn't doubt it. Grimmtown PD's forensics team was one of the best in the business and Crane was their boss. If they couldn't find evidence at a crime scene then that evidence didn't want to be found. Still, it was worth a shot. Maybe my piggy eyes would pick up on something they'd missed.

'Can I go in now?' I asked.

'Sure, it looks like our guys are packing up so there's no risk of you contaminating the scene.'

I gave Jill an 'as if I would' sort of look.

I walked around the sleigh, examining the ground carefully. The kidnappers had certainly been thorough; all footprints, hoof prints or any other kind of print had been very carefully obliterated. The sleigh itself, dents apart, looked like it had been gone over by a professional valeting service after it had landed. It was sparkling. This meant, in effect, that regardless of how hard I looked, I wasn't going to find anything.

As I examined the sleigh's interior, there was a clearing of a throat from the far side. It was the kind of polite coughing that suggested that the cougher wasn't too pleased to see me, that I was interfering with their work and that they'd much rather I was somewhere else. It had to be Crane.

I looked up into a stern-featured face dominated by a long beak and topped by an unruly mass of bright orange feathers, parted to the right. The eyes were masked by a spanking new pair of sunglasses.

'Dr Crane,' I said, grinning widely just to annoy him further. 'DI Jill said I could take a look around.'

Crane took off his sunglasses and stared meaningfully at me. 'That's Lieutenant Crane.' There was a pause – which I presumed he intended to be more meaningful as he continued to gaze at me. 'What,' another pause, 'are you doing here?' The glasses were put back on. At least now if he continued to stare at me, I wouldn't have to see it – and I was nine points up already.

Small mercies.

'Sorry, Lieutenant, I forgot.' I hadn't, I just did it to annoy him. He was very particular about his title.

193

'Hmph,' was the indignant response.

'Anyway,' I said, being even more cheerful, 'did you find anything?'

The sunglasses came off again and this time he was giving me a significant stare – which I assumed was one step up the scale from meaningful but still only garnered three points. Now I was up to thirteen and looking good.

'That, my friend,' pause for effect, 'is a good question.' Fifteen.

'I know it is. I'm a detective. It's my job to ask questions, so I'm pretty good at it.'

Another pause and stare (but I couldn't tell if it was withering, significant or another type of stare entirely). Twenty points; record here I come.

'And,' pause, glasses on, 'to answer your question, all we have found so far,' long pause (definitely for effect), glasses off again, 'is tobacco.' Twenty-six; I was on the final stretch, the record was looking good. No, I wasn't enjoying this but I still needed as much information as I could get so, if it meant I had to listen to Lieutenant Crane, then this was a sacrifice I had to make.

'Well, one of my techs found traces of tobacco just behind that rock there.' He waved one of his wings, indicating a large boulder some distance from the sleigh. 'It's ordinary pipe tobacco.' Pause. 'You can get it in any store so it's not much of a lead.' Pause, glasses on. 'It could have been left there by anyone. Once we analyse it in the lab we may know more because that, my friend, is what we do.' Thirty-one points.

'And did your team find anything else?'

I caught a hint of evasion on his face that he quickly masked with his usual blank demeanour. 'No, nothing else.'

There was something, but he wasn't willing to share. I had to find some way of making him change his mind.

'You see that lady over there?' I waved in Mrs C's direction. Crane nodded.

'Well, her husband is the owner of this sleigh and he's missing. Now her style of dress might have given this away already, especially with you being a CSI and all, but the missing man is Santa Claus and, unless we find him in the next twenty-four hours, there are going to be a lot of very disappointed children all over the world. Do you have kids, Dr Crane?'

'Yes,' he replied. 'Three.'

It was time to lay on the guilt trip. 'Do you want to be the one to tell them why they have no presents this year? Why they'll remember this Christmas Day for the rest of their lives for all the wrong reasons? It might even have a traumatic effect on them. Could you live with that? Could you?' I could see I was getting to him. The mention of his kids had made a small crack in his calm exterior and I was about to open it wide. 'This woman has hired me to track down the missing Santa and I'm going to do everything in my power to find him, do you understand?' Dr Crane swallowed once and nodded. 'Good, because every little thing that can help me might take me one step closer to ensuring your kids have a happy Christmas. I know you have to observe standard police protocol here but if you've found something else – no matter how small – it might be the thing that breaks this case.

'Imagine the satisfaction you'll get when we find Santa and you're there helping your kids open their presents, secure in the knowledge that you were the one who gave us that one vital clue.' My patter was working and I could feel he was about to reveal all – in a manner of speaking.

'Well, there was one other thing, but I'm not even sure it's relevant. I won't know for certain until I get it back to the lab.' No meaningful silences and the glasses stayed firmly on his face. Still stuck on thirty-one points: come on, Crane, cut me some slack. 'We found this.' He reached into an evidence bag and pulled something out. He held it out to me for a closer look. 'Please don't touch,' he said. 'You could compromise the evidence.'

I looked at what he was holding in his rubber-gloved wing. 'It looks like a hair,' I said. From what I could see it was a long cream-coloured hair. It looked too thick and rough to be human, and reindeer didn't have hair as long as this so it hadn't come from one of them. Dr Crane ran a feather along the hair. As he did, some particles of fine white dust fell off.

'Any idea what it is?' I asked.

'Not at the moment,' Dr Crane replied. 'It's not human – unless there was a caveman at the crash site. Based on what I know about animal hair – and I am somewhat of an expert – I don't think it's reindeer hair.'

'So what is it and where did it come from?' I mused. 'Maybe it's just coincidence that you found it; after all, it was a national park and I'm sure lots of animals live there.'

'Yes, perhaps, but animals don't have a tendency to use white powder. That doesn't seem like something you'd find in the wild, now does it?'

'True, but what is it? It just doesn't make any sense.' It was reasonable to assume we weren't dealing with something that applied talcum powder after showering; or maybe we were, this case was weird enough as it was without adding cosmetics to the equation. I really needed the results of the hair (and the powder) analysis as quickly as possible. I had a feeling that this – when combined with the tobacco – was the clue that might just break the case wide open. My heart began to thump just a little bit faster and I could feel the sense of anticipation building up inside me. I was near to a breakthrough; I could feel it. Once more, Harry Pigg was on the case.

'Doc, I have one more favour,' I said.

The sunglasses came off once more and I was given a quizzical look. Thirty-five points, we have a winner and a new world record – and without any enigmatic quips either.

'Can you let me know the results of your tests, just this once?' I handed him a business card. 'My number. Call me any time, day or night. I really need this one, and I promise I won't tell anyone about this little conversation, OK?'

The crane looked at me for a long time and finally gave me a brief nod, which I took to mean yes. Then he turned his back on me and stalked over to his team. Clearly the discussion, such as it was, was ended.

Still, I'd gotten something – not a lot, but something – and in this case any lead, no matter how insignificant, was a break. After one last quick look around, I came back over to where the others were waiting.

'Anything, Harry?' asked Jack.

I shook my head. 'Other than a trace of tobacco and a strand of hair the police found, there's nothing else here.' I described the hair to Mrs C and she confirmed that, based on my description, it didn't sound like a reindeer hair. Other than that, no one could offer any suggestions as to what it was. We were going to have to wait until the Crime Lab did their analysis.

Despite the small break we'd just had, I was becoming as frustrated as the Three Bears during a porridge shortage. Every time I thought we were on to something, the lead fizzled out almost as quickly as we got it. Would this case ever get solved? I sank down on a nearby rock and buried my head in my trotters. This wasn't good. My reputation as Grimmtown's foremost detective was at stake but, more importantly, I didn't fancy getting laughed at by Red Riding Hood and allowing her the opportunity to gloat.

After a few minutes of quality self-pity, I turned to the others. 'It doesn't look like we're going to find anything else here.' I could sense their disappointment, I think they'd been hoping for a breakthrough – or at least some solid evidence Santa was still alive. 'Cheer up, folks,' I continued. 'There's no reason to think he came to any harm and whoever brought the sleigh down seems to have gone to a lot of trouble to make sure it got down safely, so there're reasons to be hopeful.' I really wanted to get out of there and back to Grimmtown as quickly as possible and wait for Dr Crane to call me. Reluctantly, they followed me back to our sleigh and, after we were all aboard, we made our way back to the city.

11

A Rug with a View

After we'd landed back at the Claus residence I sent Jack and Basili home in a cab and wandered the streets of Grimmtown, trying to get my thoughts together.

You know those dramatic scenes in movies where the hero is happily minding his own business walking along the street when all of a sudden a really big car screeches up beside him, two burly men jump out, put a bag over his head, bundle him into the car and drive off? Well, I had one of those (sort of). I was walking along the street, minding my own business and mulling over the progress (or lack thereof) in the case. There was a strange swishing noise from above and before I could react, two burly men materialised on either side of me, put a large black bag over my head and bundled me into . . . well, more like on to . . . something soft and wavy. There was a sudden lurch as whatever I was in took off once more and then silence – apart from some whispering.

'Is this him?' This was a deep I'm-a-tough-guy-so-don't-screw-with-me kind of whisper.

'How many pigs in trench coats do you see walking around

199

Grimmtown? Of course it is,' whispered a second, just as intimidating voice.

Now I didn't recognise either voice, but I figured they were the types who would do me irreparable damage if I suddenly tried any heroics – not that I was going to try too much while I had a bag on my head.

I could still hear noises from outside the vehicle and could feel the wind buffeting my head, which suggested I was in a convertible of some kind, but I couldn't feel any vibrations or engine noise. It was a very strange sensation. I extended my arms on either side but couldn't feel any doors or walls. Mystified, I ran my trotters across the floor. It seemed to be made of very plush material; possibly a carpet.

Carpet! Of course. I wasn't in the world's quietest sports car after all. I knew exactly where I was and, more to the point, who had abducted me. Yet again I had one of those sinking feelings I knew only too well. Yes, things had gone from bad to very much worse.

'Hi, Ali, can I take the bag off now? I presume we're on your magic carpet.'

There was a brief round of slow, sarcastic applause and then a voice said, 'Of course Harry. My, my, it didn't take you too long to figure out where you were, did it?'

The bag was pulled roughly from my head and I found myself staring straight into the face of one of Grimmtown's biggest gangsters, Ali Baba. Ah yes, now the plot was really thickening. If Ali had me, then my life expectancy was dropping fast to roughly the same level as a haemophiliac's at a vampire convention.

Then, to my complete surprise, Ali said something that I never thought I'd ever hear him say, 'Harry, I need your help.'

'Excuse me,' I said, shock visible on my face. 'Could you repeat that? I'm not sure I heard it properly.'

'You heard. I need your help.' To be fair, he did look as if he was struggling to say the words.

Now this was roughly akin to the fox asking the Gingerbread Man for his assistance, so you can imagine my disbelief. 'Why exactly do you need my help?'

Ali Baba looked at me strangely. 'Presumably you've heard about what happened last night.'

'Not really, I've been out of town,' I said.

He threw a newspaper at me. 'Read the main article.'

I picked up today's edition of the *Grimmtown Gazette* and read the huge headline that dominated the front page.

Crime Wave in the City
Grimmtown Terrorised

That's what I like about the *Gazette* – it doesn't go for sensationalism! I read on.

The citizens of Grimmtown are cowering in fear in their homes today after a spectacular series of robberies across the city last night.

At exactly midnight forty of Grimmtown's wealthiest families and businesses were burgled in a series of elaborate heists. In every case, alarm systems were circumvented and security cameras picked up little or no trace of the intruders. Some blurred and very brief footage that some cameras did record shows what appears to be a single burglar, dressed in a tuxedo entering the premises. Grimmtown PD advise that there isn't enough detail in any of the footage to make an accurate identification. Despite this the police say they are following a definite line of enquiry.

As of now, no precise details of what was stolen are available but the haul is described by a Grimmtown PD spokesperson as 'substantial'.

I looked across at Ali Baba and raised an eyebrow. 'Forty burglaries, forty thieves. It's not much of a stretch, is it? Even Grimmtown PD must have been able to figure it out.'

'Except for one small detail that they appear to have chosen to overlook: I didn't do it.'

I raised my other eyebrow. 'Really?' I have to say, I agreed with Grimmtown's finest here. Even without any evidence, Ali Baba and his forty thieves surely must have been a shoo-in for the crime; the numbers were just too coincidental.

'Yes, really,' Ali Baba continued as we sped through the streets of the city. 'Although I think it's fair to say that even if I and my men had been having dinner with the police commissioner and the mayor last night when these admittedly admirable crimes were committed, they'd probably still have arrested me. Except for the fact that the evidence is, as of now, circumstantial and I have an exceedingly good lawyer, I might still be imprisoned.'

'So what's all this got to do with me?' I asked, although I had a fairly good idea what – and it wasn't something I was particularly looking forward to.

'Quite simply, I think someone is trying to frame me. I want you to find out who actually did these crimes and clear my name.'

'You're kidding, right?'

'Do I look like I'm kidding?'

Actually he didn't – but then again, he never looked like he was kidding. He had that kind of face and he wasn't noted for his sense of humour.

'But I already have a client. I can't abandon her,' I protested, knowing that it was a futile gesture.

'Well, now you have two clients,' Ali replied. 'I can't imagine your caseload is so heavy that you can't manage two clients at once.'

'Well, my current case is proving problematic. I'm not sure I can give you the time that you might reasonably expect in a case of this complexity.'

Ali gave a sigh of frustration and turned to the front of the carpet. 'Sayeed,' he said, 'if you'd be so kind.'

The pilot, who was sitting cross-legged at the front of the craft, nodded once. The magic carpet lurched forward and then began to ascend through the evening sky. In panic I scrabbled around, looking for something to grab on to so as not to plummet down into the streets below. Around me, the two henchmen and Ali Baba seemed totally unaffected by the sudden ascent as they sat on the carpet, laughing at my discomfiture. How come they didn't look scared? And, more importantly, how come they didn't fall off?

Ali must have known what I was thinking. 'Velcro,' he said.

The magic carpet continued to shoot upwards and, as the pilot increased the angle of ascent, I began to slide towards the back of the carpet. Ali Baba showed great courtesy in leaning to one side to allow me to pass him by. I looked up as I zipped past him and caught his eye. He must have taken pity on me as he ordered Sayeed to level out – just before I tumbled off the edge of the carpet. What was it with this case, all these flying vehicles and close shaves?

With an all too familiar sense of resignation – why was I suddenly detective of choice for Grimmtown's crime fraternity? – I nodded to Ali and confirmed that I'd take on the case, although it was not as if I had much of a choice, was it? I either agreed to Ali's terms or became a pork pizza on the street below.

'OK, OK,' I gasped. 'You have my complete and undivided attention. Now, just so we can be clear, you say you weren't responsible for these robberies.' Ali nodded.

'So I assume you have an alibi for midnight last night?'

Ali shifted and looked uncomfortable. 'Well, yes and no.'

'What do you mean "Yes and no"?' I knew it, it had been too good to be true. Here came the wrinkle.

'As I've already said, we weren't responsible for the forty robberies the police are interested in because we were in the process of relieving Danny Emperor's warehouse of his entire stock of gentlemen's clothes. We bypassed the alarms at ten p.m. and spent over four hours cleaning the place out. It was quite a haul.'

'Are you trying to tell me that you didn't commit the forty robberies at midnight because you were busy burgling somewhere else? What kind of an alibi is that?'

'It is a somewhat unfortunate alibi as alibis go, I will admit, but the fact remains, we are not responsible for last night's crime wave, but we can't tell the police why exactly, can we?'

No, I thought, *you were too preoccupied with a smaller one of your own.*

My thoughts were interrupted by the ringing of my phone. With a nod from Ali, I was allowed answer it. 'Hello,' I said. 'Whoever this is, it's not a good time.'

'Harry, it's me: Danny.' Oh well, there was a surprise. I suppose he wanted my help too.

'Danny, can I call you back? I'm in the middle of something here.'

'Please, Harry, just give me five minutes. I've been robbed. It's my warehouse. It's been completely cleaned out.'

'Gee, Danny, that's terrible. Any idea who did it?' Well, I couldn't really say I was looking at the culprit, could I? Not if I didn't fancy going for another flying lesson.

'The cops have no idea, but they don't think it's linked to the other robberies last night.'

'Well, that's good at any rate. Listen I really need to go, can we talk about this later?'

'Harry, please; it's my livelihood. I need your help. Please, tell me you'll take the case.'

Typical: I'd gone from zero to three cases in under a day and I didn't want any of them. Mind you, at least I knew who had robbed Danny – although I wasn't sure I'd be too successful in revealing the culprit. Then I had an idea; it might have been an idiotic idea but it might get me off the hook on at least one of the cases. 'Danny, I'll take your case. Now I really have to go. I'll catch you later, OK?' Before he could say anything else, I hung up.

'Here's the story,' I said to Ali Baba. 'I'll take your case, but my fee is that you return everything you stole from Danny's warehouse.'

Ali's eyes narrowed. 'I think, perhaps, that you may want to reconsider that last statement.'

I reconsidered (for a nanosecond) and ran the options through my head: solve one case immediately – check; give Ali Baba some of my time while I tried to solve his case – check, but then again I didn't have a choice, did I? At least it was an easy way for Ali to get out of paying in the event I did manage to sort out his problem – not that I held out too much hope of solving it; I was more concerned with how to keep Ali sweet while I investigated what seemed like an impossible case – while trying to not run foul of a police force that believed they already had the case wrapped up. Nice!

'No, Ali, I don't think so.' I wasn't sure where this sudden bout of courage had come from, but I'd had just about enough of being pushed around. 'Drop me off the carpet if you want, but my terms are that you return Danny's clothes. Otherwise no deal.' I looked into his eyes wondering if he had the same stare staying power as Rudolph – I hoped not, calling my bluff would put me in a very weak negotiating position (as in being dangled by my ankle from a magic carpet high above Grimmtown).

Ali didn't even try to argue the toss – maybe he felt that me clearing his name was more then recompense for having to part with the spoils of his latest crime. 'Very well, Harry,' he said, with a nonchalant wave, 'it's a deal. Where can we drop you off?'

I sincerely hoped that he was using that phrase as a figure of speech. 'Somewhere near my apartment would be good – and on the ground,' I managed to croak. A few moments later my feet were firmly on terra firma again. Before I could say anything – a 'thank you' certainly wasn't one of them – the magic carpet was ascending into the darkening sky once more and, for the first time in what seemed like years, I was finally on my own. Wearily, I dragged myself through the front door and up the stairs to my second floor flat. Fumbling the key in the lock, I pushed the door open and fell into the living room, almost literally as I was so exhausted I could barely stand.

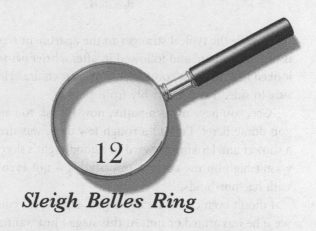

12

Sleigh Belles Ring

I'd like to say that that's why I didn't notice there was someone else in the room as any other reason would reflect badly on my detecting abilities, powers of observation and legendary senses that number above the fifth one. In truth, the room was dark, the curtains were closed, I was so relieved to be home I never thought to turn on the light and the intruder was exceptionally quiet. Until a dark voice said, 'Mr Pigg, about time; I've been waiting quite a while for your return,' I'd have probably gone straight to bed without any idea there was anyone other than me in the apartment.

With a kind of resigned how-much-worse-can-this-day-get groan, I turned in the direction of the voice. In the gloom I could dimly make out a shape sitting in my favourite chair. From what I could see, whoever it was was slightly taller than me and was either wearing the biggest turban I'd ever seen or was sporting an afro the size of a hedge. He looked like a giant microphone. Then again, maybe I was just imagining it; I was certainly tired enough. 'Who the hell are you, and why are you sitting in my comfy chair?'

He gave the typical stranger in the apartment reply, 'My name is not important,' and followed it, after a brief pause with, 'and it looked like the most comfortable of your chairs.' He shifted from side to side. 'I suffer terribly from piles.'

'Gee, you have my sympathy; now I'll ask you again, what are you doing here?' I'd had a rough few days, was tired, in need of a shower and looking forward to a good night's sleep; compassion wasn't high on my current priority list – not even for someone with haemorrhoids.

I didn't even care if he had a gun, although I couldn't actually see if he was armed or not. At this stage I just wanted to lie down. In fact, being shot might not be the worst thing that could happen to me just now – at least I wouldn't have to worry about being flung out of vehicles in mid-air any more. I collapsed on to my sofa. I was too far gone to be concerned.

'Close the door on your way out, will you, my good man? And if you intend to search my apartment, can you do it quietly although you won't find anything; I keep all my files in my office.'

'Relax, Mr Pigg. I'm not going to hurt you. In fact, I may be able to help you in your current case.'

'Which one?' I mumbled. 'At the moment, they're piling up like dirty plates in Stiltskin's kitchen.'

'I'm delighted to hear it,' said microphone man. 'But I'm referring to the case of the missing Santa.'

Tiredness rolled off me. Suddenly I was interested. 'What about Santa? What do you know?'

'Patience, patience. All in good time.'

'Look, if you don't mind I could really dispense with the game playing. It's late, I'm tired, you're in my flat uninvited and I don't have time for this nonsense. If you've got something to say, say it now and go.'

'Very well, here's what I have to say – and please forgive the nature of my statement. For reasons that I cannot disclose, it must inevitably be of a somewhat cryptic nature.'

I rolled my eyes, someone else speaking in riddles. Great. 'Go on and then get out.'

'If you need to find Santa then be aware that time is of the essence in this case,' the intruder declaimed.

To be quite honest, I was expecting something a bit less obvious and a bit more helpful. 'Is that it?' I said. 'You broke into my apartment to tell me I needed to get a move on? Tell me something I don't know; something that might actually be of some help. I don't need you to tell me that tomorrow's Christmas Eve; I'm already painfully aware of that, thank you very much.' I wasn't tired any more – apart from tired of this idiot in my living room.

The intruder stood up. 'No you misunderstand; *time* is of the essence here.' This time he emphasised the word 'time'. It didn't really matter, it was still nonsense.

'OK, that's it. You're out of here now. If I need idiotic, pointless statements of the obvious I'll visit a psychic.' I pointed at the door.

'Please, Mr Pigg, I cannot say more. Think about this conversation after you have had some rest. It may make more sense then.' The intruder headed to the door. 'Remember, the future of Christmas is at stake here.'

Really? I hadn't been aware of that either. It was good of him to continue to point these things out, otherwise I might have missed them. I was tired of this. 'Just go.'

'Very well, but consider carefully what I've said.' He walked out and closed the door behind him. He had to turn sideways to fit through.

Time is of the essence, hah! I fell back on the sofa as tiredness made a sneak attack on my recent burst of energy and forced it into an inglorious retreat. Just as I was dropping off, I had the nagging sense that there was something familiar about the intruder's voice – or maybe it was just my imagination. I didn't care any more, I just wanted my bed. Struggling to my feet, I stumbled into the bedroom. At first I was so tired I didn't even notice the low rumbling noise that greeted me when I entered. The aroma in the room, however, jolted me to my senses like a dose of smelling salts had been wafted under my nose.

Had something died in here while I was away, I wondered – and where was that rumbling noise coming from? It sounded like an avalanche was cascading towards me from somewhere. I shook my head to wake myself up and told myself to get a grip. Whatever it was, it was no avalanche.

Through the dim light from the window I could make out a large shape lying on my bed. Further investigation determined that the rumbling noise was emanating from whatever it was. Cautiously I crept towards the bed. As I neared it, the vile smell grew more intense and, accompanying the rumbling noise, I could hear a rhythmic frrppp, frrppp.

All trace of fear evaporated and annoyance took its place. The mysterious noise was the sound of the ex-genie snoring loudly and the other noise was . . . well, I think you can work it out for yourself.

Some thirty minutes later I'd learned something else about my temporary lodger: it was impossible to wake him up when he went to sleep. I'd pulled at him, kicked him, shouted at him, poured cold water on his head, threatened him, pulled all the covers off him and the best I could get from him was a mumbled 'G'way, I'm tired.'

Eventually, frustrated, angry and still very, very tired I went back to my living room and fell into a dreamless slumber on the sofa. Ah bliss; sleep at last – or at least it was until I was awakened almost immediately by a loud banging at my door. This was really turning out to be one of those days – and nights. Now I wasn't even being let have a decent night's sleep.

'Go away,' I muttered, pulling a cushion over my head. It was no use; I could still hear the banging – which seemed to have gotten louder. Whoever it was, they really wanted to see me.

'Call at my office,' I shouted. 'I should be there by nine.' Or probably much later, if I didn't get any sleep.

Strangely, I was too tired to be scared – or maybe it was just that I was all scared out by events over the past twenty-four hours. Either way, the knocking at the door didn't bother me unduly. It could have been an abominable snowman outside and I wouldn't have been too concerned; I just needed my sleep and no one (or nothing) was going to stop me. But the banging continued: **THUMP, THUMP, THUMP.**

Resigned to being awake at least for the foreseeable future, I rolled off the sofa, on to the floor and, eventually, got myself upright.

'I'm coming, I'm coming,' I shouted, trying to be heard over the noise of the knocking. Reaching the door, I went to unlock it and then paused as I decided a bit of caution wouldn't go amiss. 'Who's there? What do you want?' I shouted, hoping I'd be heard over the battering noise that was now threatening to wake up not only everyone in the building but very probably everyone in the neighbourhood too. Although the neighbours were, by now, used to strange things happening in or around my apartment, they still tended to frown upon being woken up in the middle of the night.

'Open up, Harry, it's me.' Over the thumping I could just make out Mrs C's voice.

'Do you know what time it is?' I roared. 'I'd really like to get some sleep.'

'But I've something important to tell you. I've found out who sold that jet-powered sleigh.'

Unlocking the door, I dragged Mrs C inside and pointed her at the sofa. As she sat down she sniffed the air. 'What's that awful smell? And where is that noise coming from?'

'Trust me, you don't want to know,' I said as I sat facing her in my comfortable chair. 'Now, tell me all about the sleigh.'

'Right. I spoke to the guy who makes all our sleighs, Wenceslaus King. He's been supplying us with high-quality vehicles for hundreds of years now. If anyone knows about these things, it's him. I asked him about the jet-powered sleigh and after some huffing and puffing about new-fangled devices and how he wouldn't have anything to do with them (he's a bit of a traditionalist you know), he finally admitted that he knew of one company that manufactures them. Apparently they're new on the market.'

'You don't say. Who would this high-tech sleigh company be?'

'Well, apparently it's called Sleigh Belles and is run by two very successful business women – hence the name.'

'And do we have names for these queens of industry?' I asked.

'Yes, they're called Holly and Ivy, and I've even got an address for them.' She reached into her bag and extracted a folded piece of paper. 'They have a hangar out at Grimmtown Airport and their offices are attached to it.'

'We can go there first thing in the morning. But for now I'm going to try to get some sleep.' I slumped down into my chair and rested my head on a cushion.

'Why don't you go to bed?' Mrs C asked the obvious question, but it would take too long to explain.

'Trust me, this is the best option just now,' I said and closed my eyes once more.

It seemed like only minutes later that a strident ringing woke me up. Was I destined not to get any sleep tonight? To my surprise, when I opened my eyes it was daylight and, instead of Basili's flatulence, I could smell freshly brewed coffee. What was going on? As I tried to wake up and get a grip on the situation a steaming mug was put on the table in front of me and a ringing telephone thrust into my trotter.

Blearily, I put the phone to my ear. 'Hello?'

'Pigg, it's Crane. I have that analysis you were looking for.' I looked at my watch, seven a.m.; wow, he was on the ball early.

'And?' I was still half asleep so my powers of speech were going to be a tad limited for a few more minutes.

'We've done a preliminary investigation and it's definitely not human.' I wondered whether he was taking his glasses off and on while he spoke, but I refrained from asking. 'I'd say it's animal, probably horse but I'll need to do a more detailed analysis to confirm.'

'OK, so we have what could be horsehair, I'm with you so far. Any idea what the white powder is yet?'

'That's more interesting indeed. According to the analysis, the powder is some sort of resin.'

'Resin? As in the stuff gymnasts and weightlifters use for better grip?'

'The very same. Now if you'll excuse me, I need to get this report to the investigating team.' Before I could thank him, he'd hung up. Polite as ever.

I considered what Dr Crane had told me. What did all that mean? The thought of a horse on the parallel bars – even one as graceful as Black Beauty – or doing a clean and jerk with two hundred pounds of weights was so improbable that I dismissed it as highly unlikely in this particular case, although I have to confess I would have paid good money to see it. Resin, horsehair – that combination suggested something but I just couldn't place what exactly it was. It hovered there in my subconscious just out of reach, taunting me. Well, it could wait, another more immediate mystery demanded investigation: who'd handed me the phone and, more importantly, where was the glorious coffee smell coming from?

Master detective that I was, I had the mystery solved in no time, helped in no small way by the fact that Mrs C was in my kitchen-ette, washing up what I suspected was a week's worth of dirty dishes (I'm very busy, you know, and don't always have enough time for the domestic duties. I'm usually very good around the house).

'Have you been here all night?' I asked her.

'Well, there wasn't much point in going home and then coming back in the morning was there?' Mrs C said. 'Anyway, this place needed a good cleaning. I don't know how you manage to live in squalor like this.'

It wasn't that bad. Sure, there were unwashed dishes in the sink and some underwear drying on the radiators, but I wouldn't have described it as squalor – that was a bit harsh. On the other hand, my apartment was now gleaming. All exposed surfaces had been polished, the floor had been swept and there wasn't any sign of my underwear anywhere. I hoped she'd put it away as opposed to thrown it away.

In fact, the apartment was now cleaner than when I first moved in.

'Um, thanks, but you didn't really have to.'

'Yes, I did; besides it gave me something to do while you and your sidekick snored in stereo. I certainly wasn't going to get much sleep with that racket.'

'I don't snore,' I said indignantly.

'Yes you do, just not as loudly as he does.' She jerked her thumb at the bedroom. 'Honestly, you were like a pair of reindeer. Now get up and drink that coffee, we've work to do.'

I took a sip of my drink – even that was fabulous. It seemed almost a shame to drink it; I wanted to keep it forever and worship it first thing every morning.

'Damn fine coffee.' I raised the mug in tribute.

'It should be: I've had over two hundred years of practice.'

I didn't doubt it.

I tried to drink it slowly, savouring the moment but Mrs C was having none of it. 'Come on, come on, we're wasting time here. We need to get a move on or we'll be late.'

I wanted to say, 'Serves you right for making such good coffee', but it came out as 'Yes, ma'am, just one more sip.' Don't know how that happened!

Minutes later we were in my car and heading for the airport.

'Do you know anything about Sleigh Belles?' I asked.

'Not really, we've never done business with them. We tend to be a bit more traditional. From what I've heard they're very professional and capable. Anything more than that I suppose we'll find out when we get there.'

It didn't take long to reach the airport. After making a few enquiries we were directed to a large hangar on the outskirts of the cargo area. Inside, I could see a handful of jet-powered sleighs undergoing maintenance.

'Looks like the right place,' I said as we headed to a door with a sign which read 'Sleigh Belles – Office. Please ring to enter.'

I rang, the door opened and we entered. Inside the office was warm, comfortable and empty. 'Hello, anyone at home?' I shouted as I walked over to what I assumed was the reception area.

'Just a moment, we'll be with you shortly,' came a voice through a partially open door in the back wall, which I assumed led to the hangar proper. Moments later two dishevelled ladies in oil-stained overalls came in, one carrying a large wrench, the other a welder. As soon as they saw us, they smiled broadly.

'Hi,' said one, a short brown-haired girl extending her hand. 'I'm Holly.'

'And I'm Ivy,' said her tall blonde companion.

'And we're the Sleigh Belles,' they chimed in unison, dazzling us both with gleaming smiles.

'Whether it's a commercial cargo sleigh,' said Holly.

'Or a small, private sleigh,' said Ivy.

'Then Sleigh Belles have just the sleigh for you,' again in unison. 'When it comes to choosing a sleigh, the Belles will show you the way.'

I didn't know about anyone else, but I was threatening to overdose on the saccharine diatribe of the Sleigh Belle girls. As I listened to them I could feel my blood-sugar level rising. I wondered who their PR people were so I could find them and beat them to a pulp for coming up with that jingle. It was the least I could do.

'OK, ladies, enough with the sales pitch; we're not here to buy.'

Their faces dropped but only for a moment. Within seconds their innate (and annoying) perkiness was once more to the fore.

'Well, how else can we help? That's what we're here for,' twittered Holly.

'We're interested in your sleighs, or rather in who's been buying them,' I said.

Ivy's face dropped and she shook her head. 'Oh no, I'm afraid we couldn't possibly give you that information, it's confidential.'

I tried the guilt trip once more. After I'd delivered yet another passionate speech about how Christmas would be ruined for all the children of the world and the poor woman beside me was suffering because her husband was missing (I was quite good at it by now), I was greeted by more firm shakes of the head from both girls and another definitive 'no'. Wow, they were a tough audience.

It was time for Plan B. I turned to Mrs C. 'Perhaps your powers of persuasion might be a tad more effective.'

Within seconds both Holly and Ivy were resting their chins on Mrs C's forearms while she pinned them against the wall, their legs kicking frantically. Well, I'd found it an effective means of persuasion so I was sure Holly and Ivy would too. And as things turned out I was right. Within a few seconds of Mrs C doing her stuff, we were going through Sleigh Belles records – or should that be record, as they'd only sold one jet-powered sleigh since opening for business.

'It's a very exclusive market, you know,' trilled Ivy by way of excuse. 'Not many people can afford one.'

'You don't say.' I reached for the Sleigh Belles ledger and scanned the first page. It didn't take long as the number of entries could be counted on the fingers of one finger. The only sale they'd made was to a company with a suitably generic and meaningless name, Sleigh Aviation. From the sound of it, I was sure the name was a fake and a quick call to Sol Grundy confirmed my suspicions. Sleigh Aviation didn't exist. I hadn't expected anything else, but I asked him to dig a bit deeper to see what he could find out about them. After thanking him, I hung up and updated Mrs C on what he'd found (or hadn't found if I was to be accurate). Her disappointment was plain.

'All is not yet lost, Mrs C.' I turned to Holly and Ivy. 'If someone was looking to repair one of your sleighs, where would they go?'

'Oh, it depends on the damage,' Holly said. 'What kind of repairs are you talking about?'

'A jet engine clogged up with dozens of . . . what were they called again, Manolos?'

Mrs C nodded a mournful confirmation as she recalled her shoes' fate.

The Sleigh Belles didn't bat a fake eyelash. 'Goodness, then they'd almost certainly have to come to us. We're the only ones that could do that kind of repair. It's very specialised, you know.'

I didn't doubt it. 'If anyone makes enquiries about fixing a jet engine then you're to give me a call right away,' I said. 'Otherwise you know what will happen?' I nodded in Mrs C's direction. 'And we wouldn't want a repeat of that now, would we?'

'No,' chimed both girls, clearly unimpressed at the prospect.

'Good, I'll be waiting for your call. Bye now.' I turned and headed for the door, Mrs C close behind.

For some reason the girls seemed relieved that we were leaving. Now why ever could that be, I wondered?

13

A Run Across the Rooftops

On our way back into town I filled Mrs C in on Dr Crane's call. She was just as confused as I was. 'Horsehair and resin? That's a strange combination.'

Again, the sense of familiarity taunted me but when I tried to focus on it, it slithered away once more. I knew that it should mean something, but what just wouldn't come to me. I'd have a look on the Internet when I got to the office and see if that would suggest anything. As I drove, I told Mrs C about my mysterious nocturnal visitor.

'He said "Time is of the essence." Any idea what that means?' I asked her.

She shook her head, but yet again I got the feeling she was holding something back. What was it with this case and people being evasive? I was used to criminals not telling the truth, but when it was your client or those supposedly helping you . . . Still, I couldn't really accuse her on the basis of my feeling, could I?

I caught a glimpse of something in my rear-view mirror that vanished almost as quickly. Was I being followed? I couldn't see any sinister types in any of the cars behind, nor did any of the vehicles give the impression they were tailing me. Just as I relaxed, thinking I'd imagined whatever it was, it happened again. This time I got a better look: it wasn't a car, it was a carpet. I was being tailed from above.

Ali Baba! I'd forgotten about him – and he wasn't someone you could easily forget. If I didn't show him I was doing something, I could well be falling from that selfsame carpet sometime later in the day. In desperation, I reached for the phone once more. It was a long shot but maybe Detective Inspector Jill might have some info that hadn't been released to the press; something I might be able to use.

'Hey, Jill, it's me, Harry.'

'Harry Pigg, twice in two days. This is quite an honour.'

'Look, Jill, I need another favour, I'm in a bit of a bind.'

I could almost hear her eyes roll upwards. 'What is it now?'

'I've taken on another client since we last spoke and he's very interested in me solving his particular dilemma as soon as possible.'

'Well, let me be the first to congratulate you.' Jill's voice dripped sarcasm – and I can spot sarcasm at a hundred paces. 'But how does that involve me?'

'Because you suspect him of forty robberies; crimes, I might add, he claims he's innocent of.'

There was a sharp (and, I think, impressed) intake of breath. 'Ali Baba, wow, as clients go that one's a doozy.'

That's not how I would have described him but I wasn't in a position to discuss semantics with Jill. 'Look, he says he didn't do it and he wants me to prove it. I have evidence to show that he is innocent but I'm not in a position to share it just at the moment.' Primarily because the evidence suggested he was busy committing another crime altogether – but I wasn't going to tell her that. 'I just need you to give me something to work with, anything. Please.'

The silence from the other end of the phone suggested that not only did Jill have something, but she was considering whether or not to share it with me. I tried to help her make up her mind. 'Please, Jill. If he's innocent then I need to help him. I know he's a crook, but just not on this particular occasion.' Just ask Danny Emperor!

'OK, Harry, but bear in mind that I'm putting my ass on the line here. Make sure it doesn't get back that your source was me.'

'My snout is sealed.'

'All right. Here's the weird thing about this case: CCTV footage didn't capture too much, but what it did capture seemed to suggest that the thieves were identical to each other, all dressed in tuxedos.'

I was confused. 'You mean they looked similar?'

'No, I mean identical; same height, same clothes, same shoes, same everything. It was like the robberies were committed by clones or something – but that's ridiculous.'

I had to agree with her. Whoever had committed the crime, it probably wasn't the result of a bizarre scientific experiment. 'Just so as I'm clear, you're saying that the perpetrators were exactly the same in every respect.'

'Yep, but bear in mind we only caught glimpses of the thieves on camera but what we did see suggested they were.' Now I was even more confused, but I could also see why the police liked Ali Baba for the crimes. Forty apparently identical thieves committing burglaries at exactly the same time at forty different locations: how bizarre was that? Then again it couldn't be any more bizarre than a missing Santa, a reindeer with an attitude problem and jet-powered sleighs, could it?

I thanked Jill and hung up. Where did I go from here? Neither case seemed to be on the verge of a breakthrough and both had anxious clients – although they were anxious in very different ways, it had to be said. As I mulled things over, I caught a glimpse of a huge advertising hoarding on the side of the road. It was an ad for Olé 'King' Kohl and his Fiddlers Three. They were giving a Christmas recital at the Grimmtown Cauldron later today. The hoarding showed Olé and his boys mugging for the camera and waving their violins around. My brain began to make connections. Musicians; horsehair and resin, critical components in violin bows; did I finally have a useful clue? Once more I reached for the phone. It rang twice and was followed by a 'yes' and a meaningful pause.

'Lieutenant Crane, it's Harry Pigg again.' This time I wasn't counting.

'Yes, Mr Pigg, and what can I do for you now.'

'Your horsehair and resin, I think they come from a violin bow.'

The pause this time was definitely sarcastic (remember, I can sense it).

'Violin bow? Mr Pigg, that,' pause, 'is something we're already aware of.'

'Already aware of? Well, why didn't you tell me.'

'Because, my friend, you're a detective. What kind of scientist would I be if I didn't allow you to do some detecting – and you appear to have done a fine job. It took you less than a day to discover something I knew at the crash site. My congratulations.'

I didn't give him time for any more meaningful or sarcastic pauses, I just cut him off. Smartass.

If I wasn't confused before, I certainly was now. Had Santa been kidnapped by a mad, jet-sleigh-flying, Christmas-hating musician? If so – and it did sound unlikely – then why? And more to the point, how was I going to get him back? On top of that I had to find forty identical, monkey-suit-wearing cat burglars or be at the receiving end of Ali Baba's displeasure. Some days it's just great being me.

As if someone up there was reading my mind and felt I needed some more incentive, my phone rang once more. When I answered it, I couldn't hear anything. Great, one of those calls. 'Hello, whoever you are, I'm not that kind of pig.' I expected to hear heavy breathing but instead I got what sounded like someone whispering.

'Mr Pigg, is that you?'

'Yes, who is this? Speak up, I can't hear you.'

'It's me, Ivy from Sleigh Belles, and I can't talk because . . . well, remember you asked us to phone you if anyone enquired about getting their sleigh repaired?'

I was all businesslike now. 'Yes, are they there now?'

'Yes, that's why I'm whispering; I don't want him to hear me. Holly is trying to keep him occupied for as long as possible. Can you get here as quickly as you can?'

'I'm on my way.' I turned the car and did a very unsubtle and highly illegal U-turn in the middle of the freeway and headed back towards the airport.

As I accelerated, Mrs C grabbed the door and held on tightly. 'What's going on?' she demanded.

I quickly filled her in as we raced in and out through the traffic, flirting with several traffic offences but not committing to any. We made it back to the airport in half the time and I parked the car where it couldn't be seen by anyone in Sleigh Belles. As I got out, I turned to Mrs C. 'Stay here, things might get a bit hairy.'

She snorted indignantly. 'No chance. If there's any possibility that this might lead us to my husband, then I'm going with you.' She flexed her arms, which I took as both a threat and signal of her intent. I also knew when I was beaten so I nodded and told her to stay close. 'And under no circumstances are you to go wandering off on your own, regardless of what happens.' I wasn't too concerned for her safety, I wanted to make sure that we were able to keep whoever was in Sleigh Belles conscious long enough to get information out of them. If Mrs C got her hands on them, there was a distinct possibility they wouldn't last the day.

We skirted round a large warehouse and ran towards the Sleigh

Belles main entrance, crouching low to avoid detection. When we got to the door, I stuck my head up and peered through the window. A very nervous Ivy was behind the counter casting anxious glances back into the maintenance area. I tapped on the glass gently and when she saw me she waved me inside. I opened the door a fraction and sneaked in, followed by Mrs C.

'Who's in the maintenance hangar?' I whispered.

'Holly and one of the guys who originally bought the sleigh. He wants the engine fixed and she's trying to keep him talking.'

'OK, you stay here while I take a look.' I crept to the door that separated the office from the hangar and peeped through. At first I couldn't see anything other than sleighs, bits of sleighs, sleigh engines and tools for fixing sleighs. Then I heard voices from behind a large sleigh to my left. If I wasn't mistaken (and I rarely am), it was the same craft that had indulged in the aerial acrobatics with us two nights ago. The dents certainly suggested so. Making sure I didn't step on anything that might give my presence away, I slunk up against the fuselage and inched my way forward.

Now I could make out the voices. One was clearly a nervous Holly, trying her best to stall and doing a very bad job of it. The other was a man's voice and, by the sound of it, becoming increasingly frustrated by Sleigh Belles' actions.

'Can't you be more specific?' demanded the male voice. 'To me it seems obvious: one of the engines is faulty. We collided with a flock of birds and we need to get it looked at.'

'Flock of birds,' a likely story.

'Well, um, it's not as simple as that,' stammered Holly. 'We don't have the parts here. I'll have to order them and that will take . . . um . . . a few days.'

'What do you mean, you don't have the parts? Surely, parts for a jet engine are standard operating procedure? You sell jet-powered sleighs, don't you?'

'Yes but the flange inductor has been totally wrecked and the hyperfilters look like they have what appears to be the heel of a very expensive boot embedded in them. These aren't the kind of things that happen to engines every day, you know.'

Well, that was true anyway.

'Flange inductor? Hyperfilters? There are no such things. You're making this up.' He did have a point, from where I stood it sounded like Holly was reaching a bit. It was time to do something and fast, otherwise the girl was in big trouble.

Just as I was about to finally get a glimpse of the sleigh owner there was a loud clanging noise from behind me, followed by a sheepish 'sorry'. I knew I hadn't made the noise because I was being very careful – and as a detective I was a master at sneaking around – so the noise could only mean one thing.

I looked around at Mrs C. 'I thought I told you to stay in the office,' I whispered.

'You did, but I had to see what was happening out here.' Mrs C was trying to be indignant but she knew she'd fouled up. 'Sorry,' she said once more.

'Well, you're about to get your wish,' I said as the owner of the voice raced around the sleigh to see what had made the noise. 'Who the hell are you?' demanded a very tall man in a very dapper tuxedo. 'And why are you spying on me?' Tuxedos? What was it with tuxedos and my cases? Now, however, wasn't the time to contemplate the ins and outs of sartorial elegance as a large, tuxedoed man was heading straight for me, arms outstretched – and I didn't think he was asking me to dance.

I'd like to say that my next move was planned and superbly executed, but as my attacker lunged at me I slipped on the self-same pipe Mrs C had knocked to the ground seconds before. The pipe shot backwards and I shot forwards, slipping under the clutches of Mr Tuxedo and colliding with his stomach. There was a satisfying explosion of breath and he fell backwards on to the ground. Before I could grab him – or at least fall on top of him – he rolled to one side and pushed himself upright once more. I swung an arm at him but he easily avoided it. Rather than risk further entanglements, he turned on his heels and sprinted for the hangar entrance.

'Stop that man,' I shouted, but as the only other three people in the hangar were watching him go from a very safe distance, it was a pointless request.

As I stood trying to figure out why he looked so familiar, I received a nudge – no, a jab – in the side. 'Well, what are you waiting for?' said Mrs C. 'Get after him.'

Rolling my eyes upwards in that world-famous gesture of resignation, I lumbered after my retreating quarry, hoping that the burst of speed he was displaying was just an adrenalin rush and he'd soon slow down.

How wrong was I? He must have been a marathon runner in his spare time as he seemed to go faster. There was no chance of me catching him but I figured I'd better make the effort or face the wrath of Mrs C again – not something I was too keen on. I struggled pigfully after him as he ran around sleigh machinery towards the open doors. If he got outside I'd never catch him, so I figured I'd better come up with something fast. Maybe if I could slow him down somehow . . . ah, the old throw something and knock him out trick. That might work. I grabbed a hammer off a table as I ran – well, jogged – past and, pausing to take careful aim, I flung it at the escaping well-dressed gent. It completely missed him and I groaned in exasperation.

But I was too quick with my frustration. The hammer sailed past him but then rebounded off the frame of a stripped-down sleigh, spun up into the air, deflected off the overhead light and plonked down on his head. Did it stop him? Of course not; I'd never be that lucky, but it did slow him down. I suspect having a hammer bounce off your skull will do that. The success (sort of) of my devious plan fuelled me with a fresh burst of energy and I raced after my staggering prey once more, hoping to nab him before he recovered.

Behind me, Mrs C was roaring, 'Go on, Harry, you nearly have him.' It was an exaggeration of sorts and I was also aware that she wasn't doing too much to help by way of joining in the chase either; I was still on my own. Typical.

I ploughed on, weaving through maintenance tables and bits of sleigh, hoping against hope that I could catch this guy. I really needed a break in the case and this was the only one that I was likely to get between now and a deadline I had no control over – Christmas Eve would fall on Christmas Eve regardless of what I did and it needed a Santa if it was going to work properly.

And the only link I had to getting Santa back was haring out of the hangar. If I didn't catch him Christmas was a bust.

I reached the hangar doors seconds after Mr Tuxedo. Racing out into the cold winter air I looked around but couldn't see any sign of him. Stretching away on both sides of me were other hangars, none close enough to have been reached before I got out. In front of me a short taxiing route led to the main airport runway. He wasn't running down that either, so where the hell was he? I was pretty sure he hadn't vanished into thin air – although that was always a possibility in my cases – so he had to be here somewhere. I looked around again, more carefully this time. Hangars, runway and no obvious place to hide. Or maybe I was wrong. A heap of wooden crates was stacked between Sleigh Belles' hangar and the one to the left of it. It was the kind of thing that a man on the run might use as cover.

'I have you now,' I whispered, as I approached the crates.

If he wasn't there I'd be gobsmacked, so I was gobsmacked

when I threw myself around the boxes and leaped on to . . . well, nothing actually. There wasn't a sign of him. There was, however, a ladder leading to the hangar roof and when I looked up I caught a glimpse of his heels as they disappeared from view above me. This was just so unfair: now I had to climb as well. I grabbed a rung and began to ascend. About halfway up I had a horrible thought, what if he's waiting at the top for me to stick my head up? I'd be a sitting pig. Then I'd be a falling pig, followed by a pizza pig on the asphalt below. Before I could think about it I was interrupted by a shout from below.

'He's running along the roof. If you don't get your finger out he'll escape.' Mrs C was watching out for me once more.

Well at least I knew I wasn't going to be ambushed.

I clambered up the remaining rungs as fast as I could and scrambled on to the roof – just in time to see the well-dressed man leap on to the next hangar beyond and continue running. No matter how optimistic I was, I knew I had no chance of catching him this way.

'Bring the car around and try to get to the last hangar before him,' I roared at my fan club below. 'We might be able to head him off before he gets back to ground.'

Seconds later, as I ran across the roof, I heard a screech of tyre rubber as Mrs C accelerated around the hangar and shadowed me from the ground. I waved her on, urging her to speed up and not follow me, but she just waved back, grinning broadly. It's possible she may have misunderstood my intentions. 'Go faster,' I roared at her. 'Don't wait for me otherwise he'll get away.'

I could see the 'Oh, right' expression as the penny finally teetered on the edge for a few seconds before falling into the vast chasm of her mind. Almost immediately, she gunned the accelerator and the car sped forward, racing parallel to the hangars.

Mr Tuxedo reached the edge of the roof. Did he stop and turn around with his hands in the air, acknowledging that he had no way of escaping and that I finally had him? Did he hell. He didn't even break stride as he jumped across the gap and on to the next building.

I followed and, as the gap didn't look too wide, I leaped without fully contemplating the consequences. I barely made it across to the adjoining roof, teetering on the edge, arms flailing before I managed to regain my balance.

And so we continued our not-so-merry chase across the maintenance hangars of Grimmtown Airport. He managed the gaps with a degree of flair and athleticism; I managed them by gritting my teeth, closing my eyes and jumping – all the while hoping for the best.

Now my quarry had run out of hangars to run across. He'd reached the edge of the last one and, unless he had a well-concealed jetpack under his jacket, the only way was down. Mr Tuxedo took a quick look over his shoulder to see where I was and didn't even slow down before throwing himself off the edge and disappearing from view. I ran to where he'd jumped, fully expecting to see him soar gracefully into the sky, give me a rude gesture and disappear over the horizon. I was wrong on all three counts. When I looked down I saw that his jump had taken him into the back of a truck filled with packing crates. How lucky can you get!

He didn't even waste time checking for injuries. No sooner had he landed than he was up and out of the truck and racing across the asphalt. At the same time, Mrs C roared around the corner, her eyes firmly fixed on the road ahead.

Well, if he could do it . . . I took a deep breath, tried not to think about what I was about to attempt and threw myself off the roof. As I fell, the truck driver took it upon himself to drive away and I watched in horror as my nice soft landing suddenly became something altogether more concrete.

I screamed, closed my eyes, covered my head with my trotters and prepared for the impact I didn't even think I'd feel. To my surprise and relief, instead of splattering across the ground I bounced off something and was catapulted into the air once again. I opened my eyes once more and looked down at the soft-top roof of my car which Mrs C had driven right into my path and I had oh-so-conveniently landed on. At first I was mentally congratulating her on her ingenuity and lateral thinking in coming up with such a stunning rescue plan but quickly scrubbed that train of thought when, oblivious to both my presence and her part in my rescue, she kept driving. With a horrible sense of déjà vu I spun in the air and dropped towards the ground again – luckily from not quite the same height as my first descent. This time my fall was broken by the asphalt, but at least, when I finally managed to sit up and check for injuries, it seemed like that was all that had been broken.

There was a screaming of brakes from up ahead, followed almost immediately by the sound of a car reversing. Seconds later Mrs C pulled up beside me. 'How did you get down so fast?'

I didn't bother to fill her in; I dived into the passenger seat and roared at her to drive. The car sprang forward and we raced along the asphalt, trying to spot where our quarry had got to.

'I can't see him any more,' said Mrs C. 'I think we've lost him.'

I scanned the area ahead of us and caught a glimpse of our quarry nimbly scaling a wire fence on the far side of the runway and disappearing into a maze of buildings beyond. I punched the dashboard in frustration. 'Dammit.'

Mrs C put a sympathetic arm around my shoulders. 'Don't worry about it; we're getting closer to breaking this case all the time.'

'Really? The only thing we were close to breaking this time was my spine when I bounced off the car – and he still got away, whoever he was.' As I said it, the feeling that I'd seen him some-where very recently sat in the shadows of my mind and taunted me.

'You'll catch him, I know you will.'

I appreciated her support but didn't share her confidence. 'Come on, let's get out of here.'

I sulked all the way back into town. In fact I was seething so much I almost missed it as we drove by.

'Stop, stop the car!' I ordered.

'We're on the freeway, Harry. I can't stop.'

'Well, pull in; do something. Just stop the car.'

'Why? Are you not feeling well?'

'Pull over now.'

Mrs C drove on to the hard shoulder and stopped the car. 'What's going on, Harry? You're behaving very strangely.'

I pointed up at the huge hoarding we'd stopped under; the same hoarding I'd noticed on the way out earlier. 'It's him, look. Up there.'

'It's who? Where? What are you talking about?'

I grabbed her head and pointed it at the huge poster of Olé 'King' Kohl and His Fiddlers Three. 'There? See the grinning idiot second from the left? The guy that looks like his family tree has no forks? That's him; that's the guy we were following at the airport. He's part of Kohl's band.'

'Are you sure about this?' Mrs C didn't seem to share my convic-tion.

'Positive. It's him all right. Let's get back to town. I need to find out as much as I can about these guys. I'm not sure how they fit into all this but I'm going to find out.'

14

Another Chapter in Which Nothing Unpleasant Happens to Harry

Stiltskin's Diner was the kind of place that gave good food a bad name and then got sued for slander. That was why I only ever drank the coffee there, but it was really good coffee. Mug clenched in trotter I slid into his usual booth and stared at Boy Blue, failed shepherd, dodgy musician and officially the world's worst informant. At least today he acknowledged me – if you consider a grunt to be a sign of recognition.

'Blue, you're looking good this morning.' It was a lie; he never looked good but I had to start somewhere.

Another grunt.

'Have you come across Olé "King" Kohl in your travels around the Grimmtown music circuit?'

'Kohl? Met 'im once or twice. Arrogant. Plays jazz.'

'Isn't everyone who plays jazz arrogant? Seeing as it sounds like musical vomiting I think they try to appear superior so they don't have to explain it.'

Blue nodded. 'Maybe, maybe.'

'So what do you know about Kohl?'

'Used to be known as Oliver Cole back in the day. Small-time thief who 'ad ambitions to be something bigger until he got caught. Spent some time in prison and when he came out changed his name to Olé Kohl, formed that band with his fiddling buddies and went on the circuit.'

'That's it?'

'That's it.'

'Turned away from a life of crime?'

'I didn't say that, did I?'

'Well, what are you saying?'

'All I'm sayin' is that if you checked for burglaries in the towns he's been tourin' you might just see a connection.'

So Cole/Kohl was still keeping his hand in – and his group wore tuxedos. I couldn't see a direct correlation, but I thought I'd ask anyway. 'Any chance he could be involved in that spate of robberies around town the other night?'

Blue looked at me. 'Possible, yes, but it's a bit out of his league unless he had some serious connections – and I don't think he's that well connected.'

Maybe, maybe not, but it was certainly worth following up. 'OK, Blue, thanks for your time.'

I drove back to the office and met up with Mrs C, Basili and Jack.

'Here's where we're at – or not at might be more accurate,' I said to them. 'Santa was kidnapped and the only lead we had was the jet-powered sleigh that attacked us on the way to the North Pole.'

Nods all around.

'Following up on the sleigh lead has brought us to Olé "King" Kohl and his band of merry men who, based on their track record, I like better for Ali Baba's robberies even if I still can't see how they did it or if they're actually involved at all.' I pushed myself away from the table and stood up. 'It's all so confusing. My senses say the two cases are connected in some way, I just can't see how or why.' More – slightly more confused – nods and Mrs C shifted uncomfortably in her chair. Was it my imagination or did she look just a little bit guilty? Again I had the feeling she knew more than she was telling and now, in front of the others, wasn't the time to confront her – but very soon it would be. I was hitting a solid wall in this investigation and I was getting fed up with being blocked every time I thought I had a break.

I also had Ali Baba to consider. He'd already been on the phone once today, demanding progress and issuing his usual brand of exotic threats. I knew he was keeping a close eye on me too and I needed something for him as well or face another exciting magic carpet ride.

'So where do we go from here?' asked Jack.

'Good question,' I said. 'I think a trip to Mr Kohl and his boys is in order. They might let something slip.'

'But they might know you're on to them. It could be dangerous.'

I was tempted to respond with 'Danger is my middle name,' but I refused to resort to cliché at a time like this.

Well, nothing ventured nothing gained. 'It's the only option we have at the moment. Anyway,' I said with as much confidence as I could muster, 'I can take care of myself.'

From the sceptical glances I got, I could tell they remembered the sleigh incident, the jet ski and the recent pursuit at Grimmtown Airport shambles and, perhaps, weren't as convinced as I was.

Unbelievers!

I rubbed my trotters together. 'Right, let's get cracking.'

Mrs C stood up. 'It's about time,' she said.

'Well, I'm sorry things aren't moving as fast as you'd like,' I snapped, indignation rising.

'No, you don't understand; it's really about time,' and she gave me a significant look.

Was she trying to tell me something?

About time? Time is of the essence here? What was it with these people and their insistence that time was so important?

Suddenly, synapses that had previously been on an extended holiday began to arrive back at work.

Time is of the essence here.

It's about time. No, what she meant was, it's about Time.

How could one man single-handedly deliver presents to every child in the world over the course of a single night? Time.

How could one (or perhaps four) men dressed in tuxedos carry out robberies in forty different places at the same time? Time, that's how.

It was indeed all about Time – or, more accurately, the ability to manipulate time.

Satisfied that their work was done, the synapses in my brain headed off for a well-deserved rest.

I turned to Mrs C. 'It is about Time after all, isn't it? Your husband can do something with time and that's how he does what he does. More to the point, that's probably why he was kidnapped. Kohl and his boys are using that same ability to pull off all those robberies and frame Ali Baba at the same time.'

Mrs C nodded and gave me a half-smile. 'I'm sorry I couldn't tell you about it. Each generation of Santas is born with the ability to freeze time. It's been kept a secret for thousands of years and the family have sworn a blood oath never to reveal it to outsiders – whatever the cost. If the secret was revealed, there could be terrible consequences. Think what someone could do if they found out.'

I think I knew exactly what would happen – actually, had happened – if someone found out.

'Rudolph and I probably bent the rules a little by dropping

those cryptic hints, but we can safely say that we didn't tell you outright. That way we adhere to the spirit of our vow, but I can't tell you how much it hurt me not to be able to reveal the secret – even at the expense of my husband's life.' Tears began to trickle down her face; tears that could at any second become a raging torrent.

I seized the box of tissues once more and thrust it at Mrs C. She grabbed a bunch and dabbed her eyes. I tried to reassure her, if only to try to stop the impending deluge. Then I homed in on something she'd said.

Rudolph and I? When had that arrogant herbivore ever tried to help me? Then it hit me: he'd been my mysterious midnight caller – the human microphone. It hadn't been a turban or an afro; it had been a poor attempt to disguise himself by covering his antlers. At least now things were beginning to make a bit more sense.

'Look, we've had a few big breaks this morning,' I said, trying to console Mrs C. 'All we need to do now is confront Kohl like we planned, and hopefully we'll be able to wrap everything up by this evening.' I wished I was as confident as I was making out, but it seemed like the only course of action open to us.

'I hope so,' she sobbed. 'If my husband's not in the air by midnight, there won't be a Christmas.'

I looked at her in horror; I'd forgotten it was Christmas Eve. We didn't have much time left. There's always something.

'We'd better get a move on then,' I said, trying to sound confident. 'Next stop "King" Kohl's. Everyone ready?'

More noncommittal grunts, nervous nods and general I-don't-think-this-is-such-a-good-idea type facial expressions.

'OK then, let's go.'

Jack Horner raised a tentative hand. 'Um, aren't you forgetting something?'

'What's that, Jack?'

'Well, we're about to go after a bunch of thieves and track them to their lair, right?'

I nodded. 'More or less, yes.'

'Well, I don't want to sound like a scaredy cat, but they're probably big tough guys and we're, well, we're not.'

'Now, Jack, did you honestly think that I was going to face these guys unprepared?' In fact, until he mentioned it, I was, but I wasn't going to let my veneer of invincibility get tarnished so easily in front of my team. I wasn't sure exactly how dangerous facing Kohl would be but it probably made good sense to have some degree of insurance before going in there. But who could I call on at such short notice? My usual able assistants in situations like this, Mr Lewis and Mr Carroll, had told me they'd be unavailable until after Christmas.

Aha!

I called Jack over. 'I have a little job for you; here's what I want you to do.' I bent down and whispered in his ear.

His eyes widened. 'You sure he'll be OK with it?'

'Yep, especially when you tell him why we're doing it. Don't worry, you'll be fine.'

Jack scurried out of the door. 'Where's he off to?' asked Mrs C.

'Plan B,' I said.

'Ah, so you actually have a Plan A then?'

'I always have a plan,' I replied, although I could have added: *the plan may be flimsy, improvised, not fully thought out at the time and subject to change depending on events.* It might not have been the most inspiring thing to say, especially right now.

'While Jack's busy, you guys are with me. Basili, when we get there, act the tough guy once more.'

Basili looked unhappy. 'Where is this there that we are going to, Mr Harry? And why must I be acting the gentleman of toughness once more?' This was followed by an extended and unpleasant bout of flatulence.

'We are going to the Grimmtown Cauldron and you are pretending to be the tough guy because you did such a fine job at the North Pole,' I said, and because I don't have time to get anyone else at such short notice – but I left that part unspoken; his ego was fragile enough as it was.

'Right, everyone, now that that's been sorted, let's get to the car and start making tracks.'

15

A Night at the Jazz

We left the office, tramped down the stairs (somewhat reluctantly, it has to be said) and got into the car. As we drove to the Cauldron, I could sense the unease in the other two. It was hard to blame them; I wasn't really sure what I was going to do myself. I didn't really expect them to have Santa trussed up in the front row of the auditorium, but if the guy we'd chased at the airport saw me he might panic and do something stupid. Then again, he might just beat the living daylights out of me – and I didn't think my 'minder' would do much by way of minding. I suspect his concept of minding in that instance would be running for the door as fast as he could. Ho hum.

The Cauldron itself was an auditorium that looked like a giant cauldron turned on its side. It stood on a hill overlooking the city and was the venue *du jour* for Grimmtown's musical set. It had recently seen concerts by Hubbard's Cubbard, Peter Piper and the Magic Harp Rock Ensemble. Tonight, as we were advised by every billboard on the way, it was hosting 'An Evening of Classical and Jazz Fusion by the Experimental Quartet Olé "King" Kohl and his

Fiddlers Three'. That sounded nasty. In musical terms the word fusion always suggested a number of musicians all playing completely different tunes at the same time with their eyes shut, nodding their heads knowingly all the while. The audience, baffled by what was going on on stage, would shout phrases like 'nice', 'cool', 'look at those hip cats go' and even an occasional 'groovy' (the Grimmtown musical cognoscenti were just as pretentious and anachronistic as their counterparts everywhere else).

It just made my ears bleed.

Already crowds were arriving for the Fiddlers' Christmas Eve recital. Had they really nothing better to do with their time on this particular night? Either that or Kohl and the boys were more popular than I thought – or expected. As we pulled into the car park, Mrs C asked a very obvious question – and one that I'd completely failed to consider. 'How are we going to get in? Do you have tickets for this gig?'

'It won't be a problem,' I replied, though it was distinctly possible it might be a very big problem. If the crowds were anything to go by, this was a sell-out so getting in might be a tad on the difficult side.

We pushed our way through the crowds, trying to get closer to the door. Two huge figures were checking all the tickets. There would be no way past them – or would there? If I wasn't mistaken, the ticket collectors were my two friends, Lewis and Carroll. They'd certainly deter anyone from trying to get in with a forged ticket or without any ticket at all – unless of course that person was me.

'Stick close,' I whispered. 'We might have a way in after all.' I pushed my way through the throng towards the ticket check, with Mrs C and Basili close behind. They were much better pushers than I was so I skilfully fell behind them and let them do the dirty work. It was like the parting of a human Red Sea; people just disappeared in front of them as they man- (or woman-) handled their way through, clearing out bodies like a flamethrower through a field of snowmen. Getting to the front of the line was easy after that.

Mr Lewis took one look at me and rolled his eyes upwards and gave me an 'I didn't peg you as a jazz buff' look (Mr Lewis was a man of few words).

'I'm not,' I replied. 'But I'm on a case and need to see Kohl as soon as possible.'

Mr Lewis raised an eyebrow in an 'I suppose tickets are out of the question in this instance' expression.

'You know me too well and I really need to get inside.'

Seconds later we were running through the Cauldron's huge lobby, searching for a way backstage. If Kohl was anywhere, he'd be back there getting ready. Everywhere I looked all I could see were doors leading to the auditorium proper; upper stalls, lower stalls, balcony, dress circle. There was no way I'd ever wear a dress just to get a good seat.

I spotted a nervous-looking usher and made a beeline for him. 'How do I get backstage?'

'Um, Mr Kohl doesn't like to be disturbed before he goes on stage. He's very particular about that,' stammered the usher, clearly intimidated by my friends.

'Well, I need to disturb him now and if I don't find a way backstage quickly my associates may very well set about disturbing you.'

The usher pointed to a passageway, partially hidden by a velvet curtain. 'D . . . d . . . down that way.'

'You are most helpful,' I said as we brushed him aside and headed down the passageway. 'Please don't let me find out you warned him we were coming.'

'N . . . n . . . never crossed m . . . my mind,' the usher replied.

'In that case don't ask your face to be a corroborating witness,'

I said. 'It mightn't hold up under questioning.'

The passageway led to a dimly lit corridor running the length of the backstage area. On one side were a series of doors, each with a large star in the centre. The first few were blank, but the fourth had 'Mr Kohl and Band' scrawled across it.

'We're here,' I whispered to the others.

'Great,' Mrs C whispered back. 'Now what do we do?'

'Well, let me listen for a moment, see if I can make out who's inside.' Carefully I put my ear to the door and tried to hear what was going on inside. It wasn't difficult; Kohl had a very loud voice.

'We wait until everyone's settled, play a few of the standards and when they're getting into it Santa can do his stuff. Once everything stops we make our way through the audience, relieve them of their valuables and get back on the stage. It's the perfect crime and we'll have the perfect alibi. It's foolproof, I tell you.'

'And what about Santa?' asked another voice. 'He wasn't too easy to persuade last time. What makes you think he'll cooperate again?'

'As long as he thinks we'll let him free in time for Christmas, he'll reluctantly play ball. By the time he finds out I intend to hold on to him, it will be far too late. After that we'll have to find more effective means to ensure his help.'

It was the perfect crime. Looked like we were just in time. If what they were saying was to be believed, Santa was just beyond the door.

I turned to the others and repeated what I'd just heard. 'Just give me a few minutes to come up with a plan.'

Mrs C pushed me aside. 'Plan be damned, I'm going in there,' and before I could stop her she'd flung the door open and barged into the room shouting, 'Santa, where are you? It's me, Clarissa.' Whatever that woman had in terms of devotion to her husband was more than compensated for by her lack of subtlety – and this lack of subtlety had put paid to any chance of a surprise. No sooner had she burst into the room than two of Kohl's Fiddlers Three had grabbed her and flung her back at us. As we fell in a heap like a bunch of oversized skittles, the third grabbed a large red shape that had been lying in the corner, threw it over his shoulder and made for the door with the rest of the band in close pursuit.

'Stop them, they're getting away,' shouted Mrs C at me.

'I'd love to,' I groaned, 'but I should point out that it's difficult just at the moment as you're lying on top of me.'

'Oops, sorry.' She rolled to one side and I sprang (well, struggled) to my feet, dusted myself down and raced down the corridor after them. Considering they had to carry a large body, they were certainly making good progress as there was no sign of them ahead of me.

I burst through a fire door at the end of the corridor and heard them disappear up the stairs in front of me. Stairs; good, that would slow them down a bit. Above me I could hear scuffling as their cargo finally began to weigh heavily on them. I knew I'd never be able to take them on all on my own, but if Jack had managed to deliver his message, well then things might just work out after all.

I'd like to say I raced up the stairs after Kohl, but I'd be lying, or exaggerating at the very least. I was still winded after Mrs C had landed on me and I was also being extra careful to avoid being jumped on by any – or all – of the Fiddlers Three. This meant that by the time I got to the top of the stairs and out on to the roof of the Cauldron, I was just in time to hear the screaming noise I'd become oh so familiar with recently as Kohl and the boys took off in their private jet sleigh, waving rudely out of the window at me and leaving me standing on the roof watching as they disappeared into the darkening sky.

Or so they thought.

They had barely disappeared from view when I heard a voice from above. 'Harry, are you OK?'

A magic carpet flew down and hovered beside me, Jack peering down over the edge.

'I'm fine, Jack,' I replied. 'Now shift over and give me some room.' I climbed on to the carpet and nodded at Ali Baba. 'You got my message then?'

'Your man was most persuasive.' He waved at the sky. 'Are those the people who framed me for the robbery?'

'They most certainly are, but I haven't really time to explain right now.' I fastened the Velcro strip I'd been handed onto my behind and made sure I was stuck to the carpet. I pointed in the direction the jet sleigh had taken. 'I've always wanted to say this: follow that sleigh.'

Instantly the magic carpet lurched forward and we were about to ascend when there was a shout from below. 'Wait for us.' Basili and Mrs C had finally made their way to the roof, just in time to slow us down.

'Do we wait for them?' asked Ali Baba, looking down at them doubtfully.

'We don't have a choice, I think,' I said. 'It's her husband who's behind all this, so the least we can do is take her with us.'

'Very well,' sighed Ali Baba and indicated for the carpet to stop. Seconds later both Basili and Mrs C had scrambled aboard and the carpet dropped significantly in the air. 'Not good,' I heard Ali Baba mutter under his breath but at least he didn't threaten to push them off again.

Much more slowly this time, the magic carpet ascended into the evening sky and sped after the sleigh. I could just make it out ahead of us, flying back towards the city.

'Quick, we need to catch them before they land,' I shouted pointing at the sleigh.

'That may be easier said than done,' said Ali Baba as his driver tried to urge as much speed as he could out of his cloth vehicle.

Slowly we began to pick up speed but I wasn't sure it would be enough. The sleigh didn't seem to be getting any closer.

'We're not going to catch them, are we?' said a plaintive voice from beside me. 'And it's all my fault.' Mrs C burst into tears once more.

I tried to comfort her (I seemed to spend my time comforting her). 'Don't worry, Ali Baba is a very resourceful man. I'm sure he's working on something even as I speak.'

As if he could hear me from the back of the carpet, Ali Baba said, 'We're not going to catch them. I am sorry, Harry; we are just carrying too much weight.' This provoked a new flood of tears from Mrs C, and it certainly wasn't what I'd hoped he was going to say.

'Perhaps I might be of some assistance,' said a voice from somewhere on my left. As I was sitting on the leftmost edge of the magic carpet it was fair to say that this was something I hadn't expected. As I looked around we were bathed in a bright red light and I looked straight into the eyes of Rudolph the Red-nosed Reindeer.

'What in the name of blazes are you doing here?' I asked.

'Clarissa thought I might be of help, so I got here as quickly as I could,' he replied.

'What, you think you might be able to pull us along, do you?' I wasn't sure exactly how this arrogant animal could be of any use whatsoever bearing in mind our last meeting so I didn't want to waste my time on him.

'Don't be ludicrous, my dear pig. I see no point in pulling this particular craft.' Rudolph was confirming my suspicions all the while but then, just when I figured all he was going to do was to give us vocal encouragement, he surprised me. 'But I might be able to carry a passenger on my back.'

'If you do, do you think you can catch them?' I asked.

'What do you think I do for a living every Christmas Eve? Of course I can catch them. Now are you going to hop on or not?'

Was he talking to me? He was certainly looking at me. Why was it always me that got asked these questions? Was I really seen as some kind of superhero? Everyone on the magic carpet was looking at me too – most of them with 'I'm glad I wasn't asked' expressions on their faces.

With a resigned groan I peeled off the Velcro and stood up. 'OK, Rudolph, I guess it's up to you and me now. Get close to the carpet so I can climb on your back without falling off.'

Rudolph taxied in and flew parallel to the carpet. Ever so carefully I stepped off the ornate material and on to Rudolph's back. As I did so, he turned his head and whispered, 'This never happened, is that clear? Under no circumstances should anyone ever find out I did this. It's so humiliating.'

Clinging tightly to his neck, I whispered back, 'Heigh-ho, Rudolph, away.'

16

Get Behind Me Santa

I'll give Rudolph credit for one thing: he was fast. In a matter of seconds he'd left the magic carpet far behind and was speeding over Grimmtown in hot pursuit of Kohl. I suppose speed was of the essence if you had to get around the world delivering presents over the course of one night, time being stopped or not. The drawback with this incredible burst of speed was that he had me on his back and I had nothing to hold on to by way of saddle or reins. It meant I had to get closer to Rudolph than I would have wished; wrapping my arms tightly around his neck and pressing my legs firmly against his body. With the wind threatening to drag me off and throw me away, trust me, I was clinging on with whatever bits of my body I could use. At least Rudolph smelled nice. I'd expected something mangy and pungent, but, considering how he'd been when I'd first met him, I shouldn't have been surprised that he exuded a scent of aromatic oils and expensive cosmetics.

Rudolph must have felt my panic – then again my legs were probably on the point of crushing his ribs so it wasn't too hard to miss. 'I don't suppose you could relax a little? You're not making this very easy for me,' he asked.

'Believe me, from where I'm sitting it's not too much fun for me either, but don't take it personally; it's not like we're engaged or anything.'

All I got in return was an indignant snort, but I did try to relax my vice-like grip a little – but only a little. From where I sat, it was a long trip to the ground and there were no return tickets if I slipped off.

Rudolph wove in and out through Grimmtown's skyscrapers like a supersonic bee in a flower garden, always keeping the sleigh in his sights. As far as I could make out we were beginning to gain on it – not that I spent too much time looking; mostly my head was buried in Rudolph's neck.

I leaned forward towards Rudolph's head once more. 'Are we there yet?'

'We're catching up. Whatever you've planned, be ready to do it shortly.'

Now that we were getting closer I realised that I hadn't really thought through what I was going to do next. Even if we did catch up with the sleigh, we were still hundreds of feet above the ground and lacking in certain key accessories: namely a parachute, a weapon of some sort, a way into the sleigh and, most importantly, a soft landing should things go wrong. Looked like once more I'd be making it up as I went along, only this time I couldn't afford to make any mistakes – at least not if I didn't want to spend yet more time doing some unforced mid-air acrobatics.

I took a quick glance ahead; we were slightly behind and just above Kohl's sleigh. Rudolph had done fantastically well to catch up.

From above there didn't seem like there was any way into it – not that I suspected there'd be an easy way in regardless of what angle we approached it.

'Take us down beside it,' I ordered. 'I need to take a closer look.'

Rudolph obliged and flew parallel to the craft. There was a door in the side, but I wasn't sure I'd be able – or even wanted – to try to do a mid-air reindeer to sleigh transfer and open that door from the outside. Scratch that. There was only one option left.

'Let's have a look at what's underneath.'

Seconds later we were looking up at the undercarriage This one was different from the others I'd seen in that it looked to have landing gear as opposed to skis.

'That's because it's geared for urban flying rather than polar,' Rudolph advised. 'They're becoming very popular with Grimmtown's rich set.'

'No doubt,' I replied, scanning the underside of the craft carefully. Like all the other sides there didn't seem to be any obvious entry point. The wheels nestled snugly against the surface and didn't offer any way in – not that I was prepared to try that particular route; I wasn't a slim pig and I don't think I'd have managed to squeeze through. I didn't even want to contemplate what would happen if the wheels suddenly came down while I was clambering over them. The beginnings of a plan were forming in my head, but I had to find a way in in order to make it work. If they managed to get back on to the ground I'd be sunk.

I was just about to order Rudolph away from the sleigh and have a rethink when I saw a small handle nestling snugly against the sleigh's underbelly. Urging Rudolph closer, I had a better look. It seemed to provide access to some sort of undercarriage maintenance area. If there was a way in, there just might be a way up into the sleigh proper.

'I'm going to try to open that hatch,' I told Rudolph. 'Keep an eye on me when it swings out. The last thing I need right now is some freefall training.'

Rudolph nodded and rose up against the hatch. I grabbed the handle, twisted it and pulled. The door swung down, revealing . . . well, um, a dark space actually. Without a torch I had no way of seeing what was in there. Oh well, why would this be any different from any other time?

Now came the tricky bit. As carefully as I could, I pushed myself on to my knees and then stood on Rudolph's back. 'Whatever you do, don't wobble or suddenly decide to fly away, OK?' I told him. I slowly reached up, grabbed the edge of the hatch and, with Rudolph's help, climbed into the darkness. 'Do me a favour and stick your head in here,' I shouted down to him. Seconds later, he poked his head in and the area was illuminated by a red light. Who needs a torch when you've a red-nosed reindeer?

The maintenance area itself was small and just allowed a mechanic access to the landing gear. There wasn't even room to stand up but once I was inside and crouching I saw another hatch in the roof above me. Figuring that this might open out into the sleigh proper, I cracked it open and peered through the narrow slit. I could hear laughing from the cabin above. Clearly Kohl and the boys figured they were home and hosed. All I could see through the crack were the band members' feet – and they did have very nice shoes indeed – but I imagined the rest of the band were attached to them too, so jumping into the cabin and attempting a rescue was probably out of the question unless . . .

I poked my head back down and called to Rudolph. 'Count to twenty and then cause a diversion.'

'Whatever do you mean? What kind of diversion? I'm Santa's lead reindeer you know, not some sort of performing animal,' a highly indignant Rudolph replied.

'Well, if you want to hold on to that job then you need to do something to distract the people in this sleigh so I can rescue Santa. Do I make myself clear?'

Rudolph nodded. 'Absolutely.'

'Good, start counting now.' Rudolph disappeared from view and began to count. I hoped he'd come up with something that would attract the attention of everyone in the sleigh otherwise it would be the worst rescue in the history of bad rescues.

Seventeen . . . eighteen . . . nineteen . . . twenty. I cracked open the hatch once more and waited. It wasn't a long wait. I'd barely finished the count when I heard excited shouts from above.

'Hey, what's that flying in front of us?' said a voice.

'Dunno, it looks like a big dog,' said another. I sincerely hoped Rudolph couldn't hear; I wasn't quite sure how his ego would take that remark.

'Now what's he doing?' Whatever it was I hoped it was going to be good.

'Hey, guys, come take at look at this.'

This was followed by the sound of fading footsteps as what I hoped was every member of King Kohl and his Fiddlers Three charged up front for a look.

I pushed up the hatch, clambered into the cabin and looked around. I was instantly drawn to the red shape slumped in the corner.

Santa – and he was unguarded. I ran over to him and shook him. 'Santa, wake up.' There was no reaction. I slapped him gently on the face – still nothing.

There was a shocked voice from the cockpit. 'Oh no, he cannot be serious.'

This was followed by, 'There's no way he's going to do that.'

'Oh my God, he is.'

'That's disgusting,' and finally, 'It's going to hit, taking evasive action.'

Then the plane lurched sideways. Wow, whatever Rudolph was doing, it was certainly working. All I had to do now was wake Santa up and I could put the last piece of my plan into action. The plane bucked wildly again and I was flung across the cabin. Seconds later a still unconscious Santa fell on top of me.

Panic reigned in the cockpit. 'I can't see a thing; the whole window is covered in poo. It's like tar. What did that dog have for lunch and how the hell are we going to get it off?'

I pushed Santa off me and shook him once more. He mumbled something incomprehensible and slowly opened his eyes.

'Aren't you a little short to be a member of Fiddlers Three?' he slurred.

'I'm Harry Pigg and I've come to rescue you.'

'You're who?'

'I'm Harry Pigg,' I repeated. 'Your wife sent me. I'm here with Rudolph.'

Comprehension began to register in Santa's befuddled brain. 'Rudolph, where is he?'

'He's outside, come on.' I pulled Santa to his feet and draped his arm over my shoulder. Slowly I dragged him across to the hatch and, yes I'm ashamed to admit it, I just dropped him in. Seconds later, I fell in beside him and pulled the hatch shut.

'Now what?' asked Santa.

'Now we wait for your pal to come back, which should be any second now.'

No sooner had I spoken that we were immersed in a red glow once more. 'Under no circumstances is anyone ever to know what I did to divert those people, understood?' said a somewhat shame-faced Rudolph.

'My lips are sealed,' I said with a smirk. 'Now,' I turned to Santa, 'how does this stopping time trick of yours work?'

'You know about that?' said Santa indignantly. 'How did you find out?'

'I'm a detective, it's what I do,' I said, and then as an afterthought, 'trust me, your people didn't tell me; I worked it out for myself.'

Santa gave me a disbelieving look but, after a few seconds' consideration, let it slide – at least for the moment. 'Here's how it works: you have to be touching me so you won't be affected when everything stops then all I do is—'

There was a pounding noise from above. Santa's disappearance had been discovered. We didn't have much time. I grabbed Santa by the hand and held on to Rudolph's nose with my other trotter. The reindeer gave an indignant squeal. 'Now would be a good time, Santa,' I said, raising my eyes to the commotion above. Santa nodded once to show he understood and closed his eyes.

The hatch was ripped open and tuxedo bedecked arms stretched in, trying to grab us.

'Right now would be even better,' I squealed as hands scrabbled at my head.

Almost immediately the noise from above stopped. Santa opened his eyes once more. 'That's it,' he smiled.

'That's it?' I said. 'You just close your eyes and, hey presto, time stops?'

'I've had hundreds of years of practice,' Santa replied. 'Mind you it's not quite as easy as it looks. Now I really think we should be going.'

'No argument from me.' I hopped on to Rudolph's back and helped Santa on in front of me. 'I couldn't agree more.'

Seconds later we dropped out of the hatch and flew back in the direction of the City once more.

It was an eerie sensation, flying through the night when everything around us had stopped dead still. Kohl's sleigh hung suspended in the sky like a giant Christmas tree ornament and all around us everything was silent. Below, the lights of Grimmtown's evening traffic were unmoving. The landscape looked like a giant version of Santa's house.

Once we were far enough away from the sleigh I said to Santa, 'I think we're OK now.' There was a rush of air and suddenly we were surrounded by the noise of the traffic below, the wind whistling around our faces and the distant screaming of Kohl's jet sleigh as it staggered through the sky while the passengers tried to figure out some way of clearing the poo from the cockpit windows before it crashed – and no doubt trying to figure out exactly where we'd disappeared to.

'Not long now,' I shouted at Santa, trying to make myself heard over the buffeting wind.

Santa turned back to reply and was about to say something when his face dropped. 'I'm not so sure about that,' he said pointing back over my shoulder, concern visible on his face. I swung around and saw Kohl's jet sleigh bearing down on us. Through a smeared windscreen I could see the pilot grinning as the aircraft rapidly closed the distance between us.

'Rudolph,' I roared, 'you need to get a move on. They're right behind us.'

'I'll do my best,' Rudolph puffed. 'But my load is somewhat heavier now; I'm not sure how long I'll be able to keep it up.'

'Just do your best, I'll think of something.' Though I wasn't quite sure what. This time there didn't seem to be an obvious way out. Kohl's sleigh was just too big and too fast. I remembered the damage the other one had done to our sleigh on the way to the North Pole, so I didn't think one Santa, one reindeer and an – admittedly brilliant – pig detective would offer much by way of resistance if they chose to ram us, which I reckoned would be any second now.

It was obvious that Rudolph was tiring. His flight pattern was becoming more erratic and he was beginning to wheeze. All the while our pursuers were chewing up the distance between us. I looked behind me once more. They were right on top of us. This was it – we were going to die. They were so close I could see Kohl in the cockpit mouthing 'I have you now' at me.

There was a sudden blur of movement and something flew in

between us and the sleigh. Caught by surprise, the pilot spun away wildly, careening out of control into the sky above.

What had happened? I looked around and then heard Jack Horner's voice from underneath us, 'Woohoo, you're all clear, Harry. Now let's drop Santa off and wrap this thing up.'

I looked down and saw Ali Baba's carpet flying along below us. A smiling Jack gave me a thumbs up and a very relieved-looking Mrs C applauded wildly.

'Thank you,' she mouthed and I gave a small bow in acknowledgement and almost fell off Rudolph as a consequence.

Note to self: never try flashy gestures when balancing on the back of a tiring reindeer several hundred feet above the ground.

17

Happy Christmas to All, and to All a Good Wrap Up

Two days later I was back at work.

What about holidays? I hear you say, but a detective's work is never done. Anyway, I was looking for something to occupy myself. Having spent Christmas in close proximity to a flatulent ex-genie who snored like a foghorn had left me understandably eager to get out of the apartment.

Once more I was in the office, feet up on my desk, enjoying the silence (and the lack of unpleasant odours). At the other side of the desk, Jack Horner was showing me what he'd got from Santa, which, considering the part he'd played in the rescue, was a substantial haul indeed. Apparently his mother had been more than a little surprised at the amount of gear heaped under the Horner tree on Christmas morning.

I was basking in the satisfaction of a job well done. Santa had been delivered back to the North Pole just before midnight, just in time to commence deliveries. I'd asked him how long the job would take once he'd frozen time and set off on his journey.

'About twenty-four years, give or take a day or so. Our record is twenty-one years, three months, two days and twelve seconds but we were much younger then,' he'd said, a tad ruefully.

'Let me get this straight. Every Christmas Eve it takes you about twenty-five years to get around the world, delivering presents to everyone, then you get home and start the whole thing all over again?'

'That's about right, yes.'

Wow, and I thought I had a tough job.

Jack's chattering interrupted my thoughts.

'Harry, there's a few things I don't understand.'

'Yes,' I said.

'Well, Kohl got away, didn't he? Won't the police lock up Ali Baba 'cause they still think he did it?'

'They still suspect him, that's true, but now that he knows Kohl did it, he can ensure enough evidence is planted at the various crime scenes to incriminate him.'

'You mean he's going to frame him?' Jack sounded indignant.

'Well, I don't think it's considered framing someone when they've actually committed the crime, do you?'

'I suppose not,' said Jack doubtfully. 'But what about Danny Emperor?'

'Well, you can imagine his surprise when he went to his warehouse yesterday and everything had been put back exactly where it had been before Ali Baba had taken it. That was the deal I made with Ali and, in fairness to him, he stuck to it. Danny still has a faint suspicion he might have hallucinated the robbery and who am I to dissuade him from that thought? At least we got a few suits for Basili out of it, seeing as Danny was so grateful.'

'Yeah, that's not a bad thing. Basili's yellow outfit is a bit . . . um . . . loud.'

I stood up and slapped Jack on the shoulder. 'That's true,' I laughed. 'Come on, let me buy you lunch.'

Jack sat there with a frown on his face. 'There's one thing that I don't understand though.'

'Only one?'

Jack ignored my insult. 'Well, if the time travel thing is such a big secret and only the Santas know about it, apart from us, of course,' he said.

'Yes?'

'How then did Kohl know about it? He had to know about it in order to carry out the robberies in the first place, didn't he?'

'You know, Jack, that's a very good question.' It was a very good question – and one I'd spent quite an amount of time thinking about over the previous few days. I wasn't going to tell Jack, but I had a sneaking suspicion that there was more going on here than we knew about. Somebody had tipped Kohl off and I didn't think that somebody was Santa or anyone in his immediate circle. Something told me we hadn't even begun to scratch the surface of this particular mystery. Call it a hunch if you like but my detective senses had been tingling since Christmas Eve. Something was brewing; I was certain of it and this case had only been the beginning. There was more to what went on than met the eye and I was convinced that I was going to be involved whether I liked it or not.

But today wasn't the day to be worrying about it. I needed to treat Jack to a well-earned lunch.

We were on our way out of my office when there was a timid knock on the door.

There goes lunch, I thought.

I opened the door to a very petite, very pale and very obviously frightened young woman.

'Can I help you, madam?' I asked.

The woman was clearly on the verge of tears.

261

Not another one, I thought. Why do they gravitate towards me?

'Please, Mr Pigg, I need your help. My name is Muffet, Matilda Muffet, and I'm having a terrible spider problem.'

The End

Acknowledgements

Again, a whole raft of people contributed hugely to getting this book on the shelves.

As always, thanks are due to Scott and Corinna at The Friday Project for their work in making *The Ho Ho Ho Mystery* presentable in the first place. The comments that came with with the edits were worth the admission price alone!

To my agent, Svetlana, for the support, advice and help and for educating me in the mysterious and arcane ways of the publishing industry – and she makes great jam too.

To all those who offered help, advice and assistance over the past few years: Darren Craske (great writer, buy his books now), Guy Saville (great writer, buy his book when it comes out in 2011), all at CBI, David Maybury, Dooradoyle and Adare libraries (again), and all those places around Limerick that have great coffee and a quite corner to write in. It all adds up folks.

Above all, thanks to my family, Gemma, Ian, Adam and Stephen for 'encouraging me' to be in front of the computer at 9:30 every day and for ensuring my feet were firmly fixed on the ground during the process. No chance of any airs and graces with you lot around!

Ian: please be advised that beating me once at Pro Evo Soccer does not make you better than me.

Adam: Bazinga!

Stephen: they won the Premiership and the FA Cup, Drogba ended up the top scorer by a country mile, isn't it about time you admitted that Chelsea are far superior to Manchester United in every way? No? All right then, they'll just have to do it again.

THE CURDS AND WHEY MYSTERY

To my parents, Bobby and Nancy,
from whom I got my love of reading

Contents

Contents

1

Along Came a Spider

Sometimes being a detective isn't all that easy. Actually it's never that easy. Case in point, my current client: a small lady with a big arachnid problem.

'Spiders?' I said, ushering the very pale and very frightened Miss Muffet to the nearest chair.

'Yes, spiders,' Miss Muffet nodded faintly, lips trembling. She looked to be teetering on the edge of a complete breakdown – and I didn't fancy being the one left cleaning up the shattered pieces from my floor afterwards.

'Spiders,' I said again, still trying to get my head around what she was saying. 'As in small, scuttling things with eight legs that build webs in unswept corners?'

'No Mr Pigg, spiders as in large, hairy creatures the size of poodles; spiders that eat small animals and build webs that fishing trawlers could use to haul in whales. I'm not talking about a few tiny money spiders here; I'm talking about thousands of these giant eight-legged monsters running amuck in my house. Imagine putting a breakfast on the table and then, when the guest goes to get his coffee, he comes back only to find that a tarantula or

271

somesuch has made off with his bacon,' she said. 'And not only that, spiders terrify me; always have done. I hate them. I can't even sleep there any more I'm so frightened. It's playing merry hell with my business.'

'And what business would that be?' I asked.

'Oh, sorry, didn't I say? I do apologise. I'm the proprietor of the Curds and Whey Bed and Breakfast on Grimm Road. Maybe you've heard of it?'

I gave a rueful shake of the head.

'Ah well, never mind. It used to be very popular with visitors and was very highly thought of. Until this happened, business was extremely good. I had full occupancy. Now, not too many people are keen on staying there.' Fumbling in her bag she took out a tiny white handkerchief and began dabbing her eyes just as the tears began to trickle. 'The house has been in my family for generations,' she said between sobs. 'If I can't get this sorted I'll have to close down and sell it. I can't let that happen. That's why I've come to you.' She looked up at me. 'I need you to find out who's doing this; find out who's trying to put me out of business. Can you help me, Mr Pigg?'

Now I'm normally not one to refuse a pretty lady, but there was just one teeny problem; well, a fairly big problem actually: I didn't like spiders either. Scratch that, I hated them. They were one of two things that really terrified me (and no, I'm not about to tell you what the other is; I don't want you laughing at me). Just the thought of one of those hairy creatures scuttling across my trotter sent shivers up and down my spine, along my arms and down my legs, where they stopped for a moment to catch their breath before running back up again for a repeat performance.

Miss Muffet's dilemma meant I now had to do a careful juggling act: fear of spiders versus earning money to pay some long outstanding bills – and some of my bill collectors were of the type that had a baseball bat as part of their corporate uniform. After a brief, but brutal, mental struggle, earning money came out a clear winner, actively encouraged by blind greed and aided and abetted by sheer desperation – fear of spiders never stood a chance.

I stood up and extended my trotter. 'Miss Muffet, the Third Pig Detective Agency would be delighted to take on your case,' I said, trying not to show any hint of the anxiety that was developing into full-blown arachnophobia in my head.

The look of relief on her face convinced me I'd done the right thing.

'Oh that's wonderful, Mr Pigg. I knew I could count on you.'

We'll see how much you can count on me when funnel-web spiders start doing the tarantella up and down my back, I thought, but, of course, I didn't say it out loud; I had an image to maintain, after all.

I walked my new client to my office door.

'I think the first thing we should do is to go and have a look at your building,' I said. 'Maybe we'll find some clues there.' I didn't really want to – for obvious reasons – but I had to start somewhere and the B&B seemed like a good place to kick things off, although if what she said was true I'd spend most of the time kicking off spiders.

'An excellent suggestion,' said Miss Muffet. 'There's no time like the present. My car is outside. Why don't I drive?'

On the way to Miss Muffet's B&B she gave me some more background.

'Well, when I was a young girl there was nothing I enjoyed more than eating my bowl of curds and whey on the tuffet in the back garden.'

Curds and whey? No, I'd never heard of it either. I wasn't sure what it actually was, but it didn't sound like something I'd like. Mind you, I had no idea what a tuffet was either.

Miss Muffet continued her story. 'One morning I was busily tucking in as usual when I heard a noise beside me. I looked over and there was this enormous spider hanging down – a really big hairy one – looking at me as if I was going to be his breakfast. It quite frightened the life out of me. I was so scared my bowl shot into the air and spilled all over me. It made quite a mess, and curds and whey are so difficult to get out of clothes. After that, I never really liked spiders again.'

I nodded occasionally as she told the story. I could understand where she got her fear of spiders from – that much was obvious – but how did that connect to the sudden plague of them that was apparently infesting her business premises – if it was infested at all. If she was that frightened of spiders, maybe she'd just seen one or two and overreacted. I know I probably would have.

I started asking the obvious questions.

'Miss Muffet, do you have any enemies; anyone with a grudge or who might want to put you out of business?'

'Oh no,' she said, after thinking about it for a moment. 'I'm sure I don't. Who could possibly want to do such a thing? I don't think I've ever had any problems with anyone.'

'Has anyone shown an interest in buying you out?'

'Well, I have turned down offers over the years, of course. It was always a lucrative business and people were forever looking to buy me out, but I always resisted.' She frowned as she remembered something. 'Mind you, there was one gentleman recently who did phone a number of times offering to buy the building. He was most persistent, but I kept on refusing. Eventually he stopped calling. I do remember because he had a strange, squeaky kind of voice.'

Motive, I thought to myself.

'And you have no idea who it might have been?'

'I didn't pay much attention, to be honest, and I never thought to ask for his name.'

She drove around a corner and onto a long street. 'Here we are, Grimm Road. I'm at the far end.'

Apart from yellow construction vehicles in the distance and a few cars parked outside some of the houses, the street itself seemed very quiet. But as I looked out of the window a most bizarre sight greeted me. Turning to Miss Muffet, I pointed to what I'd seen.

'Is that a . . . shoe?' I gasped in amazement.

Now I should point out that this wasn't just an ordinary shoe that someone had lost while running from the scene of the crime. This was a giant shoe; a shoe the size of the building my office was in. This was a piece of footwear that dwarfed all others into insignificance – a mega-shoe. As I gaped at it I thought I could see . . . 'Are those windows?' I asked.

'Hmm, pardon? Oh, yes,' replied Miss Muffet with a complete lack of interest. 'Those are probably windows.'

Considering what I was looking at, her response puzzled me. She was acting as if this was quite an ordinary event.

I nudged her gently. 'You don't seem particularly surprised at seeing what looks like a giant shoe at the end of your street.'

'Don't I?' she replied. 'Well, I do see it every day. It's the Shoe Hotel. It's been there for years. A little old lady lives in it. She runs it as far as I know.'

Now it began to make sense. I vaguely remembered reading about a series of themed hotels that had opened up all around the country over the past few years. This must have been one of them but, as themed hotels went, it was quite spectacular. It had been designed to look like a trainer – all white paint and blue stripes – and would never suffer from foot-odour. The huge entrance doors were where the (presumably very large) big toe would have been and the shoelaces were large plants that draped down along the walls. From the small number of cars in the car-park, business didn't appear to be too good. That was significant.

More to the point, it was just possible that the owners mightn't take too kindly to competition from a local B&B and might be only too delighted to see it close its doors.

More motive.

I made a note to speak to this 'little old lady' on my way back.

'And you've never spoken to the owner of this hotel?' I asked.

'No, I don't even think I've ever met her. Ah, here we are,' Miss Muffet said as she pulled into the driveway of a large house. 'Well,' she said as she stopped the car and we got out, 'shall we take a look?'

From the outside the B&B didn't look particularly frightening. It was a three-storey brown brick building with white lace curtains in all the windows. Very homely indeed.

But was there something odd about those curtains?

'Miss Muffet, why do you have lace curtains on the outside of all your windows?' I asked.

The look she gave me suggested she might be having second thoughts about utilising my services as a detective. 'Those aren't curtains, Mr Pigg, they're webs.'

I took a second, closer look and, to my horror, I could see she was right. What I thought were curtains were in fact giant spider webs that covered all the windows from top to bottom. This lady hadn't been exaggerating. If the webs were anything to go by, she did have a major spider problem and probably some major spiders causing the problem. I wasn't at all sure I wanted to go inside now. In fact, I was thinking about turning around, running straight back to my office and hiding behind my desk until they went away.

Miss Muffet must have read my mind as she grabbed me by the arm and pulled me towards the door.

'It's okay,' she said gently. 'They tend not to be too active this time of the day. They mostly come out at night – mostly. We should be able to look around without being disturbed too much.'

I was disturbed enough already and I wasn't sure that I particularly wanted to look around the inside any more but, for such a slight woman, she was incredibly strong; she propelled me through the front door and into the lobby before I could change my mind.

Inside, it was as if the whole interior had been redecorated by someone from Haunted Houses'R'Us. Huge strands of ghostly web hung over the stairs and all the furniture. Long wispy tentacles extended from the ceiling and drifted in the draught from the front door. One trailed across the side of my face. It felt like someone breathing gently on my cheek and I jumped in fright.

Miss Muffet laughed quietly. 'After a while you just learn to ignore it.'

As I looked around I could see that, just like she said, there didn't appear to be too many active spiders. I'd never heard of them taking afternoon naps before, but I was glad they did. Spider siesta meant they weren't going to bother me – for which I was grateful. I could see large dark shapes huddled up in some of the webs but, understandably, I didn't examine them too closely. The last thing I wanted to do was to wake any of them up.

Miss Muffet gave me a guided tour, but apart from all the webs there wasn't much to see. The ground floor comprised a large dining room, a guest lounge, a small reception area, Miss Muffet's office and the kitchen. The rest of the building was taken up by bedrooms. Other than the webs there certainly wasn't anything obvious in the way of clues and I'm a very observant pig – I spotted the giant shoe hotel, didn't I? By the same token, I was keeping a very close eye out for any spiders that might suddenly awake and decide they wanted to play with me.

As I wandered around the house a couple of things began to bother me – other than the spiders. Apart from the little ones that you'd find in any ordinary house, spiders weren't too easy to come by. So where did the thousands of spiders that had taken over

Miss Muffet's house come from? Someone must have supplied them – and they were probably very specialised, so certainly weren't picked up off the shelf from alongside the tins of beans and cereals in the local supermarket. That was certainly something to follow up. It was time to talk to my informant – although, if past history was anything to go by, he'd barely be able to inform me of his name let alone give me any useful information.

The other thing that nagged at me was Miss Muffet's mention of guests. It meant she must still have had some staying in the house. So why exactly were they staying? Unless they were keen students of spiders there was no sane reason to stay in the B&B – especially with a lovely, shiny, shoe-shaped hotel just up the road.

'How many people are actually staying here at the moment?' I asked.

Miss Muffet did a quick calculation. 'Nine, I believe.'

'And they've shown no indication of wanting to leave because of your infestation?'

'No, not at all. In fact, I haven't received a single complaint,' she said proudly.

Now that struck me as more than a tad suspicious. For someone to want to stay in a house infested with spiders, they'd need a particularly good reason – a reason that might just be connected with the case – especially when there were so many other places to stay.

'Can I have a list of your current guests and all your employees?' I asked.

'Of course, but surely you don't believe any of them are involved,' Miss Muffet replied, a bit naively I thought.

'At the moment I'm not ruling anything out,' I said, grabbing for the usual clichés as she reached behind the reception desk and opened the register.

'Here you are,' she said. 'Nine guests: Mr and Mrs Jack Spratt,

Queenie Harte, John B. Nimble, Licken and Lurkey, William Winkie, Pietro Nocchio and, lastly, Thomas Piper.'

'I'll have to speak to all of them; can you arrange that?' I said, then I focused on what she'd actually told me. 'Did you say Licken and Lurkey?'

'Oh, yes, indeed, they're a rather entertaining team.'

She might have been a savvy businesswoman but her taste in entertainment was clearly lacking. Licken and Lurkey were a cabaret act that had been run out of every theatre in town – and in most other towns in the county as well. They marketed themselves as the WORLD'S most renowned and entertaining comedy DUO (their capitals, not mine, I hasten to add), but they were about as entertaining as having boils lanced. I also had history with them. Back in the days before becoming the WORLD'S most renowned and entertaining comedy DUO, they had toured the country as the WORLD'S MOST ASTOUNDING MAGIC ACT – which had been neither magic nor astounding. I'd been asked to investigate a series of dove disappearances and had discovered that they all coincided with a performance by the despicable duo. As their act included the standard 'dove from a hat' trick and as the dove escaped during each performance, never to be recaptured, they had to find new ones for every show. Did I mention they weren't too bright? I hadn't realised they were still in town, but they'd be first on my list of interviewees as, from past experience, they were a pair who weren't too worried about getting their talons dirty.

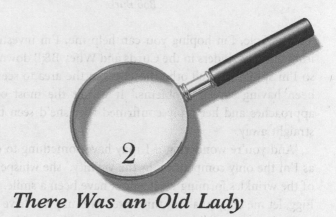

2

There Was an Old Lady

Having assured Miss Muffet that I was on the case and following a specific line of enquiry (yes I know, it wasn't exactly true, but it got me out of spider central), I called for a taxi and made my way back into town. As we drove past the giant Shoe Hotel I asked the driver to pull in for a moment. No harm in asking a few questions, I thought.

Inside, the hotel was sparkling clean and, thankfully, there wasn't a cobweb to be seen. I approached reception and asked to speak to the manager. The receptionist looked at me strangely – I suppose they didn't get pigs in every day – but when I showed her my ID, she relaxed a little and ushered me into a small office. Behind a large desk sat a tiny old lady composed, it seemed, entirely of wrinkles. She looked like an elephant's knee. As I entered she stood up and pottered around to me. She was so decrepit it seemed to take her hours.

'Mr Pigg,' she said in a wavering voice, 'I'm Mrs Sole. How may I be of assistance?' She spoke so quietly I could barely hear her. With what seemed like an enormous effort, she waved me to a chair and, several lifetimes later, pottered back to her seat once more.

'Mrs Sole, I'm hoping you can help me. I'm investigating an infestation of spiders in the Curds and Whey B&B down the road, so I'm speaking to all other hoteliers in the area to see if they've been having similar problems.' It wasn't the most original of approaches and her reply confirmed that she'd seen through it straight away.

'And you're wondering if I may have something to do with it as I'm the only competition in the vicinity,' she whispered, some of the wrinkles forming what might have been a smile. 'Well, Mr Pigg, let me tell you about this hotel. We may not have too many cars in our car-park but you've probably noticed, being a detective, that they are all very expensive cars.' I hadn't, in fact, but nodded my head in agreement so as not to give the game away. 'You see we cater for the more . . . ah . . . discerning client at the upper end of the market. At the present time, Mr Humpty Dumpty, whom I'm sure you've heard of, occupies the penthouse suite and some business partners of Aladdin's have taken over the entire second floor. So, you see, that old building at the other end of the street really doesn't offer anything in the way of competition.'

She was certainly making a convincing argument. If Grimmtown big-shots like Dumpty and Aladdin used this hotel, then Mrs Sole wasn't going to worry too much about putting Miss Muffet out of business. Besides, she seemed like a sweet, kind old lady. Surely she wouldn't have been spiteful enough?

'Well, anyway, thank you for your time. You've been most helpful.' As I stood to leave, the phone rang.

'Excuse me a moment, won't you,' said Mrs Sole and lifted the receiver. It was like watching a weightlifter doing the clean and jerk. She was having so much difficulty I was almost tempted to hold it for her when she finally managed to get it to her ear. 'Yes, this is she,' she whispered into the mouthpiece. There was a brief silence, then Mrs Sole exploded.

'WHAT DO YOU MEAN THEY'LL BE LATE?' Suddenly she wasn't such a retiring old lady any more. 'IF THOSE FLOWERS AREN'T DELIVERED IN THE NEXT HOUR, YOU WON'T HAVE A JOB. UNDERSTAND?' There was a brief pause. 'AND YOUR BOSS TOO.' Her voice rose a few more decibels. 'AND I'LL HAVE YOU RUN OUT OF TOWN; YOU'LL NEVER DO BUSINESS IN GRIMMTOWN AGAIN. UNDERSTAND?' Another pause then she changed back into 'nice old lady' again, as if by magic. It was terrifying to watch. 'They'll be here in ten minutes? Why, that's wonderful. Thank you so much.'

She heaved the phone back in its cradle and turned to me, smiling sweetly once more.

'You just can't get good staff any more,' she said.

I just nodded. I was shell-shocked and wanted to be out of the hotel before she lost her cool again – perhaps with me – and it wasn't something I thought I'd particularly enjoy. Backing away towards the door I waved faintly at her and thanked her again.

'Not at all,' she whispered. 'I've quite enjoyed our little chat. We must do it again sometime.'

Not in a million years, I thought, as I raced across the lobby and back into the taxi. Instructing the driver to get us out of there as fast as he could, I slumped down in the back seat and considered what I'd seen. Clearly, Mrs Sole wasn't quite the demure lady she appeared. That having been said, she was probably right about not caring about Miss Muffet's business. She may have been as nuts as a squirrel's winter store, but I didn't see her as the primary suspect in this particular case. It really didn't make any business sense for her to see the Curds and Whey B&B as a threat.

I needed to do some further investigating and the spiders seemed like the next best thing to follow up on. Who could have supplied them? It's not as if they were something you'd order every day. I could even envisage the conversation in the pet shop:

'Do you sell spiders?'

'Yes, sir. We do most species. Would you like one or a pair?'

'Well, I'd like ten thousand actually.'

'Well, I can manage about twenty – maybe thirty at a pinch.'

Eventually every pet shop in Grimmtown would have been emptied of spiders and they still wouldn't have had enough – whoever 'they' might actually be.

It was the best (and only) lead I had right now.

Back in the office, I gathered my team (okay an ex-genie named Basili – who couldn't do magic any more – and a little boy called Jack Horner) together and explained the current case. Jack seemed very interested in the spiders. He seemed to think that a house full of them was cool for some reason.

'If I was looking for spiders, how would I go about it?' I asked him.

'Pet shop.'

'Well, that much I'd worked out for myself. Now supposing I wanted a couple of thousand of the critters; tarantulas, black widows, all the big guys.'

Now I had his attention.

He mulled it over for a second. 'Well, not too many of the local shops would be able to supply that many.'

I noted the use of the phrase 'not too many'.

'Best guy to talk to would be the Frogg Prince. He specialises in reptiles, spiders, that sort of thing. If anyone could do it, he'd be your man – I mean frog. I got my gerbil off him; he's called Fred.'

I assumed he was talking about his pet and not the owner of the store.

'And where is this Frogg Prince likely to be found exactly?'

Twenty minutes later I was talking to an enormous frog dressed in a grey pinstripe suit. Had I not been a pig myself it might have been a bizarre experience, but in Grimmtown you tended to meet all shapes and sizes – and creatures.

Theodore Frogg was the owner of Frogg Prince Pets and apart from a tendency to *ribbit* occasionally when talking, he was relatively normal – or at least as normal as a frog in a suit can be.

'Ah, yes, Mr Pigg, we did *ribbit* get an order that exhausted our entire supply of arachnids and we still *ribbit* had to provide more.'

'Arachnids?' He'd lost me.

'Spiders dear boy, *ribbit*, spiders. Yes, it presented us with quite a challenge I can *ribbit* tell you. But we managed it.' He glowed with pride, but then again it might just have been the natural state of his skin – it was quite shiny.

I was getting that tingly feeling that I usually got when a case finally started to come together.

'Who ordered the spiders?' I asked.

'Well, strange to relate, *ribbit*, it was a most unpleasant person indeed; very small, very green, extremely smelly and with a large wart on the end of his nose. Spoke in a kind of squeaky voice. He was somewhat bedraggled and quite offensive – but he did pay in advance so I *ribbit* didn't ask too many questions. In any event, I didn't want to refuse as he had two rather large creatures with him and I *ribbit* found them quite intimidating. I got the distinct impression they weren't about to take "no" for an answer.'

This was getting stranger by the minute, but the reference to speaking in a squeaky voice hadn't been lost on me. I'd have laid money that this was the same creature that had offered to buy the B&B from Miss Muffet.

'Creatures? What kind of creatures?'

'Large grey creatures dressed in *ribbit*, well, very little actually. They did *ribbit* rather frighten me, I must say.'

Large grey creatures; probably Trolls. Someone was certainly making sure the Frogg Prince wasn't going to renege on this particular deal.

'And they just instructed you to deliver them to the Curds and Whey B&B?'

'Good heavens, no. I just had to organise the acquisition of the spiders. They said they'd *ribbit* collect.'

'And you didn't think that this was at all suspicious?'

'Not at all, no. I just assumed they were scientists and needed them for research.'

That certainly wasn't likely. One small, green, smelly person and two trolls were about as far from science as you could get. 'And I assume they paid cash up front?'

Frogg nodded guiltily, knowing he'd been rumbled.

'So once you had the spiders, how did you contact them?'

Mr Frogg rummaged around in his wallet. 'They left me a number. Here it is.'

He handed me a piece of paper with some scrawled digits on it. It looked like a mobile phone so probably wouldn't lead to anything, but I had to follow it up anyway. 'And how did they collect the merchandise?'

'They came in a big *ribbit* truck and loaded everything into it.'

I thanked Mr Frogg and walked back onto the street. As I did, a large transport truck, with an equally large bulldozer on its trailer, passed by. A yellow bulldozer, I noticed idly.

Yellow!

Construction yellow!

My mind began to make the connections and I finally began to do some serious detecting.

Construction workers – or more to the point, construction trolls – like the ones that tended to frequent Stiltskin's Diner of an evening, and very like the ones I'd seen working near the B&B.

Small, green, smelly person! Could only be an orc. And who

employed all the orcs in Grimmtown? Ah, now that wasn't so good. That was someone I particularly didn't want to upset if I wanted to keep all my body parts intact.

Things were beginning to make sense. Someone wanted Miss Muffet out of business all right – but that someone wasn't running a rival hotel; oh no, that someone wanted her out because she was in the way of something much bigger. It was all becoming very clear. Now all I had to do was prove it. I needed to pay a visit to a building site – and make sure I wasn't caught in the process.

3

Follow the Yellow Brick Road

Building sites are difficult to find your way around at the best of times. Add in some night, a sprinkling of rain, a generous helping of mud and not only are they difficult, but they become downright unpleasant. The ground that has already been excavated becomes very slippery. Pools of cold, dirty water lie in wait for the unwary pig and, if the pig is very unlucky, there are large holes in the ground just waiting for him to fall into.

This particular building site was about a mile from Miss Muffet's place. Huge hoardings announced that a new motorway, coming soon, would provide access to Grimmtown for countless commuters, blah de blah de blah. It was the usual PR doubletalk. Of more interest was the name of the construction company involved in this wondrous feat of engineering: The Yellow Brick Road Construction Company looked to be doing this particular job. Then again, as it was owned by Edna, the Wicked Witch of the West Side, an old sparring partner of mine (to put it as euphemistically as I could), the YBRCC did most building jobs around Grimmtown. To an outsider, it probably seemed amazing how they always managed to get the big building deals. As any insider would tell you, they greased politicians' palms, encouraged planners to 'share' any competitive quotes and generally bullied any other prospective contractor out of business. If they were doing this job and Miss Muffet was in the way, then chances were she wouldn't be in the way long. More to the point, if the spider strategy didn't work then they'd probably find something a tad more imaginative to encourage her to sell up.

I knew Edna of old and knew she wasn't a woman to be trifled with, especially where money or power was concerned. She was also a woman who didn't let much get in the way of achieving whatever her current objective was, so I had to tread very carefully indeed if I wasn't to become a permanent part of the motorway foundations. Not that I wasn't treading carefully already. Not only was I trying not to ruin my clothes, I was trying to make sure I didn't break any legs, arms or other vital parts of my body by suddenly falling into one of those previously mentioned large holes.

I figured if there was any information about the building work, like plans or drawings, it'd be in the construction hut. I could just about make it out in the distance, a small, cheap prefab mounted on blocks. I squelched my way towards it, unsure of what was ahead of me. In order not to alert any security I had decided not to use my torch – a decision I was now regretting as it seemed that every large puddle on the site lay between me and my destination and I was stepping into each one in succession.

Eventually – cold, wet and muddy up to my knees – I arrived at the hut. I listened carefully at the door and, when I didn't hear any obvious sounds from inside, very carefully picked the lock and slid in. Considering my history at picking locks, it was surprisingly easy. Ensuring the window blinds were closed, I was finally able to flick on my torch and a pencil-thin beam of light swept the room.

In fairness, it didn't take much in the way of detecting skills to figure out what was going on – the plans were in plain sight, tacked to one of the walls. It would have taken a pretty poor detective to miss them. They confirmed the construction of a new ring road around Grimmtown and the road ran straight through where the Curds and Whey B&B currently stood. Was it any wonder someone wanted her out? If they had been foolish enough to start work on the road without ensuring beforehand that all the land could be built on, then I could understand their urgency. Every day that the road couldn't go through Miss Muffet's house was another day of unnecessary costs to the construction company and, if I knew Edna, she wouldn't take too kindly to any unnecessary costs – or indeed any costs at all usually.

Now that I had the information I needed it was time to disappear. Unfortunately, that looked like it was going to be a futile wish as, just when I was getting ready to open the door, I heard noises from outside the hut. I could tell they were gnomes from the growling half-animal sounds they made, so it probably meant that Edna's security had been doing their rounds and were coming back to base – a base I was currently occupying and didn't seem to have anything remotely large enough to hide a pig in. I had a quick – and admittedly extremely optimistic – glance at some filing cabinet drawers, but had to concede that I'd barely get my legs into one of them, let alone the rest of my body. Once the gnomes opened the door they could hardly miss me and, stupid though they were, they would certainly have enough sense to realise I wasn't supposed to be there. Heaving a long and resigned sigh, I knew there was only one thing for it. I braced myself against the wall opposite the door and waited.

I didn't have to wait long.

'Check hut?' muttered the first gnome.

'Yeah, we check,' agreed the second.

'Got key?'

'No, you got key.'

'No, me not got key. You got key.'

At which point there was a minor scuffle, during which one or the other (it was hard to tell which) found that they did have the key after all.

Seconds later peace had broken out and the door opened cautiously. Two unkempt gnomes entered, preceded by their smell. As soon as they were in view, I let out a loud roar and rushed straight at them. It was no contest; a fine specimen of prime ham landing on two weedy security guards, who were already terrified at finding a very large and very angry creature in a hut that had most definitely been empty the last time they'd looked.

The impact took all three of us back out through the door and into a pool of mud on the ground beyond. Fortunately, the gnomes broke my fall, so they took the brunt of the landing as well as most of the mud. From the cracking noises I heard it was obvious that my fall wasn't all they'd broken. As I struggled free, one of them sank his teeth into my leg and I roared in pain.

'Pig,' howled the gnome to his companion as he recognised the taste. 'Not monster; pig.'

As I've already mentioned, gnomes are quite stupid. In this instance they were stupid enough not to realise they'd been injured, but not so stupid that they didn't recognise that their attacker was a pig. Figuring I was easier meat (possibly literally) now that they knew I wasn't a creature of the night, they seemed a bit more positive about chasing me. Staggering to their feet they lurched after me. Although I had the benefit of a fully working body, they had the advantage that they knew the terrain, so while I splashed my way across a sea of mud, they took drier, less slippery paths and slowly began to close in on me.

I have to say I was, by now, getting just a tad concerned as I was totally lost, had no idea where I was going and couldn't see my way off the building site. Meanwhile, Tweedledumb and Tweedledumber were gradually getting nearer – moving towards me in straight and presumably dry lines while I blundered around in circles getting muddier and wetter.

'That's 'im over there,' shouted one suddenly, and he scuttled in my direction.

I panicked and began to run. Heedless of where I was going, my only thought was to put as much distance between me and them as I possibly could.

Through the darkness I was just able to make out a small mound of earth. Maybe I could hide behind it. Figuring that it was a better option than wandering aimlessly around a building site in the dark, I dived over it. To my horror I found that, rather than landing on the ground beyond . . . well . . . remember those large holes I was talking about earlier? That's what was at the far side of that little mound. Bracing myself for impact, I landed with a resounding splash into a large pool of dirty water that covered me from head to toe in cold, wet mud. No need to worry about keeping clean now, but from what I could hear of my pursuers I was now so well camouflaged that they had problems finding me. They probably figured I was just another heap of mud.

'Where he go?' said one.

'Dunno,' said the other. 'Maybe he escape.'

'No, he still here. Me heard big splash.'

Clearly my new muddy ensemble allowed me to blend in perfectly with my surroundings. It may have been freezing and mucky but at least it was keeping me safe.

After a half-hearted search, the two gnomes gave up looking for me, finished their patrol and headed back to the hut. Rather than continue to wander in confusion around a dark building site, I chose to remain hidden where I was – cold and wet – until daylight. As soon as the skies began to lighten and I could see my way, I sneaked out of the building site and made my way home for a long, warm and much needed shower.

4

Revenge Is a Dish Best Served with Bacon

Later that morning – clean, dry and smelling so much nicer – I considered my options. I knew who was trying to frighten Miss Muffet out of business and I knew why. Now all I had to do was convince one of Grimmtown's most notorious criminals to back off and leave my client alone. I was more than a bit apprehensive as, even though I had something over Edna, she was a woman who didn't like to be crossed, especially if it involved her losing money – and I was quite certain that, in this instance, it would.

I required a plan; I needed it to work and, above all, I needed it fast. But I was stumped. Yes, the great detective didn't know what to do. As I sat at my desk waiting for inspiration, I had a quick read of the front page of our daily newspaper, the *Grimmtown Times*. The headlines were of the usual type:

Dumpty Wins Citizen of the Year for Third Year Running.
Grimmtown Goblins Reach Regional Finals.

Tuffet's Historic Status Confirmed by Local Archaeologist.
Mother Goose Wins Libel Case. Ugly Duckling Must Pay
   Damages.
Troll Finally Evicted from under Bridge. No More Tolls for
   Locals.

As I scanned them, the germ of a plan began to formulate. The
more I thought about it, the more excited I became. I might just
be able to pull this one out of the hat after all. I could even see
my own headline: 'Third Pig Saves the Day – Miss Muffet Stays.'
I grinned to myself and called Miss Muffet. It was time to swing
into action.

An hour later Miss Muffet and I were standing outside the front
door of Edna's massive mansion. It was a very impressive house
indeed – more like a palace. Built completely out of white marble,
it stood at the top of a hill overlooking the rest of Grimmtown.
If I were rich, it was just the kind of house I'd like to have.
Unfortunately, I had to make do with a grotty flat that gave a great
view of the local abattoir. It didn't really compare.

The massive door in front of us swung inwards and one of
Edna's personal bodyguards, a large silverback gorilla in a tuxedo,
stuck his head out for a look. There was a short pause while it
tried to figure out where it had seen me before, followed by a
spark of recognition and a very impressive accelerated leap backwards, his eyes bulging in fear. Miss Muffet was visibly impressed.
If I could scare a gorilla like that, I was clearly the right man for
the job. I neglected to tell her that, as a result of my last encounter
with Edna and her goons, I had a protective spell placed on me.
Any time one of the gorillas approached me, it began to shrink.
By the time it reached me it was usually the size of a puppy and
not in a position to do much by way of damage. It was a kind of
magical restraining order and was the only thing that was allowing

me to brazenly confront Edna in her lair. Well, would you want to take on two fully grown gorillas with bad attitude, bad breath, bad posture and bad dress sense – and that's on top of all the other representatives of the criminal brotherhood that hung around in Edna's? I'd met some of them before, during my last visit here, and it hadn't ended well for quite a few of them. I'm sure they'd relish the prospect of another visit from me.

While the gorilla disappeared – presumably to announce my arrival – another, less impressive denizen of the house came out to see who was at the door. There was a short pause while it too tried to figure out where it had seen me before, followed, eventually, by another spark of recognition. It seemed to be the day for them.

'Pig here,' he shouted over his shoulder.

'Pig from last night?' came a reply from inside.

'Yeah. Maybe now we sort him out.'

The first gnome rushed at me and then goggled in surprise as he was suddenly grabbed by the neck and swung sideways. As his colleague ran out after him, he suffered the same fate. Both had failed to notice the two rather large creatures that stood on either side of the door. We hadn't come unprepared.

'Ah, you haven't met my associates, Mr Lewis and Mr Carroll,' I said, indicating the two massive ogres each of whom was dangling a gnome by the neck. Well, did you really think I was just going to walk into Edna's unprepared – magic restraining order or not? I'm not that stupid.

Both gnomes gurgled something which might have been, 'Please let us go, we are in considerable discomfort,' or might just as easily have been, 'We are delighted to make the acquaintance of these two large gentlemen you cleverly brought with you as protection.' It was hard to tell, but one thing was for sure, they weren't in a position to do anything threatening to either Miss Muffet or me.

Mr Lewis and Mr Carroll had that kind of effect. Each was over eight feet tall and, when squeezed into a black tuxedo, looked very intimidating indeed. I had brought them with me exactly for this kind of situation.

'Gentlemen, I think you can put them down. I don't believe they will be too much trouble from now on.'

Both gnomes tried to nod their agreement – but it's difficult to nod when your neck is being tightly clenched by a hand the size of a beach ball.

At my signal, both of them were dumped unceremoniously on the ground, where they lay in a gnomish heap, blubbering and trying to skulk away. I almost felt sorry for them – almost.

'Okay chaps, let's go find Edna.' The ogres squeezed through the door after us as we entered the house. As we made our away across the wide lobby, gnomes and orcs scattered in all directions, clearly not wanting to engage our group in any form of physical contact. I can't say I blamed them; my minders had that effect on people.

Edna's office wasn't too difficult to find simply because it was the room that the loud voice screaming, 'Who the blazes is interrupting my telephone call?' was emanating from. Looking a lot braver than I actually was, I took a deep breath and swung open the office door.

Edna sat behind an ornate desk with a phone to her ear. As soon as she saw me she told whoever was on the other end of the line that she'd call them back and hung up.

'Well, well, well, if it isn't Harry Pigg, the world's greatest detective,' she sneered. Then she saw Miss Muffet. 'And look who's with him: Little Miss Muffet. Hey darling, seen any spiders lately?'

I decided that cutting to the chase was the best option. 'Okay Edna, we know what you're at,' I said. 'And just so as you know, Miss Muffet isn't selling, regardless of how you try to intimidate her.'

'Why, Harry, I have no idea what you're talking about. Why would I want to buy that tatty B&B? Tourist accommodation isn't really my style.'

'No, but building roads is,' I replied. 'I've seen the plans. Without Miss Muffet's house, your construction company can't complete that new motorway. It'll be very bad for your reputation if you don't; not to mention all the money you'll lose if the work doesn't finish on time. Maybe that's why you're trying to encourage her to sell up.'

To my surprise, Edna didn't seem at all worried that she'd been rumbled; in fact, she seemed unusually calm. An uneasy feeling started to gnaw at my stomach – and it wasn't because of what I'd had for breakfast. Something was very wrong here.

'From what I hear, things aren't too good in the local B&B trade. Strikes me that an infestation of spiders would be really bad for business,' she said. 'I could even see the health inspectors closing the premises down. Now that would be unfortunate. But if it did happen, I'd certainly feel for the owner. Losing your business is a terrible thing.'

'Indeed, but, of course, if it did close and you did buy it, you couldn't knock it down so your motorway could go through.'

'Sorry, Pigg, I have no idea what you mean.'

'Come on Edna, cut the nonsense. This is me, Harry Pigg, you're talking to. I know exactly what you're at.'

'No, I don't think you do,' Edna said, with the faintest of smiles beginning to smear her singularly unattractive features.

I decided to play my trump card so as to avoid an unnecessary 'oh yes I do', 'oh no you don't' conversation.

'Look, let's not play around any more. You want Miss Muffet out so you can build your road; she's not moving, so you're trying to scare her, but I've discovered that no matter what you do, you won't be able to demolish her house because . . .' – I whipped a copy of the day's newspaper out of my pocket like a cheap magician pulling a rabbit from his hat – 'tuffets are protected under Grimmtown bye-laws. They won't let you touch that house.' I was almost tempted to follow it with a ta-dah and a cheesy bow, but I figured Edna mightn't take too kindly to my theatricals.

To be honest, her reaction left a lot to be desired. Instead of gnashing her teeth and raging around the room in frustration at her scheme being thwarted, she sat at her desk looking at me as if I was a particularly interesting specimen of insect. The feeling that she knew something I didn't grew stronger.

'Tuffets, eh? Now that's a bit of a nuisance and no mistake,' she said. 'What specific tuffet are you talking about?'

'The tuffet in the back garden of the B&B; the one that Miss Muffet's family have been sitting on to eat their curds and whey for generations. Surely you've heard the song "Little Miss Muffet sat on a tuffet . . ." and so on. Tuffets are considered to be of immense historic importance, so they cannot be dug up, built over or altered in any way. It was in the paper. So even if you get the building, you still won't be able to build your road through it. Or if you do, I suspect you'll be neck deep in lawyers, archaeologists, environmentalists and politicians, all of whom will tie you up in enough red-tape to stall the building work for years.'

Edna grinned – the 'I have you now and you're not going to like it' grin. She slumped back into her chair and pressed a button on the desk. Seconds later a well-dressed and superior-looking gentleman entered the room carrying a folder. He had bureaucrat written all over him. 'You rang, ma'am,' he said, nose in the air.

'Tuffets, Laurence. They are protected, aren't they?'

'Yes, ma'am,' he replied. He was very well spoken.

'And that includes the tuffet in the Curds and Whey B&B?'

'Why, yes, ma'am.'

'The tuffet that we investigated when we were planning the motorway?'

'Why, yes again, ma'am.' He seemed to be enjoying this almost as much as Edna. I could sense she was about to spring her surprise and I knew it wouldn't be pleasant.

'The self-same tuffet that we agreed not to disturb and altered our plans so the motorway would go over and not through the premises?'

'Ma'am, you are, of course, correct once more.' And he looked at me and smirked.

Over the B&B?

Not through? Over?

Edna slapped the desktop and howled with glee. It was as if she could read my thoughts – which probably wasn't all that difficult as the expression on my face gave them away.

'Yes, Harry, over the B&B. So you see, we didn't need to put Miss Muffet out of business at all. In fact, she was never going to interfere with our plans. I do believe you've had a wasted journey – at least from your perspective. From my point of view, I don't think it's been wasted at all. In fact, I've quite enjoyed our little tête-à-tête. It certainly makes up for the last time we met.'

I didn't doubt it. Our last encounter resulted in her losing out on a very valuable antique and having a spell placed on her body-guards. It was payback time.

Happy that he'd been both of service to his mistress and had helped in the humiliation of one of her most hated foes, Laurence slimed out of the room, leaving me to face a gloating Edna.

'So you see, Pigg, you were wrong. Wrong, wrong, wrong. Just wait until word gets out, and, trust me, word will get out.' She was taking great pleasure in my discomfiture.

I decided that a dignified withdrawal was in order. Gesturing to Miss Muffet to follow, I stuck my snout in the air and strode purposefully out the door of Edna's office, her raucous laughter, the howling of orcs and roars of her gorillas all echoing around my humiliated head as I left.

I wasn't let be humiliated for long. We were no sooner out the door when Miss Muffet turned on me. She was, understandably, a bit miffed that things hadn't gone entirely to plan and, despite my (now battered) confidence, we were no further down the road to solving the case.

'Please, Miss Muffet,' I said in my most soothing and placatory voice (it was something I was actually good at – I regularly had to placate disgruntled clients). 'This was only the first step in solving the case. At least we've eliminated Edna and her construction company from our enquiries. Prior to this she was our main suspect.'

'Our only suspect,' Miss Muffet pointed out, somewhat miffed.

'Our only suspect for now,' I replied. 'Trust me; by the end of the day, I expect we'll have loads more.'

I didn't realise at the time exactly how prophetic that comment was going to be.

5

Jack Has a Bright Idea

I was back in the office once more. I seemed to be spending an awful lot of time there, which was probably a good indication that the case wasn't going too well. All my leads had turned out to be useless and – reluctant though I was to admit it – I was stumped. This case seemed to have more red herrings than a communist fishmonger and, to add insult to injury, even Edna had got one-up on me. Now, as if to mock my incompetence, I was depending on my two 'partners' for assistance – and that was something I never thought I'd hear myself say.

To be fair, both of them were taking the case seriously and were coming up with ideas, even if most of them were either useless or wildly impractical.

'That is most strange,' Basili mused when I told them about my visit to Frogg Prince Pets. 'I would have been most certain that a vile orc person would have been belonging to Edna.'

Another vile person, I thought. 'Well, if what she said is true then she is really out of the equation and I've no reason to doubt her. Her story is too easy to check out. And if he's not Edna's then whose is he? I thought she had the market cornered in cheap orc labour.'

'The orc is one thing, but if it's not Edna and it's not that mad old woman who lives in the Shoe Hotel, then who's doing it?' said Jack.

'That's the question, isn't it,' I replied. 'If we knew that, then we wouldn't be here, would we?'

Then Basili asked the question that set the wheels spinning – or at least rotating slowly – in my mind once more.

'Why are all those people still staying in this place?'

I know the same question had crossed my mind when I visited Miss Muffet's earlier, but I hadn't given it much thought since. Basili did have a point.

'I don't know, but it would want to be a very good reason, wouldn't it?'

'Indeed, many people are being most scared of spiders and they certainly would not be staying anywhere where creatures like that are in such large numbers.'

'If I was them, I'd have moved out ages ago,' said Jack. 'I don't mind creepy-crawlies, but it can't be a lot of fun staying there with webs and stuff.'

'That's why I intend to go back there and talk to them. If they have a reason then I need to know what it is. Maybe then I can get some idea of who's responsible for the spiders.'

'Oh, yes, once more we are doing the interviews,' exclaimed Basili, clapping his hands in excitement. 'I love when we are talking to our suspects.'

Jack raised his hand. 'But won't that sort of give the game away. If they know we're investigators, won't they just lie to us? We won't find anything out that way.'

'You know Jack, you're right. There must be another way, one that won't make it obvious who we are.'

Jack's hand was still in the air. 'I've got a great idea, Harry.'

I doubted it, but I indicated for him to continue.

'Remember when we were at the North Pole and we needed to get information from that bogus elf?'

I nodded. 'Why is that relevant?'

'Disguises.'

'Excuse me?'

'We could disguise ourselves as guests.' Jack waved his arms in excitement. 'No one would know who we are and we could mingle, talk to everyone and make them reveal something.'

I was about to point out how difficult it would be to disguise a pig, a fat ex-genie and a small boy as anything that would successfully pass muster when Basili chimed in.

'Oh, that is a most excellent idea, young Jack. We are going undercover in a secret mission. How exciting.'

And how stupid, I thought. We'd never get away with it. We wouldn't last ten minutes in the B&B. But the more I thought about it, the more the idea refused to go away. Maybe it could work. Our cover would have to be spectacular if we were to avoid discovery, but it might be the only way to find out what was going on. At least that was my justification when I agreed to it. In fact, I was so desperate and unable to come up with any other idea that, really, I had no choice.

'Okay then, we're going undercover,' I said.

Jack jumped up and down in excitement.

'But not you,' I said to him. 'It could be dangerous.'

'Yes, but you didn't say that when I was disguised as the elf, did you?' His disappointment was obvious.

'But this is much more dangerous. We won't be able to keep our eye on you like we did then and there's always the danger of blowing your cover.'

'May I be making a suggestion,' Basili interrupted.

I waved at him to continue.

'Mr Harry and I will be talking to the guests, yes?'

305

I nodded.

'Well, will we not be needing a someone to be keeping an eye on the people who are working there too?'

'Yes,' Jack shouted. 'I could be in the kitchen, helping out and stuff and, at the same time, keeping my eyes open.'

It made sense and he'd probably be safe enough there. After all, what harm could come to him in a kitchen?

'All right then team, it's agreed. Now what shall we go as?'

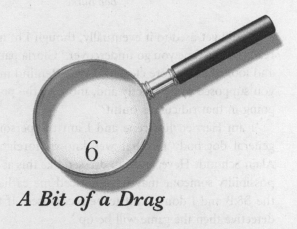

6

A Bit of a Drag

'Are you guys really serious about this?' Gloria, my receptionist, had offered to give some tips on make-up and clothes, but seemed to be having second thoughts now that she'd actually seen our disguises. At that moment she was touching up my face with mascara and gloss – whatever they were – and seemed to be finding it tremendously difficult to refrain from smirking – if not guffawing loudly. 'There,' she said, putting her magical make-up kit away. 'You're done, but I have to say it: even if you put lipstick on a pig, it's still a pig.'

With as much dignity as I could muster – which wasn't a lot considering I was wearing a long blonde wig, high heels and a black minidress – I pointed out that, as ideas went, our one had legs (and probably better ones than mine) and, if it came off (insert whatever gratuitous pun you like here), would probably help hugely in breaking the case.

I stood up and tottered around the office, teetering from side to side as I tried to keep my balance. 'How do women stay upright in these heels,' I asked. 'Is tightrope walking a genetic trait that all women have, or something?'

'You'll get used to it eventually, though I'm not sure you'll be ready by the time you go undercover.' Gloria paused for a second and looked even more closely at me. 'Remind me again, who are you supposed to be exactly and, more to the point, why are you going in that ridiculous outfit?'

'I am Harriet du Crêpe and I am the personal assistant and general dogsbody for that well-known foreign movie-director Alain Schmidt-Heye, and I'm dressed like this as there's a distinct possibility someone may have noticed me earlier when I visited the B&B and I don't want to be recognised. If they know I'm a detective then the game will be up.'

Gloria began to erupt into gales of laughter. 'So let me get this right. You, a large male pig, are going undercover as a female PA to an international movie-director who can only be—' She never got to finish her sentence. Before she could say any more, the door from my office, where Basili had been changing, opened and he entered the room. His entrance certainly had an impact, although not, perhaps, the one we might have expected. Gloria collapsed on the desk, laughing uncontrollably, tears of hilarity streaming from her eyes.

'Is your lady assistant being most amused at my outfit?' said a somewhat indignant Basili. 'I am thinking that, after studying pictures of many famous directors of movies, that it is perhaps a most accurate representation.'

I wasn't sure what illustrations he'd actually studied, but I wasn't convinced that his outfit was as representative as he thought. Brown knee-high riding boots covered tan plus-fours. On his upper body, a lurid red smoking jacket and a white silk shirt jostled for prominence. The overall over-the-top effect was completed by a white silk scarf draped casually around his neck, white gloves, a cigarette holder (with no actual cigarette) dangling from his mouth and a black beret rakishly plonked on his head. He did look a bit extreme, but time wasn't on our side. We had to make do with what we were able to pick up at Freddie's Fancy Dress Store, having sent Basili out with a shopping list.

In hindsight, maybe I should have gone myself. But it was too late now.

Gloria had recovered some of her composure. 'So you go into Miss Muffet's B&B, you snoop around dressed like that and you hope people are going to give something away – other than an award for the most ludicrous outfit in the house. And on that note, how exactly are you going to justify your presence there in the first instance?'

'Our story is that we're scouting locations for a haunted house movie that Basili – I mean Mr Schmidt-Heye – will be filming early next year. Miss Muffet's is a prime candidate, I think you'll agree.'

'I'll take your word for it, but I think you need to get in character, Harry; the voice needs to be a little higher, otherwise people will see through your disguise – assuming they don't cop to you as soon as you walk in the door.'

I puffed out my (enhanced) chest indignantly. 'I was a very talented actor when I was younger, I'll have you know. I played a leading role in my school's Nativity play and my performance got great reviews in the school newsletter.'

Gloria looked like she was biting her lip. 'If you say so,' she said. 'On a more serious note, how are you going to get to Miss Muffet's? You're going to have to look the part from the moment you arrive.'

'Hah, I knew you'd ask that. Ali Baba still owes me a favour after I sorted him out at Christmas, so he's allowing me to use one of his stretch magic carpets. It'll make quite an entrance.'

'Could you not have used an ordinary limo; you know, one with actual wheels?'

'I couldn't afford to rent one and, anyway, Ali doesn't use them; he flies everywhere, so magic carpet it is.'

'Just as long as you don't fall off,' smirked Gloria.

'This isn't one of the sporty, streamlined ones Ali normally uses. It's a big one with loads of room – and seat-belts. We should be fine. Anyway, it's a short ride when you're not on the ground.'

I gestured to Basili. 'Right Mr Director, you ready to go?'

'But Mr Harry, I know nothing about the making of the movies. What will I be saying if someone should be talking to me?'

'Look, you're a big-time movie-director so act like one. You haven't got time to speak to mere mortals like the guests at the B&B. If anyone tries to engage you in conversation, just sneer and refer them to me. As your PA, my job is to answer any questions. While we're in there, your job is to listen, okay? Just think of these words and you'll be fine: arrogant, superior, enigmatic.'

Basili nodded. 'Ah, now I am seeing. You want me to be acting just like you.'

Before I could reply with furious indignation at the slur on my impeccable character, the phone on Gloria's desk rang. 'Yes,' she said, 'they're here. I'll send them right out.' Hanging up, she said, 'Your magic carpet awaits.'

Together, Basili and I headed for the door.

'Be careful, won't you?' Gloria said, grinning. 'And remember: stay in character at all times, you don't want to blow your cover.'

'We'll be fine, daaaaarling,' I drawled in my finest PA voice.

I could have sworn I heard an 'I'm not so sure' from the office as the door closed behind us, but I couldn't be certain.

I was so eager to get to Miss Muffet's and begin our undercover operation that I made a fatal mistake as I closed the door behind me. I still hadn't quite mastered the art of woman walking, so forgetting to take off my shoes, I teetered on the landing and took a tentative step forward before stumbling over the first step and sliding down the rest of them on my backside, landing in an undignified heap on the floor below. There are twenty-four steps from my office to street level and I felt every single one of them as I bounced my way down.

Struggling to my feet, I tugged my dress down and, ignoring the smirks of our chauffeur, clambered aboard the stretch magic carpet, making sure I was securely strapped in before taking off. On our way across town, I briefed Basili some more on the dos and don'ts of being a movie-director.

'When we get there, do not get off this carpet until I say so. It's my job to make sure that everything is ready for you inside. Say nothing unless I ask you a question and nod knowingly if I point anything out. Do not open any doors; I'll make sure they are opened for you. You will eat alone at a separate table. That will give you an opportunity to study everyone as I'll be eating with them.'

Basili looked uncertain. 'I am not so sure about this. What if I am making a mistake?'

'Don't worry about it, I'll be there to clean up any mess, but, if you don't say anything, there's probably no way you'll get into trouble.' Considering his track record I wasn't so sure, but I had to build up his confidence as best I could.

The fresh air blasting our faces as we threaded our way through the buildings of downtown Grimmtown reminded me of something that, despite its obviousness, I had completely failed to take into consideration: the ex-genie's flatulence problem. 'Basili, under no circumstances are you to fart. It will completely undermine your credibility. I might be able to argue one or two of them away as sewage problems or something, but if it happens consistently it may damage our relationship with the guests.' Not to mention their lungs, vision and general well-being.

'I will do my utmost, Mr Harry, but it is a most remarkably difficult thing to do.'

As if I didn't have enough problems already.

'Where is Jack?' asked Basili. 'Surely he is being here with us?'

'He's already at the B&B, settling in. I spoke to his mother and got her okay for him to be a kitchen boy at weekends. Not only will he let us know what's going on behind the scenes with the staff, but he'll get a bit of pocket money as well. The only drawback is he'll have to work for it.'

'Ah, yes, of course, the staff. Isn't it always the butler that is doing these things? Perhaps we should be taking a closer look at this man.'

'No, Basili, it isn't, and I'm not even sure Miss Muffet employs a butler. Let's not start jumping to conclusions just yet.'

'You are right.' His face dropped. 'I am still so very new to this game of detectives. I have very much to learn.'

I patted him on the shoulder. 'But you're learning all the time. We're nearly there, so remember what I told you and, above all, please don't fart.'

Basili gave me a weak and totally unconvincing smile as the magic carpet glided to a halt outside the B&B.

'Okay, we're on. Don't move until I get back. If anyone tries to engage you in conversation just ignore them and act superior.'

Basili nodded and looked glum.

I rummaged in my handbag. 'Here, wear these,' I said, handing him a pair of sunglasses. He looked at them doubtfully.

'But we are in winter and there is no sun to be shining.'

'It doesn't matter. Movie people wear shades all the time, indoors and outdoors. It's a sort of a trademark.' And it will hide some more of your face, I said to myself.

Right, it was time to get fully into character. Chest out, balance, do not wobble and remember you're a PA. I recited this little mantra over and over as I hopped gingerly down from the magic carpet. Taking a deep breath, I stepped forward, put my shoe down very carefully and then repeated the operation with my other foot. I found that if I swayed gently from side to side it made walking a little bit easier. Balancing like I was on the deck of a small ship in a hurricane, I rolled towards the door of the B&B, opened it and stepped into the world of the movie business.

7

Quiet on Set

What did I know about being a PA? Very little. The sum total of my research had been three gossip magazines Gloria kept in her desk drawer and a quick viewing of a documentary on the Grimmtown Film Festival. It didn't make me an expert, but it gave me something to go on as I entered Miss Muffet's B&B.

'No, no, no, this won't do at all,' I shrieked as I strode purposefully into the lobby. 'Mr Schmidt-Heye must have total privacy. This area must be cleared at once.'

As there was no one there apart from Miss Muffet herself, who was manning the reception desk, it probably didn't have the effect I was expecting, but I figured I might as well get into character immediately.

'Mr Pigg, is that you?' Miss Muffet seemed to have difficulty deciding whether to laugh or to stare. Maybe I should have briefed her in a bit more detail about our plans.

'Yes,' I hissed. 'But today I'm Harriet du Crêpe, remember?'

'I know, you told me. I just wasn't expecting . . . this,' she whispered back.

I didn't ask her to elaborate; I just requested that she play along.

By now, some of the guests, attracted no doubt by my high-decibel delivery, were gathering on the first-floor landing and at the entrance to the dining room.

'Please,' I shouted. 'Can we have everyone out of here now?

'What's going on?' asked a small, old man at the dining-room door. 'Is there a fire? Should we evacuate? I'll get my coat.'

'No, no.' Miss Muffet tried to defuse the situation. 'We have a new guest arriving and he likes his privacy. Perhaps if you could all go back to what you were doing, we might get it sorted out.'

'So there's no fire then?'

'No.'

'Or any emergency?'

'Definitely not.'

'Good,' said the old man. 'I'm going back to my breakfast then.'

'Thank you, Mr Spratt,' Miss Muffet said. 'Coffee should be along shortly. That's Jack Spratt,' she whispered to me as the guests began to disperse. 'He's here with his wife. They stayed here after they got married and are revisiting now to celebrate their anniversary.'

From the look of him, that would have been about two hundred years ago. 'And they're still staying here despite the . . . um . . . difficulties.'

'Oh, yes, they're quite adamant. Apparently it has huge nostalgic value for them.'

It would want to, I thought. It's the only reason anyone would want to stay here.

Figuring that Basili had been waiting outside long enough, I decided it was time for his grand entrance. 'Good,' I announced. 'The area is clear. Mr Schmidt-Heye can enter now.' I rushed outside and beckoned at the chauffeur.

'What?' he grunted.

'Help Mr Schmidt-Heye down.'

'Hey, Ali Baba said I was only to drive you here. He said nothing about this.'

The prospect of helping a large ex-genie off a magic carpet while wearing heels didn't appeal to me. 'Just do it, okay. Do you really want me to tell him you wouldn't help us?'

With a resigned groan, he got off the carpet, walked around to the side and held out his arm. 'Okay, big guy, down you get.'

'Respect, please,' I ordered. 'This is a famous movie-director. You will refer to him as "sir" at all times.'

'No, he's not. He's that fat bloke that hangs around with you when you're not wearing a dress. He's a movie-director in the same way that I'm an astronaut.'

'Keep your voice down, you'll blow our cover.'

The chauffeur smirked. 'Oh, I think you're doing that all by yourself. You don't need my help.'

I marched up to him and grabbed him in a very unlady-like way. 'Just oblige me, okay?'

The chauffeur's face turned white as I tightened my grip. 'You're the boss,' he wheezed and turned to Basili. 'If . . . sir . . . would care to take my arm.'

'That's much better,' I said as he helped Basili down from the magic carpet. 'I'll see your boss gets a good report.'

The chauffeur glowered as he jumped back into his seat, but, sensibly, refused to comment any further. Seconds later the magic carpet shot into the sky and we were on our own once more.

'Right, we're good to go. I've cleared the reception area, so, hopefully, no one will approach us. Remember, if they do, let me do the talking.'

Basili nodded glumly and followed me inside where Miss Muffet was waiting to greet her newest guest. 'Mr Schmidt-Heye, what a great honour it is having you here in our humble abode.' Wow, she certainly knew how to fawn. Then I noticed that she was

317

looking at Basili expectantly. I nudged him hard in the ribs. 'That's you, remember?'

'Yes, you are most welcome.' He tapped his cigarette holder on the edge of the reception desk. 'Now please to be showing me my room. I must lie down. It has been a most horrendous trip.'

Wow, the ride from my office hadn't been that bad.

'Yes, of course. Your room is this way. If you'll follow me.' Miss Muffet led us up the stairs. Lining the wall all the way up was a series of paintings. I glanced at them as we passed. They all seemed to show pictures of the same person doing something adventurous. In one picture he was waving to a large group of people on the ground as he ascended in a hot-air balloon; in another he was in a speedboat waving once more at a pursuing fleet.

'Family portraits?' I asked Miss Muffet.

'Sort of,' she replied, but made no attempt to elaborate further.

I shrugged my shoulders, but decided to drop the subject, seeing as she clearly didn't want to talk about it. But something about the pictures nagged at me. For some reason, the person featured in them rang a bell, but recognition just wouldn't come.

We arrived on the first-floor landing and were led into a large bedroom at the front of the house. To her credit, Miss Muffet had made a huge effort to remove any trace of spiders, but they were already reclaiming the corners and would probably have retaken the whole room by teatime.

Basili looked around, his head in the air. 'I am supposing this will have to do,' he sniffed, running a gloved finger along the dressing table and holding it up for scrutiny.

'It's okay, Basili,' I whispered. 'We're on our own now. No one can see you. You can drop the act.'

'Thank goodness for that,' he said as he collapsed on the bed, which groaned ominously at the intrusion. 'Being an undercover operative is being most difficult.'

'You've only been undercover for five minutes and all you've had to do is walk up a flight of stairs, how difficult can it be?'

'Ah, yes, but I am struggling greatly to find my inner director and my motivation. Why am I doing this? What are this man's issues and struggles?'

He seemed to be taking his acting a bit too seriously. 'Look, you're not auditioning for a role in a real film. Just stand around and be superior like we said. Just stay shtum and you'll be fine.'

We were interrupted by a knock on the door. 'Quick, back in character,' I ordered. 'Who is it? Mr Schmidt-Heye is resting after his long journey and cannot be disturbed.'

'Harry, it's me, Jack,' whispered a voice from outside the door. I quickly opened it and dragged Jack into the room. He took one look at us and fell on the floor laughing.

'Jack, this isn't the time,' I said. 'What have you to report?'

With difficulty, Jack composed himself and sat up. 'I'm working in the kitchen, but it's not a very nice place. The cook, Mrs Hubbard, is very bossy. I don't think she likes me.'

Miss Muffet nodded at Jack's comment. 'Mrs Hubbard runs a tight kitchen. Just do as she says, work hard and you'll be okay.'

'And then there's the waiter or butler or whatever he is. He's a bit strange; won't talk to anyone.'

'Aha,' said Basili. 'I am being right, there is a butler. He is doing the crime.'

'Oh, don't be ridiculous, old Mr Zingiber has been with the family for years. He looks after serving the meals and making sure the guests are being cared for. He's certainly not responsible for this crime.'

Jack pulled at the hem of my dress. 'And I think he's made of gingerbread too. I'm terrified in case I spill something on him and he melts.'

Miss Muffet overheard. 'Don't worry about him; he's pretty stale by now. It'd take quite a deluge to soften him up.'

'Anyone else in the kitchen I should know about?' I asked.

'Just Polly. She helps Mrs Hubbard with the cooking. She's a nice girl; none too bright, but very good with food, making tea, that sort of thing,' said Miss Muffet.

It was time to bring the meeting to order. 'Right, now that everyone's here, let's go over it once more: look out for anyone acting suspiciously, don't talk to anyone unless you have to and, if you find anything out, come and tell me. Got that?' Nods all around. 'Good, now let's go and solve this case.'

Jack scurried back to the kitchen and Miss Muffet made to follow him. She turned to me as she reached the door. 'Will you be dining with us tonight?'

The thought of hundreds of spiders watching me as I ate, waiting for an opportunity to help themselves, made my stomach cartwheel, but I had to meet the other guests. 'Mr Schmidt-Heye will dine at a table alone; I will eat with the other guests.'

'Very good. Dinner is at seven.'

Yeah: me, the guests and a tribe of tarantulas. 'Lovely,' I muttered. 'Oh, by the way, where's my room?'

'I put you in the room next door. Unfortunately, we didn't have time to clean it out. I'm afraid you'll just have to ignore the spiders.'

Fantastic.

8

A Bluffer's Guide to Polite Conversation

The dining room looked like it had been decorated for a wedding. White strands of web hung in all the corners and were draped like netting across the furniture. Miss Havisham would have felt right at home here. Someone had made an effort to clean the room; the webs on the floor had been swept into corners where they piled up like indoor snowdrifts. As it was evening the spiders were more active too. Armies of them marched across the floor or dangled from the ceiling seeking out food. Miss Muffet had thought ahead though. As well as kitchen-boy duties, Jack had been drafted in, with a sweeping brush, to attack any arachnids that came too close.

He was being kept very busy.

In order to maintain appearances as well as giving Basili an opportunity to eavesdrop, I'd managed to get him a table all to himself in the corner, where he was the subject of many curious looks. If anyone tried to approach the table I intercepted them with a 'Mr Schmidt-Heye wants to be alone' and what I thought was a very forbidding stare. It seemed to work, as any would-be fans slunk away without disturbing him.

Satisfied that Basili wouldn't be talking to anyone, I left him to his meal and took my seat at the nearest table. Mr Spratt and a woman I assumed to be Mrs Spratt sat on either side of me. Across the table was a pompous-looking gentleman. 'Nimble. John B. Nimble,' he'd replied curtly when I'd introduced myself. 'Antiques.' I wasn't sure whether he was referring to his job or to the other two guests at the table. Then he went back to reading his newspaper, ignoring the rest of us.

'Charming,' I muttered.

'Oh, he's not too bad once you get to know him,' said Mr Spratt. 'By the way, I'm Jack and this is my wife, Muriel.' He indicated his wife, who was as round as he was thin, and she gave me a tiny wave. Side by side they looked like the number 10 and were in direct contrast to John Nimble in that they never stopped talking. Muriel Spratt had confirmed what Miss Muffet had said: the Spratts were celebrating fifty years of marriage by returning to the guest house they'd stayed in for their honeymoon. Miss Muffet's B&B in Grimmtown; wow, they had really pushed the boat out the day they got married.

'And how about you dear?' asked Mrs Spratt. 'Is there any romance in your life?'

'I'm firmly focused on my career,' I bluffed. 'There's no time in my life for a relationship at present', which wasn't entirely untrue either.

As I watched I couldn't help but notice that the Spratts had a strange habit of sharing the contents of their plates with each other. She'd cut the fat off her meat and pass the rest on to her husband and he reciprocated by passing the fat from his food on to her plate. They ate so fast they got to finish everything before the spiders got to it. Mrs Spratt noticed me watching them eat and giggled nervously. 'It's a diet thing,' she said. 'He likes the lean bits and I like the rest, so we never go hungry.'

I spent the rest of the meal beating spiders away from my plate as I tried to eat my salad faster than they could steal it. It was a close contest, but victory was mine – the dead arachnids scattered around my plate testament to the brutal struggle. All the way through I fielded questions about Basili's solitude; all my answers being variations on a theme of being anti-social with a fear of being touched or spoken to.

After dinner we all migrated to the lounge for 'mingling and conversation', as Miss Muffet put it. From what I could see, it seemed to mean an evening of awkward silences and everyone standing around looking very self-conscious. In fact, until one of the guests, Mr Nocchio, a tall, thin gentleman with a funny lumbering gait and skin the texture of wood, came up and quizzed me about Basili, who was standing behind me still trying to look superior, we might have all been in a very arty silent movie (in black and white, of course).

'Who eez thees movie-director you 'ave behind you?' he asked in heavily accented English.

'He's the famous Alain Schmidt-Heye,' I replied haughtily.

'Famous? I 'ave not 'eard of 'eem.'

There was a chorus of 'me neither's as everyone in the room suddenly took an interest in our conversation. It was time for some arty-type bluffing.

'Of course you haven't heard of him, unless you're the kind of discerning movie-goer who enjoys documentaries. He's very highly thought of on the global cinematic stage.' Attacking their artistic pretensions while fabricating Basili's cinematic catalogue might divert their interest. If they figured they didn't know as much about high art as they thought, they might just go along with what I was saying so as not to appear less cultured. Ah, intellectual snobbery, how I admire thee.

'Ah, yes, now that you mention it, I do recall reading something about him in the arts section of the *Grimmtown Globe*. Didn't he do that film on the secret life of Prince Charming?' said a well-dressed man leaning against the mantelpiece at the far side of the room. I was surprised he'd even noticed us; he seemed to be constantly keeping Miss Muffet in his eye line as she hovered around her guests, making sure they were comfortable. What was making her so interesting, I wondered? This well-dressed man now needed to be kept in my eye line; that was suspicious behaviour – in my book at any rate.

'Yes, that was one of Mr Schmidt-Heye's,' I replied, going with the flow. 'It was very well received and there are rumours it may get nominated for a Gifty.' If I was going to bluff, I might as well go all the way and spin out as convincing a back-story as I could. It would only have to hold up to scrutiny for another day or so. After that it hopefully wouldn't matter.

'Gifty? What's a Gifty?' asked a small, dapper man, sitting in one of the armchairs by the fire.

'It's the Grimmtown International Film and Television Awards, darling,' I said, rolling my eyes. 'Goodness, do you people know anything about culture?'

There was a brief pause followed by much knowing nodding and variations on 'Ah, the Awards. I didn't realise they were known as Giftys by the masses.' Nothing like intellectual pretension to aid in a cover-up.

Basili nodded smugly and raised his cigarette holder to his mouth once more.

The dapper man, whom, based on a process of elimination, I suspected to be either Thomas Piper or William Winkie, stood up and walked across the room towards me.

Uh, oh, I thought. This isn't good.

'I much preferred your earlier, funnier material,' he said, trying to approach Basili. 'Don't you do that kind of stuff any more?'

I interrupted and blocked the spoofer. 'Mr Schmidt-Heye appreciates his fans, but doesn't like to be touched. You may address any comments through me.'

Then, to my horror, Basili decided to engage in some role-play – and in direct contravention of orders. 'There is a favourite film of mine that you are liking? I am most gratified to meet a true fan, and, perhaps, you are telling us your name.' Nice one Basili; maybe he might turn out to be good at this after all.

The dapper man preened at being acknowledged. 'Willie Winkie's the name,' he said, stretching out a hand that I immediately slapped away, giving him a warning look at the same time.

If he was Winkie then the man by the fireplace must be Thomas Piper. Licken and Lurkey I already knew – and, fortunately, they weren't in the room – so that meant that the only person I hadn't met was Queenie Harte.

So far, so good – now all I had to do was find out what they did. 'Mr Schmidt-Heye is thinking about moving from documentaries into dramatic motion pictures. To that end he is engaging with a number of significant backers with a view to raising funds for this exciting venture. If any of you are interested, perhaps you might provide me with your details. So far, all our investors have received a significant return on their investment.'

There was an excited murmuring and a swathe of business cards was thrust into my trotters.

'What kind of movie are you considering making?' The formerly abrupt Mr Nimble sat up straight in his chair and suddenly seemed very interested too.

'We've received a very promising script for a horror film that we believe we can use to take the genre into significantly new directions. In fact, that's why we're staying here. We feel that it may be a great location for some of the opening scenes, set in a haunted house.' More nodding and knowing looks – suddenly they were all experts.

Ah, what a bit of pandering to artistic snobbery can get you.

Just as they were all falling over themselves to tell me how great Basili was, how they were secretly fans of his all along and how they'd be most interested in discussing investment opportunities, there was the sound of the front door banging and loud shouting from the hallway. Every head – except mine and Piper's – swivelled apprehensively towards the lounge door. I turned to Basili and whispered, 'Be on your toes, things might get a bit out of hand.'

He looked confused. 'Why, Mr Harry, what is happening?'

Before I could answer, the lounge door crashed open and in walked a giant chicken garbed in a clown costume, followed closely by a much smaller turkey dressed as a nun. My worst fears were confirmed: Licken and Lurkey had come home to roost – and from the way his eyes narrowed, Licken had immediately seen through my disguise. It was time for some quick action. I rushed towards him arms outstretched. 'Licken darling, it's been so long. How ARE you?' I exclaimed while grabbing him by the shoulders and attempting an air-kiss. *Mwuah, Mwuah.* 'Don't let on it's me,' I whispered into his ear. 'I'll explain later. As far as you're concerned I'm Harriet, okay?'

To his credit, Licken bought into my story and nodded vacantly, trying to catch up with what was going on.

'And Lurkey too, how wonderful!' Another air-kiss, followed up with a hug that squeezed the breath out of him before he could say anything. 'Not a word,' I hissed. 'Or I tell all about you know what.'

Before he could respond, I turned to the other guests. 'I'm sure you've all already met Grimmtown's foremost comedy duo, Lurkey and Licken,' I announced. 'They're very old and very dear friends of mine,' a statement that wasn't exactly untrue either. 'They're such darling people and I'm so glad to see them again after such a long time.' Behind me I could hear Lurkey gasping for air while Licken seemed to be whispering in his ear. Hopefully Lurkey wouldn't say anything stupid, though he was by far the dumber of that particular duo, so I wasn't sure he'd caught on. Licken, on the other hand, was giving it large.

'Ah, yes, our dear friend Harriet. Remember when she used to sell ice-cream at the Grimmtown Grand Old Comedy and then the punters used to chuck it right back at her. Ah, she's come a long way since then.' Then he caught sight of Basili. 'Is that who I think it is? Surely it can't be—'

'Yes, you're right,' I interrupted before he said something stupid. 'It's Alain Schmidt-Heye,' adding, 'the famous movie-director', when I saw the confused look on his face.

'Oh, yeah, right; him,' Licken stammered, clearly confused.

I needed to get them out of the room before they gave something away, but at the same time I couldn't leave Basili there on his own with his new fan club. He'd definitely give something away.

'Sir,' – I grabbed Basili by the arm – 'perhaps we could take these two fine gentlemen outside to catch up, so as not to bore our other friends here.'

'Nonsense,' said Willie Winkie. 'We wouldn't be bored at all. I'm sure your tales of the glamorous showbiz life you lead would be the perfect after-dinner conversation piece.'

I was about to spin out an excuse as to why we had to leave the room right that second – just as soon as I could think of one – when I saw something that sent the case in an entirely new and unwelcome direction. Above the mantelpiece, almost totally obscured by webs, was a portrait. This wasn't just any portrait, though. Oh, no, even hidden by all those strands of webbing, the face in the picture was immediately recognisable: Grimmtown's most notorious pirate, Sinbad El Muhfte. Now that I could see his face clearly, I also recognised him as the subject in all those pictures on the stairway wall.

Then the links began to coalesce in my mind.

El Muhfte. Not much of a stretch to Muffet.

Sinbad El Muhfte and Miss Muffet; the names were slightly different, but the similarity was surely no coincidence.

Now, looking more closely at the portrait, I could see the family resemblance and the awful truth struck me: Miss Muffet must be Sinbad's daughter. The daughter of one of the most famous criminals in the town's history, who was currently doing a twenty-to-life stretch in Grimmtown's maximum security prison. And in all the pictures on the stairway wall, he wasn't waving to adoring fans, as I had originally assumed; oh no, they were portraits of him taunting the pursuing police, having successfully evaded them once more.

Now I'm not a great believer in coincidences, so considering who daddy was and combining it with Miss Muffet's current predicament, I got a horrible feeling that this case had just taken a major turn for the worse – and I was smack in the middle of it.

9

At Midnight,
All the Detectives

I tried not to show any reaction, but Basili sensed something was wrong. 'Ms du Crêpe,' he whispered. 'You are fine, yes?' I waved him away. 'Yes, yes, I'm okay. I'm just a bit faint. Must have been something I ate.'

Willie Winkie grabbed me by the elbow and escorted me to one of the fireside armchairs. 'Here, sit down.' He turned to the other guests. 'Can someone get a glass of water?'

I tried to stand up, but a restraining arm kept me firmly in the seat. 'I'm fine, honestly.' It was time for some drama. I slumped across the chair and brought my hand to my forehead. 'I'm just feeling a little light-headed; perhaps if someone can help me to my room, some rest might do me good.'

A glass of liquid was thrust into my trotters. 'Here, drink this,' said Willie Winkie.

I grabbed the glass and emptied it in a single slug – and promptly nearly brought it back up again when the burning liquid hit my stomach. It felt like I was dying. My lungs heaved for breath and my eyes were streaming tears. Had someone seen through my cover and tried to poison me?

'Nothing like a glass of brandy to sort you out,' bellowed John Nimble. 'I always have a snifter after my evening meal. Good for the internal workings.'

So, not poison then. Based on what I'd drunk, I figured my internal workings would never work the same again. I waved my arms at Basili and between coughs and noisy intakes of air I managed to wheeze the word 'bed'. Basili took the hint, dragged me to my feet and hauled me out of the lounge. It wasn't the most dignified of exits, but at least it worked. Supporting me on his shoulder, he struggled manfully upstairs before dropping me on the floor of his room. I hit the ground with an undignified thud.

'Sorry, Mr Harry,' he apologised. 'I am not being able to carry you any further.'

I lay on the carpet gasping. 'Now I really do need a glass of water.' I was gasping even more when one was flung in my face. 'Please be snapping out of it,' said Basili. 'It was only a glass of brandy. Now perhaps you are explaining the meaning of your behaviour.'

Dripping, I hauled myself upright and managed to stagger to the bed. Sitting on the edge I faced the ex-genie, took a deep breath and tried to explain what I'd seen.

'Sinbad El Muhfte, pirate, freebooter and all-round bad guy is Miss Muffet's father,' I said, a tad dramatically. The effect was lessened by the blank expression on Basili's face. 'You've never heard of Sinbad?'

Basili shook his head doubtfully. 'I knew of a Sinbad many years ago when I was very young. He was an adventurer and having the most exciting time. Is it being the same person?'

'Your Sinbad was this Sinbad's ancestor, if memory serves. Sinbad El Muhfte was Grimmtown's most notorious pirate. Basically, he helped himself to the contents of any ship that tried to sail into the port. It impacted the sea-trade in and out of the city for years until he was finally captured and jailed for a very long time.'

'So?' asked Basili.

'So, the big question that people asked after he was sent down was: what happened to all his riches? He had looted lots of valuable antiques, paintings, that sort of thing. He was quite the collector. From what I remember, he didn't put it in banks or invest too much of it so as to keep the law off his trail. There were lots of rumours that he'd hidden it somewhere. Over the years people have tried to find where he'd stashed it, but eventually, when no one found anything, they began to believe that it never existed. The rumours eventually died out.'

'But why is that having anything to be doing with our present case?' asked Basili.

'It may not, but if someone got wind of where the fortune was stashed and let's just say that it was somewhere in this house – which was probably his house after all – then wouldn't it be very easy to search if the owner had been scared off the premises?'

'Is it not being stretching things just a little bit?' said Basili. 'I am still thinking that someone trying to be putting Miss Muffet out of business is a most strong motive.'

'Well, I'm not going to dismiss it just yet,' I replied. 'But I haven't been able to find anyone with any pressing need to acquire the house. We still have to follow up this lead though. I feel that this could break the case.'

'Maybe you are right. Perhaps we are following it up in the tomorrow.' Basili stood up and looked pointedly at where I was sitting. 'Right now I am most in need of some sleep.'

I stood up, glanced at the door and sat down again.

'Really Mr Harry, I am most very tired. You are going back to your room, yes?'

'Basili, if it's all right with you, I'd prefer to stay here.'

'But why is this, Mr Harry?'

'Your room doesn't have as many spiders as mine. I'd feel much more comfortable sleeping here.'

'But this is a very small bed. There is not enough room for two persons of our size.'

He was right. He'd barely fit in the bed himself. 'I'll just sleep here, in this chair.' I pointed to a very uncomfortable chair in the corner of the room. 'It'll be fine – just try not to fart or snore.'

Basili looked doubtful. 'But Mr Harry, I will be asleep; how will I be controlling myself?'

Now there was a question even I couldn't answer. Briefly I weighed up the alternatives: spiders or flatulent snoring. Yeah, not much in the way of a choice, but in the end staying in Basili's room won – but it was a close contest. Trying to make myself as comfortable as I could in a not-so-comfortable chair, I covered myself with a blanket and settled down (insofar as I could) for a night's sleep.

I don't know how long I'd been sleeping, but it seemed like only minutes before I was awoken by Basili – and not by his snoring. He was shaking me frantically and whispering, 'Wake up Mr Harry. There is being someone outside.'

Blearily, I opened an eye. In the darkness I could make out the ex-genie's huge frame towering over me.

'Wassup? Wha's goin' on?' I mumbled. 'Need sleep.' Before I could turn over, Basili had whipped my blanket away. The sudden draught of cold air over my now-blanketless body brought me to my senses. 'What's going on?' I repeated, wrapping my arms around me in an effort to keep warm.

'Mr Harry, there is much creeping noises outside the room. I am thinking someone is being most careful not to be heard, but my detective senses are picking them up,' Basili announced proudly. 'Are you investigating?'

I noticed the distinct absence of the word 'we' in that last sentence, but chose to ignore it. Shushing Basili, I slid out of the chair, padded to the door and placed my ear against the wood. Basili was right; I could make out the sound of someone shuffling along the landing, doing their best to be undetected. It definitely wasn't the sound that someone having to make an emergency midnight trip to the bathroom would make.

'I'm going to have a look,' I whispered.

'You are being most careful, Mr Harry.' It was probably a warning, but it was also a very accurate statement of my intentions.

I cracked open the door and peered out. The glow of the moon through the web-covered landing window showed a dark shape creeping across the carpet. I couldn't make out who it was, but by their actions, they certainly didn't want to be discovered. Well, it was too late for that. Harry Pigg was on the case and eager to find out who was skulking around Miss Muffet's in the dead of night.

Pushing the door open just enough to let me pass through, I stepped out onto the landing and, tight against the wall, shuffled along after the mysterious stranger. I tried to make out who it might be, but there wasn't enough light. Whoever it was stayed hunched over so it was difficult even to see how tall they were. Then again, I hadn't planned on getting close enough for any kind of physical contest. I just wanted to find out what they were up to (and possibly who they were, as long as I could discover it from a safe distance).

Just as I was contemplating my next move, the shape disappeared from view around a corner where the landing turned to the left, leading to the rest of the guest bedrooms. Maybe we were in for a spot of breaking and entering, though as the stranger was already in the building there wasn't much breaking to be done. Now that I couldn't be seen, I could at least speed up and get to the corner. Tiptoeing along, I'd just come to the turn when an arm reached out, grabbed me around the neck and with a hissed 'Gotcha!' pulled me into the nearest bedroom.

I have a very healthy survival instinct, honed by years of cowardice and reluctance to get involved in any sort of a fight, so when my assailant pushed me to the ground, I rolled away immediately and tried to get to my feet. Before I could do anything I was pushed against a wall, realising at the same time that my reflexes weren't as sharp as I'd hoped – and certainly not as sharp as those of my attacker. Pinned against the unyielding surface, I struggled to break free, but I was held in a grip like a bear-trap.

'All right, let's see who we've got here,' my assailant whispered, reaching for the light switch. At the same time, sensing an opportunity, I pushed as hard as I could and for a second the grip on my throat loosened – but only for a second. Almost immediately I felt a hand grab my hair and heard a grunt of surprise as it came loose in my attacker's grip. Yay for wigs! Anxious to maintain whatever advantage I had, I ducked and threw myself sideways, smacking painfully into a dressing table. Stunned I fell to the ground, unwilling and unable to offer any resistance. I couldn't compete against my attacker and a dressing table. It was two against one, and this one in particular knew when to give up.

I lay on the floor panting and waiting for my attacker (the one that wasn't a dressing table) to finish me off. I was more than a little taken aback when, instead of being either beaten or tied up, the light was switched on and I heard her exclaim, in a very feminine voice, 'Wow, you're one ugly lady.'

Figuring that pointing out I was male might not be the most appropriate response in the circumstances, dressed as I was in ladies' clothes, I heaved myself up into a sitting position and said, 'It's a disguise.'

'And why might someone be staying in this particular guest house disguised as a lady pig?' asked my attacker, who, now that I was getting used to the light, seemed to be a very slim, very attractive and very dangerous-looking woman.

'Maybe for the same reason that another someone is skulking around outside her room, in the dark and trying not to be seen.' Then, in a flash of inspiration, I knew who she was. 'Queenie Harte I presume.'

'Guilty as charged,' she said, raising her hands in admission. 'And you are?'

'Harry Pigg, Private Investigator.'

'Never heard of you.'

'Well, I've never heard of you either. What are you doing here?'

She fumbled in her pocket before producing her ID. 'I'm with the Grimmtown Bureau of Investigation and I'm on a case. What about you?'

'Snap,' I replied. 'But what interest has the GBI in spiders?'

'Spiders? I'm not here because of spiders and the real reason I'm here is none of your business.'

'Well, if you're not telling then I'm not telling either.'

'Okay, be like that. We'll see how secretive you'll be after a night in the cells.'

I was going to point out that it would probably be more comfortable than staying in the B&B, but if I was taken away then there was no chance of cracking the case. 'Your point is well made. Mind if I make myself more comfortable; your floor isn't doing my back any good.'

'Please.' Queenie pointed to another of those uncomfortable armchairs that seemed to be part of every bedroom in the building. Maybe the floor was better after all. I remained there and looked up at Ms Harte. She had obviously gone through her special-agent-doing-undercover-work-at-night checklist: black trainers, black pants and a black top would make her very difficult to see in the dark. She looked like she shopped at SpiesMart.

'Look, I'm here because Miss Muffet asked me to investigate why her premises were being infested with spiders. Initially, I thought someone was trying to put her out of business, but after I discovered who Dad was, I'm fast beginning to think it may be connected to him in some way.' I gave Queenie as sincere a smile as I could. 'Now come on, give me something. I was straight with you. Who knows, I may even be of some help.'

Queenie gave me a disdainful I'm-a-Federal-Agent-how-could-you-possibly-be-of-any-help look, but seemed to relent a little. 'Okay, okay. Here's what I know. Sinbad isn't getting released any time soon. We believe that he hid his fortune somewhere in this house before he was captured and never had a chance to dispose of it properly. He left home when Miss Muffet was very young and hasn't spoken to her since. I think there's bad blood there, so she isn't going to inherit the loot any time soon.

'Now, here's where things get a bit murky. We believe that one or more of the gang members are hoping to double-cross him by trying to find the loot for themselves. With Sinbad locked away, it's an ideal opportunity to make a break for it if they're successful.' Queenie sat on the edge of the bed and sighed. 'As a result, I was sent in to try to integrate myself with the other guests so we could catch the bad guys in the act.' She looked down at me. 'When I heard you following me, I thought I'd got my first break. I knew you weren't for real as soon as I saw you pull up to the front of the house earlier.'

'How?' I asked, my sense of righteous indignation bubbling up.

'Oh, come on, did you really think you could fool anyone with those ridiculous disguises, all that air-kissing and luvvy-this, luvvy-that. There are kids' amateur dramatic groups that are more convincing.'

'Try telling that to the other guests,' I retorted. 'They were falling over themselves to help us finance our latest project. We certainly fooled them.'

'Yes. But, then again, most of the other guests are idiots.'

She had a point.

Something was still nagging at me, though. 'Here's what I don't get. Sinbad has been in prison for the best part of twenty years. So why now? Why wait all this time? It's a bit odd, don't you think?'

'Yeah, we thought that too, until we met George P. Etto.'

'Excuse me? Who's Etto?' I'd never heard of him and wondered how he figured in this.

'Etto was Sinbad's cellmate, in for antiques forgery. He was released about a week ago. Celebrating his new-found freedom he was in the Blarney Tone and, while very drunk, let it slip that Sinbad talked in his sleep. One night Etto had heard him mumble about his fortune, the house and a secret room. We believe that somebody, possibly one of Sinbad's gang, heard him, persuaded him, somehow, to be quiet and is now trying to use that information to find the stash.'

I had no illusions about how Etto might have been 'persuaded'. 'And you have no idea which of the guests is the gang member – or if there is more than one?'

Queenie shrugged. 'So far all their stories check out – sort of. The only ones that seem harmless are Mr and Mrs Fussy Eater; all the others are more than a bit dodgy.'

I hadn't had time to really investigate them so now was a good time to get some background information. 'How so?'

'Well, John Nimble is into antiques and is trying to get Miss Muffet to sell her collection of candlesticks, chandeliers and cutlery. We believe he's also a fence and deals with lots of local gangs, helping them to offload stolen goods. So far, though, he seems to be on the level in this particular instance.'

'Okay, that's Nimble. What about Winkie?'

'So far as we're aware, he's just a travelling salesman, but he has a history of breaking and entering. He's gone straight now, or so he says, but that may just be a front.'

'Thomas Piper?'

'Another businessman; buys and sells almost everything. Had a lucrative sideline smuggling animals years ago and did the time.'

'Smuggled animals? So he might be able to lay his hands on a few million spiders?'

'Possibly, but he's been keeping his nose clean these past few years.'

I made a mental note to check out Piper in more detail. He certainly sounded a likely suspect.

'And then there's Nocchio, self-styled arms dealer.'

I looked up with interest when she said that. 'Arms dealer, now he sounds very shifty.'

Queenie smiled. 'Not really. He also deals in legs, torsos and heads.'

Were we talking about some kind of mass-murderer and, if so, why was he still on the streets? 'Are you serious?' I said.

'Yep, as well as making superb wooden toys and sculptures, he's a supplier of parts to puppeteers and toymakers. He also has quite a reputation for furniture and antiques restoration. Apparently he's quite good. He has a large customer base in Grimmtown. Again, a bit of a shady past. He was involved in that whole Punch and Judy situation. A very messy business. Punch is still doing time.'

So I was no further down the road really. It looked like any of the guests could be responsible for the spiders. I needed some time to think. Reaching for my wig, I stuck it back on my head and ignored Queenie's snigger.

'I'll be heading back to my room now. Goodnight, Ms Harte.'

'Goodnight, Mr Pigg. Or should that be Miss du Crêpe? No doubt I'll see you tomorrow. And if you need some pointers on applying make-up, don't hesitate not to call me.'

I gave her an indignant stare as I marched out the door and back to Basili's bedroom. The look of relief on his face as I closed the door behind me gave me a little reassurance, but I noted that he'd made no effort to follow me and see what had happened.

'Oh, Mr Harriet, I was so worried,' he exclaimed. 'You are being okay, yes?'

I quickly explained what had happened and the newest wrinkle in the case.

'The GBI?' Basili said. 'That is most ominous. Perhaps it would be better if we were leaving things to them.'

'Oh, I don't think so, Basili,' I replied. 'You see, she's not GBI after all.'

'She is not? Now I am being very confused. You have just said that she was.'

'Nope. She said she was, but her ID was as fake as my wig, and I should know, I've used a fair few over the years. I can spot a dodgy ID at fifty paces.'

'But if she is not GBI, then who is this Ms Harte?'

'I don't know yet, but one thing is for sure; she'll need to be watched.'

This case had suddenly become a lot murkier.

10

Breakfast at Matilda's

Next morning, as I sat at the breakfast table, I viewed all the guests in an entirely new light. To be fair, none of them looked remotely suspicious. At a table on their own – which I suspect was deliberate – Licken and Lurkey exchanged bad jokes, practised juggling with their cereal bowls (which meant there was quite a mess around them) and howled hysterically at how funny they were. It was no coincidence that no one else was laughing.

As he placed my fruit bowl in front of me (PAs don't do cereals; calories darling), Jack Horner asked me if there had been any developments. 'Later,' I whispered and he nodded his understanding. Meanwhile, I watched Mr Zingiber as he waited on the other guests. Jack was indeed correct: he was a giant orange cake in the shape of a man, but he didn't seem to let that inhibit him in any way. He served up food and drink with aplomb, but seemed to be especially careful when pouring the guests' tea or coffee. Can't be too careful when you're a gingerbread man I suppose.

This morning I was eating alone, so took the time to go over the events of the day (and night) before. Assuming Queenie Harte was being up front with me, most of the guests had a less than honest reason to be staying in the B&B. Of course, that didn't mean they had motive – it just made them suspicious. If I could connect any of them to the spiders – which seemed to have been fruitful and multiplied overnight, the dining room now looked like it had been caught in a snowstorm – it might just bring me one step closer to cracking the case.

But which one?

I had eliminated Licken and Lurkey as I knew them of old and didn't think they had the sense to pull off a job like this. They might have been rubbish entertainers, but they certainly weren't master criminals. Mr and Mrs Spratt didn't seem like law-breakers either, but I wasn't eliminating them entirely just yet. The rest? Well, take your pick. Any of them could have been the culprit; I just needed to investigate a bit more. Piper was certainly acting strangely. And as for Queenie Harte . . .

As I sat there staring at the webs on the far wall wafting gently in the breeze, I thought about our encounter the previous night. What brought her here? She certainly wasn't GBI, so who was she – and why was she here? I didn't have any reason to disbelieve what she'd told me about the other guests as she was trying to gain my trust, but anything she said or did from here on would be viewed with suspicion. Of course, this also begged the question: would she be as helpful as she'd promised? I didn't think that, when the chips were down, she was going to be as accommodating as I hoped. Then again, I had no intention of helping her either, so I couldn't really afford to get too precious about it.

Maybe it was time to get to know the guests better. After last night I was at least on second-name terms with most of them, so I figured I had enough to get a chat going. Who knows, maybe they'd let something drop in conversation.

As I speared an apple slice and prepared to eat it, a particularly large spider at the far side of the room caught my eye. He swung from side to side on a tendril of web like an arachnid Tarzan and seemed to be staring at me. If I hadn't known better, I'd have said he was thinking about having me as his next victim – he was certainly scary enough. It was time to nip that in the bud. Grabbing a plum from my bowl, I flung it at the spider. He didn't have time to react before it hit him full on, squashing him against the wooden panel on the wall behind. I smirked as I resumed my breakfast. Pig 1, spider 0.

As I settled back to enjoying my fruit, the spider incident bugged me. I knew I was missing something, but right now, it just wouldn't come. It wouldn't be the first time this had happened, so I figured I'd just let it fester in my head and eventually – usually when I least expected it – it would explode fully formed into my mind, screaming 'look at me, look at me'. Whether it would help me break the case was another thing entirely – it might just as easily turn out to be a recipe for cookies. Well, if it was, Jack would be happy.

'Mind if I join you?' said Willie Winkie, sitting opposite me before I could reply. Pouring himself a coffee, he settled into his chair and looked across the table at me. 'Feeling better?'

For a second I didn't know what he was referring to, until I remembered my little 'episode' from the night before. 'Oh yes, darling, so much better. It's amazing what a good night's sleep can do for one' – as opposed to engaging in a midnight skirmish with a fake GBI agent.

'Good, we were all so worried about you,' Winkie said, without a hint of sincerity.

'Well, I'm fine now and eager to check out this house properly. It has such an ambience don't you think? It's such an ideal location for our movie.'

'Ah, yes, the horror film. What's the plot?'

'Plot?' I was on dangerous ground as I hadn't thought that far ahead. 'Well, um, some kids – we have some of the finest child actors lined up already – creep into a haunted house in the middle of the night and scary things start happening to them.'

'Like what?'

'Ghosts, things that go bump in the night, that sort of thing.'

'You know, it's funny you should mention bumps in the night. I could have sworn I heard noises outside my room after I went to bed. I think that's what woke me up.'

'And did you find out what was making them?' I asked, trying not to look as guilty as I felt.

'Nah, I just put it down to the age of the house. In a place like this you must expect lots of funny noises.'

'And speaking of the house, if you don't mind my asking, what convinced you to stay here?' I waved my trotters at the cobwebs. 'It's hardly the most comfortable.'

'It's a bit unorthodox, I'll grant you,' he replied. 'But it's cheap and, more importantly, it's very close to the Rag District.'

'Excuse me? Rag District?'

'Yes, where all the clothes shops are. That's my business you see, I sell clothing; in particular, I deal in nightwear: dressing gowns, pyjamas, nightgowns, that sort of thing. In fact, if you're looking for costumes for your film, I might just be able to sort you out with a good deal.'

'Ah, that won't be necessary, our Costume Department look after that kind of thing. Anyway, I don't think there'll be much need for nightwear in this movie.'

'But you've said it takes place at night, so you never know,' Winkie replied. He was certainly persistent.

'Tell you what, I'll take it up with the producers; see what they say.'

'I'd be grateful.'

'So,' I said, putting my metaphorical detective's hat back on. 'Have you been in the clothes business for long?'

'Yep, I'm an old hand at it now. I started off with a small stall in Grimmtown Market and built it up from there.'

'I imagine in the sales game you must meet all kinds of interesting people.'

'Over the years I've met all sorts. Maybe if we get an opportunity later, I could tell you a few stories.'

Oh, yes, now that would be fun: listening to a travelling salesman bore me to tears with his tales of tailors and seamstresses. 'Well, Mr Schmidt-Heye is toying with making another documentary after he finishes his horror movie. He's looking at Grimmtown's criminal underworld and its characters. You must have come across a few in your time.'

Was it my imagination or did a shifty expression cross Winkie's face?

'To tell the truth,' he stammered, 'I've been very lucky. I've never bumped into anyone shady in my years selling clothes.'

'Oh, I do find that hard to believe, darling. Surely you're being far too modest. A man of your wide-ranging experience must have encountered a shady character or two.'

'No, not really. As I said, I've been lucky.' He stood up from the table. 'Now if you'll excuse me, I really must be going.'

'But you haven't finished your coffee,' I pointed out.

'I'll take it with me,' he said, grabbing the mug in both hands and almost dropping it again it was so hot. 'The caffeine helps me focus.'

Not to mention your burnt hands, I thought. 'Have a good day.'

Well, he had started acting very strangely once the conversation veered into the criminal. Then again, that didn't necessarily make him guilty. He would need further investigation though. Spotting

Jack serving at another table, I waved him over and pointed at Winkie as he disappeared out the door.

'See that guy?' I asked.

Jack nodded. 'Yes, that's Mr Winkie.'

'I want you to follow him and see where he goes. Be careful and make sure he doesn't see you.'

'I'll be the invisible man,' Jack replied, proud to have been given a real mission.

'I don't doubt it,' I said.

As Jack scurried off after his target I watched the other guests. Mr and Mrs Spratt were dividing up their bacon, Thomas Piper was pretending to read the paper, but I could see his head move back and forth as he followed Miss Muffet's movements in and out of the room as she served breakfast. At a separate table, Nocchio and Nimble were deep in conversation. In fact, from where I sat it looked like they were having an argument. Detecting antennae went on full alert as I stood up and edged towards them, in the guise of getting a newspaper from the rack on the wall beside them. As casually as I could, I stood within hearing distance and pretended to scan the front page.

'No, ees madness,' Nocchio whispered, staring at Nimble.

'What choice do we have?' Nimble replied. 'It has to be done now.'

'But 'ow? We don't know where eet is.'

Now that could quite easily be a conversation about Sinbad's fortune. Had I finally got a break in the case?

'But we'll find it soon, I know it.' Nimble spotted me hovering and waved at Nocchio to be quiet.

'Morning daaaarlings,' I bluffed. 'And how are we all this glorious morning?'

'Fine, fine,' Nimble blustered and Nocchio nodded agreement.

'Great. Well I have a location to examine, so I'll see you darling gentlemen later. Time is money you know.' I made my way back to my table and finished my breakfast, mulling over what I'd just heard. Winkie might have been shifty, but the conversation I'd just eavesdropped upon was downright dodgy. Those two gentlemen would warrant further observation – but they were now looking suspiciously across the room at me, so I figured they'd be very careful around me. I needed someone else to do the listening.

Just as I was mulling over my dilemma, Queenie Harte strode into the room and made for a table in the corner. The best way to keep an eye on her would be to invite her to share my table. As she was oblivious to the fact that her cover had been blown, I might even be able to get more information out of her. It meant sharing what I'd seen this morning, but I figured it was worth the trade-off.

'Ms Harte. Oh, Ms Harte, would you care to join me, darling? We haven't had a chance to talk yet.'

Queenie glanced over her shoulder at me and would probably have ignored my request had I not made it out loud. Unwilling to be seen to be anti-social in front of all the other guests, she sat down in the seat recently vacated by Willie Winkie. 'It's Ms du Crêpe isn't it? We haven't been formally introduced, but I'm aware of your charge's reputation. It's a pleasure to meet you.' The expression on her face suggested otherwise, but I didn't care.

'Ms Harte, the feeling's mutual. Please, have some breakfast.' I waved Mr Zingiber over and he carefully filled Queenie's cup with hot coffee. As she sipped, I updated her on the morning's events. To my surprise, she didn't seem too interested in what I'd overheard.

'Come on,' she said. 'They could have been talking about anything.'

'Maybe. But considering our current situation, don't you think it might have some bearing on the case?'

'It's possible, I suppose.' She mulled it over as she drank. 'But I'm not going to waste time on something that might just turn out to be a red herring.'

She seemed very casual about it. I wondered if she had something more important to do – something that she was keeping from me despite our conversation of the night before. Yes, I know, I'd have done the same, but that didn't make it any easier to stomach.

'You know something, don't you?' I jabbed a trotter at her. 'Something you're not telling me.'

'Of course I don't. Don't be ridiculous. I told you last night that I'd pass on any information, didn't I?'

'You did, but I'm starting to think you might have been leading me on.' I stood up from the table. 'Anyway, I've more important things to be doing.' In the interests of keeping up appearances, I walked around and air-kissed her (I was getting quite good at it by now), whispering at the same time, 'If I find you've kept something from me, I'll —'

'You'll what?' she snapped. 'Remember who you're talking to. If I want I can have you detained for obstruction of justice. You wouldn't do too much investigating then, would you?'

I stepped back, pretending to be suitably chastened. 'You're right, of course.' I bowed my head in mock-humility. 'Carry on with whatever you're doing. I'll just scoot off and scout locations for the day, shall I?'

'Yes, you carry on with your PA work. I'm sure you're very good at it.' Queenie's voice dripped sarcasm, but I ignored it. Better people than her have been sarcastic towards me, so she'd have to be really good to get any kind of response. I left the table and went upstairs to Basili's room. I'd instructed him to order room service and wait until I got back – it was a form of damage limitation. By now I was beginning to think that our cover story wasn't quite as well thought out as we had originally planned. Maybe next time we'd just go in as ordinary guests (in disguise, of course). Well, they do say hindsight is 20-20 vision and, based on our current success rate, we must have been very short-sighted.

I was just about to knock on the door when I spotted something on the floor. It was lying where the carpet met the wall and must have been missed by the cleaning staff – although if the cleaning staff amounted to one gingerbread man then it would be easy to see why. Curious, I bent down and picked it up. It looked like a raisin but had a rubbery texture. I was still examining it when I entered the room.

Basili was still there, stretched out on the bed.

'Have you any plans to get up today?' I asked, rolling the strange object around in my trotter.

'But of course, Mr Harry. I am waiting for you to be returning so we can discuss our strategy.' Basili got off the bed and began dressing in character once more.

'Ah, strategy. Here's where we are: Jack is following Willie Winkie to see if he's on the level. Nocchio and Nimble looked to be having a row at the breakfast table, Thomas Piper is watching everything Miss Muffet does and Queenie Harte is threatening to put me in jail. There, have I covered everything?' I had briefed Basili about my encounter with Queenie the night before, after I arrived back at the bedroom bruised, tired and with my wig askew. The ex-genie contemplated what I'd said, nodded sagely and said . . . well . . . nothing.

'That's it, that's all you have to offer: a nod?' I screeched.

Basili had the decency to blush. 'I am most sorry, Mr Harry. There is nothing that I am offering at this moment. I am sure that I am being most disappointing to you, particularly when our small friend, young Jack, is being a most practical detective.' He looked curiously at what I had in my hand. 'And what is that you are playing with?'

I looked at the object again just as Basili sat at the dressing table and began to dab some make-up on his face. As he did so, my brain finally decided to wake up properly and start making connections.

Make-up; rubbery raisin-like object.

'It's a wart, Basili,' I said.

'That is very disgusting. Why are you playing with such a thing?'

Oh, it's not a real wart. It's fake. Someone else in this house has been disguising themself. And what kind of person might have a wart?'

'Ah.' The ex-genie's face lit up. 'An orcy person. You are thinking that perhaps someone is making the disguise and visiting the froggy man to buy his spiders?'

'That's exactly what I'm thinking.' And I was thinking very hard indeed. Things were starting to come together at last. Basili's comment about Jack, the fake wart, the guests and Frogg Prince's statement all began to link together in my head. There might be more of the guests involved in the crime, but I was starting to narrow down my list of definite suspects. At last I had something to go on.

11

A Secret Revealed

Leaning forward, I kissed Basili on the forehead. 'You're a genius,' I said to the puzzled ex-genie. 'I think we may finally have a breakthrough.'

'I am? We do?' Basili didn't know whether to preen or be confused. 'Perhaps you are explaining it to me.'

'Well, remember Frogg Prince's description of the orc that came into the store?'

Basili's face was a study in concentration. 'He was saying that it was a most unpleasant creature: very smelly, very green and with a wart.'

'Yes, but he also described him as being small, remember? And how many small guests are staying here at the moment?'

I could see Basili counting them out one by one. 'Two?' he ventured.

'Exactly. Jack Spratt and Willie Winkie. Everyone else is just too tall.'

'But Mr Spratt is being such a jolly person.'

'Indeed, but that's why you should never let emotion get in the way of good detecting. Everyone is a suspect until proven otherwise.'

I was still finding it hard to believe Jack Spratt could be involved in this. Basili was right in that respect: he just didn't seem the type. But now that he was a likely suspect I'd have to pay more attention to him – and possibly even his wife. The 'perfect 10' would now be under my unwavering gaze from here on in as well. So many suspects, so few eyes. It was very possible that I'd have to enlist Basili in taking a more active role in the day-to-day operations of the Agency, though I shuddered to think of him trying to shadow a suspect. It wouldn't be shadowing so much as a total eclipse. The only way he'd manage to stay unseen would be if someone managed to cast an invisibility spell on him – and even then he'd probably end up barging people out of the way like a mini-hurricane as he followed his target down the street. He certainly wouldn't be unobtrusive.

'You know, it's a bit stuffy in here.' I headed towards the window and pushed it open. Considering two of us had slept in the room (or tried to sleep, in my case), one of whom suffered from flatulence, fresh air was very much the order of the morning. A cool breeze wafted through the window, blowing the cobwebs that were evidence of the spiders' attempt to reconquer the room. Some of the strands floated across the room and settled against the wall on the far side.

As they drifted to the floor, my brain, already fully charged having sorted out the disguised orc issue, decided to go for broke and head for a touchdown. Why did the webs moving suggest something to me?

Wafting webs.

Webs in a draught.

Just like those I'd seen in the dining room at breakfast – which were nowhere near any draught from the door. Something else had made them move. Maybe air escaping from something like a hidden door or secret passage.

My brain hit the end-zone and the crowd went crazy. 'Basili.' I grabbed the ex-genie and hauled him to his feet. 'Get ready to act like you've never acted before. I think I know where Sinbad's fortune is hidden, but I need you to get everyone out of the dining room.'

To his credit, Basili didn't ask any stupid questions – for a change. He finished dressing in his Acme Director's Outfit™, flicked some imaginary dust off his shoulders, straightened his back and got back in character.

'Mr Schmidt-Heye will be looking most very hard for some actors for his most magnificent movie. Perhaps I am holding auditions in the lounge.'

And by extension, no one would be in the dining room while I investigated the wafting webs.

'Basili, you're excelling yourself today – and it's still only morning,' I said, thumping him on the back. 'We might make a detective of you yet.'

'I am learning much from such an excellent tutor as yourself,' he said proudly. I didn't doubt it; with someone like me to learn from, even Basili could pick up a tip or two.

Now it was time to see if all his learning could be put to some practical field use – and, more importantly, would he be able to carry it off on his own. I needed him to keep the guests distracted while he remained in character. It was a big ask and, to tell the truth, I was more than a bit apprehensive. He wouldn't have me interfere for him, or be there to prompt him if he ran into difficulty. He needed to be Alain Schmidt-Heye and to do so he'd have to ignore all my advice of the previous day; he'd be talking for an extended period of time and I suspected there would be a certain amount of physical contact. Well, it couldn't be helped; he was on his own and there was nothing I could do about it.

After passing on a few last-minute tips I headed downstairs

into the dining room, took up what I hoped was a casual pose at the mantelpiece and waited, casually ignoring everybody and trying to look superior. Fortunately, Basili swung into action immediately, so no sooner had I adopted Superior Look No. 7 – I'm in the Movie Industry and You're Not, Insignificant Worm – than there was a loud thumping as he tested the stairs' tolerance limits with his feet as he descended and headed into the lounge.

'Can I have everyone's attention please,' I ordered – as opposed to asking (PAs don't ask). 'Mr Schmidt-Heye is not only extremely excited about the ambience of these premises, but he also feels that, as sometime residents, having you in the movie might add to the overall sense of realism that he is striving for. Accordingly, he will be holding auditions for the role of guests, starting,' I glanced at my watch, 'well, now actually.'

There was a stunned silence followed almost immediately by a mass exodus. Ah, the lure of the movies, I thought. It gets 'em every time. Even Mr and Mrs Spratt had gone out for a look.

I scanned the room once more, just to be sure it was empty, and turned to where I'd seen the webs move. As I studied them, they once more fluttered gently in a breeze of some description. My initial hunch was correct: it wasn't a draught from the door. Something else was definitely blowing the webs. I ran my trotters along the wooden panels beside the fireplace. At first I thought I'd been mistaken, but I felt it on my second pass: a gentle gust emanating from what seemed to be a slender vertical crack in one of the panels. It didn't look like natural wear and tear, which suggested only one thing to my rapier-like mind: a secret passage of some description. All I had to do now was figure out the mechanism to open it.

Of course, I'd come across secret doors, passages and tunnels before and had built up quite an expertise in figuring out how to open them – which was just as well as Basic Techniques 1–3 (pushing, pressing and pulling) failed miserably. Conscious that someone was eventually going to come back into the room, I moved onto Techniques 4–7 (finding a trigger, cracking a combination, solving a mysterious message and my own addition to the pantheon: hitting everything and hoping for the best). To my surprise (and the bruising of my ego) none of the classic steps worked. I was figuring that maybe there wasn't a secret passage there at all when, as I stepped back for a better look, I stumbled over the fire irons. Grabbing at anything that might keep me upright, my trotters gripped onto a circular carving cut into the stonework of the fireplace itself. Instead of offering support, it twisted under the pressure and, as I hit the ground, I was rewarded with the sound of wood scraping on wood as the panel slid aside to reveal a dark space behind. Forgetting about my injured dignity, I stood up and peered cautiously into the opening. It did occur to me as I did so that Sinbad's fortune, if that was indeed what was hidden behind the panel, wasn't going to amount to much as the secret passage was barely bigger than a cereal carton and not really large enough to store more than a gold bar or two.

In fact, now that I could see into it, there wasn't any gold inside either. A small wooden box nestled snugly in the hole. It didn't look like much; no runes, mysterious carvings or strange inscriptions. By the same token, it didn't look booby-trapped either.

It wouldn't be long before I wouldn't be on my own any more. Throwing any hint of caution aside, I grabbed the box and pulled it out waiting for the explosion, release of gas, or some strategically placed spring-loaded metal spike to assail me. When none of the above occurred, I cracked the lid on the box and pushed it ever-so-carefully open. Inside there wasn't a treasure map, nor a letter from Sinbad, and there certainly wasn't any treasure. Nestling snugly on a velvet cushion was a small blue bean. More importantly, it wasn't a runner bean, green bean, baked bean or kidney bean. I recognised the sparkly aura that surrounded it; it was the type of aura that screamed 'I'm a magic bean. Look at me and observe my magnificence and my suggestion of things occult.' Any time I came across any kind of magic object, I much preferred to observe its suggestion of things occult from a safe distance – preferably another continent – and this particular magic artifact was no exception. I've made no secret in the past of my hatred of all things magic as, when they got involved in my cases, things generally didn't turn out well. Looking at the particular magic bean posing proudly in its case, I figured this would be no exception.

I'd like to say that I wasn't surprised then, when I heard a voice behind me whisper, 'Thank you so very much, kind lady. I knew there was more to you than met the eye.' Before I could react, there was a sharp smack to the back of my head and I stumbled forward, striking the front of it against the mantelpiece. Faced with a double-whammy of head trauma, my system decided enough was enough and slowly began to shut itself down as I slid to the floor. The last thing I saw before I blacked out completely was a gloved hand taking the box from my trotter.

12

Bean There, Done That

Basili was bending over me, shaking me (a bit too violently for trying to wake up someone who'd just been mugged, I thought).

'Mr Harry . . . I mean Miss du Crêpe, are you okay?' Now he was trying to drag me to my feet. Did he know nothing about the basics of first aid?

I waved him away. 'I'm fine,' I mumbled. 'Just give me some space.' My head ached all over courtesy of the symmetrical strikes it had received, my vision was blurred and I think my skirt had ridden up over my thighs. I quickly tugged it back down to a more acceptable level before worrying about my physical well-being. A girl's got priorities after all. 'Who else is here?'

'Oh, no one. I have given them all a scene to prepare. They are being most busy with the rehearsals, so I am taking a five before I am having to return. I was being most concerned when I saw you on the floor.'

The mugging was coming into clearer focus now. 'Basili, when you were talking to the guests, were they all there, or did anyone leave during your act?'

The ex-genie mulled it over for a second before giving me a rueful stare. 'I am sorry, I am not really noticing.' As he spoke he seemed to observe something. Raising his head he sniffed the air carefully.

'What is it, Basili? What can you smell?'

'There has been some apparatus of magic in this vicinity very most recently,' he said. 'I can sense it.'

Of course, being an ex-genie he could probably detect the lingering aura of the magic bean. Quickly I explained about what I'd found and he nodded his head. 'Yes, that is it. Definitely pulse magic. Very powerful.'

I reached into my handbag, grabbed my phone and punched in a number.

'Good morning, Directory Enquiries, how may I be of assistance?'

'I need you to put me through to Beanstalk Control right away,' I demanded.

'Of course, sir, please hold the line.' There was a brief pause followed by the number being connected.

'This is Beanstalk Control. For details of licensed beanstalks in your area, please press 1 now. For details on how to register your beanstalk, please press 2 now. For help with beanstalk removal, please press 3 now. For information on unregulated beanstalks in your area, please press 4 now.'

I punched 4 on my keypad and waited.

'Your call is important to us. Please hold and a Beanstalk Engineer will take your call as soon as one becomes available.' Seconds later a sanitised version of one of Hubbard's Cubbard's very early hits, sounding like it was being played by a hippo on a toy keyboard, came down the line – presumably to help me relax while I waited for the next available Beanstalk Engineer. I ground my teeth in frustration while listening to how important to

Beanstalk Control my call was; all the while wondering was it actually possible that so many people with unlicensed beanstalk issues had called at exactly the same time, thus putting everyone else on hold.

'Come on, come on,' I muttered. 'I don't have time for this.' Then I noticed something: was it as a result of my injuries or did the dining room seem darker? Before I could consider it further, Beanstalk Control finally decided that I was, in fact, actually important to them after all and assigned an operative to my call.

'Hi, this is Fred in Unlicensed Beanstalks. Thank you for your patience and understanding. How can I help you today?'

'Well, Fred, I was wondering if there have been any reports of unlicensed beanstalks in the Grimmtown area this morning?' I asked.

'Just a moment, sir, and I'll check,' Fred put me on hold once more while he went off to investigate. This time, however, I wasn't waiting long. 'Yes, sir, in fact we have reports of one such plant this morning and – whoa, it's a biggie. I don't think I've seen one that big since—'

As he spoke I suddenly understood why exactly the room had become darker. A large shape outside the window was blocking most of the light. 'Thanks, Fred, you've been a great help,' I said.

'But don't you want to know where it is?' Fred was being a true professional right to the end.

'It's okay, Fred, I think I have a fair idea.' Outside the dining room window, I could make out a giant leaf and part of what I now knew to be a beanstalk trunk. This particular plant was in Miss Muffet's backyard. Whoever had taken the bean from me had acted fast.

I was just on the point of hanging up when I thought of another – and very vital – question. 'Where's this particular plant going to?'

'Ah, now there's an interesting thing: it's going all the way to Neringus's Castle.'

Now at this point I need to present a little Beanstalk 101. Most of you probably already know that they grow from magic beans, extend quite a bit into the sky and are tricky to both climb up and chop down. What you probably don't realise is that these beanstalks connect to a number of cloud kingdoms, mostly small ones, that hover in the skies over Grimmtown. As a result, all beanstalks are both registered and licensed with the good folk of Beanstalk Control to ensure both the safety of air-traffic above the city and to control access to these cloud kingdoms. The people in these aerial fiefdoms – usually giants – have an arrangement with Grimmtown Corporation: in return for prompt payment of taxes they are assured of privacy and managed access via registered beanstalks. As you can imagine, they aren't overly keen on tourists and prefer that most other people – especially brave young adventurers – just stay away. In fact, if one was to hide a large treasure trove, a kingdom in the clouds would be the perfect place – assuming one of their rulers let you enter in the first place. Then again, if treasure was involved, chances were a small bribe might help those selfsame rulers get over any rampant xenophobia they might have and allow it to be stashed somewhere safe.

Bearing that in mind, if Sinbad's fortune was in Neringus's Castle, he couldn't have picked a safer place to stash it. That particular edifice hovered in the highest section of clouds above Grimmtown. This made it difficult to get to in normal circumstances. On top of that, it was ruled by a particularly unpleasant member of the giant community named Neringus. Usual advice, where he was concerned, was to stay well away. Stories abounded – some probably true – of those above-mentioned brave young adventurers who fancied their chances against him only to find that legends didn't always tell the whole truth and favour the small guy. Apparently, back in the old days it was a common occurrence to find bits of the more unsuccessful adventurers raining from the sky after the latest failed quest – so much so that Grimmtown Police Department placed a blanket ban on any further expeditions to the clouds, after a particularly unpleasant experience when the mayor of Grimmtown was hit on the head by a falling leg while giving an outdoor speech on pollution and the importance of clean air.

If deciding what to do once you got to a cloud kingdom – apart from actually staying alive – was a problem, getting there was fraught with even more difficulty. The only approved access was beanstalks, which was all very well if you were young, fit and able to climb for extended periods of time. All aerial transport in and around them was banned and the ban was strictly enforced: on the ground by Beanstalk Control, through legislation, and in the air by the giants – usually through shooting down any aircraft that wandered too close. The giants' method was generally considered to be the more effective of the two, and that was causing me no end of concern as I left the B&B to take a look at the beanstalk.

As beanstalks went it was a particularly fine example of the species. Shooting out of the ground where the magic bean had been planted, it towered above us, twisting its way into the sky to disappear from view among the clouds. Giant leaves the size of cars shaded us from the sun and the plant's trunk was as wide as the house beside it. I took one look at its size and knew there was no way I was climbing it. For one thing, climbing is murder when you have trotters and, more importantly, I wasn't as young as I used to be; even if I managed to get a foothold I'd probably only make a few feet before giving up in pain and exhaustion, with very sore legs.

Beside me Basili looked apprehensively at the towering green structure. 'We will not be climbing that, Mr Harry?' His gaze stretched up further. 'Will we?'

'I don't think so, Basili, but, as always, I have a plan.' I pulled out my phone and made a quick call. 'Ali, it's me, Harry. I need another favour and this time I promise it'll be the last one.'

'If you say so, Harry,' came the weary voice from the other end. 'What is it this time?'

'I need to borrow another of your carpets; one of the long-range ones that can travel at altitude.'

'And where would this particular magic carpet be travelling to?'

'Well, we have a new beanstalk in town and I need to get to the top.'

Ali Baba laughed. 'No chance, Harry. None of my carpets – in fact no magic carpet – is capable of travelling at that altitude. They're just not designed for it. And even if they were, there's no way I'd lend you one. It wouldn't last five minutes once it got up there. Those giants aren't too friendly, you know.'

'You think? Okay, thanks anyway, Ali.' I turned to Basili. 'Well, scratch that plan. We won't be travelling by magic carpet this time.'

'So, how will we be getting there?' asked the perplexed ex-genie.

'That, my good friend, is an excellent question and one to which I still haven't figured out an answer,' I replied, looking once more at the intimidating mass of greenery that stretched into the sky above.

'Well, I am most confident that you will, very, very soon,' Basili said, and he placed a comforting arm around my shoulders.

I was encouraged by my partner's confidence in me, but I still had no idea how to get to the top of the beanstalk. Any aircraft we might use would probably be blown out of the sky before we got near it.

Then other, more important short-term thoughts struck me. Who had planted the magic bean? And, having planted it, had they climbed up to the clouds above? Well, there was an easy way to find out.

'Basili, stay here and get into character again. I need to get everyone out here to see who's not around any more.'

'But of course, Mr Harry,' Basili replied. 'I will be ready.'

I rushed back into the house and shouted, 'Mr Schmidt-Heye has been most impressed with your performances. We've set up an outdoor set for some more testing, so if you could all step outside into the garden that would be lovely.'

There was a flurry of bodies as the guests decamped *en masse* outdoors. 'Anyone left inside?' I screamed. 'Anyone else want to do a screen test.'

'There's no one left here,' said an unfamiliar voice behind me. I spun around to face Zingiber, the gingerbread manservant. 'They're all outside now. All that's left here are the staff.' Turning his back on me, he skulked back towards the kitchen.

'Charming,' I muttered, as I made my way back outside once more.

In the garden, the guests were swarming around, gazing up at the beanstalk and chattering excitedly. 'Gosh,' said John Nimble. 'That's a most elaborate set; how did you set it up so quickly?' He slapped the nearest leaf. 'Wow, it feels so lifelike.'

'That's set designers for you,' I said. 'They work fast and try to make it as real as possible.' I looked around the garden, checking off the guests as I went along. I'd just seen Nimble and had checked Queenie Harte off my list on the basis of the previous night's activities. Thomas Piper was talking to Pietro Nocchio and Miss Muffet, and Mr and Mrs Spratt were examining the beanstalk with interest. Maybe they were figuring out how best to eat it. That only left Willie Winkie, who was being tailed by Jack Horner and wasn't even in the building when I'd been attacked.

Now I was confused. I'd eliminated all the guests and there was still no sign of who had stolen the magic bean.

Or had I?

As I stood there something fluttered down from the beanstalk and came to a halt at my feet. I looked down at a large white chicken feather and realised that I'd badly miscalculated. I'd never even considered Licken and Lurkey as possible culprits because I figured they weren't bright enough and I'd known them for years. I'd been misled. Now that fowl duo were climbing the beanstalk, trying to get to the top and lay their hands on Sinbad's treasure.

There had to be some way of getting there before them; there just had to be. Maybe someone could cast a magic spell and teleport me there. Basili quickly poured water on that particular scheme. 'All cloud kingdoms have a magic-damping field around them to prevent the very thing that you are being suggesting, Mr Harry. There is, of course, much magic once you arrive, but alas it cannot be used to get there.'

Well, scratch that as a plan. Unless I came up with something quickly, Licken and Lurkey would get away, but what could I do? Just as despair began to creep over me a thought struck me: 'maybe the (fake) GBI could be of assistance.'

Queenie Harte had slid up beside me.

'What can the GBI do to get to the top of the beanstalk? Do you have super-fast climbers or something?'

'I'm afraid not,' Queenie replied. 'We'd need to go through channels, just like everyone else.'

Then an offer of help came from a most surprising source.

'I think I might be of some assistance,' smiled Miss Muffet. 'Just wait here, I'll be right back.'

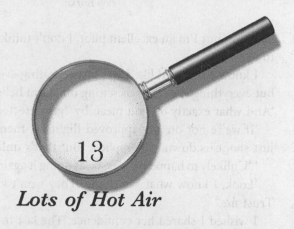

13

Lots of Hot Air

'Are you crazy?' I said to Miss Muffet. 'This has no chance of working.' I looked disbelievingly at the hot-air balloon that was being prepped for take-off as I spoke. 'Oh, yes it will,' Miss Muffet replied. 'My father used to use them when he needed to approach the cloud kingdoms under the radar, so to speak.'

I remembered the picture of Sinbad in the hot-air balloon that had adorned the stairway wall. 'But how?' I asked. 'Any unauthorised aircraft approaching them is destroyed.'

'That's the beauty of balloons,' Miss Muffet said. 'Firstly, they're quiet. Secondly, if they ascend close to the beanstalk they don't usually get detected. The beanstalk's own mass helps to mask their approach.'

'Usually,' I interrupted. 'You said "don't usually get detected". What does that mean exactly?'

'Well, it doesn't always work,' Miss Muffet replied with a rueful expression. 'Sometimes the balloons get caught in the branches; other times they stray too far from the beanstalk's cover and get detected; but I'm an excellent pilot, I don't think that will happen to us.'

I know I sounded like I was just repeating everything she said, but everything she said was setting off alarm bells inside my head. 'And what exactly do you mean by "get detected"?'

'If we're not on any approved flight list then they'll probably just shoot us down,' she replied. 'But that's unlikely to happen.'

'"Unlikely to happen"?' Yes, I was doing it again. 'Unlikely how?'

'Look, I know what I'm doing. They won't know we're there. Trust me.'

I wished I shared her confidence. The last thing I needed was an angry giant gunning (possibly quite literally) for me while I floated around in a very big, very obvious and very defenceless target.

'And there's no other way,' I asked, resigned to the inevitable answer.

Miss Muffet shook her head. 'Not if you want to get there now. If we have to go through official channels and get approved flight plans, visas and travel permits we'll be tied up in paperwork for days. By then the culprits will have gone to ground and we'll never find that treasure.' She turned and looked at the balloon. The red globe was filling with hot air and struggled against the guy ropes that were securing it to the ground. 'Oh, look, it's nearly inflated. Time to get on board.'

'You're absolutely sure about this?' I asked as I nervously approached the basket that would be keeping us safe for the duration of the trip – a very delicate and fragile-looking basket, I have to add.

'Absolutely; we'll be as safe as an . . . um . . . ah . . . very safe thing,' Miss Muffet said as she clambered up the rope ladder that dangled from the basket's edge. Her reply did nothing to reassure me.

'Are you getting in, or what?' she shouted from above.

'Just a moment,' I said. 'I need to do something first.' I rushed back into the B&B, up to my room and grabbed my case. Seconds later I was out of my costume and back in my detective's clothes. Well, my cover had been blown anyway; I might as well get comfortable. Glad to be wearing civvies once more, I ran back to the balloon where an agitated Miss Muffet was waiting impatiently.

'Hurry up, we haven't got all day.'

I gritted my teeth, muttered, 'Here goes nothing,' and ascended the rope ladder, only managing to get tied up in it twice before dropping into the basket.

Inside it was a lot roomier than it looked from the ground. Clearly Sinbad hadn't skimped on his comforts when in the field (or over it in this case). A carpeted floor was covered with cushions and seatbelts hung loosely from the walls. A small control desk allowed someone to pilot the craft and the burner that heated the air, keeping the balloon airborne, spurted flame over my head.

'It's certainly a bit more snug than a magic carpet,' I said as I sat down and strapped myself in.

'Nothing but the best for my father,' said Miss Muffet.

As I made myself comfortable, I became aware of raised voices from outside the balloon.

'No,' said one. 'You can't go; it's too dangerous.'

'Oh, yes I can,' replied Jack Horner. 'Harry needs me. I'm the one who keeps him out of trouble.'

'And I am being flying too,' said an indignant Basili from outside, also getting in on the act. 'Please be standing aside.'

Although I couldn't see what was going on, I didn't imagine anyone was going to stand in Basili's way. No one's life would be worth that. Minutes later, after much huffing and puffing, he fell into the basket, followed almost immediately by a very happy Jack Horner.

'Well, the gang's all here,' he said excitedly as he looked around.

'Indeed we are,' I said. 'It's good to see you again. How did you get on following Willie Winkie?'

Jack's face dropped. 'It was really boring. He just wandered around clothes shops talking to people and shaking their hands. Next time give me something more interesting to do.'

'I'll see what I can find.' I rubbed his head affectionately. 'At least your work may have helped eliminate him from our enquiries.'

Jack's face lit up. 'It did? Wow.'

I shifted around on my cushion and asked Miss Muffet when we'd be airborne.

'Any second now,' she said.

There was more commotion from outside the basket.

'Let me through,' roared a man's voice. 'I need to be on that balloon.'

I looked over the side and saw Thomas Piper furiously pushing people out of his way as he raced towards the ladder.

'I'd suggest we leave now,' I said. 'I don't know what his problem is, but I'd prefer that he not come with us.'

'Right you are,' said Miss Muffet, and she released the moorings. There was a lurch and the balloon began to ascend. With a roar of frustration, Piper leaped up to grab onto the ladder and missed it by inches. He waved his fist angrily at me as the balloon gathered speed. I refrained from waving back – or making any other gestures either.

'Why is the Piper gentleman so eager to ascend with us?' Basili asked. 'Does he like balloons?'

'I have no idea,' I said. 'But based on his behaviour since we arrived in the B&B, I don't want him here with us.'

Jack stood up to look over the edge of the basket. 'Look at Miss Muffet's. From up here it looks tiny.'

I wasn't too concerned with events on the ground; I was far

more worried about the giant green plant that seemed to be far too near us. Miss Muffet was taking the 'flying close to the beanstalk' tactic as literally as she could. If I stretched out my hand I'd be able to grab a leaf.

'This isn't too bad,' she said, spotting my concern. 'There are no dangerous air currents and we're ascending nicely. We should be at the top before too much longer.'

'And what then?' I asked. 'A balloon will hardly be inconspicuous poking above the clouds.'

'Ah, but it won't be going above the clouds.' Miss Muffet made some adjustments to the balloon's ascent. 'Once we reach the top, we'll moor ourselves to the beanstalk just below cloud level and finish the journey on foot. There will probably be an immigration post that we'll have to avoid; other than that I don't envisage any problems.'

No, apart from hiding a large hot-air balloon, navigating a beanstalk thousands of feet above the ground and avoiding immigration security on a cloud. No problem at all.

I was enjoying the quiet and resisting all temptation to check out the scenery below and above when, as is usual with these things, events began to take a turn for the worse.

'Uh – oh,' announced Jack. 'That doesn't look too good.'

'What? What doesn't?' I scrambled to my feet and looked in the direction Jack was pointing. Heading towards the balloon at great speed and with deadly intent was a flock of birds with what looked to be very sharp beaks.

'Well, they're not coming to escort us,' said Miss Muffet. She caught me by the arm and pulled me over to the controls. 'Here, you pilot.'

'M-m-me? I don't know how to drive a balloon.' I looked blankly at the small control panel.

'There's nothing to it, just keep an eye on those dials and if we start to veer off course or to descend, just fire off the burner there.'

'What will you be doing during all this?'

'Attending to our visitors,' Miss Muffet replied, grimly, as she opened a long wicker box at the side of the control panel and took out a very mean-looking crossbow. 'Unfortunately, I don't have too many bolts so I hope there aren't too many birds out there.'

She took up position beside Jack, loaded a bolt and took aim. I wasn't able to watch – not because I was frightened, although I was – but because I needed to keep the balloon steady. I used Jack's shouting as an indication of how successful Miss Muffet's aim was.

'Got him, good shot.' Well, that was positive. One down already.

'Oooh, unlucky, you just missed him.' Not so good. 'But not that time.' She was obviously a good shot.

'Quick, now they're flying around to the other side.' The balloon lurched as the other three rushed around to that side of the basket.

'Oh, another good shot, Miss Muffet. You're great at this.' Frankly, I was hoping she was. All it would take was one sharp-beaked bird to evade the crossbow bolts and we would be in big trouble.

Seconds later we were in big trouble.

'Shoot! shoot!' shouted Jack.

'Dammit,' grunted Miss Muffet, which I took to mean she'd missed.

'Oh dear,' said Basili, and this was followed by a loud hissing which I first thought was him farting. When the balloon's ascent started to slow I knew that flatulence wasn't the issue this time. The craft's envelope had been punctured somewhere above us.

'Now what do we do?' asked Jack, a not-unreasonable question in the circumstances.

'Plan B,' replied Miss Muffet, reaching into the same wicker box she'd removed the crossbow from and lifting out a smaller, wide box.

'What's that?' I foolishly enquired.

'I'm glad you asked, Harry,' she said, handing the box to me. 'It's a puncture repair kit and you're going to have to be the one doing the repairing. I'll have to try to keep the rest of those birds away while attempting to stop us from crashing at the same time. There's no one else who can do it.'

I looked at my two accomplices. She was right: Jack was too young to risk doing something so dangerous and Basili was just too fat. It was me or certain death – or possibly certain death for me and survival for the others. 'What exactly do I have to do?' I asked, not that I really wanted to know the answer.

Miss Muffet pointed up at the huge mass of the balloon's envelope above. 'You'll need to climb up on the outside of that, find the hole and repair it as fast as you can. The envelope is surrounded by netting so you'll have something to hold on to.'

This was sounding worse by the minute. 'Outside, as in outside?'

'Afraid so, and you'd better be quick; we're losing altitude.'

The balloon's envelope was already starting to sag where it had been punctured and, of course, the birds hadn't been so considerate as to pierce it near the basket. Oh, no, they'd gone for maximum effect by making the hole near the top, right where it was at its most inaccessible.

'Harry.' The urgency in Miss Muffet's voice brought me back to a reality I didn't want to know about.

'All right, all right, I'm going.' I grabbed one of the steel supports that secured the basket to the burner and hauled myself up onto its edge. It was then I realised just how high we actually were. The entirety of Grimmtown sprawled below and tiny clouds drifted by. Beside me, the huge mass of the beanstalk twisted and turned as it stretched away from us towards a large cloud mass above.

371

'This isn't a good idea,' I muttered as I pulled myself upright and balanced on the basket.

'Here you are, Mr Harry,' said Basili from below. 'Perhaps you are tying this to yourself in the event that you are falling.' He reached up and tied some rope around my waist.

'Thanks, Basili,' I said. 'Whatever you do, don't let go.'

'You are depending on me,' Basili replied proudly. However one interpreted that sentence, it was correct in every respect.

I pulled on the rope to make sure it was secure then, taking a deep breath that was part terror, part resignation and part I'm-probably-going-to-die-now, I took firm hold of the netting around the envelope and began my very careful ascent of the balloon.

Initially, it wasn't too bad. I was able to work my way upwards by grabbing the next strand of netting above me, digging in with my trotters and pushing myself up. Just when I was about to shout down to the others that this wasn't too difficult, I reached the spot where the balloon's surface bulged outwards and quickly corrected myself as I began to edge out, my body hanging parallel to the ground far below, clinging on for dear life.

Inch by desperate inch, I crawled along the balloon's surface making sure each next grip was secure before letting go the previous one. Slowly, I made my way around the curve until I had passed the equator and was lying on the envelope once more. Above me, I could see where the bird had punctured the surface. I focused on that spot and tried not to look down as it got closer and closer.

I was concentrating so much on the hole in the balloon that I almost didn't notice the birds dive-bombing me. Sensing what I was trying to do they launched an all-out attack to try to knock me off the netting, but I saw their approach at the last minute and waved my arms furiously – which almost had the desired effect as I lost my balance and swung away from the balloon, only grabbing on at the last second.

Above, the birds screeched their frustration and were preparing for a second assault when one of them dropped out of the sky in a flurry of feathers. Miss Muffet had hit the target once more.

That gave the rest of the flock something to think about as they circled the balloon warily, waiting for the chance to have another go at me. At the same time I was gradually getting nearer the puncture, pushing my way along the envelope step by very careful step.

At last I reached my destination. The hole didn't look too big and I didn't anticipate any difficulty in fixing it. Removing the repair kit from my pocket, I opened it and took out a large tube of glue. I quickly applied it to the area around the puncture before cutting off a strip of material from the roll provided and using it to cover the hole. Easy, just like repairing a bicycle wheel – except bicycles tended not to develop punctures while thousands of feet in the air with the wind whistling around the repairer, threatening to blow him into oblivion.

I was patting down the patch, making sure it was secure, when I heard a shout from below. 'They've punctured the far side of the balloon. Quick, Harry, get going.'

And so it went on. I'd no sooner repair one hole than another would appear somewhere else on the balloon, despite Miss Muffet's best efforts to keep the birds at bay. I travelled around the surface of the balloon, doing repair after repair, conscious of the fact that I was running out of both glue and patches, when I heard the phrase I never thought I'd hear spoken again.

'It's okay, Harry, I think we're here.'

I finally took the time to look around. I'd been so caught up in my role as a porcine puncture repair kit that I hadn't realised how high we now were. The balloon was nestling snugly against the beanstalk just below a huge mass of grey cloud that stretched in all directions. Typically, just when I thought we were safe, the birds made one last attack – this time on me. The flock of feathered fiends flapped around my head, pecking and clawing. In panic, I tried to swat them with both arms, forgetting for a second where exactly I was. Losing my balance I slid down the balloon's surface so fast I was unable to grab onto the netting while the birds squawked triumphantly – and possibly even mockingly – as I fell. With a howl of terror I plummeted off the balloon, seeing the concerned passengers in the basket pass me by in a blur. Anticipating a long and painful fall, I covered my head with my arms – not that it would make much difference really. Fortunately, Basili's knot held and I came to an abrupt halt, swinging gently from side to side, looking up at the basket as three heads peered over the edge and down at me.

'Mr Harry, you are being okay, yes?' asked a concerned Basili.

'I'm fine,' I replied as they hauled me up. 'But the next time, I think we'll climb.'

14

Cloud Kingdom

Happy that we were temporarily safe, Miss Muffet threw out a small anchor that bit into the trunk of the beanstalk and secured the balloon.

'Okay, gentlemen, we climb from here. It's not too far to the cloud, so keep quiet and try not to be seen. As soon as the beanstalk broke the cloud-cover, chances are the giants set up a temporary border control to manage any visitors, so we'll have to get by them first.' She climbed out of the basket and held it steady. 'Everyone out.'

Jack hopped nimbly out of the balloon, followed, somewhat less agilely, by Basili who had to receive some help from me (which basically meant me standing under him and, with much huffing and puffing, pushing him over the edge). Seconds later I stood on a large leafy branch beside the others. Above us the cloud-cover blocked out the sun, forcing us to finish our ascent in semidarkness.

'The branches are wide enough so you shouldn't be in any danger,' Miss Muffet advised. 'Just be careful and you'll be fine.'

Slowly we climbed through the foliage towards the fluffy mass above. 'I thought clouds are just made of water,' I whispered to Miss Muffet. 'What's going to stop us from sinking through them once we get there?'

'The giants have magic powers and one of the basic ones makes the clouds solid. It only works on those clouds they live on, though; otherwise they'd play havoc with air traffic control.'

She had a point.

'So now what?' I asked as we reached the point where beanstalk and cloud met.

'Let me take a peek and we'll see.' Cautiously, Miss Muffet poked her head up through the clouds, took a look and quickly pulled her head back down. 'Just as I thought,' she whispered. 'There's a heavily guarded immigration post covering all access from the beanstalk. They look pretty mean and are keeping a very close watch. We're going to have to come up with some sort of distraction.'

'What kind of guards are they?' Our success rate at distracting them very much depended on their level of stupidity. In my experience it ranged from mildly dull (ogres) to extremely thick (gnomes) with degrees of dimness in between.

'Not sure. I think they were goblins,' Miss Muffet said after thinking about it for a moment.

'Well, that's good.' It was too. Goblins featured just above gnomes on the stupidity scale. Any half-decent distraction would probably work on them. Obviously they were the best the giant could muster at such short notice.

'And speaking of distractions.' She looked at me and, from the expression on her face, I just knew that whatever diversion she had in mind would somehow involve me. 'You're going to have to go up there.'

'Why me?' I said. 'Haven't I been through enough already?'

'Yes, but you're the smooth talker. If anyone can distract them it's you.'

'Fine, whatever you say,' I replied. There didn't seem to be any alternative.

Bracing myself to strut my stuff, I looked up at the clouds once more. 'I have another question,' I said.

Miss Muffet rolled her eyes. 'This really isn't the time, Harry; we've got other things to worry about.'

'I know but, if the clouds are supposed to be solid, how did you manage to stick your head up through them? What's stopping me from banging mine when I go up there?'

'They're magic clouds, Harry; they allow access up through them but are solid for everyone on the surface. How else would the beanstalks get through?'

A few minutes later, a bit dishevelled and only slightly presentable, I poked my head up through the clouds and shouted at the goblins, 'Oi, you lot, my craft has broken down and I need some help.' Pulling myself up to cloud level, I reached into my coat, grabbed my wallet and waved it at them. 'I've got money.'

At the immigration post, all four goblins took a look at me (or maybe it was my wallet) and, as one, they rushed to my assistance. As the first two arrived I grabbed them and, before they could react, banged their heads together. As they collapsed on the ground I threw myself at the other two, who had stopped in confusion as their colleagues fell (see, thick, like I said). There was a satisfying crunch as I crushed them beneath me and, moments later, with my team's help all were securely bound and gagged and dropped into the basket of the balloon below so they'd be out of sight.

'You'd have thought that if they were that concerned with security, giants would have a brighter militia than goblins,' I said, as the last one disappeared from view.

'I suspect they were a short-term solution because the beanstalk appeared so suddenly. Normally, immigration is a lot tighter,' Miss Muffet said.

'If you don't mind my saying so, you seem very well versed in this whole area,' I said to her.

'It was my father,' she replied. 'He used to sit me on his knee and tell me about his adventures. He spent a lot of time in places like this. Anyway, it's the kind of thing you need to know when you run a B&B. Guests are always asking how to visit.'

Now that we'd successfully – if somewhat illegally – crossed the border, I finally had a chance to look around. In the distance, the skyline was dominated by an enormous castle. It was so huge it made Aladdin's look like a hut. Towers stretched upwards, gigantic walls encircled the castle's base and the moat that surrounded it was the size of a large river.

'So this giant's a big fellow then?' I said, looking apprehensively at the massive edifice.

'Neringus? Yes, he's one of the biggest, I believe. Rumour has it he's about seventy feet tall. That's the thing about giants, they're giants.'

'Seventy feet?' I was gobsmacked. 'That's big, even for a giant.'

'That's because he's managed to live to be over three hundred. Most giants don't get to survive that long. There are too many adventurers just waiting to have a go. Giants spend their lives constantly looking over their shoulders, waiting for the next hero to try to steal their golden goose or magic harp. This guy's one of the greats.'

'And what about Licken and Lurkey, are they in league with him?' If they were it would be quite an achievement. I still wasn't sure how they'd managed to pull it off. Not only had they managed to infest Miss Muffet's with spiders but they'd stolen the magic bean and made a beeline for Neringus's kingdom without any fear for their lives. Mind you, I still wasn't convinced. They just weren't that imaginative.

'I shouldn't think so,' Miss Muffet said. 'Remember they didn't know the treasure was here either until a short while ago. There's no way they could have planned this. Still,' she looked around carefully, 'there's no sign of them here. Unless they had something to bargain with, they'd have ended up on a spit, being the goblins' dinner, once they popped their heads above the clouds. Goblins are quite partial to poultry.'

I considered what Queenie had said. 'That's what worries me. Neither of them is too bright, or so I thought, and I've known them for years. They're not smart enough to pull something like this off. They must be getting help.'

'From who?' asked Miss Muffet.

'One of the other guests,' I said. 'I'm still not sure which one, though I have my suspicions' – which included most of them right about now.

Other than the castle, there wasn't much to see. Gigantic trees dotted the landscape like green skyscrapers and the only obvious road (and it was very obvious as it was about a mile wide) bisected the cloud and led straight to the castle. There were no villages (the giant had probably eaten all the villagers) and no other signs of life. All told, it was a pretty desolate place.

I pointed to the castle. 'Well, it looks like we're walking.' In fact, after having worn heels for a day, I found I was able to manage the cloud's grey, spongy surface without any difficulty. The others weaved from side to side, having trouble maintaining their balance. It would be a while until they found their cloud-legs.

Together we made our way along the road towards the architectural monstrosity ahead. As we walked, I tried to formulate a plan. What would we find in the castle? Would Licken and Lurkey be waiting with the giant, ready to make a meal of us (literally and metaphorically), or would we manage to find the treasure and get it back to sea level? As the fowl duo was dumber than a bucket of gerbils, someone had to be helping them; but who? Questions, questions – and not an answer in sight.

Then a far more important thought struck me: we were walking towards a large castle, occupied by a very unpleasant giant and, other than the occasional tree, there was no obvious cover to stop us being seen by any lookouts. We were sitting ducks, so to speak.

'Well, to be honest we don't have much choice,' Miss Muffet pointed out when I mentioned it. 'We could try to disguise ourselves as goblins, but it would mean climbing back down to the balloon to undress them and I really don't think there's any chance their outfits would fit us.' She looked pointedly at Basili and me.

'So, what do we do?' Jack asked. 'I don't want to end up being eaten.'

'I don't either, Jack, but maybe we can use the trees as cover.' As plans went, it wasn't up to much owing to the scarcity of actual vegetation, but at least it was a suggestion – albeit a relatively useless one.

'Perhaps we are being continuing with the film plan.' Basili had been quiet up to now and when he said that I wished he'd stayed quiet.

'That's the most—' I began, before being interrupted by Miss Muffet.

'The most brilliant suggestion I've heard,' she said. Clearly she didn't hear much by way of brilliant suggestions in the course of running a B&B.

'No, listen,' she continued. 'Why not try it? What have we got to lose?'

'Our heads for one thing,' I pointed out. 'We're here illegally; Licken and Lurkey know who we are; and do I need to point out that a giant, with a healthy appetite for meat and who isn't too fussy about what type, lives here?'

380

'And I suppose you have a better idea?' Miss Muffet said.

'Well, there's always the old standby,' I said. She raised an enquiring eyebrow. 'Wait until dark.'

Miss Muffet was about to say something, clearly thought the better of it when she realised she had no other suggestions and wisely chose to remain silent.

'There, that's settled then. Now let's find somewhere to shelter.' I headed towards the nearest tree and sat down against the trunk. Branches that were so big they could have made a successful living as trees in Grimmtown overhung our location and provided the perfect cover. As long as we stayed here, we'd never be seen from the castle.

Beside me, Jack looked up through the leaf cover at the sky as he huddled against Basili for warmth. 'Well, at least it's not ra . . .' He had just opened his mouth when there was a loud clap of thunder and the skies above, clearly intent on inflicting as much misery as possible on us, unleashed a deluge that could only loosely have been described as rain, such was its intensity. Although the tree provided great cover from prying eyes, as shelter it left much to be desired. Torrents of water flowed down leaves the size of umbrellas and submerged us in a cascade of freezing rain.

'Thanks, Jack,' I said, as water streamed down my face, ruining what was left of my make-up.

'Don't mention it,' he said miserably as he tried to shelter under Basili's jacket.

'Look on the bright side.' Miss Muffet stood up and tried to wring out her hair (it didn't make much difference). 'With rain this heavy, the guards won't be too keen on keeping watch and it'll provide decent enough cover. And we can't get any wetter now, can we?'

'I suppose not. Okay, gang, let's walk.' I stood up, watched water flow off me in mini-streams and squelched forwards towards the castle. Grumbling loudly, Basili followed with Miss Muffet and Jack bringing up the rear.

Miss Muffet was right about one thing: the rain certainly provided enough cover. It pummelled us relentlessly as we walked, cascading down around us and soaking us through. It was like being underwater. At least there was one benefit: no one was interested in talking much. We trudged on, wrapped in our own silent miseries, hoping all the while that the castle was getting nearer – we certainly couldn't see it through the deluge, large though it may have been.

I don't know how long we walked for. It could have been minutes, it could have been hours. Time seemed to pass differently under the incessant downpour. All I knew was that, out of nowhere the road ended and I was suddenly walking on wood. I held out my arms to block the others. 'Everyone, stop right now. I think we're there.'

Ahead I could just make out a large dark space which I imagined was the castle entrance. That meant that we were now standing on the huge drawbridge that extended over the moat. From what I could make out, the entrance seemed to be unguarded. Was it going to be that easy? Just to be sure, I indicated to the others to stay where they were and crept forward for a closer look. Once I was under the huge arch at the far end of the drawbridge, I was sheltered from the rain, for which I gave a silent prayer of thanks. Ahead of me, the arch opened out into a huge covered lobby with doors in all the walls and a gigantic staircase leading to the upper levels. On the far side of the arch, almost hidden from view, was a guard post. Sensibly, if somewhat against orders, the guards had obviously elected to perform their duties from inside the comfort and warmth of their hut. In other circumstances I may have been appalled by their cavalier attitude to their work; today I was mostly grateful. Just to be sure, I sneaked over to the hut, crouched under the window and very cautiously took a look in. It seemed, from what I could observe, that the security goblins' idea of keeping watch amounted to huddling around a table, playing cards and accusing each other of cheating.

I crept back to the others and advised them of the situation. 'If we're very quiet we should make it past that hut without any difficulty. After that, as I don't know where we're going, I suggest we head for the nearest door and then decide what to do next.' My plan was greeted by a round of ragged and less than enthusiastic nods.

Single file and crouched down, we sneaked past the guard hut, along the wall towards the first door. When we got there I realised we had a problem.

'Anyone got any ideas how to reach that?' I looked up at the door handle. It was the perfect height for a giant, but, some thirty-five feet above us, it was more than a little inaccessible.

'Well, if we had some rope we could make a lasso and pull it down,' Jack suggested.

'Rope anyone?' I asked, to be greeted by much shaking of heads. 'Okay then, it looks like we'll have to invoke Plan B.'

'Plan B?' Basili said. 'What is Plan B?'

'Something that you'll play a vital role in.' I waved him forward. 'Stand there.'

Basili did as instructed. 'Now, I'm going to climb up on your shoulders.' This was a lot more difficult than it sounded. We were all so wet, every time I attempted to clamber up on Basili's back, I slid back down again.

Miss Muffet was becoming exasperated. 'The longer we hang around here the more likely it is that one of those guards will come out for a quick smoke or the giant will decide to go for his evening constitutional. We'll be pretty defenceless then, balanced one on top of the other, won't we?'

Her powers of persuasion were very effective. The thought of the castle's owner finding us gave my mountaineering skills a temporary boost and seconds later I was balancing precariously on Basili's ample shoulders and extending my hand down to Miss Muffet.

I hoisted her onto my shoulders. She teetered back and forth for a second, but, thankfully, regained her balance before she could bring the whole tower down.

'How far to the handle?' I asked.

'It's still out of reach,' Miss Muffet said. 'Once Jack is up here, he might be able to grab it.'

I looked down at Jack who was waiting expectantly down below. 'You're up.'

He must have had monkey ancestors as he shinned up all three of us and balanced on Miss Muffet's shoulders like he was going up stairs.

'Can you reach it?' I asked.

'Maybe, if I jump,' Jack shouted down from above. 'But it's very big. I can't pull it down. I'll have to hang off it. Just a sec.' There was a brief pause, then he said, 'It's on its way.' Followed seconds later by, 'Oh, no.'

Oh no? Why the 'oh no'? 'Jack, what's going on?' As I spoke the door opened inwards and our tower collapsed onto the (fortunately) soft carpet inside. Other than a few bumps where we landed on each other, everyone seemed okay. I did a quick headcount. Basili was lying under me, pushing me off. Miss Muffet sat on the ground rubbing her back. And Jack – where was Jack?

'Help,' came a voice from above. 'Someone help me.' Jack was still dangling from the handle. 'I can't hold on much longer.'

'Quick,' I said to the others. 'We need to find something to break his fall.' Anxiously the three of us looked around the huge room. Furniture the size of houses towered above us; the carpet stretched off to walls that seemed miles away. There didn't seem to be anything that we could use.

'There, look.' Miss Muffet pointed at a small white bundle partially hidden by a chair leg. She ran over and pulled at it. 'Perfect.'

We followed her over and looked at what she'd found.

'Why is there a sheet on the floor?' Basili asked as he helped her pull it across the room.

'I don't think it's a sheet; I think it's a handkerchief.' Miss Muffet panted as she heaved the mass of cloth along the carpet.

I grabbed the other end and helped. 'I hope it's clean,' I said.

'Don't even go there,' Miss Muffet said through gritted teeth. 'That's the least of our worries right now.'

When we'd reached the door, Miss Muffet and I grabbed a corner, Basili seized the opposite edge and we stretched out what I now saw was a clean hanky.

'Everyone hold on tight,' I ordered and looked up at the small figure dangling above us. 'Jack, let go the handle. We'll catch you.'

Either he was very trusting or he couldn't hold on any longer. I had barely finished speaking when he dropped into the taut hanky, bounced up once and landed in the middle again.

'Wow, that was fun,' he said, poking his head out of the tangle of cloth.

I checked him for any injuries, but he seemed none the worse for his experience. 'Are you okay?'

'Yep,' he said. 'What's the plan?'

Before I could reply, there was the sound of applause from the far side of the room and a female voice said, 'Marvellous, absolutely marvellous. Can you do it again?'

15

Fee, Fie, Foe,
Something-or-Other

The only thing I was sure of as I swung around to see who had spoken was that it almost certainly wasn't the giant. If he'd been in the room he could hardly have missed our amateur acrobatics and rescue stunt – and we'd probably have noticed him by now anyway. That didn't mean we weren't in danger, though: chances were, anyone living in the giant's castle probably wouldn't be friendly.

'Okay everyone, be on your guard,' I whispered. 'See if you can spot who's doing the talking.'

Miss Muffet pointed. 'I think it came from over there, somewhere near all those musical instruments.'

'How incredibly observant of you,' said the voice once more. This time it sounded as if it was taunting us. 'Maybe you should take a closer look.'

Huddled together, we crept carefully across the wide expanse of carpet, towards the array of instruments Miss Muffet had pointed out.

'I am opinioning that we are being in the music room,' whispered Basili.

'You think?' I said. 'What was your first clue?'

'Quiet, the pair of you,' Miss Muffet hissed. 'This isn't the time or the place.'

'I'd listen to the lady,' said the mysterious voice once more. 'She knows what she's talking about.'

Miss Muffet turned towards me. 'I think it's coming from behind that harp.'

'Oh, you're so warm. Have another guess.' Now the voice was starting to irritate me.

I looked over towards the instruments. A huge, definitely giant-sized wooden harp towered above us. The instrument's front column had been carved into the shape of a woman in long flowing robes, arms clasped above her head. The harp was a bit worse for wear. Long, deep scratches ran the length of the column and it looked as though chunks of wood had recently been cut out of the base. It had clearly seen better days. A stool – presumably for the absent harpist – sat to one side. If there was someone hiding behind the harp, I couldn't see them. All I could make out was a collection of other instruments, all on display stands. Cellos, violins and basses stood to one side, brasses dominated the centre and a large grand piano took up the left-hand side of the display area.

I nudged Miss Muffet. 'Are you sure you heard the voice from behind the harp? I can't see anything.'

The carved woman on the harp turned her head and looked down at us. 'That's because it is the harp, you dunderhead,' she said, her voice dripping sarcasm. She unclasped her arms and positioned them on her hips. 'You're not too bright, are you?' She took a closer look at me. 'And are you wearing make-up?'

'Take it from me, you're not seeing us at our best,' I said wearily.

'That much is certain,' Basili added.

'More to the point,' I interrupted, before the conversation went further off the rails. 'Who exactly are you?'

'Why, I'm the famous magic harp.' The harp drew herself up to full height. 'Of course, you've heard of me.' It was more a statement than a question.

'The harp that Jack the Giantkiller stole?' There seemed to be a lot of Jacks cropping up in this particular case.

'No, no, no!' The harp's face twisted angrily. 'Do you honestly think anyone would be capable of stealing me? I'm not exactly convenient to carry, am I?' She had a point. From where I stood she looked very heavy indeed. I imagined it would take a small team of men and an industrial crane to move her.

'So what did he . . .'

The harp interrupted as if anticipating my question. 'He stole a lyre okay, L-Y-R-E. Not a harp, a lyre – and a pretty cheap one at that.' She shook her head. 'Giantkillers: thick as soup. It's not as if it's easy to confuse us.'

Once more the conversation was threatening to derail and plunge into a canyon of digressions.

'Look Miss Harp, Harpy or whatever your name is. We're looking for a chicken and a turkey that might have arrived here earlier today. Have you seen them?'

The harp smirked. 'And I thought giantkillers were stupid. Those two make most other adventurers look like geniuses.'

'So they were here then?' I asked.

'Oh yeah, they were here. They even whispered about trying to steal me, until I warned them off. I told them I'd tell Neringus what they were at. That sorted them out. But before they ran off they did this.' She pointed to the scratches and damage to the harp's base. 'Vandals. I'm going to need some repair work and a new coat of varnish because of them.'

'And where are they now?'

389

'Oh, they headed off with my master. Knowing him, I expect they're chicken soup by now.'

I didn't think so; they were here for a reason and I suspected the giant was tied up in it. It was possible they'd be dinner eventually, just not yet. 'Where did he take them?'

'His study is on the first floor. Top of the landing, turn left, first door.' The harp smirked. 'Will you be doing your team pyramid act to get up the stairs? If you are, can you leave the door open, I'd love to watch.'

Now that presented a problem. We'd had enough trouble just opening the door to the music room; getting up a flight of stairs presented a challenge an order of magnitude more difficult – and we had to do it without being seen.

'Anyone got any suggestions?' I asked the others. Silence greeted my question. Team Harry clearly weren't on the ball right about now. 'Anyone?'

'I think you might not need to climb the stairs after all,' the harp interrupted. 'If I'm not mistaken the owner of the house is on his way down.'

'What? The giant is on his way? We need to hide. Now!'

From outside the door came the noise of something very large and very heavy descending the stairs. I looked around in panic. Other than the furniture there wasn't much by way of hiding places. Maybe we could take cover behind a table leg and hope we weren't seen. It was a long shot, but it was the only option we had.

'Everyone, get to the table,' I shouted and ran towards the towering wooden structure. Basili crouched beside me. The other two had taken cover behind the large percussion section. I looked at the harp. 'And if you say a word or do anything to attract attention, I'll carve my initials into your pretty wooden head. Are we clear?'

The harp gulped once and nodded. 'I already need some restoration work; I don't fancy needing more.'

There was a loud crashing from above as the giant pushed the door fully open and entered the room. I felt the floor vibrate as he walked across the room and paused beside our hiding place. Peeping out, I could see a gigantic boot and the bottom of Neringus's trousers. Slowly, he bent down towards me. How had he seen us?

I was caught between cowering where I was and making a futile attempt to run for the door when a loud voice proclaimed, 'FEE, FIE, FOE, FU—, oh there it is,' and the giant picked up the handkerchief we'd used to rescue Jack moments earlier. As the giant turned to leave the room he paused once more and I heard him sniff loudly. 'FEE, FIE, FOE, FUM, I SMELL THE BLOOD OF AN . . . well, I'm not exactly sure, but I do smell something. Unless I'm mistaken, we have intruders. How inconvenient. I shall have to talk to those goblins. They seem to be less than efficient.' He began to prowl around the room, sniffing constantly, trying to pinpoint our location.

'Sire, if I may.' The treacherous harp pointed at the table. 'I think you'll find what you're looking for behind that table leg there.' Before Basili or I could run, the giant reached down, picked us up in each hand and dangled us in front of him. 'Now, what have we here, hmmm?' He scrutinised us carefully, turning us around and examining us from all sides. 'How unusual: a most unattractive male of the pig species and a large gentleman with a faint echo of magic. I suspect you have quite an interesting story to tell and I do so look forward to hearing it before dinner.' He smiled. 'Then again, as you probably will be dinner, I expect that you'll be finished telling it long before that.'

As the giant took us from the room, I managed to grab Miss Muffet's attention, waving at her to stay hidden until we left the room. I couldn't say whether she got the message before the door was slammed behind us and, firmly in the giant's clutches, we ascended the stairs.

16

The Not-So-Great Escape

Suspended fifty feet above the ground, we were carried along a landing and into the giant's study. He walked towards a huge desk and sat down, dropping me and Basili into a glass bowl under a reading lamp. As he studied us, I took the opportunity to take a closer look at him too. Long brown hair hung down around his shoulders, green eyes stared at us in fascination and his nose bore evidence of more than one confrontation (though whether with other giants or human adventurers, I couldn't say). Judging by the frilly shirt, puffed at the sleeves, I was getting a definite New Romantic vibe from him. His smile wasn't especially friendly, not that I expected it would be. As a rule, anyone with a penchant for eating his visitors probably wasn't the friendly type.

'Well now then, and who do we have here, hmmm?' Even when he spoke quietly it was like standing beside a jet engine as it prepared to take off. I covered my ears to deaden the sound – it didn't make much difference.

I decided that, as it had worked reasonably well up to now, I'd go for the film crew ruse once more; well, we still sort of looked the part, although perhaps a little more dishevelled than I might

393

have liked. 'I'm Harry du Crêpe, personal assistant to Alain Schmidt-Heye, world-renowned film director. This is he.' I waved at a terrified Basili who was cowering beside me. 'Snap out of it,' I hissed at him while kicking him none too gently on the ankle. 'Our lives depend on this.'

Neringus's smile stretched even wider. He seemed to be very amused at us. 'Movies, eh? How nice. Are you sure you're not perhaps Harry Pigg and his assistant Basili, the former genie, hmmm?'

Busted!

I looked up at Neringus, 'Licken and Lurkey?'

The giant rubbed his stomach and belched loudly. It was like being caught in an unpleasant-smelling wind tunnel. 'Indeed, the feathered fowl duo. I must confess, I am so looking forward to having them for dinner. I'm feeling a tad unwell and I'm told that chicken soup does wonders for a cold.'

'You're going to eat them?'

'But of course; they were trespassing, as, I must point out, are you.' Now that wasn't something I wanted to hear. It wasn't that I was overly concerned as to their fate; I was more concerned that we were likely to meet the same end. 'In fact, why don't you wave to them; they're over there.' He pointed to a shelf on the far wall. Sitting in a covered bowl the size of a truck, very like the one we were in, only much bigger, were a very unhappy-looking Licken and Lurkey. They gave me an abashed wave. I didn't return it.

'So now what?' I asked the giant.

'Now? Why you're going to be dinner, like I've already told you. Why? Did you have something else in mind?'

To be honest, all thoughts of solving the case had vanished once Neringus had mentioned we were on the menu. The only thing on my mind now was trying to escape, initially from the bowl and eventually from Neringus's kingdom. I wasn't sure right now which was going to be tougher.

Neringus stood up and walked towards the door. 'Don't go anywhere now. I'll be expecting you to be here when I get back.' He smirked as he left the room. I was starting to dislike him deeply.

Once he was gone I turned to Basili. 'All right, let's get out of here,' I said. 'It shouldn't be too hard.' When I tried to clamber up the walls of the bowl I found out just how difficult it was going to be. Trotters and glass were not a good combination. No matter how hard I tried, I couldn't get any purchase on the surface and kept sliding back down. Even if we tried a cut-down variation on our human pyramid of earlier, we still weren't tall enough to reach the bowl's rim. Every attempt either resulted in another slide down the glass or me collapsing in a heap on top of poor Basili.

'Oh, Mr Harry,' he moaned after our latest attempt had ended in failure. 'I am not wanting to be a giant's evening meal. What are we to do?'

'I'm thinking, Basili. I'm thinking.' Which was true. I just wasn't coming up with anything remotely resembling an escape plan. As I lay at the bottom of the bowl, out of the corner of my eye I caught something moving: Licken and Lurkey were waving frantically at me. As they were partly responsible for me being in this mess, I chose to ignore them, but it wasn't to be. Basili nudged me in the ribs.

'Mr Harry, I think they are trying most hard to communicate with us.'

'How? Semaphore? Morse Code? Interpretive Dance?' I really wasn't interested.

'No, Mr Harry, they are writing something.'

'Writing? On what?' I still wasn't interested.

'On the glass.'

I suspected there wasn't anything that Licken and Lurkey might say that could possibly interest me, but I took a quick look. Their first attempt at communication seemed to confirm this. Using what I suspected was something out of his make-up pouch, Licken had written: 'DON'T CLIME GLAS WE TRIED THAT TO IT DUZENT WORK.'

Well, that really encouraged me. We were trapped in glass bowls in a giant's stronghold and all they seemed to be interested in was stating the blindingly obvious. Well, we weren't going to get much help from that direction. I urged Basili to ignore them. 'Unfortunately, they won't go away, but we can look in the other direction.'

'But Mr Neringus will be eating them,' he wailed.

'Better them than us,' I replied.

'Oh, Mr Harry, that is being very cruel.' Basili slumped down beside me. 'Look, they are being writing another message.'

'Let me guess: "we're all going to die," just spelled very badly.'

'No, it is something about a trezzar. What is a trezzar?'

'Trezzar?' I looked over at the other bowl. 'WE NO WHERE TREZZAR IS.'

'I don't know anyone called Trezzar,' I said to Basili. 'Do you?'

'I am not aware of anyone with that name,' he replied after thinking for a moment.

'So what are they try . . .?' Then it struck me. 'It's not a who, it's a what. They know where the badly spelled treasure is. They've found Sinbad's fortune.' Then an even worse thought struck me. 'If we get out of here, that means we'll now have to rescue them, too.'

'But, of course, that is meaning that we must be getting ourselves out of here first,' Basili pointed out, taking his 'stating the transparently obvious' cue from the other two.

'Well, that's true,' I replied. 'But I confidently expect that we'll be out of this bowl imminently.'

'You are having a plan?' Basili jumped up and down in excitement and it wasn't a pretty sight.

'I'm not.' Basili's face dropped once more. 'But I suspect they are,' and I pointed up to the huge anglepoise lamp that overhung

396

the bowl. Perched on top, lowering a rope, were Miss Muffet and Jack. The cavalry were here.

'Good work, guys,' I shouted as the rope descended.

'Sorry it took so long,' Miss Muffet replied. 'The stairs were a bit tricky.'

'Yeah,' Jack piped in. 'I'd have been here quicker only for her.'

Miss Muffet rolled her eyes and wisely chose to ignore him.

'I'm glad you're here now,' I said as I grabbed the rope – which was actually a piece of giantish string – and clambered up the side of the bowl.

Basili wasn't as limber as I, so it took a more concerted effort to get him out, all three of us dragging the rope upwards while he dangled uselessly. Eventually, he was able to grab the rim and pull himself up onto it. 'Now what?' he asked.

'We lower you onto the desk then I follow you down.' More grunting, groaning and near-misses ensued until the ex-genie was, finally, safely on the giant writing pad that the bowl rested on. Once he was safe, I shinned down after him and waited for Miss Muffet and Jack to join us.

'Okay,' Miss Muffet said, 'let's get out of here.' She stopped when she saw the expression on my face. 'Uh oh, I suspect that doesn't mean good news is about to follow.'

I pointed at Lurkey and Licken. 'We need to get them out too; they know where the loot is.'

Miss Muffet stamped her foot on the desk. 'Dammit, there's always something.' She looked across at the bowl. Although it was only at the far side of the study and a short walk by giant standards, to us it would be like negotiating an assault course. 'Do we have to?'

'I'm afraid so,' I said. 'Without them we're stuck. Mind you, I don't know how we're going to get over there.'

Miss Muffet scanned the desk. 'Maybe we don't have to.'

I raised an enquiring eyebrow.

'Look, it could take us the rest of the day just to get up to that shelf and, after that, we'd still have to get them out of the bowl.'

I nodded for her to continue.

'What if we could just break the bowl from here?' She ran over to the side of the desk and forced open a large paper box. 'Ah, just what I was looking for.' She reached into the box and hauled out a long rubber band. 'Here, give me a hand to take these out.'

The rest of us looked blankly at her.

'Now, please,' and her tone of voice suggested that arguing with her would not be a good idea.

'You heard the lady,' I said to the others. 'Let's go.' Together we dragged a number of rubber bands from the box and formed them into a big pile on the desk.

'Right, now we tie them together – and make sure they're proper knots. I don't want them coming loose at a crucial moment.'

'Care to elaborate on the plan?' I asked, mystified.

'In a moment; just keep tying.' She ran to the far side of the desk. 'I'll be back shortly; I just need to find something.'

Jack looked at me. 'Harry, what's she doing?'

'Your guess is as good as mine,' I said to him, 'but she seems to know what she's at.'

By the time Miss Muffet came back, carrying a large stone, we'd tied the rubber bands into a long strand. 'Paperweight,' she announced and looked at our work appreciatively. 'Not bad, boys; not bad at all.' She grabbed one end of the strand. 'Now if we tie this to here,' she muttered as she wrapped it around the stem of the lamp, 'and this end to . . .' She looked around the surface of the desk. 'Ah, good; this will do nicely.' Taking the other end of the rope of rubber bands, she secured it to a giant marble pen holder. Once both ends were tied off she grabbed the middle of what had become an improvised catapult and hauled it back. As the bands began to stretch, she struggled to keep it taut.

'Harry. Genie. Help me.'

The two of us stood beside her and took the strain. Together we pulled the rubber rope further back until our muscles were straining to keep the tension on it.

'I don't think we can hold this much longer,' I grunted.

'Jack,' Miss Muffet shouted. 'Grab the stone and put it on the rubber band – and hurry.'

Jack scurried around to where Miss Muffet had dropped the stone and rolled it over to where we stood. 'It's very heavy,' he said.

'I know, Jack, but just try your best, okay.' I could hear the tension in her voice. She wouldn't be able to hold on much longer.

Jack put his arms under the stone and slowly began to lift.

'That's it,' Miss Muffet encouraged him. 'Just a little bit more. You're almost there.'

Inch by painful inch, Jack raised the stone until it was level with Miss Muffet's arms.

'Now, drop it on the elastic band on top of my forearms and stand well back. We'll only get one shot at this.'

Jack eased the stone onto the rubber band as instructed. 'Stand well back, Jack,' she ordered. 'On the count of three, everyone let go; one, two, three.'

To be honest, I wasn't able to hold on any longer anyway. As soon as she said 'three' I let go and watched as the stone flew across the room towards Licken and Lurkey's bowl. It was obvious almost as soon as it was fired that it was going to miss by some distance.

'Dammit,' Miss Muffet shouted. 'I thought I'd aimed it correctly.'

'Don't be hard on yourself,' I said to her. 'It was a one in a million cha . . .'

'And one that might just pay off,' Jack interrupted. 'Look.'

We followed the stone as it sailed through the air. Although it missed the bowl by the proverbial country mile, it cannoned off a picture frame on the shelf above, deflected sideways and smacked into a vase that sat on the edge of the shelf. The vase teetered from side to side before falling off the shelf and bouncing onto the bowl on the shelf below as it plummeted to its destruction on the floor. There was a loud crash and the bowl began to break. We watched in fascination as the glass cracked and shattered around Licken and Lurkey. Fortunately (or unfortunately, depending on your point of view), neither of them seemed to have been injured in the process.

Miss Muffet turned to us proudly. 'Of course, I meant it all the time.' She looked at our disbelieving faces. 'Yes, really.'

But she didn't get too much opportunity to bask in her glory.

'Um, Mr Harry, I am believing that the bird people are leaving us behind.'

'See ya, suckers.' Free at last, Licken and Lurkey were using their wings to glide to the floor. I certainly wouldn't have called it flying.

Miss Muffet looked on as the pair of them reached the ground safely and scuttled out the door, giving us a quick wave as they did so. 'There's gratitude for you,' she said.

'They're criminals who were facing death by digestion; I don't think gratitude was high on their list of priorities.'

'Maybe not, but if they get away they'll get to the treasure before us.'

'I don't think so,' I replied. 'They're obviously not in league with the giant, even though I suspect they thought they could talk him around when they climbed the beanstalk. I think their first priority will be to get out of here and report back to whoever hired them.'

'And who do you think that is?' Miss Muffet asked.

'I'm not sure yet, but, as our brothers in blue like to say, "I'm following a definite line of enquiry."'

'So you do know who's behind this?'

'I have a fair idea, but I don't want to say just yet; I need some more information first.' I'd finally started to piece together the case based on what I'd seen and heard over the past twenty-four hours and was pretty sure I knew who was behind it all – but I could still be wrong.

What? I hear you say, Harry Pigg wrong? I know it's highly unlikely, but I just needed to be certain – assuming I could get out of here alive. And that was my current priority; solving the case could wait a while longer, until I'd evaded an angry giant with non-selective carnivorous dietary habits and his mangy bunch of goblin guards. At least I knew Sinbad's fortune was definitely here somewhere – if the chicken and turkey were to be believed.

Now, I had to come up with another plan. I gathered the others around and briefed them on our current situation. 'We're on top of a table that's thirty feet off the ground; any second now, Neringus will probably be back for his soup and sandwiches and will be a bit miffed when he discovers the main ingredients have flown the coop. His state of mind probably won't be appeased in any way when he sees that we're out of the bowl, so we need to get out of here soonest.' Nods of agreement all round.

As it turned out, getting down off the desk wasn't too difficult. A combination of the rope Miss Muffet and Jack had used to rescue us, together with the rubber bands, allowed us to climb down without too much difficulty – although in Basili's case it became more like a bungee jump than a descent. It took three bounces before we were able to snag him and lower him safely to the carpet.

'Now what?' whispered Jack.

'Now we head for the wall and try to keep out of sight until we get to the door,' I replied. 'Everyone, follow me.'

The four of us crept along by the skirting until we reached the door which, thankfully, the giant hadn't closed when he left the room. It was a small break, but one we were grateful for. Over the past hour we had done more acrobatics than an average circus troupe and I wasn't keen to add any new tweaks to our act. Motioning the others to stop, I peeked around the door frame. The landing appeared empty. It stretched ahead, doors on both sides and the stairs to the lower level at the far end. The trip back to the front door would be an endurance test.

I turned to the others. 'Looks like it's clear. Let's go. And remember, stay close to the wall.'

Miss Muffet tapped me on the shoulder. 'Remind me again, where are we going?'

'The plan is to get out of here. It's too dangerous to hang around, so I suggest we make for the front door and head back to the beanstalk,' I said.

'And then what? Do you really think that Sinbad's fortune will be here when we come back – assuming we do come back?'

I looked pointedly at Jack Horner. 'It may not be, but my priority now is to get the others back to Grimmtown before they come to any harm. If that means we don't find the loot, then so be it. Ready?' I ran out of the door and, tight to the wall, began to make my way down the landing towards the stairs. I'd only taken a few steps when I heard music wafting up from the ground floor. From the sound of it, the harp was singing for her metaphorical supper while the giant applauded enthusiastically. It was like listening to a thunderstorm. Then another thunderstorm, as metaphorical as the harp's supper, set off lightning bolts in my head. It was something the harp had said and I'd only now registered the significance of it. Considering the giant's innate hostility to any kind of visitor, I was fairly sure the only person in this whole scenario who'd be able to visit Neringus's castle without fearing for their life was the mastermind behind the whole caper. All I needed to do now was to escape and unmask them – and see how I keep referring to the villain in the plural? – that's just to keep you guessing, assuming you haven't figured it out yet.

17

The Axeman Cometh

The stairs proved to be easier than I expected; then again we were going down. Even Jack was able to hang off the edge and drop to the lower step each time. It took a long and tiring time to get to the bottom and by the time we did we were barely able to stand. Between us and freedom was a huge lobby, a guard hut, a drawbridge, a longer walk across the clouds, an immigration post (hopefully still unoccupied) and a short beanstalk descent to our balloon. I just hoped we wouldn't collapse from exhaustion before we got to it.

Basili had dropped to his knees. 'Oh, Mr Harry, I do not think I am making it to our balloon. You must be leaving me here and be going on without me.'

Before I could give my heroic reply about never leaving a man or ex-genie behind, Jack fell down beside him. 'Me neither,' he gasped, 'but please don't leave me here and go on without me.'

Miss Muffet bent over, struggling for breath and put her hands on my shoulders for support. 'They're right. I'm tired too. We need an alternative option, otherwise we'll never get back.'

Privately, I was glad they were exhausted; I was too. I just didn't want to be the first to admit it. 'Okay, find someplace to hide while I see what I can come up with,' I ordered. I wasn't sure what I was looking for, but I had to find something and fast. If the giant or one of his goons spotted us we were toast – or maybe soup.

I scuttled away and, still hugging the wall, made my way to the room adjoining the giant's music room. The door was slightly open so I was able to peer through the crack and take a look around. From what I could see, I was looking at the dining room. A huge table and chairs dominated the centre and pictures of Neringus and the rest of what looked to be a very ugly family indeed adorned (if adorned could be said to be the correct word) the walls. My quick examination revealed nothing that might be of assistance and I was wondering if I'd find anything useful when I became aware of a raucous noise coming from the far end of the lobby. It wasn't loud enough, or even sophisticated enough, to belong to a giant and sounded like whoever was making it was having a good time.

The goblins! Of course; the giant's guards had to have someplace to live while they were off duty. They were hardly going to commute up and down from Grimmtown on a daily basis – and they had to have some way to get quickly to and from any rogue beanstalks that might suddenly appear in the giant's domain. Imbued with a fresh, albeit faint, sense of hope, I headed towards the source of the noise, alert for any stray goblins.

As I got close I could see the source of the goblin revelry was a small wooden cottage, nestling snugly under the stairs out of sight. I wasn't too bothered about checking it out, though. Oh, no, all I needed was the rat-drawn cart that was secured to a post outside the cottage. Now, in normal circumstances, the fact that the vehicle was drawn by two giant rats that seemed to be all teeth, fur and drool might be a cause for concern, but, in my current circumstances, I couldn't really afford to be choosy. It was the cart or nothing. At least, being goblins, they hadn't bothered with any guards outside the cottage. This wasn't really carelessness; if I had been them, I wouldn't have been too worried about anyone breaking in and stealing anything belonging to me. It was a giant's castle after all – who'd be mad enough? Apart, that is, from me.

Oh, so carefully, I sneaked up to the rats and, mindful of the teeth, gently untied the reins all the while muttering, 'easy boys' and 'there, there'. I know they weren't horses, but I wasn't sure how exactly to address a giant rat. All I wanted to ensure was that they didn't decide I looked like a very appetising meal. Fortunately, either I didn't look appetising or they'd already been fed because I managed to undo the reins and step up onto the driver's seat without any difficulty. The difficulty, of course, happened imme-diately afterwards. No sooner was I on the cart than the door to Goblin HQ opened and one of them came out for a smoke or a stroll or something. It didn't take him long to spot that his personal fleet was being hijacked.

'Oi, you,' he bellowed. 'Get down off that. It don't belong to you.'

I didn't stop to discuss the ethics of robbery when in a desperate situation. I just grabbed the whip from the holder beside me, cracked it over the rats' heads and yelled 'mush, mush'. The rats bounded forward, almost toppling me off balance as the cart lurched beneath me. I heaved on the reins and tried to force the rats over to where the others waited. For a few seconds it was rat against pig; they wanted to go one way, I another. Bit by bit I managed to force them in the direction I wanted and once they saw I was stronger (and had a whip), they caved in and raced away towards the foot of the stairs.

'Everyone, get ready to jump,' I roared at the others. 'I'm not sure I can get this thing to stop.' To their credit, when they saw me bearing down on them in a rat-powered cart, they didn't bat an eyelid. In fairness, they'd seen so many strange things that day this was just one more – and one that they could grasp.

I pulled back on the reins, shouting, 'Whoa boys' at the same time (well, in fairness, my only exposure to animal-drawn vehicles was what I'd seen watching Westerns, so my grasp of commands was based on what I'd heard cowboys say). The rats didn't really 'whoa', but they did slow down enough to allow my friends to clamber in the back. Once they were safely on board, I cracked the whip once more – now that I was getting the hang of it – and the carriage raced towards the drawbridge.

'Faster, Harry,' Jack shouted into my ear. 'The goblins are coming after us.'

True, but as they were on foot, they had no chance of catching us. I was far more concerned about those in the guard hut at the drawbridge, who, even now, were swarming out. Either the card game was over or they'd been alerted to our presence.

'Goblins ahead,' I roared. 'I'm going to need help up here. Anything in the back we can use.'

'We're onto it,' Miss Muffet replied. Seconds later she appeared on the seat beside me.

'Well?' I said hopefully.

'There isn't much by way of weapons, but there is lots of fruit and veg – most of it rotten. It's not great, but,' she hefted a head of cabbage in her hand, 'it's better than nothing. Okay, everyone, grab something and prepare to pelt.' There was a scuffling from behind as the others burrowed into the rotting pile to find the best weapon.

Out in front, the goblins were forming a ragged line and bringing weapons to bear. Seconds later they were running for cover as a barrage of rotten tomatoes, cabbages and what looked like a very solid head of cauliflower ('that one was mine,' Jack yelled gleefully) rained down on them. To tell the truth, I think the vicious snapping of the giant rats probably had more of an impact, but, either way, it cleared them out of our path. The cart bounced across the drawbridge and onto the road that led back to the beanstalk. Surely nothing could prevent our escape now.

Of course, as soon as I think something like that, inevitably some new obstacle presents itself in our way – or in this case, right behind us. From the music room, I heard the urgent shouts of the harp as she alerted her master to our escape. Damn, she had seen us.

This was followed by a bellowing like an explosion and the giant roared, 'FEE, FIE, FOE, FUM, I SMELL THE BLOOD OF AN . . . UM . . . AH . . . PIG, TWO HUMANS AND SOMETHING ELSE. BE THEY ALIVE OR BE THEY DEAD, I'LL GRIND THEIR BONES TO MAKE SOUP, BREAD, A NICE PIE AND SOME LEFTOVERS FOR SUPPER.'

I hoped that if he did catch us that I would be dead before he decided to use us for some cookery, though my priority was to make sure we weren't actually caught at all. I cracked the whip once more, trying to get as much speed as I could out of the rats. To be fair, they were tearing along the road at a fair lick; I just didn't think they'd be able to outrun the giant with his huge strides.

The ground shook as the giant started to run.

'He's catching up,' Miss Muffet's voice was on the edge of panic. 'Can't you go any faster?'

'I probably could, but the rats can't,' I shouted over my shoulder. 'Is there anything left you can use to slow him down?'

'It's fruit, Harry, not a tactical nuke.'

'Well, throw it at him anyway. Maybe it'll distract him.' I know, it was a stupid suggestion but it was the best I could come up with.

'No, wait.' Jack had decided to enter the conversation. 'I've got a brilliant idea. Just do what I do.'

407

Unable to look at what was going on behind or risk crashing the cart, I kept my eyes firmly on the road ahead, hoping that Jack's idea would work.

'Everyone, throw the fruit on the road in front of the giant, maybe he'll slip on it.' I could hear the desperate enthusiasm in Jack's voice, but, as ideas went, it wasn't the worst. Mind you, it wasn't the best either. The chances of Neringus slipping were . . .

'Whoops, there he goes,' Jack shouted. This was followed immediately by a loud crash as the giant hit the ground. The vibrations bumped the cart into the air and it bounced around wildly for a few seconds before I could get control once more.

'What's he doing now?' I asked, wondering if Jack's idea had given us enough time.

'He's getting up, but very slowly,' Miss Muffet said. 'He looks a bit dazed.' She paused for a second. 'Oh, no. He's after us again, but at least he doesn't seem to be moving as fast.'

Onwards we raced, pursued by the stunned giant. From the confused commentary in the back of the cart, he seemed to be gaining, just not as speedily as before.

Ahead, I could see the tip of the beanstalk getting nearer and nearer; I hoped we'd make it in time, but, just when I thought we were going to do it, I noticed that the rats' pace had begun to flag. In fairness, I'd driven them hard all the way from the castle and they hadn't let me down. By now their tongues were dangling from their mouths and their fur was covered in sweat. They were probably on the point of collapse and I couldn't really blame them; they hadn't much left to give.

'How near is he?' I roared.

'He's almost on us,' Miss Muffet replied. 'Can't you go any faster?'

'The rats have had it. There's nothing in the tank.'

'There's got to be something you can do.'

The rats were almost at walking pace now. 'There's only one thing for it,' I said.

'What?' exclaimed the others in unison, clearly expecting another great idea.

'We get out and run,' I replied, to groans of disappointment. That was a clear signal my idea didn't entirely meet with the approval of the group. Then again, some of us weren't exactly built for running; at a pinch – and this was most definitely a pinch – we might just be able to manage a brisk walk. 'Like, now.' I jumped off the cart and ran – well, lumbered – towards the bean-stalk. Following my example, the others followed, Jack in the lead, then Miss Muffet and, at the back, a less-than-mobile Basili.

Freed of their passengers, the rats lurched sideways off the road, dragging the cart behind them. It was a small diversion, but might just be enough. As the giant pounded after it, we raced towards the beanstalk, arriving just as Neringus realised his mistake and changed direction again – only this time straight at us.

Without looking, I jumped straight down through the cloud-cover, hoping that the balloon hadn't drifted away. It hadn't and, as an added bonus, I had a soft landing on the bodies of the goblins we'd dumped there earlier. Pausing only to throw them out of the basket (and onto a large nearby leaf – I'm not that cruel, you know), I undid the mooring rope just as the others fell into the balloon behind me.

'How fast can this thing drop?' I asked Miss Muffet.

She pushed me aside. 'As fast as ballast and hot air will allow. Now let me drive.'

The balloon drifted sideways, away from the beanstalk, and, as Miss Muffet made adjustments, slowly began to descend back towards Grimmtown.

'Can't it go any faster?' I asked.

'Give me a chance,' she replied. 'I have to make some very precise calculations.'

'Maybe if I climbed back out there and pulled off one of those patches, would that work?'

'Unless I get it right very soon, you might just have to.'

Bluff called, I skulked back over to the basket's edge and looked up. As I did so, a huge foot planted itself on the beanstalk and, seconds later, the rest of the giant followed, climbing down after us, his eyes focused on the not-so-rapidly-descending balloon.

I looked over at Miss Muffet once more. 'I know, I know,' she said. 'You don't have to tell me. He's up there isn't he?'

I nodded.

'Okay, time for extreme measures.' She pulled a cable and the parachute valve at the top of the balloon opened, releasing hot air. The balloon began to drop more rapidly.

'That's more like it,' I said.

'Just keep an eye on how fast we're dropping,' Miss Muffet replied. 'I'd prefer a gentle landing as opposed to a crashing one.'

'You're okay; the ground's a good bit away yet.'

'And we're moving towards it a little bit faster than I'd like,' Miss Muffet pointed out. 'And what are we going to do when we land? The giant won't be far behind us.'

Her point was well made. Think, Harry, think.

When the obvious solution struck me, I slapped myself on the forehead for taking so long to come up with it. I grabbed my mobile and made a call to Ezekiel Clubfoote. Zeke supplied me with whatever equipment I needed – and could afford. If he didn't have it, it probably didn't exist, and in the past I'd asked for some very strange stuff indeed. This time, however, my request was a simple one. Zeke listened, told me he could provide it and it'd be there when we landed. I thanked him and hung up.

'I have a plan,' I said. 'But it's contingent on getting to the ground before he does.' I jerked my trotter in the giant's direction.

Miss Muffet looked at Neringus, took a quick glance over the edge of the basket and announced that it would be a close thing – which wasn't exactly what I was hoping for.

I followed her example and looked down. A large crowd had gathered around the base of the beanstalk, all of them looking up at the bizarre chase going on above. Apart from the usual crowd of rubberneckers, I could see the police, operatives from Beanstalk Control in their bright green uniforms and, unless I was very much mistaken, most of the guests from the B&B. I wasn't surprised by the gathering; even by Grimmtown standards, a hot-air balloon being chased down a beanstalk by a giant wasn't something they saw every day. Although most of the onlookers were a safe distance away, of course, there was also a smaller, more gormless, crowd closer to the base of the beanstalk looking up at us in fascination. Unless they got out of the way soon, they risked being crushed by the rapidly descending balloon.

I waved my arms frantically. 'Get out of the way, you idiots.' Being the polite citizens they were, they happily waved back at me, seemingly oblivious of their impending demise.

'Morons,' I muttered. 'Well, if they can't be bothered to listen, anything that happens to them won't be on my head.' Which was true, it'd be on theirs – and in a matter of seconds, judging by our rate of descent. Miss Muffet was right: it was going to be close. The small sea of faces below grew closer and closer and it would have been funny in other circumstances to see the way their expressions changed from bland looking-up to the sudden realization that they were in imminent danger of death. This was quickly followed by a scattering of bodies and a crash as the balloon hit the ground recently vacated by the idiot spectators.

I didn't waste any time checking everyone was okay, I just

hurdled over the basket's edge and roared, 'Did anyone leave a package for me?'

Almost immediately, Queenie Harte and Mr Zingiber struggled forward carrying a large trunk between them. 'Is this what you're looking for?' the gingerbread man grunted.

'I expect so,' I said, as they gratefully dropped the trunk at my feet. I quickly undid the large clasp and opened it. 'Oh, Zeke,' I whispered, as I looked inside, 'you've excelled yourself this time.' Turning back to the balloon, I yelled at the others to get out of the basket as fast as they could. With Neringus almost within grabbing distance they didn't need any encouragement.

'Everyone stand back, this beanstalk is about to come down,' I shouted.

'Cool,' I heard Jack say. 'Have you an axe, just like the Giantkiller?'

'Axe be damned,' I said grimly, heaving a large chainsaw out of the trunk and revving it up. 'I don't believe in wasting my time and energy.' With the last remnants of my strength, I strode over to the beanstalk and held the chainsaw against the trunk. Bits of wood sprayed in all directions as the saw bit in. Above, the giant saw what was happening and stopped climbing down. Once I saw I had his attention, I pulled the chainsaw away and looked up at him.

'Now, I'm not normally a betting man,' I said, trying to sound more confident than I felt, 'but if I was to guess, I'd say I could cut this baby down before you got to the ground.'

'You wouldn't,' Neringus said; a trifle uncertainly, I thought.

I revved up the saw once more. It made a very reassuring roar. 'Try me.'

Behind me the crowd had begun to chant, 'Cut it down! Cut it down!'

'See,' I said. 'Even the crowd is on my side.'

'What do you want?' the giant asked. Good. At last he was starting to see sense.

'I want you to head back up to your lovely castle in the clouds and not bother me again,' I said, swinging the chainsaw towards the beanstalk for effect.

The giant flinched. 'That's all?'

'No. Did you really think that would be all?' Now that I had him where I wanted him, relatively speaking, I had to make the most of it. 'Some nice people from Beanstalk Control, along with representatives of our police service, will probably be along to pay you a visit and relieve you of Sinbad's treasure, which as we know, doesn't actually belong to you.'

'But I was only minding it for him,' the giant stammered. 'He asked me to.'

'And now you can make sure that it's returned to its rightful owners, seeing as Sinbad won't be needing it for quite some time yet. Do we understand each other?'

Neringus nodded. 'Good,' I said. 'Now toddle back up there and leave us alone, or else . . .' I revved the chainsaw up one last time. I must say, I quite liked the noise it made.

Fearful of plummeting out of a chopped-down beanstalk, the giant climbed quickly away, to the accompaniment of the cheers and applause of the onlookers. Soon he was out of sight and hopefully back where he belonged. Since that he was out of our harm's way, I handed the chainsaw to one of Beanstalk Control's representatives. 'I know it's an unlicensed growth and needs to come down, but, before you cut it down, the cops will need to go up there. That guy's been hiding Sinbad's treasure since he went to jail, so it needs to be recovered and returned to the original owners.'

The BC rep looked confused, but nodded anyway; he probably didn't know what else to do.

'And now,' I announced to the crowd with a flourish, 'I just need to wrap this case up once and for all so, if the police would be kind enough to escort all the B&B's guests into the house and make sure they don't try to escape,' I did a quick headcount just to be sure everyone was still there, 'I'll explain everything.' Then another thought struck me. 'And if one or two of the police could remain here, I suspect that two more refugees from above may be arriving at any second. If they do, assuming they haven't become a giant's nourishing bowl of soup, they're to be arrested immediately.'

18

A Surprise Ending

Once everyone was sitting down in the lounge, I stood beside the fireplace and began. 'Now, this may come as a surprise to you all, but I'm not actually Harriet du Crêpe, PA to Alain Schmidt-Heye, but Harry Pigg, Grimmtown's foremost detective.' I didn't get the gasps of astonishment I was expecting. Maybe it was the remnants of the make-up, which was still liberally smeared across my face.

'Miss Muffet hired me to find out who was behind the spider infestation in her house. Initially, I believed someone was trying to put her out of business, but after some rather brilliant detective work, I came to the conclusion that the real reason was that someone wanted to lay their hands on her father's fortune, which they believed was hidden somewhere in the house. You see, Miss Muffet's father is Sinbad the Sailor, whom I'm sure you've all heard of.' This revelation was greeted with some gasps of amazement (now that was more like it) and muted nods. 'And this, though I'm reluctant to admit it, is where I made my first mistake.'

'Only the first?' asked Queenie, but I chose to ignore her cheap shot.

'You see, I didn't realise that Sinbad's treasure was never hidden in the house,' I continued. 'All that was actually here was the means to get to it.'

'The magic bean,' Jack shouted.

'Yes, Jack, the magic bean.' I said. 'Once that was found, thanks to some more superb detective work by yours truly, it led to the kingdom in the clouds and the actual location of the treasure.'

Miss Muffet stood up. 'Okay, Harry, we know all this now. What we need to find out is who's behind it.'

'Patience, good lady; all will be revealed shortly.'

She sat down once more, an impatient look on her face.

'It seemed clear to me that one of the guests had to be masterminding the whole caper. The question remained, which of you was it?'

This was greeted with indignant harrumphs and denials from the guests.

'For reasons I won't go into, I eliminated Mr Winkie from my enquiries early on. Mr and Mrs Spratt seemed to be on the level too, so I focused my attentions on the remaining guests, all of whom had something to hide.' Much guilty shifting about followed this statement. 'Yes, all of you.'

'I made one fatal assumption at this point: as I knew Licken and Lurkey of old, I hadn't considered the possibility that they might be involved. Of course, being both stupid and short of cash, they made ideal stooges for the brains behind the operation. All they had to do was keep an eye out for any sign of where the magic bean might be hidden and report back.'

'But report back to whom?' Miss Muffet asked, clearly puzzled. 'How did you know it wasn't Licken and Lurkey?'

'Once our fowl friends recognised me last night, they must have immediately told their boss who I was and what they thought I was up to. When I found the magic bean, someone knocked me out and grabbed it,' I said. 'The last thing I saw before I blacked out was a hand picking up the box – not a wing, a hand. This obviously meant there was a human involved.

'Once the magic bean was located and triggered, it became obvious where the treasure was, but this also presented a problem, as giants don't obviously like uninvited guests and it would have taken too long for a visitor to get an official visa – especially for an unapproved beanstalk. Therefore, whoever wanted to get their hands on the treasure needed to act fast and come up with a good reason to visit Neringus's kingdom.' I was getting to the good stuff now and I could sense the growing anticipation in my audience – at least, in those of them that weren't involved. 'And what better reason than to repair the giant's most treasured possession.'

Jack jumped to his feet. 'The magic harp; she was all scratched and she said she was due for repair and revarnishing.'

'Yes, Jack, Licken and Lurkey were sent up there with explicit instructions to damage the harp. As she was the giant's favourite and as he probably couldn't bear to listen to her complain about the damage, he needed her to be attended to urgently, and who better to do it than someone who's familiar with working on and restoration of the most delicate of wooden antiques and carvings.' I pointed my finger at Pietro Nocchio. 'I'm, of course, referring to you, Mr Nocchio.'

The wooden man jumped to his feet. 'That eez ridiculous; I've never 'eard anything so absurd 'een my whole life.'

'Working with puppets, I'm sure you have,' I replied. 'They're not known for their common sense.'

'That eez an outrageous accusation,' he shouted. 'I am only 'ere to meet some puppet dealers.'

'Of course you are; and no doubt you knew nothing about Sinbad or his treasure, did you?'

'Absolutely not! Before I came 'ere, I 'ad never heard of Sinbad, heez treasure or George Etto.'

'And who said anything about Etto?' I asked, smiling, knowing that I had him. 'I don't recall mentioning his name during any of this.'

Nocchio looked at me, horror-stricken. By mentioning Sinbad's former cellmate, he'd effectively sealed his fate. He sat at the table, his head in his hands.

'I thought no one would cotton on. I was dreenking in the Blarney Tone weeth some buddies and we 'eard thees Etto guy ramble on about how 'e 'ad 'eard Sinbad talking een hees sleep. At first I didn't pay much attention, but when he said something about the secret to his treasure being hidden een the house, then I got very interested. I bought heem some more drinks and 'e kept telling the same story: somewhere in thees house was the key to get to Sinbad's fortune. All I 'ad to do was find eet.

'I thought that by scaring Miss Muffet away, I'd have the place to myself. I couldn't believe eet when thees bunch of cheapskates and nostalgia junkies just wouldn't leave, so I 'ired Licken and Lurkey to help me look around. Once they realised who you really were, I figured that eef anyone could find the secret it'd be you.'

I preened when he said this.

'The rest you know. I was so close to getting up there. Once I did, I planned to make a deal with the giant and give eem some of the treasure. With Sinbad in jail for the foreseeable future, I figured I'd be long gone before 'e found out.' Nocchio sighed heavily and extended his arms. Seconds later he was led away in cuffs.

Chalk up another success to the Third Pig Detective Agency. But there was one last aspect of the case to consider. 'Oh, and considering what I heard at breakfast this morning, you might also want to talk to Mr Nimble here,' I said. 'I suspect he's also involved, as the man who'd help dispose of this massive fortune to collectors all over the world in return for some highly lucrative commission, as well as being the man who, disguised as an orc, organised for the supply of the spiders.'

Nimble stood up and blustered, 'This is an outrage. I won't stand for this slur on my good character.'

Miss Muffet walked up behind him and pushed him back down into his seat. 'Sit,' she ordered. 'I bet Nocchio will be quite happy to make a deal in return for telling us exactly how much you were involved.'

As she spoke there came the sound of wings beating from outside, followed immediately by a loud and indignant squawking. 'Ah,' I said, 'I do believe Licken and Lurkey have returned to ground level and have met their welcoming committee.'

After the police had escorted Nocchio and Nimble away, Miss Muffet rushed over and hugged me. 'Thank you, Harry,' she said. 'I don't know how I can ever repay you.'

'It's okay,' I said. 'Just pay me out of the reward money.'

'Reward money?'

'Some of the stuff Sinbad stole over the years is very valuable indeed. I fully expect there'll be a reward for its safe recovery and as the magic bean was found in your house and the beanstalk is on your property, I think you have a reasonable first claim on the loot. Spend it wisely. As a first step, I'd suggest a pest extermination service. Although I suspect that Mr Frogg Prince might be only too delighted to take the spiders off your hands. In fact, being a frog, he may very well double up as an exterminator considering the length of his tongue.'

'I think you're right. Thanks again, Harry.'

'My pleasure. But before we go, there are a few things I'd like to get answers to.' I looked at Thomas Piper. 'What's your story? You haven't taken your eyes off Miss Muffet since you arrived.'

Piper shuffled his feet guiltily. 'It's nothing sinister; I was watching out for her on her father's instructions. Once he got word of the spiders he asked me to move in and make sure nothing happened to her.'

'And what's your connection to Sinbad?' I asked.

'Let's just say we worked together in the past,' Piper replied.

'You mean you were part of his gang,' I said.

'I can't comment on that; however, I'm sure Mr El Muhfte will be suitably grateful that this situation has been resolved.'

'How grateful?' I asked hopefully, figuring he might throw some cash in my direction as a reward.

'Alas, now that his treasure has been recovered, actual monetary recompense might not be as forthcoming.'

Dammit, I'd shot myself in the foot there.

'And as for you, Miss Harte,' I said, turning to face her. 'You're about as likely a GBI agent as I am. I saw through you almost immediately; what gives?'

Queenie gave a rueful shrug. 'Sorry about that. I really didn't mean any harm. I was only here on behalf of the Grimmtown Spider Preservation Society. I'm a private detective too, and like you I was trying to find out what had happened.'

'But why the fake ID and the GBI story; wouldn't it have been just as easy to say who you really were?'

'This coming from someone who disguised himself as a woman in order to solve the case?'

'*Touché*,' I said. 'But remember who it was that solved the case.' Well, I couldn't let a gloating opportunity go by, now, could I?

'Come on,' I said to Jack and Basili, 'our work here is done. Dinner is on me.'

Together we walked out of the lounge, down the hall to the front door. Just as we were about to open it, it swung inwards and three burly policemen entered followed by a large fly dressed in a very smart grey suit.

'You're too late,' I said. 'You've just missed the others. They're probably on their way to the station right now.'

'Harry Pigg?' said the leading cop.

'That's me,' I replied, extending my trotter. To my surprise, he snapped a handcuff around it.

'You're under arrest for murder,' he said, his face expressionless.

I looked at him in shock. 'This is a joke, right? Who put you up to it? DI Jill?'

'This is no joke, sir. You're under arrest for the murder of Geoffrey Coque-Robben. Please extend your other arm.'

I realised that this wasn't a joke after all. 'You must be mistaken. I haven't killed anyone,' I said, as the handcuffs were snapped onto my other trotter.

'Sir, please, if you'll just accompany us to the station.' The other two policemen grabbed an arm each and escorted me out the door and towards a police car that was parked on the road outside the B&B.

'What's going on, Harry?' Jack cried. 'What are they doing?'

'It's okay, Jack, I'm sure it's some kind of mistake. We'll get it sorted at the police station.'

'It's no mistake, sir,' said the policeman to my left. 'We have a witness.'

'What witness? Who?' This was becoming more unreal by the minute. How could anyone have possibly seen me commit a murder I obviously hadn't done.

The fly, who up to now had been maintaining a discreet distance, stepped forward.

'I,' said the fly. 'I saw him die, with my little eye; and you were the one that killed him.'

The End

Acknowledgements

This has been a strange year (to put it mildly). Unexpected things happened and I truly became aware of the meaning of the word family. The word 'Thanks' doesn't even begin to express my gratitude for the support of my wife, Gemma, my three boys, Ian, Adam and Stephen, my parents, brothers and sister. Here's looking at you, folks.

Gem, words can't express . . .

Ian (assuming you're actually awake and out of bed), I truly appreciate your offer and the fact that you volunteered immediately.

Adam, you've had a great year. Cool stuff has happened and you're beginning to realise your potential. I sense great things (or a disturbance in the Force or it might be just indigestion).

Stephen, think of this as a time machine of sorts. As I write, Munster are in the HC quarter-finals. By the time you read it, they may be champions – or may have been defeated on the way. Who can say (right now)? Hopefully, we'll get to see (have seen!!) them on the rest of their journey.

As always, my gratitude goes to my agent, Svetlana, and to Scott and Corinna at The Friday Project for the editing and other publishy type stuff that ensured this story actually got to print.

Harry Pigg doesn't believe in thanking anyone other than himself so his acknowledgements will be conspicuous by their absence this time around.